The Church Series Book Four

Tiya Rayne

Young Ann Publishing, LLC
Colfax, North Carolina

Copyright © 2024 by Tiya Rayne.
Cover Designer Haelah Rice Covers
All rights reserved. No part of this publication may be reproduced, distributed or transmitted in any form or by any means, including photocopying, recording, or other electronic or mechanical methods, without the prior written permission of the publisher, except in the case of brief quotations embodied in critical reviews and certain other noncommercial uses permitted by copyright law. For permission requests, write to the publisher, addressed "Attention: Permissions Coordinator," at the address below.

Tiya Rayne/ Young Ann Publishing, LLC
PO BOX 365
Colfax, NC/27235
www.tiyarayne.com

Publisher's Note: This is a work of fiction. Names, characters, places, and incidents are a product of the author's imagination. Locales and public names are sometimes used for atmospheric purposes. Any resemblance to actual people, living or dead, or to businesses, companies, events, institutions, or locales is completely coincidental.

Ordering Information:
Quantity sales. Special discounts are available on quantity purchases by corporations, associations, and others. For details, contact the "Special Sales Department" at the address above.

Beast; Part One/ Tiya Rayne. -- 1st ed.
ISBN 979-8-9865803-4-0

Act One

How it Started.

CHAPTER ONE

How it Started

Summer

Five Years Earlier...

"You fucking slut." my sister's high-pitched voice pulls me out of my foggy sleep.

I open my eyes and the blaring sunlight from the open blinds causes them to water. Closing my lids, I try to rub the blurriness away. I'd only been sleep for an hour. The nightmares were bad last night, and I was entirely too sober to deal with them.

"It's too early for this shit, Rai," I whine as I sink my head back into my pillow.

It's been a full day and a half since I got high. The early signs of withdrawal are starting to creep up. My pillow is soaked from sweat and I'm exhausted. However, even if I was high, I wouldn't want to wake up to my overly dramatic sister screaming at me.

"I can't believe you, Summer." Her teary voice tells me something is different about this wake up.

I'm used to being shouted at by Raina for any slight inconvenience. I'm staying at her place, and she likes to remind me of that. But she doesn't usually cry when she's chewing me out about something.

Sitting up in the small twin bed, the room spins before I can focus. If I don't find some blow or pills, this day is only going to get worse.

1

When my head finally stops spinning, I look toward the doorway to find my very pregnant sister in her pink kitten scrubs standing beside her asshole boyfriend. I know immediately what's going on.

"What did he tell you?" I ask Raina.

She swipes a hand under her brown eyes. Even though at twenty-three, I'm the oldest by three years, many people always assume she was. Probably because she's 5'7" and towers over my 5'3" height.

"I told her the truth," Mitch yells from behind her. The black eye I gave him last night is swollen and nearly closed shut.

I roll my eyes at him. Mitch hasn't told the truth a day in his life, I don't even think he knows what the word means.

"You tried to get my boyfriend to sleep with you?" Raina scoffs.

Those that truly knew me, would know that was a lie. My best friend, Trina, would laugh her ass off at the accusation if she were here. I'm many things— most of them not good—but I'm not a soulless whore that would try to tempt her sister's lowlife boyfriend to my bed. Even I have standards.

"Is that what he told you?"

"Of course, that's what I told her, it's the truth," Mitch continues to sell the lie.

I glare at the asshat that got my sister pregnant. I don't judge people, I'm in no place to do so. However, everyone knows that Mitchell Kane can't keep his dick in his pants. At the moment, he has three other girls pregnant. My sister doesn't know about any of them. I tried to tell her once, and it ended in an argument where she called me a jealous crackhead.

I figured if she wanted to play Boo Boo the Fool, why should I discourage her.

"Let me get this right," I say, throwing the covers back and sitting on the side of the bed. "I came on to you, but you ended up with a black eye?"

Raina looks over her shoulder at him. I wonder did that even register to her, or did she automatically believe the worst of me, like our mother.

Mitch stumbles over his excuse. "You got mad when I turned your skank ass down, so you hit me." Clearly not hard enough.

My mouth drops open, there is no way she can believe that. Yet, when she turns back to me, I immediately know she does. I laugh, not at the situation, but at how I've always been considered the dumb one in the family.

I could tell Raina the truth. I could explain to her, that from the day I moved in here two weeks ago, Mitch has been trying to fuck me. I've turned him down every time. Last night, after she went to work, he got drunk and got a little forceful. The black eye was my reminder to him that no means not in a million fucking years.

"Are you seriously laughing right now?" Raina shouts.

Tucking my lips in, I shake my head no.

"I can't believe you're joking about this," she whines.

That's another sign that tells me my sister doesn't fucking know me. Making light of horrible situations is my default setting.

Exhaling my frustration, I rake a hand down my face. "What do you want me to say Rai? It's not like you'll believe me anyway."

They never do. Her and mother are always quick to expect the absolute worst from me. If I told her the truth, she would still find a way to blame me. I'm the druggy fuck up of the family. Just like daddy, as they like to remind me. Anytime anything goes wrong, I'm the one to blame. The facts never matter to them.

Raina's mouth sinks into a frown as she looks to her left to stare at the wall. "Mama told me not to take you in. She said that you were just a leeching lowlife, but I tried to help you. I was hoping you would change before your nephew came. But now I know, it's going to take a lot more than me to save you, Summer." Her eyes, so familiar to mine, cut back to me.

Raina likes to think she's the good child. The one with her shit together. If you compare us side by side, I guess that makes sense. She's the CNA, and I'm the homeless addict.

I know she took me in only because she wanted to be the one that saved me. Not for me. She couldn't care less if I'm sober or not. She wants to do it because she enjoys the accolades that come with the good girl status. She likes being the hero in her stories. Only I know how far from the truth that is.

"I want you out," she whispers.

I would say that her decision hurts me, but I'm used to it. I'm not a saint. Hell, I'm not even easy to get along with, but I've never betrayed my family. Despite what they think.

Her decision inconveniences me, especially now, but I'll figure something out. I always do. Trina says I must be part cat because I have nine lives. If I am, I'm the unluckiest fucking cat in the world because of those nine lives, so far all have been shitty.

"Fine, give me a few days. I'll be out of your hair."

I stand, stretching my arms over my head. I'm wearing a ratty T-shirt and gym shorts.

Even with everything covered, I still feel exposed in front of Mitch. I head to my borrowed dresser to find some jogging pants.

"No," Summer says stopping me halfway. "You're leaving now."

My mouth drops open. "Are you fucking serious?" I look at the clock on the nightstand. "It's 7:30 in the morning. And it's Saturday. I have nowhere to go."

Plus, what she doesn't know, is that I can't be on the streets. The whole reason I asked to move in with her is because I've made an enemy. A very dangerous one.

She wipes away the tear that falls down her cheek. "You should have thought about that before you tried to sleep with my boyfriend."

Okay, I was babying her before. I didn't want to hurt her feelings about her piece of shit baby daddy, but forget that.

"You can't be that fucking dumb, Raina. Do you truly believe I tried to sleep with him, and he turned it down, so I punched him in the face? Does that really make logical sense to you?"

"Shut up, Summer," Mitch yells. Even he knows how absurd it sounds.

"Mitch has community dick and has practically fucked everyone in Hammel projects, but you believe all of a sudden, he has found morals and turned down free pussy?"

She scoffs and wipes at her newly falling tears. "You are a lying bitter bitch, and you're just as fucked up in the head as daddy."

If she'd used a knife, she couldn't have cut me any deeper. Yet, no matter how cruel she is to me, I still could never hate her. Beat her ass, maybe, but I couldn't hate her.

My shoulders collapse as defeat embraces me. "Give me an hour, I'll be out of your way."

Raina and Mitch leave, and I get busy tossing my few measly possessions into a trash bag. It only takes me twenty minutes to get dressed.

I walk into the living room. Raina is crying in Mitch's arms and he's scrolling through his phone behind her back. He looks up at me when I walk in and smirks. The sad part is, he told me this would happen last night. He said if I didn't have sex with him, he was going to make Raina put me out. I guess he won.

Ignoring him, I place her spare key down on the little glass coffee table. Before leaving, I stop for a moment, hoping my sister would change her mind. Not because I need a place to stay, which I do, but because I hope she will come to her senses and realize I would never hurt her that way.

When she continues to avoid me, I shake my head as I turn to leave. After all these years, I still believed there was hope for us. Maybe one day I will learn that the damage my mother did to our relationship is irreparable. When I storm out of the door, I make sure to slam it.

Although I left without a fight, I really don't have anywhere to go. I doubt anyone else in my family will take me in. I have only one true friend and that's the first place my enemy will check.

I don't make good first impressions. Hell, I'm not really good when you get to know me either. And I damn sure can't afford my own place.

After taking the subway toward Queens, I climb on the bus and head to the only place I'd be welcomed. Leaning my head against the window I shut my eyes. The cool surface of the glass soothes my clammy head.

The lack of sleep last night starts to catch up to me. The moment I let my guard down, and sleep starts to lull me, my brain conjures up the images. Blood is everywhere, all over my hands and painted against my pink nightgown. I pop my eyes open quickly, placing a hand against my rapidly beating heart. I count to ten and try to do the breathing exercise my therapist taught me. Eventually, the remnants of the nightmare start to recede.

I pinch my arm to keep myself from falling back to sleep. Until I get my hands on a Perc, it's best I stay awake. I stare out the window as the city flies by.

Stepping off the bus, I toss my trash bag over my shoulder. Pulling the hoodie over my head, I keep my eyes fixed on the pavement in hopes no one recognizes me. Making the short trip to my only friends' small blue house, I walk up the steps and knock twice on the white door. After three minutes pass and no one answers I knock again. The door swings open, and a very angry Trina is standing in front of me in a red silk robe.

"Who the fuck is knocking on my…. Summer? What the hell are you doing here?" She asks once she sees it's me.

She looks over my head back out onto the street, before grabbing my arm and pulling me inside.

She shuts the door and glances up the stairs. "What are you doing here? You know Nic has goons all on this block looking for you."

I flinch at the name of my ex. The one time I tried to do the relationship thing it backfired on me. Typical.

"Raina kicked me out," I say, pushing the hoodie off my head and dropping my trash bag at my feet.

Trina's eyes narrow and she folds her arms over her chest. "What did you do?"

I love that my best friend knows me enough to know that nine times out of ten, I fucked up.

I snort, "Tried to sleep with Mitch."

She stares for a moment and then we both burst out laughing. "Is she serious? She actually believed that bullshit?"

"Apparently, her and mommy knew it was coming."

Movement on the stairs has me looking up. A tall slender white man is coming down the steps, pulling his blazer on. He looks to be in his late forties. He has a dusting of gray hair at his temples and lines around his eyes and mouth. He glances nervously at me before turning back to Trina.

"You're leaving?" she purrs at the man.

I look away when she runs her hand over his chest. I don't do well in awkward or high-pressure situations. Hell, I just don't do well period.

"I have a flight to catch at noon. I left your money on the nightstand," he says the last part low as if I don't know how my best friend makes her money.

What Trina does would be considered prostitution to some. She calls herself a sugar baby. She dates older men that provide for her financially.

"Okay. I'll see you the next time you're in town?"

The man smiles and nods his head up and down. He turns to me. "Nice to meet you."

"Uh, you too. I hope you enjoyed the services." I flinched as I realized what I'd just said.

The guy's eyes widen. Trina groans and places her hand to her forehead. He quickly makes his exit after that. As soon as the door shuts behind him, Trina turns to me.

"Really, bitch?"

I shrug. "You know how I get when I'm nervous. Plus, he reminded me of one of my old substance abuse counselors," I say, shivering as the memory of their resemblance replays in my head.

"Well, he's not." She turns around and heads into her living room.

I follow behind her, leaving my belongings in her foyer.

"I swear whoever created Viagra needs their ass kicked. I don't know why everyone wants to fuck all night."

She flops down on the couch and picks up a half smoked blunt out of the ashtray on her coffee table. I sit down beside her and place my head against the back of the sofa. Trina fires the L and the sweet smell of cannabis fills the air. My mouth waters for a hit.

She passes it to me, and I place it to my lips taking a long drag. The smoke fills my lungs and I immediately feel my body relaxing. I exhale and choke, passing it back to Trina.

"You look like shit," she says taking another hit. "When's the last time you slept?"

Shutting my eyes, I let the weed do its job. "I got about two hours last night."

I don't have to open my eyes and look at her to know she's watching me. I can feel the heat of her stare on the side of my face.

"You can't survive like that. You need to sleep."

"I'll sleep once I get a pill."

Her huff of breath alerts me that this conversation is about to get serious. "You need to talk to someone."

"I've tried that remember," I say cracking my eyes open to look at her. "Didn't work."

When I was nine, my mother took me to see someone about the nightmares. Not because she cared, but she got tired of me waking up crying and screaming in the middle of the night.

They tried to put me on medication, but by then I was terrified of medicine. To avoid going back to the shrink, I started to act out before every appointment. Mommy got fed up and stopped taking me. She stopped caring all together after a while.

"Something has to give, Summer. You can't keep living like this."

"Trina," I groan, pinching the bridge of my nose. "You know I usually love our little pep talks, but I'm running off two hours of sleep in three days. I need a place to crash until I find another alternative."

Look, I know I have a problem. Trust me, no one feels the effects of my life choices more than me. I've tried to get better, I've even been clean a few times, but that shit never lasts.

"You can crash here for the night until we find something else. It's too risky for you to stay here longer than that. He's been here once looking for you and that black Tahoe drives by at least twice a day."

"There is nowhere else for me to go," I say, sitting up placing my elbows on my knees.

"I just got paid, I can help you get a hotel for about two weeks."

I shake my head, "You have your own bills to take care of. I'm not taking your money."

She passes me the blunt and I sit up straight, taking another drag of it.

"I need to get out of town and start over in like Kansas or someplace," I groan, allowing the smoke to puff out with each word. "For that, I need money. A lot of money." Running my hands through my damaged hair, I place the green to my lips again. "Maybe I should just turn myself in to Nic. At least if I'm dead I can sleep, and I won't be anybody else's problem."

Trina snatches the blunt out of my fingers.

"Hey," I argue.

"If you're going to be talking that type of bullshit, you don't need any more weed." She places the blunt back down in the ashtray.

She turns to me, tucking her leg under her butt. "You're right about one thing. You need to leave New York. Nic is never going to stop looking for you. Rightfully so," she adds with a smirk.

I roll my eyes flopping back against the couch. "I know. But unless you have a stack of cash lying around that you don't want, that's not going to happen."

Trina's head tilts to the side as she watches me. "I might have a plan, but you're not going to like it."

"Well, I'm not feeling encouraged right now about it," I laugh.

She leans forward, placing her hands in a prayer position. "Alright, I know this guy—"

"No."

"Summer," she starts to plead but I don't want to hear it.

I stand from the sofa, but she grabs my hand and yanks me back down.

"Sit your ass down and listen," she demands. Her tone has my head snapping in her direction.

Trina runs a hand through her gorgeous lace front wig.

"I've known you since we were six years old. You're like a sister to me and I've sat back too long watching you battle with this addiction, but enough is enough. I don't think you understand, Nic is going to kill you. And I know you talk a big game about dying and giving up, but I also know you're not ready to die."

I turn away, but her finger under my chin brings my attention back to her.

"It's time to put your big girl panties on and do what you need to do. This is your only chance to save your life. Because I'm not ready to be here without my bestie."

As much as I hate to admit it, she's right. Death has come knocking at my door many times and I always find some way to avoid it. There has to be a reason for it. Clearly, I have a purpose here, and it's not to give up now. If I'm going to survive this latest fiasco, I can't stay here.

"Ugh," I grunt. "Tell me about this client."

She smiles and claps her hands together. "Okay, his name is Gregory Matthews and he's some kind of CEO or something. He's been trying to get me to do this role-playing thing with him for the longest, but he's a friend of my current sugar daddy and I didn't want to muddy the waters."

I scrunch my face in disgust. "What does he want you to do?"

"Don't make that face. Everyone has a kink, plus his isn't even that bad. He only wants to be tied up and spanked."

What the hell is wrong with people?

"Anyway," she continues. "From my understanding, he spends the entire night tied up leaving you with full control. You just have to belittle him a little. Once he's fully aroused, you climb on top, ride him to completion a few times, and get out of there first thing in the morning. It's that simple."

Already I can feel the clawing in my chest just thinking about sleeping with some random. I don't have any hang ups with sex or anything. However, I feel that intimacy on that level should be shared with two people that actually give a shit about each other. Is it ironic that I abuse my body on a daily basis with drugs, but have morals when it comes to sex? Yes.

Trina places a hand on my shoulder. "Breathe, Summer. I promise it won't be bad. As long as you don't start being yourself."

By "being myself" she means being a klutz or by having mouth diarrhea.

"I can't make any promises," I admit.

She shakes her head. "I'll call him and see if I can set something up for tonight. We can even negotiate the payment. And then this time tomorrow, you'll have a pocket full of money and you can catch a bus to anywhere you want to go. Trust me, what could go wrong?"

CHAPTER TWO

It Went Wrong

Summer

I once again pull down the hem of Trina's dress. I can only imagine what I look like in the outfit.

Years of mistreatment has me way below the required body mass for my height. I don't have nearly enough hips and ass to pull this black leather skintight dress off, so it constantly rides up. The lack of sleep has my eyes puffy and red. My skin looks yellow and dull. And although Trina worked her magic with this wig, it still looks like one of those costume ones you get at the Halloween store. I didn't need a mirror to tell me I looked a hot mess.

I tug at the thong she forced me to wear, hoping to relieve the feeling of dental floss in my ass crack. I can already feel a panic attack creeping up as I stand outside Gregory's door.

I know the code to unlock the door. Trina gave me the rundown before I left. I am to let myself in and walk down the hall to the last bedroom on the right. Mr. Gregory will be lying on the bed, naked, gagged, and waiting for me to tie him up. All I have to do is go in.

However, my feet refuse to move as I stare at the silver numbers on his penthouse door.

"Come on, Summer, you can do this. It's not like you've never had sex before," I say out loud in the empty hallway.

Exhaling a deep breath, I shake my hands out, punch in the five-digit code, wait for the green light, and then open the door. I don't know what I was expecting, but it definitely wasn't this.

The foyer opens to a French country style living room. Everything is whitewashed and rustic with beige furniture. The place looks as if someone ripped it from a Southern Living magazine. It's almost too normal.

I head down the hall, following Trina's directions. With each step I take my heart pounds faster and faster. I stop in front of the door of the last room on the right. Once I walk in, there will be no going back.

Look, I've done some shitty things for a my next high. Things I'm not proud of, yet this is one line I've never crossed. However, this is my last option to save my life, there are no other avenues for me. This cat has run out of lives it seems.

Closing my eyes, and taking a deep breath, I push open the door and walk as far into the room as I can.

"You've got this." I give myself one final pep talk before taking a deep breath and opening my eyes.

I expected to come face to face with a naked middle-aged man. Yet, that is not what I find. In front of me, in clear sight, is a scene straight from my nightmares.

I start to shake, my vision gets blurry, and my breathing becomes labored. Right now, is the worst possible time to have a panic attack, but it's too late to stop it. I shut my eyes tight, trying to fight to gain control. My demons are riding me hard, and I can't shake them.

Behind my eyelids my dreams start to play back through my mind. My memories of that night wash over me like a tsunami rolling over a shore. I'm back in my childhood bedroom with the big bloodstain on my wall.

The scene I walked in on is a lot different from the one that threatens me every time I try to sleep. In my dreams, there is no tan skinned giant with mint green eyes. Here, the giant is staring at me with a terrifying look in his eyes. In this reality, blood is everywhere. On the walls, on the bed, some even on the carpet underneath my feet. In my dreams it is only on my wall. Also, I feel no pain here, unlike my dreams.

I reach for my shoulder as an old ache starts to form. My heart beats even faster and no matter how hard I try I can't seem to get enough breath in my lungs.

When I open my eyes again, the golden-haired giant is standing in front of me. He towers over me, his wide chest reaching the top of my head. The frown on his face tells me he isn't happy to see me. I imagine not, considering I just walked in on him brutally murdering someone.

I should run. Some part of my brain is telling me to get the hell out of here. But my feet are glued to the bloody carpet because my panic attack won't let me think rationally.

Even though this man is obviously dangerous and clearly a killer, I stare into his pale eyes as if they are a lifeline. Even he is more suitable than my memories.

"Please," I plead, not sure what the hell I'm asking for.

What I wouldn't give for some coke right now. Hell, I don't even do heroin, but I'd take that over this.

"Breathe," his gruff voice says.

His pale green eyes gaze directly into my brown. When I was twelve, we went on a field trip to the zoo and one of the zookeepers warned us of the dangers of looking the large silverback gorilla in the eyes. For some reason that memory is brought back to me. My brain is screaming for me to look away, but I can't.

The giant grabs my hand and places it on his chest. Underneath my palm, his heart beats strong and steady. Nothing like the frantic beating of mine.

"Focus on me," he says, when my eyes start to shut again.

I gaze back at him, taking in his features like an art critic examining a painting. Never have I seen such a gorgeous specimen. He looks unreal. His face has an oblong shape with eyes so hauntingly beautiful they send a shiver up my spine. They are heavy-lidded and almond shaped, but it's the intensity of the light mint green orbs that draws you in. His nose is very Greek, and his plump lips are enticing despite the pale line that cut into the bottom one.

I notice there are a lot of old pale lines on his face. One cuts into his brow; another is under his right eye. He has a long one on his forehead that seems to go back into his hair line. This man has been in some fights, or accidents, I don't know which. His dark blonde hair is pulled up into a lazy messy bun on top of his head. For a moment, I wonder what it would look like hanging down.

"You're so beautiful." The dumb words fly out of my mouth like diarrhea. I can't be held accountable for what I say, my brain is fighting through little sleep and a panic attack. The fact that I'm forming actual words is a miracle.

The giant's brow pinches as he watches me. He lets my hand go so suddenly it falls from his chest back down to my side.

"I'm sorry. I shouldn't have said that." I gasp.

This is the problem with me. It's why Trina warned me not to be myself. Where normal people would scream or run for help, my brain seems to think of the most random and stupidest things to say.

The giant takes a few steps back, keeping his narrowed gaze on me as if I'm the murderer in the room. He then turns his back to me, his fist tightened at his side and his wide shoulders lift and fall rapidly. Is he about to have a panic attack too?

I take a step in his direction and the bloody carpet underneath me squelches.

His head turns slightly to his right shoulder.

"Don't." The word comes out like a whip striking through the air and I immediately freeze.

It's then I realize, while I've been distracted by my own shit and his looks, I forgot that the man is obviously a killer and I'm trapped in here with him.

My gaze bounces around the room for a weapon, there aren't any. Well, unless you count the hammer, hack saw, and power drill on the bed. But all of those are on the other side of the room and I would need to pass him to get to them. My only other option is to turn and run out the door. Hopefully, the size and height of the giant means he's slow.

I don't second guess myself. I turn and sprint out of the room as fast as my skinny legs will take me. I'm so close to the front door, I can taste the first sign of freedom. However, it sours on my tongue when my arm is nearly ripped out of its socket.

He turns me around and shoves me so hard against the foyer wall that I see stars. When they clear, the face that was once staring so intently at me, is now frowning as if it's going to eat me alive.

The giant draws in close, his hard body pressed up against mine.

"You ran," he growls down at me through clenched teeth.

What the fuck did he think I was supposed to do? He's recreating the scene from Hellraiser on the bed back there and he thought I was going to stick around to see the final act. I don't think so.

"Don't kill me, please," I plead.

I don't know what Greg did to this man, but I don't want to set him off in the same way.

"You ran," he repeats again like I missed it the first time.

"Of course, I ran," I gently argue back as I gaze up at him. "I don't want to die."

His light eyes narrow as he watches me. I'm shaking so bad my teeth are chattering.

"I have no choice."

"You always have a choice," I sprout the bullshit words an addiction counselor said to me during one of my failed treatments.

"No, I don't." His words are so calmly spoken I actually believe he may not have a choice in killing me.

He places his forehead to mine and shuts his eyes, then one of his calloused hands wraps around my throat. The pressure is light at first, almost gentle, but it steadily increases, making it harder to breathe. If someone were to see us, they'd think we were in a lovers embrace the way his forehead is pressed to mine and his lips hover so close to mine.

So, this is how it ends? I wish I could say I'll be missed, but I doubt it. It would be a relief to my mother. She probably wouldn't shed a tear at my funeral just like at daddy's. Raina would somehow find a way to make my death about her. The only person who'd truly care would be Trina.

Despite knowing there is no use in fighting, my reflexes still kick in and I attempt to pull his hands away. But he's so strong that he doesn't budge.

I gasp for air. His eyes open, and those beautiful orbs lock in on me. I'm not sure if it's the lack of oxygen to my brain or if I'm hoping to see something that isn't there, but it looks as if sorrow and sadness dance in his gaze.

Black spots appear in my vision, and I close my eyes hoping my death will be swift.

CHAPTER THREE

Her

Beast

"Look at the way she's dressed. She's a whore. A filthy dirty slut. Cleanse her of her sins. Kill the tramp," My mother's voice roars in my head.

My hand tightens around the small beauty's throat. I've never felt as disoriented as I did when she walked into the room. Her brown eyes took in everything around her.

It took me a second to scan through all the emotions I've memorized over the years. I try to keep track of them, so I'll be able to recall them if I see them again. Lucien taught me the trick my first year as a Deacon.

Panic. That was what the look on her face showed. Not fear, or disgust. Her delicate features pinched as her mouth fell open. I wasn't expecting her to plead for help, but what was even more startling was my aggressive need to answer her call.

"Then why the hell are you killing her now?" Right on time, Priest voice steps in.

"Because she's a whore," Mother replies.

I stare down into her face; her eyes are closed, and her mouth is open. Death is so near her I can feel him breathing down my neck.

"You don't want to do this, Kid." Priest's inner voice says.

"*Kill her.*" My mother counters.

I groan and slam my free hand against the wall beside her head. The hand around her neck loosens and then drops down to my side.

She gasps for breath, falling to the floor at my feet. I watch her fight to suck in enough air to survive.

I need more time. I can kill her later.

"Get up," I tell her. I don't like seeing her on the ground.

She rolls over to her back and glares up at me. I scan my rolodex of facial expressions. She's angry.

"You tried to kill me," her voice is raspier than before.

I do not reply to this obvious statement. I pull her to her feet by her arm and walk her back into the bedroom, depositing her up against the wall. I then head back over to my menu.

He's been dead for a while now. I had more plans for him, but I no longer desire the fun. The sound of the carpet squishing behind me has me turning to glare at her. She's on her knees inching toward the door.

"If you try to run again, it will not end well."

If she attempts to run this time, I will have a legitimate reason to kill her.

"*You have a reason now. Look at her, she's without morals. The good book says the wicked shall be cut from the earth.*"

Turning away from her, I gather my weapons. Using a towel, I wipe down the head of the hammer and then drop it back into my duffle. Although my attention appears to be on cleaning my tools, I listen intently for all sounds behind me. Other than heavy breathing, she does not try to leave again. Good.

The silence is interrupted by her raspy voice. It's not light and airy like it was before. I don't like it.

"What did he do to you?"

I pause, before grabbing the hack saw off the bed and wiping it down. Did she know him? Was he her lover the way Passion is for Priest? The thought of it has me turning my head in her direction.

"Nothing," I snap.

She shrinks back against the wall as if I've struck her. I go back to cleaning my tools.

"Then why did you kill him?" Her question is a lot more hesitant this time.

I want to tell her to stop talking. I don't like a lot of conversation. Plus, I don't owe her a reason for doing what I did. However, when I open my mouth those are not the words that come out.

"It's my job."

"Is your job being a serial killer?"

Shaking my head, I stuff my blade down in the bag. Grabbing the drill next, I remove the bloodied broken bit, clean it, and then toss it in the bag as well before moving on to the power tool.

"No." I once again find myself responding when my mind is telling me to be quiet.

I'm waiting for the point where the sound of her voice starts to annoy me. Even with Priest and my brothers I can only talk to them for so long before I become irritated. However, I don't like her silence.

She didn't run. Mother said they would all run, but she didn't at first.

"You're an assassin?" Her voice is even lower now, almost a whisper.

"Yes."

Silence sits between us, and I fight my instincts to turn around and look at her. The burning urge to constantly keep my eyes on her bothers me.

"Are you going to kill me?"

"Yes," I don't lie.

Though I spared her for now, she will die tonight. I ignore her soft whimpers in the corner. Tears won't save her life. After zipping up my duffle, I take my phone out and make a call. The line connects but no one speaks.

"Placing an order for one. Menu five." I hang up the phone and drop it in my pocket. The fifth item on my menu is done.

Grabbing my duffle off the chair, I walk over to her and glare down. She's in a tight ball, her back is to the wall and her knees are pulled up to her chest. Her face is buried in her hands. The fingers on my free hand twitch at the urge to touch her.

"Time to go," I say, balling my hand into a fist.

She takes her hands away from her face and looks up at me with upturned brown eyes.

"No," she says through clenched teeth.

I take a moment to study her expression. I do not immediately recall the look. It frustrates me when it takes longer than usual to figure out an emotion. Letting out a deep breath, I reach down and once again grab her by the arm, yanking her to her feet.

Her small fist beat at my chest as I escort her out of the room and into the hall.

"Let me go. I said let me fucking go," she shouts as she continues to fight me.

I stop walking and swing her around to face me. "Stop," the word is spoken lowly, but she immediately quits fighting against me.

Closing my eyes, I focus on my breathing.

"The disrespectful whore doesn't even appreciate your kindness." Mother's voice quickly points out. "You should march her back in the room and peel the flesh from her whore face."

"No," I say out loud.

"Weak. You are weak." Her voice taunts. *"The scripture says those that are in the flesh can not please God. You have not learned your lesson, Boy. Do what you are called to do."*

"Shut up," I shout.

When I open my eyes, I find her staring at me. This time it does not take me long to decipher her expression. Fear. She's afraid.

"You will behave," I tell her.

She doesn't respond, but she also doesn't try to pull away when I grab her arm this time. Until I'm ready to end her, I will have to keep her with me. There are three more people on my menus. After I've dealt with them, I'll deal with her.

"Come."

I walk her out of the apartment, my hand still wrapped around her bicep. The cleanup crew will be here soon, and I need to be long gone by then.

CHAPTER FOUR

Monster

Summer

The giant walks me through the streets of Manhattan like I'm a miss behaving toddler. His grip on my arm doesn't loosen one bit. If it did, I would definitely run.

We don't talk as we head to Grand Central station. He doesn't even let my arm go as he pays the toll. We board the train heading back toward lower Manhattan and take a seat near the back. He places the black duffle bag down at his feet.

A man across from us watches me warily, I try with all my might to ask for help with my eyes.

"Don't," his gruff voice comes from beside me.

I turn to see him staring at me. How is it possible someone so beautiful could be so deranged?

"You will only get him killed."

I wholeheartedly believe this monster will kill this man if he tries to help me. I mean it isn't hard to believe, he peeled poor Greg like an orange.

"Do you enjoy taking people's lives? Do you get some sick satisfaction from murder?" I ask curtly.

No, I'm not quiet with my question either. I want people to hear. Although, I know it won't help. I'm on a New York subway, people are trained to ignore their surroundings.

"Yes," he replies easily as if I asked him if he's enjoying the weather.

That was not what I was expecting him to say. Although, when I think about it, I don't know why I thought he would respond any other way. You can't do what he did if you don't enjoy it.

Shaking my head to clear my thoughts, I say. "Look, you can let me go. I won't tell anyone what I saw. I promise." Yes, I've resorted to pleading. I'll try anything to get me out of this situation.

"You would. Eventually, you would tell."

He leans forward in his seat placing his elbows on his knees. His eyes seem to watch every person on the train. They bounce from one face to another. Short pieces of his hair have fallen from the high bun and down into his face covering the old scar in his hairline. It bothers me that I notice it.

Taking a deep breath, I lift my shoulders and drop them on my exhale. I need to think and do it quickly. This isn't the first high risk situation I've been in. I escaped from Nic that night, and he had a gun to my head. I just need to be smart.

What do I know about this guy so far? Well, there is the obvious, he's a killer. He seems to also be battling some type of mental issue. The way he started talking to himself at Greg's house proves that all the screws aren't tightened in his head. I need to be patient with him.

At some point he's going to let his guard down and I'll be able to get away. I need to make him think I'm going to cooperate with him. Something made him not kill me when he had the chance. It leads me to believe this killer has a conscious. I need to make myself seem as human as possible to him. People don't kill things they connect with.

With my new plan in place, I lean back against the glass seeming to relax.

"You know, today has been a really shitty day for me." I laugh to lighten the mood a little. "First, my sister kicked me out of the house for trying to sleep with her man and then I took a prostitution job for my best friend. Only to end up here."

"You seem to make a lot of bad choices," he says in that emotionless deep voice of his.

I turn to look at him. He looks to be still hyper focused on his surroundings, yet I can tell he's listening to me.

"Wow, never thought I'd be judged by a serial killer."

Those light green eyes cut to me momentarily. "Assassin," he corrects.

As if there is a difference.

"Just so you know, I didn't try to sleep with my sister's boyfriend." I don't know why I felt the need to clear that up instead of the prostitution thing. Probably because I was guilty of attempted prostitution.

He again looks to me, his gaze running up and down my body before turning back to everyone else.

"I don't believe you."

Wow, this motherfucker's got a lot of nerve. "You know what, fuck you," I say sitting up straight. "You don't even know me—"

"I know you showed up at an apartment to have sex with a man that has made billions of dollars by poisoning children in third world countries just so he can get his skin care medications approved."

My draw drops and hangs there for a moment. "I didn't...... know that about him."

His gaze narrows on me. "Even if you did, would it have made a difference?"

I open my mouth to tell him yes. To explain to him that I would never lay down with a man that could hurt others, especially children. However, no words come out.

Because the truth is, I needed the money to get out of town. Although what Greg was doing was horrible, I couldn't see the children he was hurting. I didn't know them. I probably would have pushed their plight out of my mind to save myself. It's shitty to admit, but I'm honest enough to tell the truth. Does that make me a bad person?

Sitting back once again, my shoulders slump. "No. It probably wouldn't have made a difference."

"As I thought," he says, his gaze going back to scanning the crowd.

I could go off on him, remind him that he has a lot of judgement for someone that gets paid to kill people. However, that wouldn't be smart. If I want to survive the night with this killer, I have to stay calm. Same way I did the night with Nic.

Suddenly a muscle cramp hits my stomach and has me clutching my side. I take slow breaths in. Fuck! Trying to stay clear headed and survive while going through withdrawals will not be easy.

Once the cramp subsides, I relax and lean back in my seat. I ignore the heated gaze on my face. I know he's watching but I won't acknowledge him.

The computerized female voice on the subway tells us our next stop.

"Let's go," the giant says, standing and grabbing his bag. Before I can climb to my feet by myself, he wraps his large hand around my bicep and yanks me out of my seat.

"You don't have to handle me like this," I argue.

His green eyes cut to me and without a word, his grip loosens only a little. Don't get me wrong, it still feels like a python is wrapped around my upper arm, but at least the python is no longer trying to kill me.

The train car pulls to a stop, and we are off as soon as the doors open. We trot up the steps and out onto the streets. He's walking at a fast pace and my legs are moving twice as fast as his, trying to keep up.

I do notice that he doesn't slow down or move for anyone. Everyone in his path just glides out of the way for him. It's like they can feel the danger rolling off him.

We walk about a block and a half before my body and the damages I've done to it over the years start to catch up with me.

"Stop, please. I have to stop."

I pull up short and he swings around to glare at me. His eyes narrow as he watches me fight to get air into my lungs.

"You're out of shape," he states the obvious.

I roll my eyes but ignore his dig. "Where are you taking me?"

"Menu," he simply replies.

"I'm sure that's some kind of serial killer lingo, but can you dumb it down for us regular people."

Those beautiful eyes tighten at the corners. "How about I use the language of your people. I have another John."

My mouth falls open. I should be offended. He's basically calling me a whore. Not to mention he has kidnapped me and threatened to kill me. However, he is speaking my language which is Ill-timed humor and dark jokes.

I fight the laugh that wants to come out and stand up straight. "Look, if you think I'm going to help you go around this city killing people then you're crazier than I thought."

If it's at all possible, it feels as if he somehow gets bigger. His nostrils flare, his chest expands and the vein in his neck throbs. The eyes that are so striking turn even colder. He takes a step closer to me, blocking out the glow from the streetlight behind him.

"Do. Not. Call me crazy."

Okay, duly noted. I nod, taking a step back from him. He turns and yanks my arm, dragging me with him.

I don't say another word to him as we speed-walk another three blocks. By the time we stop again, I'm sweating profusely.

We stand on the sidewalk near a bunch of old abandoned textile mills. Across the street is a brick building that is meant to blend in with its surroundings but stands out like a sore thumb. It has dark gray brick siding, and black reflective glass mirrors that allow you to see out but never in. Low light wall lanterns line the front of the building like an old English manor, and then there is the unmistakable black door.

"Aces?" I say, recognizing the symbol on the black door. "What business do you have in a sex club?"

He turns to me, more of his short hairs have fallen from his man bun and are now framing his forehead and cutting through his eyesight. Even with his obscured vision I don't miss the way his gaze roams up and down my body.

He doesn't have to say a word, I can read what he's thinking a mile away.

"First of all," I say with my free hand on my hip. "Take that look off your face. My best friend has a membership here. That's the only reason I know this place." That's a lie, but he doesn't have to know that.

He smirks before turning around as if he doesn't believe me. Smug bastard. He pulls me off the curb and heads for the front door of the building.

"Wait," I call out, attempting to stop him.

I step in front of him, risking nearly getting trampled. Placing my hand to his chest, he looks down at it as if it's something I picked up off the ground. I quickly remove my hand and place it at my side feeling a bit disheartened. I push forward with the reason I stopped him.

"They're not going to let you just roll up in there. This place is entrance by membership only. And the waiting process for that membership takes months while they vet you."

I remember the process very well while Trina was waiting for her card to come in the mail.

"I'm good," he simply says and starts walking.

I obediently follow behind him, not like I have a choice. The death grip he has on my arm hasn't loosened.

After getting to the door, the giant rings the doorbell on the wall. It's at this weird moment that I realize, I don't know his name. I've been calling him giant all night. As I said, my goal is to survive the night. In order to do that, I have to connect with him.

"My name is Summer by the way."

Silence fills the space. I wait for him to acknowledge me or say something. Yet he doesn't.

"I'm not a huge fan of the name. I never felt like a Summer. I don't even like Summer. It's too damn hot. I prefer fall. The weather is much better and the colors the leaves turn are absolutely gorgeous. Although, I guess Fall as a name doesn't really sound good. Although Autumn would have been cute—"

"Gabriel," his deep voice cuts me off.

"What was that?" I heard him just fine, but I wanted him to say it again.

"My name is Gabriel," he says, glancing over his shoulder at me.

"Gabriel," I repeat it.

He doesn't look like a Gabriel. He strikes me as a Thor, or Axel. Something tough and strong.

"I like it," I admit.

He doesn't respond. The door to the club opens and a familiar large man steps out. He has an earpiece in his ear and a tablet in his hand. Well, this won't end well.

I take a step closer to Gabriel, hiding behind his wide back. Of all the bouncers at Ace's it had to be Curtis at the door.

"Name?" Curtis asks in a gruff voice. He hasn't noticed me yet.

"Aleksander Sidov."

Curtis scans his tablet before looking up at Gabriel. "Alright, I see you. And I see you have a guest." He peeks around Gabriel. I hold my breath hoping he won't recognize me.

"Wait, is that Summer?"

Look, I've already hit rock bottom tonight, at least that's what I thought. How the hell could I get lower.

I step from around Gabriel, no need to hide now.

"Hey Curtis," I wave awkwardly. "It's been a while."

He scowls at me, shaking his head. "You know I'm not letting your ass in here. Not after last time. Get the fuck away from this door."

Gladly. I turn to leave, but the grip on my arm tightens.

"She's with me," Gabriel says in a way that brokers no argument.

Curtis narrows his gaze at Gabriel. As long as Gabriel's name is on that list, he can bring whoever he wants into the club. Despite Curtis's trepidation—and don't get me wrong he has a right to not want me inside—he has to let me in.

"Alright man," Curtis says stepping back and opening the door. "But if she starts her shit, it's you that will be held responsible."

Gabriel tugs me behind him as he walks into the club. The temperature is cooler inside and the smell of leather and cleaner assails my senses. The bass to the music vibrates my chest as I follow Gabriel down a long narrow hallway toward the main room.

We walk into the first floor of Ace's, also known as the main area. If you were to stumble into this part of the club by accident, you would think you were at any other upscale bar in Manhattan.

Dark leather couches sit across from each other allowing for great conversation. Dark wood panels and black paint coat the walls. In the center of the room is a large rectangular bar that is stocked with only the most expensive and top shelf liquor.

I had hoped that whatever business Gabriel had at Aces would be in this room, but those hopes are dashed when he bypasses the bar and heads for the elevator to the lower level.

We climb into the elevator. He hits the button for the fifth floor, the lowest level. My heart sinks to my feet. He remains quiet on our slow decent down.

"I've only been here one time," I try explaining my run in with Curtis. "Admittedly, I wasn't in my right mind."

I was higher than the Empire State Building. It was the first and only time Trina was able to get me to go to a place like this. The night ended with me being tossed out by Curtis after nearly stabbing a man in the throat for grabbing my ass.

"I'm not a bad person." Despite all the evidence that's been presented against me.

Usually, I don't give a shit what others think about me, but for some reason I don't want this killer thinking I'm a bad person. I like to think it is because I need him to see me as someone that deserves to live. However, I'm not a hundred percent sure that is the reason. Which proves, I'm more fucked up in the head than I thought I was.

I wait for him to say something, but he remains silent, not even acknowledging my conversation.

Scoffing, I shake my head. "Whatever, believe what you want."

I catch the smile that lifts his lips in the reflection against the elevator doors. He's getting a kick out of toying with me and I'm falling right into his trap.

The elevator dings and the doors slide open. The smell of sweat and pussy overpowers my senses. The bass from the music pounds my chest. I know what I will face when I walk out these open doors. There is a reason Trina wouldn't bring me back to Aces. My vice runs rampantly in this place. My mouth waters and my muscles clench at the thought of what's nearly available to me.

Gabriel hauls me out of the elevator into the main area. Unlike the upscale elegant vibe on the first floor, the theme on this floor is pure sin. All the lights are red, giving the room a sexual vibe. Drapes hang from the ceiling sectioning off the areas. Chaise lounges surround tables no one would dare eat off. Well, I guess it depends on what you're eating.

Even though the music is loud, nothing will drown out the sound of pleasured moans. Naked waitresses walk around with trays filled with Lube, condoms, and toys.

We pass a section where one woman is being serviced by three men. My eyes connect with the female, and she smiles blissfully at me.

In the next section, a man is receiving a blowjob from a female and a very enthusiastic man. On the table in front of him are a few lines of coke. My feet stop moving on their own accord. That burning itch hits the back of my throat. The sight of the white powdery substance has taken over my thoughts so much, that I forget where I am and who I'm with.

"Feeling left out?"

I jump at the sound of his deep voice close to my ear. Glancing over my shoulder, I shoot him a narrow-eyed look. He thinks I'm staring at the threesome; he has no idea what I'm really craving.

"I was just looking," I say, glancing back at the group.

"Yeah right. Come on." He tugs my arm, and we continue to speed walk through the many sections.

We leave the common area and head to the back where the private rooms are. We come to a red door and stop. While he fumbles with the lock, I glance around. No one is really paying attention to us.

We kind of blend in. I mean, it's hard to fade into the background when you're as huge as Gabriel. However, this place sees celebrities, so a giant Viking and a skinny chick dressed like a cheap whore aren't very memorable. However, the camera over my head will definitely be able to recognize us.

Gabriel gets the door open and shoves me inside. The silence in the room is a welcome relief. I turn to see him placing his black duffel down on a table.

Glancing around the room, I notice that there isn't much in here. A massage table is in the middle of the floor. Beside it is a tray of oils along with a variety of dildos including one so big there is no way humanly possible it could fit in anyone's body. Laid out on another tray is a collection of colorful mesh material. Soft music plays in the background.

On one side of the room is a narrow door and another door is at the back of the room. This is my first time seeing the rooms. When I came that one night with Trina, we stayed out in the common area.

"Put this on," Gabriel says.

I turn to him and get smacked in the face with something soft. Pulling the material away from my face I hold it up to get a better look at it. It's one of the outfits on the tray.

"I'm not putting this shit on." I toss the completely see-through neon green dress to the floor.

Not only do I not have the body to pull this off, but I'm also not walking around naked in front of this man.

"You have a client coming in. Get dressed," he demands, walking past me as if this topic is finished.

Fed up with his attitude and this entire night, I pick up the fabric at my feet, ball it up and throw it at him. It hits him in the back and falls to the floor.

"Fuck you," I shout.

He spins around on his feet and glares at me.

"If you're going to kill me, then you might as well get it over with because I'm not helping you commit murder."

I'm praying this outburst goes one of two ways. Number one, hopefully I call his bluff and he in fact doesn't have plans to butcher me the way he did Gregory. Number two, and this may be a little far-fetched, he realizes I won't be useful and lets me go.

Gabriel shuts his eyes, and his breathing becomes labored. That feeling comes over me again, the one that screams you're now trapped in a room with a wild animal.

I turn and take off for the door. I hit the wood surface with a thud and immediately flipped around so that my back is against the barrier. A very irate Gabriel is staring down at me, his nostrils flaring as those intense eyes focus in on me.

He crowds my space, placing his large body up against mine. He wraps his hand around my throat, but he doesn't squeeze. I swallow, and I imagine he can feel the movement underneath his palm.

"Don't hurt me," I plead.

Yes, I know this is a big jump from my last statement. But hell, have you ever stared up at the devil before.

"Never try that again."

"Okay," I answer quickly.

I have no idea if he's warning me against throwing something at him or running, but in this moment, I will agree to anything.

He doesn't let me go immediately. Instead, he continues to watch me, his attention solely on my face as if he's found something interesting about it. He stares so long I start to feel uncomfortable. It isn't until someone squeals right outside the door that he releases me.

Gabriel steps back, shaking his head as if he's dislodging thoughts.

"You don't have time to change. Wait here." He turns away from me and heads to the narrow door on the other side of the room.

"What am I waiting on?" I call out to his back.

He stops at the door without turning to look at me. "His regular masseuse won't be able to make it tonight. But he doesn't know that." he turns to glare over his shoulder at me. "So, make him comfortable."

With those words, he disappears behind the door and I contemplate running again. That thought only lingers for a few seconds before the door to the private room opens. In steps a tall well-dressed man in a suit. His dark brown hair is gelled back off his head. He has yet to notice me.

"I told you I don't give a shit what the voters think. I've already been elected. My morals lie with the highest bidder and right now, his money is winning. Besides, what the hell are they going to do with more school funding?" He pulls up short when he spots me. His blue eyes raking up and down my body.

"Jim, I have to go. Set up the meeting for tomorrow." He hangs up the phone placing it in his pocket. "Where's Kim?"

I don't know who the hell Kim is. But thankfully I'm quick on my feet and have years of lying under my belt.

"She called in sick today, and they asked me to take her spot."

Could I have told him about Gabriel and maybe have him get me out of here? Sure. However, being in Gabriel's presence for an hour has shown me that he's fast on his feet, good at what he does, and probably doesn't take kindly to being betrayed. And just two seconds of meeting this guy showed me that he's a sleazy politician, and most likely wouldn't help me. Better the devil you know than the devil you don't, right?

He scoffs. "They replaced my Kim for some junky black girl with a bad weave."

Rude. I look down my body at myself as if I don't agree with his assessment of me.

Cocking my hip, I ask with a neck roll, "Do you want the massage or not?"

One of the things I've learned from my best friend over the years is that confidence can get you a long way in this world. The other thing she taught me is pussy is pussy. A man can talk about preference all day, but when it comes to getting his dick wet, he will stick it in anything warm and available.

Mr. Politician squints while wrinkling his nose in disgust. "You better not fuck this up." He says undoing his tie and walking past me to the massage table.

Immediately relief hits me. I have no idea why I was fighting to pull this off. I'm officially aiding a serial killer. There is clearly a life sentence in my future.

Glancing over to the door, I once again contemplate leaving. Surely Gabriel wouldn't risk exposing himself to the politician. With my mind made up, I head in the direction of my freedom.

"Where're you going?" Mr. Politician asks.

I spin around on my heels only to come face to face with a naked man. When did he take off his clothes? I take a step back.

"Get your ass back over here and start with my usual."

"Your usual?"

"Smallest to largest," he says pointing at the variety of dildos on the tray. "And I like a lot of lube."

My stomach heaves, and this time it has nothing to do with withdrawals. This was my cue to get the hell out of there.

"Sure, just let me go grab something." I turn to leave, but gasp when he grips my arm and hauls me up against his chest.

I freeze in fear. Look, I talk a big game and I'm good at compartmentalizing. I've been living on the streets long enough to know that you have to adapt fast and put your emotions to the side. However, this is the second man tonight to grab me like this. A girl deserves a mental breakdown.

"Where do you think you're going?" Mr. Politician sneers down at me. "I wasn't feeling the whole druggy look, but now I kind of like it."

Told you, all they need is a wet hole.

"Let me go," I say between clenched teeth, pulling against his grip.

He yanks me back. "Stop fighting."

Using the heel of my borrowed shoes, I stomp them on his bare feet. He yells before releasing me. However, my victory is short lived because he backhands me so hard, I crumble to the floor from the blow. My jaw is on fire and I'm sure I'll have an ugly bruise tomorrow.

I look up just in time to see an Axe cut through Mr. Politician's head. The crack sounds like an egg hitting the pavement. Blood sprays out in an arc, splattering across my face. Mr. Politician slumps forward but doesn't fall to the ground. Gabriel is behind him holding him up with one hand. His eyes stare down at me, while his shoulders rise and fall rapidly.

Standing before me is not a man. When I walked in on him with Gregory, I didn't pay attention to him, but now I can see it. He looks possessed. His eyes, that are truly stunning, look vacant. I've never been more afraid in my life.

Gabriel removes the axe from the politician's head and then repeatedly beats him with it. Blood and chunks of brain matter fly everywhere.

My body is stuck. My brain can't send the message to my limbs to move. As terrifying as this moment is, it's also beautiful. I think that signifies I'm fucked up in the head, but he looks like an avenging angel in the way he kills.

Summer, get your ass up and get the hell out of here. The small, sane, sober voice in my head yells. I haven't heard from her in a long time.

Without second guessing my conscious, I clamber to my feet, kick off my heels, and take off toward the door. Not stopping to check if he's behind me, I sprint out the room. I don't give a shit who sees me leaving that crime scene. Bypassing the elevator, I head for the stairs. I run as fast as my legs will take me. Once I get to the top level, I burst into the main floor nearly knocking over a waitress in my haste.

"Watch it, bitch," she shouts.

Ignoring her, I race for the side exit. Freedom wraps me in its embrace when I open the door and step out into the alley. I pull in a lungful of fresh air. Spotting a homeless man rummaging through the trashcan, I start toward him.

"Help," I plead. "Help me." Rushing toward him, I grab his arms. I try to push him out the alley. We need to get as far away from this place as we can.

The elderly man looks over my body, his gaze landing back at my face. I imagine he's noticed the blood. When his attention goes behind me and his eyes widen, my heart drops.

The old man is snatched away from me and tossed to the opposite wall. I turn just in time to see Gabriel standing behind me. He grabs me by the neck and shoves me against the brick wall. I hit it so hard the breath leaves my lungs. I feel like half of my night has been spent shoved up against a wall.

He crowds my space, slamming his fists against the wall on both sides of my head. I scream, before trapping the sound behind my hands.

"Don't. Ever. Run. From. Me." He punctuates the sentence with another fist to the wall.

"I'm sorry. I'm sorry," I beg for his forgiveness.

He doesn't respond, instead he leans his forehead against mine and takes deep breaths.

I have no idea what the hell to do. My heart is knocking against my chest like one of those old cartoon characters.

"I know you're mad," I start.

"Don't. Speak."

I immediately stop talking, hoping and praying this won't be my last few minutes alive on this earth. Silence surrounds us as he continues to catch his breath.

When I was in school, every report card stated that I talked too much. None of that has changed. I'm even worse in stressful situations. "Are you going to kill me—"

My words are cut off when his fist slams against the brick wall again. He takes a step back, allowing me some space. I don't dare make any sudden moves. He lifts his hand and I flinch before he cups my cheek. He then uses his thumb to wipe something away, most likely blood.

"You need to shower. Come," he demands, grabbing my arm in a strong hold again.

As we make our way back into Ace's, something becomes painfully clear. I will not get away from Gabriel by running. He's just too fast and too clever for that. I will have to rely on my first plan of making him see me as human and maybe start to like me. However, I'm not really known for my charming personality. So, I don't see this working out well.

CHAPTER FIVE

Her Eyes

Beast

After calling the cleanup crew, I slide my phone back in my pocket. I stare down at Victor Royal's lifeless body.

Although my job is complete, I feel the itch for more. The desire to remove his organs and hang them up around this room starts to make the red haze cloud my mind.

"Swine," my mother's voice in my head snarls. *"You should cut his lying tongue out of his mouth. No swift deaths."*

I reach into my bag to bring out my reciprocating saw, but stop when the bathroom door opens. She walks out using a paper towel to dry her hands. Her focus is on cleaning herself and not yet on me. As if she could feel my gaze, she looks up and stares at me.

"What?" she asks, wiping at her face. "Did I miss something?"

Turning away from her, I put my attention back on Victor. The urge to cut his body up disappears. My job is finished.

"Let's go," I demand without looking at her. Zipping my black duffle, I toss it over my shoulder.

"Wait," she says, causing me to face her. "Don't you need to clean this shit up? I mean the cameras saw you come in here. You're not worried about going to jail for this?"

Seems like she's come to terms with her death. Her questions are no longer about her surviving the night. This should be a good thing. The less she fights me on this the easier it will be. Yet, I don't like the hollow feeling that comes with this thought.

"It's handled." Again, I turn away, this time heading to the door.

"Gabriel."

I flinch when she calls my name. The only person that ever called me that name was mother. I killed the name a long time ago, yet when I went to give her my name, that is what came out.

Glancing back at her over my shoulder, I find her standing with her hands on her narrow waist. She's too skinny. I didn't notice it before, but I can see it now.

Although I've never been allowed to sample the women from the Nunnery, I have seen them. Their skin looks healthy, and it tends to glow, it never matters the color of it. However, Summer's is dull and sickly looking.

"She's a hideous whore." Mother taunts. *"You know what's wrong with her."*

"Look, I know I'm not living past tonight, but can you at least let me in on what the hell is going on? I do have family that I don't want caught up in this bullshit," she says the last part pointing at Victor.

I owe her no explanation.

"They won't. The cameras have not worked since we walked in, and the room will be cleaned."

Why the hell does this keep happening. Just like the name thing, when I open my mouth, an answer to her question falls out.

"Well, at least you're an organized killer," she says, crossing her arms over her chest.

The urge to smile at her antics tugs at my lips.

"Kill this whore. Do it now. She is a hindrance. She eats the bread of idleness. Spill her ungodly blood."

Just as fast as the urge to smile arrived it disappears. Mother's voice has that ability.

"Not now," I counter in my head.

"Weak," Mother hisses. *"Kill her. Kill the whore, now."*

"Shut up, shut up, shut up," I growl, as I pull at my hair fighting to clear mother's voice out of my head. My frantic breathing is loud in my ears as I close my eyes and shut out the world.

"Focus, Kid. Breathe." Right on time, Priest's voice steps in. *"Block that bitch out. She no longer gets to live in your head rent free. She's not here."*

Slowly, I gain control of my thoughts. Silence surrounds me. Opening my eyes, I come face to face with a pair of brown ones. Although dark circles make them look tired, her eyes turn upwards at the end giving her a feline-like look. Her irises aren't as dark this close up, I can see the lighter hues of brown. Her eyes are beautiful.

I frown as that thought runs through my head.

"You good?" she asks.

"Yes."

She steps back, looking in every direction but at me. She hugs her body, hunching her shoulders. I scan through my rolodex of memorized emotions. Embarrassment. This is peculiar. Why is she embarrassed?

"So, what's next?" she asks, pulling my attention away from her odd behavior.

"We eat," I turn toward the door and head out. Her soft footfalls follow behind me. I don't grab her arm until we are on the other side of the door.

We head out of the club. I have only nine hours to finish my menus, and then I have to kill Summer.

CHAPTER SIX

Beast

Summer

Two train rides and a bus later, we're in the Bronx at a diner.

Staring down at my French fries and chicken sandwich, my stomach turns over. My appetite is somewhere between Gregory's loft and the politician at the sex club. It also doesn't help that my body is craving something else.

However, it seems Gabriel does not have the same issues. One arm protectively wraps around his plate, his back is hunched over the table. He's shoveling mashed potatoes in his mouth with his fork as if someone will come and snatch his food away.

As focused as you would think he is on his food, his eyes have not stopped scanning the restaurant. Every sound draws his gaze. Every time the bell over the door dings, his focus shifts.

"Do you ever take a break?"

He stops stuffing food into his mouth, his attention landing on me. One dark blonde brow raises in confusion.

"We're in a diner in the Bronx, no one is going to attack you. Besides, I'm pretty sure you're the most dangerous person in this room."

I hate that I notice the minute smile that lifts his lips.

Gabriel leans up from his plate pushing it away. Using a napkin, he wipes his mouth before placing it back down on the table.

"No," he says.

It takes me a moment to figure out what he's replying to. When I do, I find it hard to believe. Clearly, he isn't scanning the room for intruders while he's getting his dick sucked.

"So even when you're…" I make a circle with one hand and use the pointer finger of the other to imitate the deed. "You don't stop being alert?"

He doesn't speak at first, just stares at me. I grow uncomfortable for a minute waiting for him to answer. Maybe that was too personal. I doubt most people ask their potential murderer about their sex life.

After the longest most uncomfortable second passes, I realize he's not going to answer my question. Rolling my eyes, I ask another one.

"What are you scanning for anyway? Threats? You think someone's going to pull a knife out and stab you over your smothered porkchop?"

He narrows his gaze slightly. "Beside us, the man in the tie. He's married, but the woman with him isn't his wife."

I look to my left to the dark-haired man with the goatee.

"How do you know that?" I ask, looking back at Gabriel.

His eyes close mid-way as if he's determining if he should give away his secrets to me.

"There is an indentation on his left ring finger that tells me he recently took his ring off. She has no ring or any signs of having a ring. Plus, he's found some way to touch her from the moment they walked in. As if he doesn't get to do it often."

I glance back at the couple sitting across from us. How the hell did he see all of that? I mean, I noticed how touchy they were, even going as far as sitting beside each other in the booth. They're acting like two drunk teens on prom night. Still, I wouldn't have guessed he was a cheater.

"How do you know she isn't his wife? Maybe they're madly in love." I ask turning back to him.

He smirks.

"Watch his cellphone," his head dips in the direction of the phone on the table.

It lights up and the picture of a smiling brunette holding a small child appears. The man looks to the phone and sighs before flipping it over, face down on the table. Asshole.

I look back to Gabriel and shake my head. "Wow, that's some talent you have there. If this serial killer thing doesn't work out for you, you could always get a job using your superpowers to catch cheaters."

He stares for a long moment. His head tilted to the side as he watches me. "Sarcasm." He finally says.

I laugh. "Now you've found my hidden talent. Although it's not as marketable as yours."

The laughter dies on my lips when I notice the way he's staring at me. It isn't sexual or anything. It's more like the way someone would stare at a difficult math problem.

"You should eat," he says, pointing at my untouched food.

I grimace as I glance down at my plate. "No, thank you." I push the plate aside and lean forward on my elbows. "I'd rather talk."

The confused look from earlier intensifies. I think I've caught him off guard.

"About what?" he grumbles.

"You. How did you get into a job like this? I'm pretty sure they didn't visit your local high school during career week."

He leans back in his seat. His chest expanding with a deep breath before letting it out.

"No, they came to my house," he answers and his gaze floats around the restaurant again.

That's believable. As gorgeous as Gabriel is, and he is stunning, he is also quite terrifying. He has to be close to seven feet tall and is as solid as a boulder. He screams danger when he walks into a room. If I were hiring an assassin, I'd definitely pick him.

"What did you do before this?"

His eyes snap back at me as if my question was connected to his pupils by a rubber band.

"Nothing," he answers.

I chuckle. "Oh, come on. You had to do something. I'm going to guess you had a desk job. Maybe something in customer service where people called and complained all day. That would probably make me want to be a killer too."

"I was seven," he cuts my rant off.

My eyes widen and my brain sputters. Maybe I didn't hear him correctly.

"Seven? As in seven-years-old?" I repeat for clarification.

He doesn't reply.

This poor man was basically raised to be a killer. I mean, I know all about a shitty childhood, but jeez. I couldn't imagine the damage this must have done to his mental state.

"I'm sorry."

He slams his hand down on the table causing me to nearly leap out of my skin and the plates and silverware to rattle.

"I don't require your pity nor your apology."

His outburst caught the attention of a few other people in the diner. The heavy-set cook with thick eyebrows glares at Gabriel. The two waitresses stop taking orders to stare at us. Even the cheating husband and his date turn in our direction. The question in all their eyes ask if I need help. If only they knew. However, for the first time, I do not attempt to ask for help.

"I didn't mean to offend you."

The fire in his green eyes simmers as he leans back in his seat and looks away from me. Slowly, everyone goes back to minding their business.

The diner isn't that packed tonight. Other than the couple beside us, only two other people are in here. An older man reading a paper and another younger guy that's wearing a trucker hat.

"It saved my life."

His words catch me off guard and I turn back to him. He isn't looking at me, but I don't doubt for a minute he isn't paying attention to me.

"How so?" I ask, truly interested in how becoming a killer at seven saved him.

This time he does look over to me.

"I was different from most kids my age. Troubled. I needed this." His gaze runs from me, finding something else to look at. "It feeds my darkness."

I understand that more than he thinks. I know what it's like to have a darkness inside you. One that calls out to you and beckons for your attention every time you let your guard down. I feed my darkness with pills, coke, weed, and even alcohol sometimes. My vices are less bloody than his, but at least he's not inflicting the damage on his own body.

"I can understand that."

Those sharp intelligent eyes flick back to me. His brows draw together, and his face tightens. He doesn't believe me. I laugh.

"Come on, Gabriel. The only reason we met tonight is because I walked into a man's house willing to sleep with him for money. Clearly, I have some shit going on too."

His smile spreads slowly but turns his already attractive face to downright stunning.

"The bad wig gave it away first," he says.

I burst into laughter covering my mouth. He watches me laugh; the smile still planted on his face. The door to the diner opens setting off the bell over the door. Gabriel focuses on the newcomers. From the way he watches them, I can guarantee he's taking in everything he can about them. When his gaze falls back on me it narrows. "Is it my turn now?"

Not sure how I feel about this. However, I've been asking him questions and I guess it's only right I allow him to do the same.

Sitting back in my seat and folding my arms across my chest, I say, "Go ahead."

He doesn't speak right away, which makes me squirm a little.

"Who did you see die?"

My body stills so suddenly, chills run up my spine. The images of blood on the wall and on my favorite nightgown flash through my mind. I shut my eyes and try to catch my breath as I fight back the memories of that night. My lungs seem to shrink in size as I struggle to get enough air flowing through them. The old ache in my shoulder flares up.

The harder I attempt to push the images away, the faster they come back to me. The sound of my father's voice calling my name has me gripping the table.

I'm startled when a heavy hand lands on top of mine. When I open my eyes, green irises are staring back at me. He takes my hand off the table, leans forward in his seat, and places my hand over his heart, palm down. The steady beat pulls me out of my memories like a life buoy.

For what seems like forever, we are suspended in time. My hand to his chest, his gaze locked in on mine, and complete silence.

I don't know anything about this man other than he's a killer that is hellbent on killing me. However, as dark as it may seem, I have more of a connection with him than I've had with anyone in the last fourteen years. Maybe, it's because he's just as damaged as I am.

Our waitress comes back, breaking into our moment.

"Can I get you anything else?" She looks between the both of us as if we're the weirdest people she's ever come across.

Removing my hand from his chest, I place it in my lap.

"No thank you. I'm good," I say without looking up from the table.

"Bring her a coffee," he says.

Lifting my head, I look back at him. His gaze is back on the room. I wonder if that moment meant anything to him. Without a second thought he knew what I needed and provided it for me. Yet, now he looks as if he only offered a brief smile to a passing stranger.

"I don't really drink coffee," I say, forcing those thoughts out of my head.

"You will tonight," he says in a tone that brokers no argument.

His eyes rest on me momentarily before going back to the room.

"Black, two sugars and a cream," he says to the waitress.

She looks to me for approval. I nod my head. She shakes hers in pity and walks away. I'm starting to believe these people think I'm in an abusive relationship.

"We have a long night; you're going to need the caffeine boost."

I roll my eyes at him but don't argue. The waitress sits my coffee down on the table. I take a sip and frown. I've never been a fan of coffee. I go to spit the bitter drink back in the cup but stop when I find Gabriel watching me. His brow raises as if he knows what I was about to do. I swallow what's in my mouth and cringe.

The bell over the door goes off letting us know someone else has just come in.

"What the fuck are you talking about? I was hitting that shit before you," the voices of the newcomers are loud.

I turn in my seat to see who they belong to, but immediately turn back around. My skin prickles with fear. I'm not shocked when I look up and Gabriel is watching me.

"We should go," I say, gulping as much of the hot coffee down my throat as I can.

I go to stand, but crash into the waitress knocking her tray out of her hand. The commotion has everyone's attention swinging in my direction.

"Summer?"

If the ground could open and swallow me right now it would be great.

"Jay, hey." I wave lamely.

"Hey?" He says, frowning. "That's all you have to say to me?" He and the three guys with him head in my direction.

Holding my hands out in front of me in a posture of surrender, I back up. "Okay, I can explain."

"Explain?" Jay repeats. "Bitch, you almost got me fucking killed."

I can't really argue with that.

"That wasn't my intention. I had no idea Nic was going to blame you."

I did know Nic would blame him. Hell, I was hoping for it. However, I didn't think I would have to witness it.

Jay grabs my arm, hauling me toward him. "Oh yeah, well I know just how to get back in his good graces." He turns to Tony, one of his friends. "Call Nic."

True fear sets in. Before I could argue, I'm snatched away from Jay and a hulking Gabriel is between us. Jay steps back, looking Gabriel over. I can tell he's trying to size him up, see if he's a threat.

Jay and his crew start to laugh. "I see you got another victim," Jay says looking past Gabriel to where I'm standing. He turns back to Gabriel.

"If you know what's good for you, you'd leave that bitch where you…"

I don't know what else he was going to say. Faster than the strike of a cobra, Gabriel chops Jay in the throat, grabs his head and slams it on the edge of the table. I'm not sure if it was bones breaking or just the rattling of the dishes, but something was loud and prompted a scream from Jay.

Tony pulls a gun and aims it at Gabriel. Before the gun is fired, Gabriel snatches the gun out of his hands, and slams it across his face. Tony falls to the ground. Gabriel takes the clip out of the weapon, using only one hand and tosses it beside Tony.

The other two men with Jay both take hesitant steps back. I don't blame them. That shit was incredible. Everyone else in the diner is completely still staring at us. The cook has one hand on the phone on the wall and the other hand clutching a butcher knife.

Gabriel turns around and takes a hundred dollar bill out of his pocket and drops it on the table. He grabs his black duffle off the bench seat and then takes my arm.

"Let's go."

I don't argue. He walks me out of the building and down the street a little way before stepping into a dark alley. He releases my hand, dropping his duffle, and starts pacing.

"I know that," he mumbles as he pulls at his hair. "I know."

I stand helplessly watching him battle whatever demon he hears in his head. I look to the opening of the alley. The thought of running hits me again, but it's fleeting. I learned my lesson about running at Ace's. Besides, I owe him to at least help. He saved my ass back at that diner.

"Gabriel," I call his name. He stops pacing but doesn't turn to me. "Look at me."

His heavy breathing and the pounding of my heart in my ears are the only noises in our little bubble. Eventually, those extraordinary eyes I've grown used to, land on me.

"We're okay. I'm right here." I step up to him, not knowing if this move will end up with my head smashed against the brick wall or not.

Luckily, he doesn't make any sudden movements. Reaching for his hand, I move slowly until I wrap my fingers around his wrist. The entire time our eyes are linked together. I move his hand from his head and place it against my chest. My heart is nowhere near as steady as his is when he does this.

His gaze falls to where his hand is pressed against my chest. For a moment we remain that way. It isn't until we hear the sound of sirens passing by that the both of us turn toward the opening of the alley. Gabriel removes his hand and goes over to pick up the duffle.

"Come on," he says over his shoulder. "I need to make a quick stop at home." I step up beside him and he starts walking. This time he didn't grab my arm. We walk side by side down the street, an assassin, and his victim.

CHAPTER SEVEN

Withdrawals

Summer

We stand outside a typical brick walk up apartment building. The type where they can charge four thousand in rent for the location, but the apartments look no better than the shit in the projects.

"For some reason, I thought the killing business would be a little more lucrative," I say, as I gaze up at the red brick building.

"No. It's only a step up from homeless prostitute."

I swing my head to look up at him. His face is stoic as he too looks over the building.

"That was a good one," I say, chuckling. "You can add standup comedian to your list of things to do when the killing gig tanks."

His green eyes land on me and his lips lift a minuscule of an inch upward. I guess that was as close to a laugh as I'll ever get.

He turns back to the building and heads inside. I follow. We skip the elevator and go straight for the stairs. I think he gets a kick out of making me suffer. By the time we make it to the 8th floor my body is on fire and I'm sweating like I've been running a marathon.

Gabriel looks over at me and frowns.

"I'm alright. I just need to sit down," I try to explain.

He opens the door to his apartment and steps aside for me to enter. The size of the place doesn't shock me. I've lived in New York most of my life. I know how tiny these apartments can be. This is a studio no larger than 400 sq ft. As soon as you enter, you're in the galley style kitchen. The dark oak cabinets and faux granite counters are bare.

The kitchen lets out to the main area of living space. A simple couch is placed against the wall with a plain rectangular coffee table in front of it. There is no other furniture in the room. Not a television, side tables, not even a plant in the corner. I would say it's the bare minimum, but this isn't even the minimum.

"Were you robbed?" I don't turn to look at him, but I feel him pressed up behind me.

"No," he replies, before walking past me to the folding doors on the other side of the room.

When he opens the doors, I can tell it's a closet. A few measly shirts hang on hangers along with a large hoodie and some shorts. There is no way this is his true apartment.

Gabriel yanks his shirt up over his head, exposing his wide back with all its cords and muscles. Damn! I didn't realize they made backs like that. Not even the crisscross of old scars can detract from the beauty of this man.

He quickly replaces the old shirt with a black long sleeve thermal. He grabs the hoodie off the hanger and then picks up a pair of black combat boots and turns to me.

"Put these on," he says, tossing the black fabric at me.

It smacks me in the face. He then tosses the boots at my feet.

"This thing is going to swallow me whole," I hold the hoodie up and it looks as wide as a bed sheet. "And there is no way I'm fitting those boots."

"You're very picky for someone in a borrowed dress."

I widen my eyes before looking down at my dress. "How did you know it was borrowed?"

His brow quirks up, and even though he doesn't say anything, I can read the word 'really' loud and clear.

"Whatever," I grumble, putting the large hoodie on.

As suspected, it swallows me. The bottom hits me right below the knees. After kicking off the heels, I put on the boots. I have to wrap the string around the ankle a few times to get them to tighten.

I look like a child playing dress-up in her daddy's clothes. Holding my arms out at my side, I drop them back down as I glare at him. He eyes me up and down before grimacing.

"I told you."

"Take off the shoes," he says, before turning back to the closet.

While his back is to me, I discreetly bury my nose into the collar of the hoodie and take a whiff. His scent is all over the fabric. It's a clean smell, with undertones of oak and sandalwood. Nothing overpowering, but I wouldn't expect anything else from him.

"Tell me about the guys in the diner?" he asks without turning to look at me.

He moves the clothes to one side in his closet, exposing a fancy keypad. Clearing my throat, I shift my weight from one foot to the next in order to take the heavy boots off.

"There's nothing to tell." I slide my feet back into my heels. They aren't the best, but at least they fit.

"Who is Nic?" he asks as he presses a few buttons on the keypad.

The back panel of the wall slides open. Oh shit. This man has a wall of weapons. There are guns, knives of all sizes, a freaking sword, and almost every power tool you can name. He opens the duffle bag and starts adding in a few more tools along with a couple of knives.

I'm so wrapped up in his arsenal that I forgot he asked me a question until he looks back at me over his shoulder.

I cringe. Would it have been too much to ask that he didn't pick up on anything that was said during that incident.

"I guess you could consider him an ex-boyfriend." I mean we were together for six months. That's a lot longer than any other relationship I've had.

He zips the bag up and starts out of the hidden room.

"Why are you afraid of him?"

"What?" I ask, rubbing the back of my neck, stalling. "Who told you I was afraid of him?"

He lifts one of his dark blond brows at me. I'm starting to get really irritated with that look. Sighing, I drop my arms by my side.

"I'm really starting to hate this talent of yours." Taking a seat on the couch, I lean back. "I burned down his stash house by accident and now he's determined to kill me."

With his arms folded across his chest, he only stares at me silently. Unlike him, I don't have the talent of reading people, so I don't know what he's thinking. I push forward.

"Sorry to spoil it for you, but you're not the first person to want to kill me. I have people lining up to do me the favor."

"Is that why you're so agreeable now?"

I wanted to argue that I'm agreeable because his big ass keeps chasing me down, but that wouldn't be truthful.

"Honestly, I was supposed to be dead a long time ago. I've been cheating death since I was a kid. I'm not surprised that bitch finally caught up to me. I guess I figured, why keep running when it's going to happen anyway. Might as well be you that does it."

After my first overdose at fifteen, doctors told me I was lucky to be alive. With the amount of Tylenol in my system I should have died. I feel like ever since then I've had one foot in the grave. If I'm being truly honest, death has had its stink on me since I was a child.

Gabriel hits the computer panel on his wall and the secret door closes. He steps out of the closet and shuts those doors too. He carries the black duffle over to the kitchen putting it on the counter. He then turns to the microwave.

"What happened to you when you were a kid?" He asks, without looking over to me.

"You're asking a lot of questions about someone you're going to kill."

Those seafoam green eyes turn to me briefly before going back to his task. After pressing a combination of five numbers on the keypad, the entire front of the microwave pops open. There's another hidden compartment. It's not a microwave at all but instead what looks to be a cool looking safe. Clearly, this shitty apartment is a lot more than it seems.

Gabriel pulls out a stack of money that has my eyes bugging nearly out my head. He places the stack into this black duffle. He then pulls out a computer that he places on the counter as well.

"Answer my question," he demands.

I roll my eyes. "No."

He gives me another one of his brief warning looks.

"Since you're in a talkative and sharing mood," I say, sitting up placing my elbows on my knees. "Who do you hear in your head when you're having an episode."

His entire body goes still. The fingers that were once flying across the keys on his laptop stop moving as well. For the longest time, he doesn't speak nor move. It lasts so long, I start to feel bad about even asking the question.

"Never mind. You don't have to answer—"

"My mother," he says at the same time I speak.

Silence once again surrounds us. I wasn't expecting that answer, but I'm not shocked.

I shrug and lean back on the couch. "Yeah, well mothers can be bitches sometimes."

If I wasn't sitting here watching his shoulders jump, I never would've believed that he could actually laugh.

Standing to my feet, I look for a door to the bathroom. I spot it in the kitchen. Before I can take one step in that direction, Gabriel turns to look at me.

"Where are you going?"

"Bathroom," I answer as I continue to my destination. "You can't hold a girl hostage without giving her a piss break."

"There are no windows in the bathroom."

I stop in my tracks and turn to him.

"Well, that's a fire hazard." When he doesn't react to my joke I sigh, and say. "Relax, Gabriel. I'm not trying to run. You and I both know I wouldn't get far." I continue my trek to the restroom closing the door behind me.

I press my back to the hard surface and take a few deep breaths. As cool and casual as I'm keeping it, this shit isn't easy.

There is a bit of level headedness that is required when you are facing your mortality. Knowing that tonight could be my last night on this earth, I start to reflect back over my life at all the things I would have done differently.

For instance, I wouldn't have asked my mother to let me stay with my father that night when I was eight. Some of the blame is on her. She knew he was in the midst of a psychotic break. I'm a hundred percent sure she wouldn't have left Raina in his care if she'd asked. Another thing I would have changed, was this outfit choice for the night.

Pushing away from the door, I quickly do my business and then wash my hands. However, nausea coils my stomach causing me to dive back for the toilet. I release everything I've eaten in the last few hours which honestly isn't much. Clutching the toilet as if it's a lover, I lie my head against the seat. I've officially hit the middle stage of my withdrawals.

Suddenly, a cold rag is pressed to my head.

"You have vomit in your costume wig," his deep voice rattles my chest.

I chuckle. "Don't make me laugh, my throat burns."

He pulls the wig off showcasing my two cornrows underneath. If I was even remotely trying to seduce this man, all that went out the window. I look like an extra in the Color Purple.

"I usually don't take the wig off, at least not until the third date," I try joking to relieve the embarrassing moment.

Gabriel doesn't respond. Instead, he tosses the fake hair onto the counter and continues to wipe my face.

"You should have eaten," he says.

I snort. "Food's not going to cure this."

"What's wrong with you?"

Taking the rag from his hands, I wipe my mouth before standing.

"Nothing," I say. "Let me finish cleaning up and I'll be right out."

He doesn't move at first, just watches me closely. I wouldn't be surprised if he could read every secret I'm holding. His gaze, no matter how short, gives you the feeling he sees you. Truly, sees you.

Gabriel leaves, and I finish cleaning up. Thankfully, I find a bottle of mouth wash under the sink and rinse out my mouth. I forgo the wig, there's no saving it. I walk out of the bathroom to find him waiting for me with the duffle bag in his hands.

He slings the bag over his shoulder. "Let's go."

We walk out of the apartment, again with Gabriel in the lead and me following behind him.

CHAPTER EIGHT

The Brother

Beast

"Submit yourselves therefore to God. Resist the devil, and he will flee from you." Mother's voice grows louder in my head with each step I take. *"You are weak. Kill the whore before she corrupts your soul."*

"Did you hear what I said?"

My attention turns to Summer. Her brown eyes soften as she gazes up at me. After vomiting, her skin looks even more dull, almost gray in appearance. The bags under her eyes are heavier and she's starting to sweat.

"She is sick with her sin. Let the Lord judge her and cast her into the pits of hell."

Stopping on the sidewalk I shut my eyes and try to force her words out of my head. I try counting, but it isn't helping.

"Rip her flesh from her body and force her to swallow it. She lives in the flesh she shall die by it." The haze starts to cloud my thoughts. The Beast is hungry, and it wants to be fed. I need to kill something.

"Tell that bitch to shut the fuck up."

My eyes pop open. I expect those words to come from my Priest voice, but it doesn't. Summer is smiling at me, her hands on her hips as she watches me.

"What?" I ask.

"I said, tell that bitch to shut the fuck up. She's interrupting our conversation."

Just like that, the clawing need for blood dissipates.

"Better?" She asks with a smile.

I nod, unable to speak.

"Good. As I was saying," she turns, and we continue to walk. "How many of these menu things do you have?"

For the first time in forever, my head is silent. There are no voices of my mother or Priest. There is only Summer.

"Only eight tonight."

She dips her chin to her chest as if she's verifying if this information is true or not.

"How many have you done so far?"

"I have only two left for the night."

"How do you determine who needs to die?"

We were told not to share this part of our lives with the outside world. Up until this point, I've never broken a Church rule. I've never had a reason to. However, whenever she asks me anything, I can't help but tell her the truth. Is this what my brother's feel when they are with the women at the Nunnery?

"Bishops assign us the jobs. They are the ones that decipher who need to be eradicated. Our job is to follow through with the kill."

"Do you ever question it?" She stops in the middle of the sidewalk to turn and look at me.

"I mean, if I know one thing, whenever man is involved with anything something is likely to be tainted. How do you know for sure that the people you're killing actually committed the crimes?"

Before answering her question, I give it a good thought. Lucien asked this once when we were still young boys. Priest told us that he'd thought of it too. He said that when he was younger, he made a kill that he regretted.

Something about a woman hiding children. Its why he always taught us to do our own research.

Everyone on my menu tonight has been verified, except one—my last kill for the night.

"I know," I explain to her.

She seems to mull over my answer for a moment, before nodding. We go back to walking, a lot slower than I'd prefer. Her gait is shorter than mine, she's out of shape, plus those shoes are preventing her from walking faster.

"You need shoes," I observe out loud.

Her laughter has my eyes cutting down at her. I like the way her face changes when she laughs. Even the sound of the high pitch noise is soothing.

"What? You're not a fan of the stripper heels?" She asks and her teeth chatter. It's a brisk fall night, but with my hoodie on she shouldn't be shivering the way she is.

"Don't be stupid, Boy. You know what's wrong with her." My mother's voice taunts. I ignore her.

"Come on."

Placing a hand on Summer's shoulder, I steer her down a different street. We walk three blocks out of the way to get to one of those fancy boutiques that sells shoes. She stops in front of the glass doors.

"Gabriel, you're not seriously about to buy me shoes from here?"

I don't answer. Instead, I head toward the door.

"It's nearly eleven o'clock. The sign on the door says they close at ten."

Looking through the glass doors I spot a woman inside moving around the store.

I tap on the glass, and she looks up at me. Her face pulls down into a frown.

"I hate to break this to you," Summer says getting my attention. She folds her skinny arms over her chest. "But even if she does decide to open back up for you, they're not going to allow me to go in there."

"Why?"

She looks down at herself and then back up to me as if it's obvious. It's not. I try to study her face in hopes that her emotions will give away why they won't allow her inside this store.

She rolls her eyes and sighs. "Never mind."

I knock on the glass once more causing the woman inside to roll her eyes. However, she walks over to the door and unlocks it.

"I'm sorry, but we're closed," the woman says.

"We will be quick, and I'm paying in cash," I tell her.

The woman hesitates for a moment, but then she steps back allowing us inside. I hold out a hand for Summer to enter first. She shakes her head but walks in. I follow behind her.

"Just so you both know, I'm not here alone and there are cameras."

Neither Summer nor I comment.

"What are you looking for?" The saleswoman directs her question to Summer.

I wait for her to tell the woman she needs help finding shoes, but she doesn't speak. Instead, she tugs at the hem of my sweater and touches her fuzzy hair. She's nervous. I pull the word from my rolodex of emotions.

"She needs shoes." I tell the woman in the black pants suit.

The sales lady looks Summer up and down, her lips curl up and her brow pinches.

"Maybe she would prefer something at a different store. I don't think we have her type of shoes here."

Summer's shoulders drop and she turns to leave. I hold out a hand barring her exit.

"She needs shoes," I say once again to the saleswoman. I don't like having to repeat myself.

The dark-skinned girl rolls her eyes before turning on her heels and walking away. I look to Summer and tilt my head in the direction of the salesclerk. She too rolls her eyes but follows the sales lady.

"What kind of shoes are you looking for?" The woman's voice tells me she isn't happy to be helping Summer.

Her stance is closed off and she looks more annoyed than anything. I still don't know why. It angers me that I can't read emotions and situations as easily as my brothers. Why would she not want to help after letting us in?

"Something comfortable and less pointy," I tell the lady when Summer doesn't reply.

She sneers and picks up a pair of black and white cloth tennis shoes. "How about these?"

Summer's eyes widen. "Um, maybe we should—"

"Those work—" Summer and I speak at the same time.

Both the women turn to stare at me with open mouths. I again feel as if I'm missing something. I hate this feeling. For the first time tonight, I wish my brothers were here to guide me.

"Gabe," Summer says.

"These shoes are $1600," the sales lady interrupts what Summer was about to say.

I wait for the problem to be announced. However, neither woman says anything else.

"Do you need to try them on?" I ask Summer.

She shakes her head but turns to the woman. "Size eight, please."

The saleswoman looks a bit stunned, but I do notice she's happier now. She's even smiling as she grabs the shoes for Summer and hands them to her.

"Can I get you anything else?"

I look to Summer to see if she needs anything else.

"No thank you," she glares at me before sitting down to put on her new shoes.

I follow the woman to the counter. Placing my bag on the register, I pull out two stacks of bound twenty-dollar bills and hand them to the lady. As she goes to ring up the box the shoes were in, I spot a collection of silk scarves behind her. One catches my eye.

"Add that to my order," I say pointing to the dark gray and black scarf.

The woman turns to see what I'm pointing to.

"That's one of our top sellers." She grabs my added item bringing my total to $2200. I give her the extra stack of twenties and she hands me the scarf. I forgo a bag.

"What do you want me to do with these shoes?" Summer asks coming to stand beside me.

"I'll toss them in the trash for you," The clerk says, trying to hand me my change back.

I don't miss the pointed look Summer gives her. I take the shoes from her and place them in my bag.

"Keep the change," I tell the sales lady before turning away.

We head for the door. As soon as we step outside, I stop her and hold out the scarf. She looks down at it but turns away instead of taking it. I expected to see her smile the way I like. Why does she not smile?

"You shouldn't have bought me all this stuff. That was too much money to waste on someone you're only going to kill."

I don't like being reminded of what I have to do. I'd grown fond of her not fighting me about it anymore, but now it seems she remembers who and what I am.

I know that she was only pretending to be nice and normal to make me not want to kill her. Yet, I still enjoyed the game she was playing. Balling the scarf up in my hand, I turn away from her.

"Let's go," I demand.

Before I take a step away from the building, I spot a familiar face coming around the corner. Even though I know that Hawk won't be able to get a good look at her, there is still sufficient enough streetlights for him to recognize her shadow. I shove Summer back against the shop door and walk forward to meet Hawk.

"Hawk," I call his name.

He easily turns to find me.

"Hey, Beast. How's it going?"

Looking over my shoulder, I spot Summer still standing beside the shop door. At least she didn't try to run. However, her attention is on us.

"Good," I reply to Hawk.

"How's your night going?"

"Decent."

"Okay. Do you want to go grab some dinner? I was heading to Red's, but I can…"

"No."

Hawk takes a step back. His gaze roams over me and then suddenly, he looks over my shoulder. I don't have to turn to see what he's looking at. I shift to my left, cutting off his view of Summer.

"Maybe we can catch up tomorrow morning before I check in. You can let the others know."

A smile appears on his face. This seems to appease my brother and it gets his attention back on me.

"Absolutely. I think Seth will be around. We can all catch up."

Tilting my chin to my chest briefly, I tell him. "Good. See you tomorrow, brother."

"Alright. I'll see tomorrow."

I wait until Hawk walks away, following his well-known route to one of Albany's houses.

"Who was that?"

Summer is standing beside me watching Hawk.

"My brother."

She turns to me, and her mouth falls open. "That fine ass specimen is your brother?"

Every muscle in my body tightens. I don't like her describing Hawk in that way. It makes me want to grab my brother and smash his head against the concrete.

"The good book says brother will deliver up brother to death. Send him to the pits of hell," Mother sneers in my head.

"Damn," Summer's voice draws my attention away from my dark thoughts. "Your mother might have been a bitch, but she pushed out some good-looking boys."

I don't correct her on how Hawk and I are related. My thoughts seem to linger on something else she referenced. It's the second time she has mentioned finding me attractive. I chalked the first time up to her panic attack.

I've always known my brothers were desirable. They often tell me of their run ins with outside women and the women of the Nunnery.

However, I don't get to have those experiences. Most women I encounter on my times outside of the Church are afraid of me. Just like mother said they would be.

"Because you're an abomination. A stain upon the earth. My sin in human form."

Summer doesn't think so. The thought comes quickly causing the haze from earlier to ease.

"Shouldn't we be going?" Her voice continues to soothe the anger that was once brewing inside of me.

"Yes."

Before I take a step, she grabs my arm.

"Give me the scarf."

I cock a brow at her. She rolls her eyes.

"No need to let it go to waste."

Her lips lift on the sides into the smile that I enjoy seeing. I hold out the scarf toward her. She takes it from me and runs her hand over the fabric. She then wraps it around her head, tying it in a ball at the front.

"Now I don't look too much like somebody's southern Grandma."

I have no idea what she's talking about, so I don't say anything. We set back off to our next destination.

CHAPTER NINE

Menu Seven

Beast

"And so, I told Raina that she's crazy if she thought I would ever sleep with Community Dick Mitch. But of course, she didn't believe me."

Summer has talked nonstop since we left Hawk. She told me about her sister and mother. She even talked to me about her best friend Trina.

I don't think anyone has ever talked to me this much. Most people assume I'm not listening or interested, but Summer doesn't seem to care if I respond or not. She just wants to talk.

She finally pauses in her ramblings when we get to the assisted living facility.

"How are we going to get in there? It's almost midnight. They aren't going to let us just walk through the front door." She points to the glass doors that I know are sealed up tight.

I don't answer her. Instead, I go around the side of the building to what I know is the staff entrance. She follows. Using the key card I made earlier today, I scan it and step inside holding the door open for her. She walks in and looks around at the stark white walls and linoleum floor.

"Just to be clear," she says with a deep sigh. "I'm not helping you in here. You know I can't stomach that shit."

"Don't worry, you have a very important role this time," I say.

Her gaze narrows. I step over to the nearest storage closet. Using the same key card, I open the door and shove her inside.

"Stay here until I come back."

"Gabe, wait."

It's the second time she has called me that nickname and the tight feeling it causes in my chest has been the same.

"Can't I just wait outside the room. I told you, I'm not going to try to run." She folds her arms across her chest.

"I'm not putting you here to keep you from running. When I do this, I let her in my head. I don't want you near me when she's in my head."

I didn't like to admit that—not in front of Summer. Only Priest truly knows where my thoughts go when I kill. Telling this secret to her makes my face hot and my chest tighten. I shift my gaze away from her.

A soft touch on my arm has me looking back down at her. The smile I'm starting to crave grows across her face.

"I get it."

The only person I thought that truly might understand my plight is my brother Lucien. He too deals with a darkness that takes over him. However, standing in front of Summer with her dull skin, sunken eyes, and frail body, tells me she has demons too. Ones she's trying to exorcise.

Dipping my chin, I take a step back. Her hand falls to her side. She walks into the closet, and I shut the door. I stand in front of it for a moment staring at the barrier between us. My breathing quickens and my chest tightens.

Before I can think about it, the keycard is back out ready to swipe over the sensor to let her out.

"Get ahold of yourself," Mother taunts. *"You have work to do."* She's right.

Stepping away from the door, I hoist my bag on my shoulder and put distance between me and Summer. Slowly I allow myself to fade into the background and allow the dark part of me to step forward.

"You will punish the world for their evil, the wicked for their sins. You are the wrath of the Lord almighty. You are his burning anger. Do what you were born to do, Boy."

"Yes, Mother."

I don't worry about the cameras. I cut those off before we left the apartment. I've learned a lot from watching Lucien over the years. I've picked up traits from all my brothers. I use my memory of the layout of this place to find the administrator's office.

He usually wouldn't be here at this time of night, but a message about a potential client needing a lung will have him rushing back to his office. And when you make the kind of money he does selling body parts and anything else you can take from the elderly on the black market, you don't wait around.

Placing my bag on the desk, I take out the tools I'll use for this kill. Part of me wants to make this quick, but the dark part of me—the one my mother helped create—needs to be fed. It is this part most people see when they look at me.

Not her. My unbridled thoughts taunt.

I catch my reflection in the blade of my hacksaw. A smile lifts one corner of my lips. Summer thinks I'm handsome.

"The whore is a liar. Do not allow her to corrupt you," Mother warns.

Shaking my head, I ignore mother's words. The sound of footsteps nearing has my attention drifting to the door. I make my way across the room to stand on the opposite side of the closed barrier.

James Tillbury walks into the room. He heads straight to his desk. He's so focused on his task he has yet to recognize my black bag in the chair. I use his distraction to close and lock the door.

He finally looks up and notices me. Immediately, his face pales and his eyes widen. He doesn't speak for a moment, just stares at me.

"Sit," I demand.

He drops down in the chair behind his desk. Walking over to him, I pick up the roll of duct tape off the desk.

"What....what do you want?" James asks in a shaky voice.

I don't answer. Unlike Seth, I don't like to do much talking when I work. I don't desire or require a confession from my victims. By the time I've gotten here, I've already proven their guilt. It is not my job to give them absolution, it is my job to send them to seek it.

"Is this about the girl?" James continues to ask as I make my way behind his chair.

I grab one of his hands and tape it to the arm of his seat.

"I didn't know she was thirteen, alright. I thought she was older than that." He goes on to admit more of his sins.

"For the wages of sin is death. Send him to the pits of hell."

I tape his other arm down to the chair, ripping the end of the tape with my teeth.

"This isn't about the girl," he says more to himself than to me. "Then, what is this about?"

"His sins are so plentiful he doesn't even know why he's here. He is wicked, just like your whore." Mother snarls.

"No," I say out loud. "He is nothing like Summer."

James starts to squirm in his seat. The panic is starting to set in.

"Help," he calls out. "Someone help."

I thought it peculiar when I studied the floor plan and realized the director made his office so far away from everyone else. It made sense when you found out he was killing his occupants and harvesting their organs. However, now I bet he wishes he didn't isolate himself from everyone else.

Tearing off one last strip of duct tape, I take the stress ball off his desk and stuff it in his mouth before taping over it. His screams are muffled, allowing me silence to work in peace.

Glancing at the clock, the time reads 12:10 am. I attach my 2in x 3.5in Forstner bit into my drill.

I walk behind James' chair. He fights against the tape, trying to get out of his restraints. Placing one hand on his shoulder, while holding the circular drill to the back of his neck, I hold him still.

"Don't move," I say, as I drill a hole into the base of his spine.

By the time I'm finished with James and the red haze has officially lifted, the clock reads 1:30 am.

My thoughts go immediately to Summer. I hurriedly pack my things and call the cleanup crew.

When I get to the janitor's closet, I quickly swipe the card. My heart races in my chest at the time it takes for the lock to turn green and the door to open.

Summer is still here. She's sitting on the floor, her knees pressed to her chest. She's shaking and sweating profusely. She looks up at me, and her face looks even more pale than before.

She wipes at her running nose. "For a moment I thought you forgot about me," she says, with chattering teeth and a weak smile.

"Put her out of her misery. There is no cure for her sickness. The whore must pay for her sins." Ignoring Mother's voice, I help Summer stand.

"We should go."

She nods and obediently follows me out of the building.

CHAPTER TEN

Daddy Issues

Summer

"Gabriel, please. I have to stop."

My body is on fire, and I feel as if I'm going to pass out. We've been walking for damn near thirty minutes. Even though we aren't going nearly as fast as I know he would like to go, it's still too fast for me.

Gabriel turns left, leading me into a park. I take a seat on one of the free benches not occupied by a homeless person. He sits beside me, his wide body taking up most of the seat.

Leaning my head back, I allow the cool breeze to wash over my clammy skin. I wish I could say this is the worst of my symptoms. However, by tomorrow I'll feel like my body is trying to reject itself. That's if I live to see tomorrow.

"At the moment, death doesn't seem so bad," I say with a chuckle.

He doesn't reply, instead he looks over to me briefly.

I stare up at the sky for a moment. Taking my time to enjoy the beauty of it. You will be surprised at the number of things you don't take the time to acknowledge in your everyday life. It isn't until you're at death's door that you stop to smell the roses.

"What demons are you running from?" His voice breaks through my calm, bringing me out of my somber thoughts.

"Have we gotten to that part of our date? The part where we start revealing intimate details?" I joke, but it is met with the same silence as earlier.

Glancing over to him, I notice one thick brow is lifted and a frown turns his full lips down.

I sigh, sitting up in my seat, I tuck my legs to my chest and cover them with the oversized hoodie.

"Do you remember when you asked me who I knew that died?"

He dips his chin but doesn't speak.

"It was my dad."

That seemed to be enough of an answer for him. However, if this is going to be my last night on this earth I might as well share my truth with someone.

"I was a daddy's girl. Family and friends all said that I was his shadow. Wherever Terence Jones went his mini-me followed."

I laugh reminiscing on my good times as a child. Despite how much of a fuck up I am now, I did have a fairly normal childhood up until about six years old.

"I looked just like him too. He, like me, was what the old folks called high 'yella'. We even have the same freckles," I say pointing to the smattering of brown spots across my face.

My smile from earlier falls as I think about how things turned out. "I was about six when I first noticed something wasn't right with him. I tried to talk to mama about it, but she kept telling me it was nothing. She told to me to stay in a child's place."

"You see, daddy would have moments where he would be so high on life and funny, that he'd seem like he was floating. He would pull me out of school on those days just to get ice cream or go for a walk. Then there were the days when he couldn't get out of bed. At first mama tried to explain it away as his artist's soul. My father was a painter."

I look over to Gabriel and although his gaze is bouncing around the area on high alert, I know he's listening to everything I'm saying. So, I push forward.

"I was seven years old when I first learned of his bipolar disorder 1 diagnosis. The doctor put him on pills to keep him levelheaded. But, he often complained that the pills affected his creative mind." I pause at this point in my story because it all goes downhill from here.

Gabriel's warm rough hand wraps around mine, squeezing it gently. I stare at the way his large palm swallows my hand. I don't pull away and neither does he. I allow the comfort of his touch to give me the strength to keep going.

"By the time that day happened, it had gotten bad in our house. We moved out on my eighth birthday. Daddy nearly burned the house down with all of us in it trying to make me a cake. That day mama found out daddy wasn't taking his meds anymore. As the weeks went by, he'd gotten worse. He was going through phases of hypomania."

I let out a deep breath, fighting down the tears and the memories. "That day, we went by to check on him and to get some mail. The house was a mess, and he had paint everywhere. He wanted us to stay. Even begged my mother to sit with him for a while, but she refused. But I was a daddy's girl, so I asked to stay with him. She didn't even argue," I say with a chuckle even though it isn't funny.

"I often think back on that day. I wonder if Raina had asked to stay, would my mother had said yes."

That thought has always stayed with me. Why did she care so little about me to allow me to stay. She knew he was dangerous. She even admitted once that she figured he would take his life soon. Yet, it never crossed her mind to keep me away from him.

"What happened that night, Summer?" Gabriel asks, pulling me from my last thought.

Leaning my head back on the bench, I once again look up at the sky.

"He wouldn't sit still. He kept talking and pacing. He repeated over and over that someone was coming, and we had to run. Eventually, I got him to calm down and try to sleep. I woke up from my bed in the middle of the night. My father was standing in my doorway with a gun.

"He shot me first. The bullet went through my shoulder and out my chest missing every vital organ in its path. As I lay there bleeding and in pain, he told me he loved me more than anything in the world. He then turned the gun on himself."

I didn't realize I was crying until Gabriel wipes the tears from my face.

"I see him every night I try to sleep. I remember the pain in his eyes as he pulled the trigger both times. He was fighting a losing battle with demons I couldn't help him with. And what's worse, I think I have the same demons."

I break down, allowing the many years I've kept my fears to myself to catch up with me. The first time I went to see a therapist I was so afraid of her telling me I was going to be like my dad that I would freak out before the appointments.

I didn't want to be him, but then I'd feel guilty because he was the only person in this world that truly loved me. The only person in the world that gave a damn about me was so fucked up in the head he didn't even know up or down sometimes. What does that say about me?

"Breathe, Summer," his deep voice sounds low in my ear.

Sucking in breaths of air, it helps to calm my nerves a little.

"Do I get a pass on the death penalty now since I have a sad story?" I ask, only half joking.

Those seafoam green eyes narrow and he shakes his head twice.

I snort and have to use the sleeve of his sweater to wipe the snot from my nose. "It was worth a try, right?"

"If it were up to me, I don't think I would kill you."

Okay, I'm definitely suffering some kind of psychotic break because that was kind of sweet. I mean, knowing the little I do know about Gabriel, I don't think he gets to make many decisions on his own. So, for him to choose to not kill me, means he actually kind of likes me.

"Aren't we a pair. The killer with mommy issues and the hooker with a possible bipolar disorder."

For the first time tonight, I get a real laugh from Gabriel. Not the shoulder shaking silent thing I think I witnessed back in his apartment, but a real chuckle with actual sound.

We sit for only a few more minutes, allowing me to catch my breath before we are on the move again. We take another train back down to Queens.

After hopping off, we walk a few blocks before the smell of grilled steak and spicy peppers has my stomach growling. Without a word, Gabriel grabs my hand, and pulls me over to the restaurant. The only option for sitting is a little table situated under the awning near the register and some outdoor dining space.

Stepping up to the counter, the smell intensifies. I actually start to crave something other than a high for the first time tonight.

"How can I help you?" The Hispanic man asks with a genuine smile.

Gabriel looks at me and I don't hesitate to answer.

"Can I have two of your grilled steak tacos, two chorizo tacos, and two carnitas tacos." I turn to Gabriel. "You want something?"

He smiles down at me, before turning to the man behind the counter. "Double her order."

"And two lemonades, please." I kindly add.

The older man places our orders and Gabriel pays willingly. We step aside allowing the two young men behind us to place their orders as well.

"Where to next?" I ask, sipping my drink through a straw.

I'm starting to come to terms with his job. I don't want to ever witness it again, but so far the men he has killed all deserved it. Gabriel ran down his victims' crimes to me on one of our train rides. These were awful people. I'm not a fan of violence and killing, but they needed to die.

Gabriel looks at me briefly before turning back to his job of scanning the streets.

"John Smith."

I dip my brow and crinkle my nose. "That sounds like a made-up name. What's his crime?"

"Murder," he simply says.

So far tonight he's killed a cult leader that preys on young girls, a man that has orchestrated hundreds of hate crimes in the US, a pharmaceutical mass murderer, a soulless politician, and an organ harvester. This guy seems like a saint compared to them.

"Who did he kill?" It must be someone special for him to be on an assassin's hit list.

"I don't know." This time when Gabriel speaks on the subject he frowns.

Our order is called. Gabriel picks it up and then directs us to the outside eating area. We take a seat separating our food. After taking a bite of the delicious chorizo taco, I close my eyes and moan at how the flavors burst on my tastebuds. When I open my eyes, Gabriel is watching me. I'm too hungry to be bashful.

"What did your research say about this guy?" I ask, picking back up on our conversation.

I'll never get over the way Gabriel eats. In the time that I have taken two bites of my taco, he's finished one and is almost done with the second one.

"This is a special case. It was handpicked for me. I don't have much on him."

I pinch my brows together. "That doesn't raise any alarm bells for you?"

When he told me about the other men on his menu, he had so much detail. He told me about their crimes, their personal lives, and even some of their few good contributions to society. I concluded that Gabriel was big on doing his own research. It kind of made me feel as if he wasn't just out here killing because someone told him to. Don't get me wrong, he's definitely a rule follower, but he isn't a mindless sheep. That's why his response seems odd.

Instead of answering me, he grunts. I don't harp on it. He knows more about this shit than I do. Maybe this is a special case, and he doesn't need any details. I go back to enjoying my tacos.

After I've made it through about three of them, he cuts into the silence.

"Why did you eat this, but not the food at the diner?"

I look up to find his eyes on me. He's finished his food, but he isn't rushing me to finish mine. Which I appreciate.

Using a clean napkin to wipe my mouth I reply, "I wasn't hungry then. But also, I love Mexican food. It's about the only thing I'll never pass up."

"You pass up food often." He doesn't phrase it as a question, but I answer it anyway.

"Sometimes," I say, clearing my throat nervously.

As I've said, I haven't necessarily been good to my body.

I finish the rest of my food while telling him all about the best Mexican restaurants I've visited. I wrap my last taco up, too full to eat another bite. I go to place it in the tray we were using for trash, but he holds out a hand to block it.

When I look up at him, he cocks a brow at me. Without saying a word, I know what he wants. Sighing, I drop the taco back down in front of me and unwrap it.

It only takes me a few more minutes to finish the last one. Once I'm done, I ball the paper up and toss it in the tray.

"Happy now?" I ask.

"Yes." He grabs our trash and takes it to the trash can.

Standing, I try to grab his black duffle off the ground, but the thing has to weigh at least fifty pounds. How the hell has he been carrying this around all night so effortlessly. I try again to lift it using both hands.

He comes over, knocks my hands away, and easily lifts the bag up. I don't miss the slight tilt of his lips.

"Whatever." I roll my eyes. "I could have done it."

"You will need a few more tacos before you can lift this."

I stick out my tongue at his little dig. He swings the bag over his shoulder and starts to walk off. I follow like the obedient captive that I am.

"Tell me about your mother?" I ask after another block of walking and talking.

I've talked so much about my life, trying to appeal to his humanity, that I haven't found out anything about him. Will knowing more about him help me stay alive? Doubtful. But at this point I'm kind of interested.

His shoulders tighten and he has yet to respond to my question. This is usually when I would let him off the hook. However, I did admit to him that I'm possibly batshit crazy like my father. I'm not going to be the only person exorcising demons tonight.

When he still hasn't responded after three minutes, I ask another question.

"Is she dead or alive?"

This time, he cuts his eyes over to me and I can read on his face he doesn't want to discuss this topic. Tough luck.

"Oh, I see. You can ask me about my shit, but I can't ask about yours. Good to know where we stand in this relationship."

"This isn't a fucking relationship," he growls as he spins around to face me.

I stop in my tracks. It's not like the fear of this man has ever dissipated. However, being around him and talking to him made me a little more comfortable with him. But having him glare down at me the way he is reminds me again of his capabilities.

"We aren't on a date, nor are we friends. Despite your blatant attempts at it. Need I remind you that you will die tonight by my hands."

For a second his words cut me like glass shards. I'm not crazy enough to believe that we were bonding or anything, but I did think that my plan to make myself more human to him was working. I even thought maybe we were cool, and he somehow understood me.

Although Trina has been my bestie since forever, she has no idea the demons I fight daily. No one does. Well, except Gabriel. He has been the first person since my daddy died that has ever truly listened to me. I thought maybe that meant something. I guess I'm an idiot or maybe it's Stockholm syndrome.

I lower my head ready to give up the fight. Then a thought hits me. Gabriel is doing exactly what I do when someone is trying to get too close. Usually, I fuck things up. Like, try to cook on a stove knowing damn well I'm too high. One of my rehab councilors called it self-sabotage.

"Fine. You want me to be your silent victim. We can do that."

I start walking even though I have no idea where we're going. This could very well backfire on me. Despite what he said, I think he has enjoyed my talking all this time. So, going silent could speed up his ire and cause him to strangle me. However, it's worth the risk.

Gabriel walks past me taking the lead. We walk about four blocks in complete silence. It's probably harder on me than it is him. I'm a talker.

I no longer stand beside him when we stop at crosswalks either. I make sure to put about six feet of distance between us. At the fourth crosswalk, Gabriel sighs.

"She's still alive."

I don't allow any outward change to appear on my face. I keep it cool and stay stoic. However, inside I'm cheesing hard. Keeping my gaze locked on the red hand sign across the street, I remain silent.

"Every day I ask myself why I haven't killed her yet," he admits.

His hand tightens into a fist down at his side. This is a hard topic for him. The way his breathing sounds labored and the veins protruding in his forearms are clear indications he's uncomfortable.

I wrap my hand around his fist. He loosens his grip. I slide my fingers in between his. He looks down at where our hands interlock but doesn't comment. It's a bold move. Not sure if I did it because I'm still trying to survive the night, or if I did it just because I know he needed it.

"Why haven't you killed her?"

My goal was to stay silent. I planned to let him get it off his chest at his own pace, but I want to know the answer to that. He is more than capable of killing his mother. The man is a trained assassin. There has to be more to the reason he hasn't done the deed.

"I don't know," he admits.

That's a lie. I think he does know, and he just doesn't want to admit it. Maybe it's because at the end of the day, despite how awful our parents can be and how they can fuck us up royally, they're still our parents. No matter how hard we try to not be bothered or to get their hurtful words out of our heads, we are still children needing the love of our parents.

I know there's nothing I can do to make my mother love me. She has said on multiple occasions that I'm the worst thing that ever happened to her.

Even before I became her problematic druggy daughter, I was always the misbehaving child. The one that hardly sat still, the one that asked all the questions and liked to get dirty. It's why my father and I bonded so well. I was like him. My mother has always hated that about me, and yet, I still long for her love.

"Well, if you kill me, maybe I can come back and haunt her for you," I say to lighten the mood a little.

My comment has those pale green eyes looking down at me with a smirk.

"Maybe," he says.

The little walking symbol appears on the sign giving us the right of way. Before I go to step off the curb, the loud sound of rap music has me looking to the left.

A large black SUV pulls up to the light. My heart skips a few beats and then starts to race in my chest. My belly fills with rocks and my limbs refuse to move.

It's him. I know it's him. I want to run and hide but I can't get my body to respond. Eventually the light turns green, and the SUV speeds off down the street.

Finally, I can breathe and my heart stops dancing in my chest. When I look up, Gabriel is staring at me suspiciously. He then turns in the direction the black SUV went. I swear this man doesn't miss anything.

"We should go," I say, before he starts asking questions.

He inclines his head, and we cross the street. Despite the red hand on the crosswalk telling us not to.

CHAPTER ELEVEN

Last Hit

Summer

We come up to a small white house with barred windows. A chain link fence surrounds the little yard.

Gabriel goes around the back of the house. He tosses his duffle across the chain fence. It hits the ground with a thud. He then turns back to me expectantly. Without a conversation, he swoops me up in his arms as if I weigh nothing. He cradles me like a bride, lifting me up over the fence. He doesn't let me go until my feet hit the ground.

He then places one hand on the metal rail and then easily leaps over the fence.

"Come on," he says, grabbing his bag and leading me to the screened in back porch.

"What if someone is home?" I ask, even though the house is pitch dark and silent.

"The owner isn't due to get home until another two hours. He's on a red eye flight right now."

I don't know why I even second guess this man.

Gabriel uses two skinny pointy tools to get into the locked door. Instead of walking right in, he stops and listens to the empty house for a moment. I assume he determines the coast is clear because he enters the home. I follow behind him, shutting the door quietly.

We enter through what looks like a kitchen, and then cut through the dining room. The house smells fresh and clean with a lemony scent as if someone recently mopped.

We walk into the living room, but Gabriel stops abruptly causing me to bump into his back.

"Gabe, what's the deal?"

A light comes on suddenly and I'm forced to close my eyes at the sudden change of brightness.

"You brought company on a menu?" An unknown voice says from in front of Gabriel.

Glancing around Gabe's wide back, I notice an older gentleman sitting in a wooden chair. A shot gun is across his lap, and a cool demeanor is painted on his face. I squeal before burying my head in Gabriel's back.

"Who's your friend?" The older man asks.

Gabriel doesn't respond. That doesn't shock me, the man hardly ever speaks. However, he isn't the one with a shotgun. We can't ignore this man.

"I'm Summer," I say, still hiding behind Gabriel.

The man chuckles. "Hello, Summer. I'm John Smith, but you can call me by my code name, Gambler."

The name meant nothing to me, but from the way Gabe's back stiffens more, it definitely hit home with him.

"You can relax," Gambler says as if anything about this situation is relaxing. "I only want to talk, Beast."

I let out a deep breath, feeling slightly better about the situation. He only wants to talk. Besides, if he wanted us dead, he could have shot us when we walked in. Stepping away from Gabriel, I go to walk around him. He quickly steps to the side placing himself right back in front of me.

"If you only want to talk then put down the gun," Gabriel says, making a good point.

That's why he's the killer and I'm just the unfortunate victim.

The heavy silence circles the room once again. It feels like two large predators are sizing each other up before they strike. Finally, the silence is broken when the stranger speaks.

"I think we both know why I can't put this gun down. Not only are you part of the Church, but you are the Beast after all."

Beast? His brother called him that name too. I'm assuming it's a nickname or codename like Gambler. Wait, do they work for the same organization? Damn, my brain is working slow as hell tonight.

They have another one of those silent standoffs. I take the opportunity to move around Gabe again. Before I can get too far from him, he grabs my arm pulling me back to his side. The action is quick, and no words are spoken, but I know it's him telling me to stay close.

The older gentlemen's gaze falls on me. A small smile turns his lips up. The lines around his blue eyes are prominent and tell of his age. He looks to be in his sixties although he's in great shape. The black fitted T shirt he's wearing stretches across defined muscles.

"That's how it started for me too," Gambler says before putting his attention back on Gabriel.

Gabe doesn't respond even though the man pauses for him to ask the question.

"How what started?" I ask.

Look, Gabriel may not want the information, but something about this older man intrigues me. None of the other victims tonight saw Gabriel coming, but this guy got the one up on him. That's talent. Plus, I want to know more about this organization they're part of.

"My revelation," Gambler says briefly to me. "I was a little older than you when I met my Maggie."

The moment he says the name, I notice the abundance of pictures. There are framed pictures everywhere. I start with the ones on the mantle.

Without thought I walk over to the framed photos. The first picture is a black and white photo of a young couple. The woman has long hair parted down the middle. She's holding up the peace sign giving me hippie vibes. The guy beside her with a look of awe, is the younger version of the man sitting.

Moving to the next photo, Maggie is wearing a white lace dress with bell bottom sleeves. Around her head is a crown of daisies. Again, Gambler is staring at the woman with stars in his eyes.

Often, you hear people talk about being with their soul mate. Looking at these pictures of this couple tells me this is what being with a soul mate looks like. Along the walls, on side tables, and bookshelves are tons of framed pictures of this couple's life.

There are pictures of them everywhere in the world. Pictures of her alone smiling seductively at the camera. Pictures of the two of them, always with him staring longingly at her. I also notice at least four pictures of her with a full belly, yet there are no photos of children.

"What happened to Maggie?" I ask turning to face Gambler.

However, it isn't him that answers the question.

"Dead," Gabriel replies bluntly.

Sadness fills Gambler's eyes. A type of sadness I've seen only once in my life. It was the day my father stood at the door of my bedroom with a gun.

"Breast cancer," Gambler says. "By the time we caught it, it was too late. It has been two months now since we buried her."

"I'm so sorry."

I didn't even know these people, but looking at these pictures made me feel as if I watched the movie of their love life. It feels as if I was a part of it and I truly grasp his loss.

"Thank you," Gambler says looking over at me.

"What does this have to do with me?"

Okay damn, Gabe. I mean I understand he's a little emotionally detached. I've figured that out during our time together, but he could at least pretend.

Gambler chuckles, not seeming to take offense. "I was like you. A dutiful soldier for the Church. I believed I owed them everything. They took an orphaned boy with anger issues, stellar cognitive skills, and made him feel as if he belonged and that he was special." Gambler pauses, his gaze seeming unfocused as if he is reliving something.

Gabriel shifts so slightly toward me that if I hadn't been looking at him, I would have missed it. The movement seems to get Gambler's attention. His grip on the gun tightens.

"That's the thing I loved about the Church," he continues as if he never paused. "The courage and the confidence they give to the youth in the program. But, like anything that has been around as long as the Church, it becomes tainted. I met my Maggie because she was on my menu."

I gasp at that realization. The woman that he looks at with such adoration was supposed to die by his hands. I ignore the hopeful flutters in my belly. Despite that little bit of excitement that tried to sneak its way into my thoughts, Gambler's story is not Gabriel's.

Hell, I don't even want it to be. Do I think Gabe is a great guy? Sure. A little off, but I've met worse. Do I want to travel the world with him and take pictures like the ones surrounding me here? Hell no.

"How did you get out of killing her?" Despite just having that rational conversation in my head, I still ask the question.

For the first time since that light came on, Gabriel takes his attention off Gambler. Those seafoam green eyes turn to me and narrow. I look away, ignoring the heat on the side of my face. It isn't until Gambler starts speaking again that the burning goes away.

"She didn't fit what they told me," he says with a laugh to himself. "Her folder said that she was a death angel. Someone that preyed on the weak and innocent. It painted her as a stone-cold killer that inherited money from her dead victims."

Gabriel doesn't respond, only tilts his head to the side.

This doesn't stop Gambler; he continues with his story. "I watched her from my scope that day, but something about her files just didn't sit right with me. I started watching her and doing my own research. It was then I realized it was all a lie.

"Maggie was the daughter of a man named Jeremiah Smith. The Smiths could trace their ancestors all the way back to their passage on one of the first ships over to this country.

"Their wealth went back even further. I learned that he had put the hit out on his youngest daughter. She'd committed no crimes and had done no harm. The only reason she was going to die, is because her father had the power and the money to get the Church to do it."

"That's not how it works," Gabriel says, his jaw tight and his hands are fisted at his side. "The Church vets everyone on our menus. We don't do hire for kill."

Gambler scoffs. "I thought so too, but they hide it well. I guarantee, 99% of the people on your menu deserved the death you dealt to them. But I'm telling you, not all of them. Me included. They painted my ledger red and told you I committed atrocious acts in order for me to be placed on your menu. The only crimes I committed were for them. They are using us."

Gabriel turns away from Gambler. His eyes are closed so tightly the scar over his brow turns pink.

"And they have been for centuries. They cut us off from society and make us believe they give a shit about us. All the while, the people that are stuffing your pockets are worse than the ones you kill. Half of the men and women that end up on your menu, were once the Church's Allies."

Gabriel begins to pace. He tugs at his hair yanking at the strands. The man bun comes loose, and his golden locs fall around his face and cascade down his back.

"Gabe, what's wrong?" I step toward him, laying a hand on his arm.

He draws away from me as if my touch is fire. Gambler continues to speak, ignoring the frenzy Gabe is in.

"The people they protect would make your skin crawl. They tell you Pope runs the Church, but that's not true. When they broke away from the Catholic Church, they didn't go independent, Beast. They aligned with something much worse."

At this point, Gabriel is losing his shit. He's pacing the room like an angry bull and having those conversations in his head with his mother. Although he has always been terrifying, he seemed more human as the night has gone by. However, now he reminds me of exactly what Gambler has called him—a beast.

"You're lying. Don't say that." He growls, smacking himself in the head. I want to touch him, but I'm afraid.

"It's the truth. I can prove it," Gambler says loudly over the noise Gabriel is making.

"Shut up. You're not helping," I shout down to Gambler. I don't like the calm look on his face.

The man shrugs casually as if all this is normal. "I'm not trying to."

Glass being shattered against the wall turns my attention back to Gabe. He's picking up the picture frames and throwing them.

"Gabriel, look at me." I approach him slowly as if he's a wild animal.

When I'm right behind him, he spins around on his feet, grabs me by the neck and yanks me off the ground. My toes are the only thing still brushing the floor.

"Gabe, please," I croak out, wrapping a hand around his wrist hoping he will let me go.

"You might as well forget it. That red haze got him now," Gambler says as if he's bored.

I don't give a shit what he says. I know my Gabriel is in here. Yes, I started this faux friendship to save my life, but I discovered the real man behind those green eyes. He's still just a boy with mother issues that they trained to kill. He's wounded, just like me. He isn't this Beast they made him.

"Please. Don't," I try again to reason with him.

Though I was initially shocked about his hold around my neck, I realize he isn't choking me. He's only holding me. He drops his forehead to mine for a brief second before releasing me. I fall to the ground hitting it with a thud.

Gabriel goes back to breaking shit. From my viewpoint on the ground, I can see him storm out of the room and down the hall. The sound of splintering wood and shattered glass following him.

"Why did you do this? What do you gain from this?" I ask from my spot on the floor.

Gambler's blue eyes soften as he peers down at me, and I recognize the sadness from earlier. The one that reminds me of my father. His gaze goes to the mantle behind me.

"Because I'm a coward, and I want him to finish what I started."

The ruckus down the hall stops. Gambler's and my head swing in the direction. From our location in the room, we can't see anything down the hallway. Suddenly, without a sound, Gabriel appears at the entrance. He stares down at me; his pale eyes bore into mine.

I don't speak nor make a move toward him. I wish I could read him the way he easily reads the world. I want to know what he's thinking as he looks so intently at me.

"It's time, Beast," Gambler says, drawing Gabriel's attention.

Gabe turns to the man that has yet to get out of the chair. In one swift move, he pulls a gun from behind his back and aims it at Gambler.

"No," I shout, but it's too late.

He fires the gun and the bullet hits Gambler directly in the forehead. The impact knocks his head back. The gun in his lap clatters to the ground, his head falls forward, and his body goes limp. I stare in horror as droplets of blood drip from the wound and down to his shirt.

The memory of my father's lifeless body slumped against my bedroom wall comes into focus. My heart starts to pound faster, and the room spins a little.

Gabriel walks over to the gun on the floor. He picks it up, presses something at the top and lowers the barrel of the gun. With one hand, he tosses the weapon onto the floor.

"Let's go." He turns to me and speaks.

"You killed him."

I'm not stupid. I knew that was the game plan when we walked in here, but he wasn't like the others. He wasn't guilty. The only way I've gotten passed what he's been doing all night, was knowing that the people he killed were bad. This is different.

Gabriel grabs his black duffle off the ground and swings it over his shoulder. He then grabs my arm and lifts me to my feet. Once I'm standing, I yank away from him.

He watches me wearily, but he doesn't say anything. He turns his back to me and makes his way out of the home the same route we took to get in. I follow quietly with my mind racing.

We make it almost three blocks before I refuse to go any further. I stop on the sidewalk. Gabriel is about ten steps in front of me. Yet, when I stop he does too. He turns to look at me.

"You're going to kill me, aren't you?"

He doesn't respond.

I shake my head and cross my arms over my chest. "I thought I could reason with you. I even for a minute thought that maybe you and I had formed some kind of fucked up friendship, but you have no feelings."

He frowns at my words. "I told you what I was. It's not my fault you formed some delusional version of me in your head."

I scoff, but he's right. He's never tried to make me believe he was anything other than a heartless killer. However, I have a hard time believing that. Call me delusional or stupid, but something deep inside me tells me that isn't who Gabriel is.

Shaking my head, I reply, "No, that's not who you are. It's who they made you believe you are."

Those green eyes that are so intelligent narrow at me. "You don't know what you're talking about."

"I know Gambler was telling the truth. And I know you know it too. Yet you still killed him. You didn't even consider letting him live. You're just a follower and now I know my fate is the same as his. So do it, Gabriel."

I step closer to him, cutting away some of the space between us.

"Get it out the way. Gun me down in the street and leave me here like trash. You're going to do it anyway."

He stares at me, his face not moving an inch. My heart gallops in my chest. Even though I mean the words I'm saying, it doesn't make death any less frightening.

"Keep walking," he says turning his back to me.

My next move can be chalked up to lack of sleep, witnessing the death of Gambler, or hell, you can put it on my drug use. I run up to his back, ball my fist and start pounding away. He doesn't even stumble at my weak blows.

"You're a monster," I shout, feeling defeated. "Just kill me. Just do it."

He turns around and grabs both my wrists in one of his hands. "Stop," his words come out with more emotion than anything else he's said all night.

My chest heaves up and down while he and I have a stare off.

"Gambler had been hidden from the Church for forty-six years," Gabriel says looking down at me. "They had no idea where he was. Two weeks ago, he shows up out of the blue like a beacon on every damn radar they have."

I scrunch my nose trying to figure out what all that means.

"He wanted them to find him." It's a statement, not a question.

Gabriel nods. "There were no bullets in his gun."

I close my eyes and place myself back in the house. He surrounded himself with pictures of his wife. He never tried to run or talk Gabriel out of killing him. The sad look in his eyes that reminded me of my father.

"This was a suicide mission. He wanted to die."

"Yes," he sighs.

I think back on Gambler's last words to me. He said he told Gabe the truth because he was a coward and he wanted him to finish the work he had done. I think he believed himself a coward because he didn't want to remain in this life without his wife. It would explain why he surrounded himself with pictures of her, but not his kids.

The fight leaves my body and I slump against Gabriel. He lets my hands go and allows me to bury my face in his stomach. He doesn't touch me or push me away. I stay there, allowing his warmth and hard body to ground me.

"We have to keep moving, Summer."

Lifting my face from his body, I look up at him. A thought crosses my mind, one I chase away like a raccoon at my back porch. However, it doesn't stop the thought from returning. I wonder what his lips would feel like on mine.

I think about this for so long, I find myself lifting on my tip toes drawing closer to his mouth. He stills but doesn't move. His green eyes move back and forth across my face not focusing on one area too long. When I am only a deep inhale away from pressing my lips to his, the sound of booming rap music has me pulling away rapidly.

This time, I'm not so lucky. Nic's large black SUV comes up beside us. The doors fly open before the Tahoe stops. Nic and five members of his crew climb out of the truck.

"Nic, hi," I say, stepping in front of Gabriel. "I was just coming to see—" my words are cut short when his fist flies across my face knocking me to the ground.

Gabriel takes a step in Nic's direction. The five guys with Nic pull their large guns out and aim them at Gabriel. He stops moving, his head cocks to the side as he stares directly at Nic.

"Imagine my surprise when Jay called and told me you were walking my streets with another dude. How do you think that made me feel?" Nic shouts at me.

I spit the blood from my split lip out onto the pavement before getting on my hands and knees.

"In my defense," I rasp. "I thought you holding a gun to my head meant we had broken up."

Nic grabs me by the hood of Gabriel's sweatshirt and hauls me to my feet. He then draws back and slaps the shit out of me again. This time, I bend at the waist but don't fall to the ground.

Gabriel must've moved again because the guys with the guns move in closer, surrounding him.

"So, you're the bitch ass muthafucker that's screwing my girl now?" Nic shouts. "Tell me why I shouldn't dead your ass on this pavement."

Despite all the guns aimed at him and being outnumbered, not once does Gabriel show any sign of fear. In fact, a slow smirk spreads across his face.

"You think this shit funny?" Nic snaps. "Light his ass up, Benzo."

"Wait," I shout jumping in front of Gabriel.

What the hell are you doing? My inner more rational voice shouts. It's the first time she's made an appearance tonight. "If Nic kills Gabriel you can possibly get away from Nic. You've done it before. Then you'll be free." Rational me made a lot of sense, but I couldn't let him kill Gabe.

He is the first man other than my father to show me kindness without wanting anything in return. Yes, he said he was going to kill me, but he's fed me when I've been hungry. He's given me clothing when I've been cold, held my wig when I was throwing up, and protected me. He may not be normal, I won't deny that, but Gabriel is my friend.

"We're not together. He's just a mark," I turn and look into Gabe's green eyes.

I'm pleading with him to follow along.

"I was going to get him to take me back to his place and then rob him." Gabe's eyes narrow down at me. The men around us laugh.

"This fool thought he had a new girlfriend," One of Nic's guys taunts, and they all laugh.

"Tonight's your lucky night, big guy. You can keep your money and your life," Nic says. "Bring your ass, Summer."

I look to Gabriel one last time and a sad smile lifts my lips. "You were going to kill me tonight anyway, right," I whisper to him. "Now you don't have to worry about it."

Nic yanks me away from Gabe and toward his black SUV. The thing my rational mind didn't know is that I got away from Nic once by chance. He's not letting me get away again. Once I climb in this truck, I'm good as dead.

"For what it's worth," I shout to Gabriel before Nic can shove me in the car. "I had fun tonight."

"Get your dumb ass in the car," Nic says pushing my head down and into the back seat.

His henchmen climb in too, and the doors shut. I look out of the tinted windows as we pull away from the curb. Gabriel watches me while I stare back at him. We don't look away from each other until I can no longer see him.

With a death grip on my thigh, Nic leans into my ear and whispers. "I'm going to make you choke on this dick before I put a bullet in your head."

Ugh, I'd much rather he shoots me first.

CHAPTER TWELVE

Mine

Beast

Watching the black SUV pull away has my head spinning. My mind is working overtime. So many voices are speaking at once.

"*Let her go. Let him kill the bitch,*" Mother shouts. "*She's a worthless whore.*"

"No, she's not," I say out loud.

"*You're going to let that shit slide, Kid?*" Priest argues. "*They disrespected you.*"

"*Evil will slay the wicked; the foes of the righteous will be condemned. She is no longer your problem,*" Mother argues against Priest.

In the back of my mind something else stirs. Something I've kept hidden for years. Something that if anyone knew about, they would lock me away. I fight to keep that side of me tapped down.

"*Control it, Boy. Don't let the evil out,*" Mother warns.

Clutching a hand to my head I try to quiet my head. I can't think when everyone is talking at the same time.

"*You don't need to think,*" Mother snarls. "*Look at you, you're weak. You think she wants you. You're a shit stain upon this world. I should have aborted you the moment I found I was cursed to carry you—*"

"*Will you shut the fuck up!*" This time, it isn't Priest's voice that appears in my head to respond to my mother. It's Summer's.

Shutting my eyes, I can almost see that playful smile on her face as she looks up at me. The way she bites into her bottom lip right before she says the most unusual thing. The way her eyes looked hooded as she stared at my lips only seconds before the SUV came.

Silence fills my thoughts. It's only me in my head now. Dropping my hands down to my sides, I open my eyes.

My decision is made. Squatting down, I look in my black duffle. A few guns, a couple knives, some power tools, rope, and my night goggles are all that I have with me. This will do. Grabbing my laptop out of the bag, I pull up the tracker embedded inside the hoodie.

Lucien gave me the hoodie one year for a birthday gift. I found the tracker immediately. I never let on to him that I knew it was there.

At first, I hesitated giving Summer the sweatshirt. I didn't think she would run anymore. Not when she was hellbent on making me befriend her so that I wouldn't kill her. I caught on to the act when we were at the diner. However, if I'm being honest, the fear of her running wasn't the reason I gave her the hoodie.

The laptop picks up on her location. The SUV stopped only a few blocks from here. I transfer the tracking information to my phone, place the laptop back in my bag and then take off running.

I found the black Tahoe at a blue house. It's similar to Gambler's place and I'd studied that layout for a week. As I near the house, the sound of loud music pours out of the home along with muffled shouting. I hop over the short fence at the back of the yard. There is a window on the side of the house and if I'm correct, it should give me a view into the living room.

I peek through the broken and bent blinds, finding there are no curtains to block my view. Four men are in the living room. They seem to be playing a video game. The volume is turned up so loud it sounds as if bombs are going off. Four TEC-9's are on the coffee table in front of the three men.

Moving to the other side of the window gives me a view into the dining room. Two more men are at the table counting large stacks of money.

Although I can't get a clear view of the third man at the table, I know he's there because his arm comes into view briefly.

Moving around to the back of the house, I search the area. A light on upstairs in one of the bedrooms leads me to believe that is where they are keeping Summer. Since I didn't see the ex-boyfriend, I'm assuming he's up there with her.

In the back yard is a wooden crate turned upside down. Picking up the worn crate, I yank off a few of the loose boards. Carrying the boards and my duffle over to the back door, I place the bag down along with the wood.

Searching through my bag, I pull out my power drill and some long nails. Checking the hinges of the back door, I make sure that it would open outward. Seeing that it does, I quickly drill the wood planks into the door and the frame. It won't hold forever, but it will slow anyone down from going out the back.

Once I've put three planks into the door, I put my drill away and grab my duffle heading to the front of the house. Before hopping the fence again, I take out my preferred tools from my bag and then stash the bag on the side of the house.

"You got work to do, son," Priest's voice says in my head. *"In and out, make it quick. This isn't a job for your mother."*

I take a deep breath. There are two ways I've learned to channel the red haze. One, is letting the Beast feed. I allow my mother's words to fill my head and direct my actions. It's never pretty when the Beast is loose. The second way I channel the haze is Priest's way. Get in, get out, get the job done.

The front door opens and one of the men from the living room walks out. He's on the phone with someone. He turns his back to me and lights a cigarette. Silently, I walk up behind him.

"Are you going to let me come see—" the rest of his words are cut off when my hatchet split the back if his head open.

I yank it out and hold him up by the back of his shirt as I bring the metal edge down into the side of his neck. It lodges in the bone of his shoulder blade.

I pull out my gun from the back of my waistband. Holding the weapon in my right hand, with my left, I use the handle of the ax to drag his body back up the steps to the front door. I step into the house and all eyes turn to me, everyone freezes in shock, which is what I was banking on.

In their moment of confusion, I take in the scene. Everything is as I remembered. Glass beer bottles scatter the living room, and a large flat screen TV is sitting on top of a stand.

One man is to the right of me sitting in a chair, he is the furthest away from the weapons, but closest to the door and escape. He is not an immediate threat. The two men on the couch are closer to the guns. They are a high threat. I scan the three at the table, and only one has a gun at his hip. He is also an immediate threat.

Their moment of confusion wears off. One of the men on the couch leaps up reaching for the TEC-9's. I toss the guy on my hatchet onto the coffee table causing the wood to splinter. He covers the weapons, slowing down their attempt to reach them.

I move through the living room as I simultaneously fire my weapon taking out the guy at the table with the beretta on his hip.

The most immediate threat has been taking care of. The other two at the table take off running for the back door I'm assuming. I ignore them.

I place a bullet in the throat of the man in the chair that was attempting to run toward the front door. Before he falls, I yank the hatchet out of the neck of the guy on the coffee table.

One of the guys from the couch was finally able to yank the TEC-9 from under his friend. He aims it at my head, but I knock the gun to the side with the ax causing him to spray the TV with his bullets. I place my gun at his forehead and blow a hole in the center.

The other guy that was on the couch tries to make a run to the front door, but my hatchet lands dead center in his back. He drops to the ground and starts to crawl the rest of the way. I make my way over to him and stand over his body. I rip the weapon out his back and put a bullet in his head. I then turn toward the kitchen to where the other two ran off.

I find them ramming against the door trying to get out. Without hesitation, I put a bullet in the side of one of the guys' head. The other turns to me with tears in his eyes and drops to his knees.

"Ay, man, I'm sorry. I told them not to take that girl. She ain't even all that cute."

"How many more?" I ask him.

I didn't care what he had to say or what he thought of Summer. She is mine. He looks confused at first, but then answers.

"Only two more upstairs with your chick."

Nodding, I turn to walk away. His audible sigh of relief is short lived. I turn around and toss my hatchet into his head. He slumps against the door with his friend.

I head upstairs.

Summer

"You fucking bitch," Nic shouts down in my face.

His hand is wrapped around my throat and he's squeezing the shit out of me. Despite how the situation looks, I'm not worried. I have no doubt Nic is going to kill me tonight, but he's still too in his feelings right now. I have about another hour of him berating me and kicking my ass before he actually does the deed.

It's how I got away the last time. He was so caught up on calling me every name in the book that he got distracted and I climbed out the window. No chance of that this time though. We're not at his other house, where it was only one level.

"It was an accident, Nic."

He frowns at me. "You think this is about that fucking house?"

Wait, isn't this what it's about? I mean, he lost about a hundred grand in drugs that night. He pulls me away from the wall and tosses me on the bed. I hit it like a ball before bouncing off to the floor.

"I fucking loved you, Summer. You told me you were clean."

Ohhhh. He's mad about that. When I met Nic, I had just gone through one of my many sober stints. They happened every now and again. I'd hit rock bottom and eventually check myself into rehab for a while. I'd come out and stay clean for about a few months, and then go right back to using. It was a cycle.

When I met Nic, I'd only been out of rehab for two weeks. We were together for four months before the memories and that feeling of spiraling hit me. His friends tried to tell him I was using again, but he didn't believe them.

I'm a little caught off guard about his admission of loving me. Nic was fun, but even sober I knew I was too broken to love. I think in his mind he thought he loved me, but he didn't. He didn't even know me.

"I tried. It just got hard," I admit.

He shakes his head. "Naw. You didn't love me enough to stay clean. Hell, you don't love yourself enough to stay clean."

He's not wrong.

The door opens, and Rico walks in holding a large bag of pills. My mouth waters at the sight.

"Is this enough?" Rico asks tossing the bag to Nic. He catches it with one hand.

"Yeah, this is good." Nic turns to me with a sneer. "This is what you like, ain't it?"

My heart starts to race, and I don't take my eyes off the bag in his hands. I don't have to answer because he knows what I like.

Loud gunshots come from downstairs. Nic and Rico pause and turn toward the door. Since we got here the noise has been on a level close to torture. Between the rap music, the Call of Duty game, and the shouting, my ears have been ringing.

"What the fuck are they doing down there," Nic asks.

"On that damn game. That shit sounds loud as hell."

Both men turn back to me. Nic comes over and squats in front of me, he grabs my jaw and squeezes hard. I whimper.

"Since you want to be a druggie so damn bad, you're going to take this entire bag of pills."

My eyes widen. There has to be fifty or more hydrocodone pills in that bag. I'll be dead within twenty minutes if I take that many.

"Rico, open this shit up. I'm going to hold her mouth open."

I immediately start to fight. Rico walks over to take the bag. Suddenly, the door bursts open. Standing in the doorway with blood splatter on his chest and his hair hanging down curtaining his face, is Gabriel.

"What the fuck," Nic shouts turning to face Gabriel.

Rico goes for his gun, but he's too slow. Gabriel fires one shot shooting Rico directly in the eye.

He walks further into the room. Nic pulls me up off the floor and places me in front of him. The next thing I know, there is a gun pressed to the side of my head.

"Take another step you big muthafucker, and I'll blow this bitch's head off."

Gabriel stops walking forward. He's about five steps away from Nic and I. His gaze is solely on Nic.

"Toss your gun to the left," Nic tells Gabriel.

For a second, Gabe doesn't respond. He tilts his head and stares at Nic. I try to plead with my eyes for him not to get rid of his gun. It's his only chance of getting out of here alive. I don't know how he got past all the guys downstairs, but if he loses that gun Nic will shoot him.

Gabe's eyes cut to me. I subtly shake my head at him. I'm dying tonight regardless. This isn't an act of selflessness. I'm not saving him over myself. I'm being realistic. Either way, I'm dying tonight, no need for him to die too.

Nic presses the gun even further into the side of my head. I wince when he hits a tender spot.

"Do it," Nic shouts.

Gabriel easily tosses the gun away from him. It hits the wall with a thud. I shut my eyes. The only hope he has now is prayer.

Nic starts to laugh. "Damn, dude. You know, I feel sorry for you. You're just another victim of Summer Jones. What did she do to you? Is it the pussy?" Nic asks.

Gabriel doesn't respond.

"That shit does have a tight grip, I won't lie. Probably some of the best I've had. Especially when she does that shy act like she doesn't know what the fuck she's doing."

Little does he know, it's not an act.

When Nic's words don't seem to get a rise out of Gabe, he switches gears.

"Or maybe it's that desperate look in her eyes. The one that calls for you to save her. That's what got me." Nic's tone lowers and there is no playful bite in them. "I took one look at her, and I knew I needed to rescue her." He goes quiet for a moment. I'm assuming he's reflecting.

Gabriel is watching Nic so intently I wonder what he's thinking. I wonder if Nic's words are registering to him. Is that what Gabe sees when he looks at me? Is it why he showed up here. Do I just scream damsel in distress.

"I'm going to let you in on a secret," Nic continues. "She doesn't want to be saved. I tried. Do you know what she wants?" he lets go of me for a split second to transfer the bag of drugs to his gun hand. His grip is back on me, before I can even consider running.

"This is what she wants. This is all she gives a fuck about. She doesn't deserve love. She's incapable of loving or caring about anything else."

Embarrassment makes my face hot. I don't like Gabe knowing my secret. I felt when I was with him, he viewed me like a human and not the fuck up that I am. I guess it's stupid because he is a killer, but he didn't know my truth and I didn't want him to.

Nic once again releases me. He transfers the bag of pills to his free hand before he turns the bag over and spills the pills out onto the floor.

I stare down at the white oblong pills scattered at my feet. My mouth waters and my heart beats rapidly. All my shit starts to fill my head. I see my dad's lifeless body against my wall. His sad eyes when he pulled the trigger plays back in my head. Even Nic's words seem to chase after me.

Am I incapable of love? Do I not deserve it? Is that why my mother hates me so much? The voice in my head is telling me to escape. She's pleading with me to take one of those pills and silence all the sad and depressing thoughts.

"Don't."

His deep voice causes me to look up from the meds on the floor. My brown eyes clash with his green.

I lick my lips, before glancing back down.

"He's right," I whisper.

"No, he's not."

Lifting my gaze back up to Gabe's, I stare at him.

"You're not your father, Summer. Take it from someone who is more fucked up than you will ever be. You're better than this." He points to the drugs on the floor.

I want to be. God, for the first time in forever, I want to be better than this. Tears start to stream down my face. The earlier visions bombard my thoughts again. The look on my father's face, the therapist telling me that bipolar disorder could be hereditary, all the words yelled at me by my mother play in slow motion in my mind. I just want to clear my head.

"What if I'm not?" I ask Gabe, connecting our gazes again. "What if the demons are too strong."

"Then I'll carry them for you. I'll fight whatever demons you have."

I believed him. This man has battled every monster he's faced tonight. He came for me when no one else would have. He's protected me, listened to me, took care of me. He has done more in one night than anyone else has done in my entire life. I truly believed that Gabriel could defeat my demons.

"Okay," I say.

I'm not dumb enough to believe it will be that simple. I've been fighting this battle since I was fifteen. I knew it was going to take more than one no to defeat this monster of mine. But, for the first time, I ignore the voice in my head pleading with me to self-medicate.

Nic scoffs. I almost forgot he was here.

"I see you're like me and you won't learn," he says to Gabriel before turning to me. "You'll thank me later."

Nic lifts the gun up and points it at my head. I shut my eyes knowing that this will be it for me. Just my luck, the day I decide to make a change would be the day I die. I wait for the gun to go off or for the pain, but nothing happens.

When I open my eyes, Nic is still beside me, but there is a knife sticking out of his throat. Gabriel walks over to Nic, he pulls the knife out, and in quick succession brings it back down on him five times. When he lets him go, Nic's lifeless body falls to the ground. Blood pools out of his neck wound.

I turn to look at Gabriel and his gaze is on me. His chest heaves up and down, but he doesn't say anything. Then, he scoops me up in his arms, again holding me like a bride on her wedding day and carries me out of the room.

"Close your eyes," he whispers as we go to descend the stairs.

I'm pretty sure what he is trying to keep me from seeing is more dead bodies. Honestly, I've seen so many tonight I should be immune to the sight. However, I still shut my eyes and tuck my head against his large chest listening to the steady beat of his heart.

CHAPTER THIRTEEN

The First

Summer

We make it back to Gabriel's apartment, not without a few curious stares. He held me the entire trip, even on the train ride.

Once we got back to the apartment, Gabe called some kind of cleanup crew and then went and showered. When he came out, I went in. It felt good to wash the night off me.

As soon as I walked out of the bathroom, I spotted a shirtless Gabriel sitting on the sofa. He was leaning forward with his head down between his shoulders, his body slowly rocking. He didn't move when I sat down beside him.

"Are you alright?" I ask, breaking the silence of the apartment.

"She's loud right now," he says in a low voice.

"What is she saying?" I don't have to ask him who. I know he's talking about his mother.

He turns his head slightly to look at me, his long hair covering most of his face. "She wants me to kill you."

That bitch. I don't panic. Taking a deep breath, I tuck my legs underneath me. Gabe gave me a shirt when I got out of the shower, but I preferred his hoodie. I didn't have any underwear so I'm ass out underneath this thing.

"What do you want to do, Gabriel? I'm not asking what she wants or what that organization wants you to do. You are capable of making your own decisions. So, what do you want?"

Those gorgeous intelligent eyes stare at me. I want to touch him so bad but I'm not sure if I should.

Beats of silence flow between us. I hold my breath waiting to hear what he will say. I pray that he won't kill me. It's kind of still up in the air. When he finally speaks, I'm completely blown away by what he says.

"You. I want you."

Heat fills my body in a way that it never has before. Nic mentioned my shyness and inexperience in sex. Before him, I'd only been with one other guy. It was a guy in high school. We weren't dating. I met him at a party and wanted to try another vice to exorcise my demons.

It was awful. After that, I wasn't interested in sex. It wasn't until Nic that I realized how pleasurable it could be. Even still, I never initiated it. However, right now, all I can think of is how Gabe would feel inside me.

Standing from the couch, I step in between his legs. He sits up straight, watching me intently. I don't break eye contact with him as I plant my right knee on the couch beside his left thigh. I quickly swing the other knee on his other side, straddling him. Gabe sinks back into the sofa, as I hover over his lap.

"Summer," he whispers my name. I can't tell if it's a warning or a plea.

Placing a finger to his lips briefly, I quiet him before planting my mouth to his. His body tenses beneath me. I go to pull away thinking maybe I'm reading this wrong. Maybe he doesn't want me this way. I mean, I'm not looking my best. These ratty braids are still in my head and although I've showered, I can imagine I still look like a woman going through withdrawals.

Before I can remove my lips from his, he opens his mouth and swipes his tongue against my bottom lip. I quickly follow his lead.

The kiss goes from chaste and soft to passionate and overpowering. Our tongues intertwine in a dance that's thousands of years old. I moan as I cup my hands at his jaws before easing to the back of his neck. I grind my hips down into his lap. If I doubted how he felt before, the impressive bulge in his shorts tells me he is enjoying himself.

However, something stands out. He is kissing me back, and my hands are all over him, but he isn't touching me. Pulling away from the kiss, he follows me. Apparently, he's not willing to let my lips go.

I chuckle, before breaking our kiss.

"Why won't you touch me," I plead, staring down into his heavy-lidded eyes.

He breaks eye contact. Bringing his hands between us, he cups them together as if he's offering me something.

"My hands, they aren't meant to be gentle. They are only for hurting and breaking things," he says, looking down at his palms as if he's holding trash.

I've come to realize; I hate that fucking organization. I know Gabriel thinks they saved him, but what they did was take a broken boy and patch him up with tape and glue. They didn't help him.

Shaking my head, I fight back tears. "No, Gabe. That's what they want you to believe. Let me show you how gentle you can be."

Grabbing his hands in mine, I place a kiss to the back of each. I then bring them to my thighs. Gabriel watches my every movement. His palms are rough and calloused against my skin, but I like the way they feel. Slowly, with my hands covering his, I move them up each side of my thighs. The motion lifts my hoodie, and my pussy comes into view. Thank goodness Trina made me shave all body hair before I went to meet Gregory.

I can almost feel his gaze on my wet center. I move his hands further up my body, stopping at my ribs. His grip tightens on me. For a moment, I start to wonder if I've taken him too far too fast. Wrapping my arms around the back of his neck, I bring our mouths together for another kiss. His tongue rolls against mine, pulling a soft moan from me.

This time, his hands stay on my body, and he rubs small circles against my skin with his thumbs.

"Gabe, I need you," I say, breaking our kiss for only a moment as I reach between us to pull him out of his pants.

When my hand wraps around his girth and I bring him out feeling the tip bounce against my navel I stop and look down.

Holy fuck.

I have to admit, some of the enthusiasm wains when I see the size of him. I guess I shouldn't be surprised, he's a big dude.

"We can stop," he says getting my attention back on his face. "If you no longer want me, we can stop. I still won't kill you."

He might not have to kill me. By the time I finish impaling myself on his length I might be dead. Well, you only live once.

"I want this," I say, before lifting up so that I can hover over the tip of his dick.

I'm so wet that it's leaking down my thighs. Yet still, making room for him inside me feels like I'm remodeling my vagina. His grip on my side tightens even more, but I don't complain. I have a feeling if I tell him he's hurting me he will get triggered and stop.

"Fuck," I moan when I realize there is an entire fist worth of him still not inside me. Yet it feels as if I've ran out of pussy for his dick. The dick to pussy ratio is clearly off.

Meanwhile, Gabe's face is flushed red and the vein in his forehead is throbbing, but thankfully he remains still.

I take a deep breath and slowly work my hips in circles attempting to get lower on his pole. Finally, after some work, I'm seated fully in his lap. If I didn't know any better, I would say this man is in my fucking cervix.

Slowly again, I roll my hips forward and then back whimpering at how full and good he feels inside me. I finally find a rhythm that works for me. I open my eyes, not knowing when I closed them, and stare at him. His focus isn't on my face, but where our bodies connect.

Pulling the hoodie off and over my head, I drop it on the floor behind me. Gabriel's gaze rakes over me with a hunger that has me feeling hot. I place my hands on his shoulders and continue to ride his massive erection. My moans fill the apartment along with his grunts of pleasure.

He whispers my name as if he's worshipping at my altar. Too soon, his body stiffens, he tosses his head back, and a roar fills the room as he spills his seed inside me.

I won't lie as if I'm not a little disappointed. This was over entirely too soon for me. I stop moving when he lifts his head to look at me. His nostrils flare as he heaves deep breaths. However, he doesn't speak.

I go to climb off him. His grip on my side keeps me in place.

"You're done. It's okay."

He shakes his head. "I'm not done."

In an instant, he grows inside me stretching my walls once again. My eyes widen. Before I know anything, I'm lying with my back on the couch, Gabriel is between my legs. One hand is on the arm of the sofa over my head, and the other is at my hips. He draws back and then slides into me as deep as he can go.

I cry out his name at the beautiful ache. My toes curl up so tight they make a popping noise.

"Gabe." Fuck me, he's deep.

He stops moving immediately. "Am I doing this right?" he asks, his brow pinched in concern.

It takes a moment for his words to register. My gaze bounces all over his face.

"Wait, is this your first time?"

He nods. I drop my jaw. There is no way this fine ass man has not had sex before.

"My brothers," he goes on to say. "They shared stories and showed me magazines."

I don't speak because my head is still trying to wrap around this being his first time. I don't think I'm worthy enough to be taking anyone's virginity.

"You will tell me if I hurt you, right?"

The concern in his voice isn't missed on me. Cupping his face, I lift up and he meets me halfway with a soul snatching kiss.

"It feels wonderful. Don't stop," I moan into his mouth. "No matter what, just don't stop."

He obliges moving his hips in and out of me. My eyes roll back in my head as he stretches me to fit him. I wrap my arms around his neck pulling him closer to me, my legs lift higher around his waist. He fucks me so good I forget about tonight and everything that happened. In this moment, it is only me and Gabriel.

He speeds up his strokes. The noise of my wetness echoes around the room. He hikes my leg further up his arm and angles my pelvis up from the couch. He pushes into me at a new angle, and I scream.

"Fuck. Shit," I cry out random swear words. He slows down, his brows pinched. "Don't stop, Gabriel. Don't you dare fucking stop."

He smirks before pulling all the way out of me and then slamming back in. I whimper his name and claw at his back as he continues that movement going faster and deeper with each stroke. I reach down between us with my free hand and stroke my clit. He watches my movement.

The first sign of an orgasm pummels me causing my body to shake like I'm going through an exorcism. Shutting my eyes, I let loose and scream as euphoria takes me on a high that rivals any drug I've ever tried.

He plants soft kisses over my face as he continues to rock through my orgasm. Tears leak from my eyes, and he licks them away.

"You're mine, Summer. All mine," he whispers in my ear.

For the first time ever, I truly felt I was where I belonged. In his arms, with him nestled between my legs, is the first place I've ever been that quiets the storm in my head. I've finally found my peace.

CHAPTER FOURTEEN

Fem

Albany

I finally find a parking spot about a block away from the Church headquarters.

Climbing out of my car, I run a sweaty hand down my pants leg.

When Nathaniel called me and told me to meet him at Church headquarters my heart nearly stopped beating. Did he know? Had they told him what I did?

When I first went to the Pope and offered my services for Hawk, I didn't think he would accept it. I knew it was a risk that he would decline my offer and tell Priest, but it was a risk I was willing to take because Hawk needed out. He was going to get himself killed. And though I see him as my brother and would have mourned him, I know what his death would do to the man I love.

As soon as I walk around the corner and the headquarters come into view, I spot Nathaniel 'Priest' Otella pacing in front of the door. I take a moment to take him in. This man has had my heart for so long I don't know how I remain alive without it.

Taking a deep breath, I bury my emotions under my usual mask.

"I hope you have a good reason for getting me out of bed at the butt crack of dawn," I tell him as I approach.

When he swings around to look at me, I wipe the playfulness off my face.

"What's wrong?"

He grabs my arm and walks me inside the building. "Something is up with Beast. He checked in this morning, but he's unsettled."

When we walk into the building, I notice a few of the Deacons and guards seem to be in a hurry to either get out of the building or toward the elevator.

"What do you mean unsettled?" I ask.

He doesn't stop as he continues to march me to the stairwell.

"I've never seen him like this," Nathaniel says as we make our way up the stairs to the upper level.

I've worked with all of Nathaniel's boys, but not Beast. I asked the reason for this once. Why did he want me to keep an eye on all the others except Beast. He simply said, Beast isn't like the others. He wouldn't appreciate the games.

At first, I was offended, especially with him calling my skills a game. But I realized quickly after meeting Beast that he was right. Beast would consider it playing.

"He won't calm down. We've tried everything I can think of. He's killed seven guards already and two Deacons that have tried to restrain him."

"Can't you talk to him," I ask as we get to the Ninth floor.

I'm assuming we're heading to one of the debriefing rooms. Sometimes, depending on your menu, the Church requires you to run down your kill after you're done.

As soon as he opens the stairwell door, the noise is epic. It sounds like a war is raging minus gunshots.

Deacons and guards fill the hallway. We push past them, Nathaniel shoving a few to the side as we make it to one of the open doors down the hall. Nathaniel shoves the few Church members in the doorway out of the way. We walk into a small room with bare walls and a rectangular table that has been upturned. And, judging from the hole in the wall, it's been tossed.

I don't focus on the room for long. I turn my attention to the scene before me. Beast is standing in the middle of the floor. Guards are around him, their guns aimed at his head. Pope is behind the guards, warning them that if any of them shoot Beast they will pay.

Nathaniel turns to me, and I pull my eyes away from an irate Beast.

"I need you to calm him down."

"Excuse me?" Is he insane.

I'm not going to lie, Beast has always scared me. The few times I've ever met him, I could never get a read on him. That never happens.

"He's never been this way. Something has him spiraling." There is true fear in Nathaniel's eyes.

Despite how young he was when he took the boys in, they are like his children. If they can't get Beast to calm down, they will eventually put him down.

Even though I know this, and I want to help, it doesn't change the fact that he terrifies me.

"This seems like a job for you, or maybe Lucien. He doesn't know me." I try to reason with Nathaniel.

He shakes his head. "Any other time, you would be right. But something tells me that right now, you are the only person that can find out what is going on. Please Fem, I need you."

I hate the control this man has over me. I love him so much that I would be willing to walk into a lion's den for him. Which is definitely what I'm about to do. Seeing the fear and desperation in Priest's eyes, tells me there is no other option.

I let out a deep breath and shake out my hands. "Okay," I say with little confidence. "But are you sure it's safe to talk to him in here? What if it's something big?"

"These rooms are soundproof and have no cameras. Everything he says will be safe. You got this."

I wasn't so sure about that.

Nathaniel walks me closer to the group surrounding Beast. Beast's wild eyes seem vacant. There is blood on his face and covering his shirt. His body heaves as if he's trying to catch his breath. His long golden blond hair hangs in his eyes.

"Beast," Nathaniel calls out to him. Those light green eyes turn to us and recognition sparks for only a second. "Fem is here, she wants to talk to you."

"What the hell are you doing, Priest." Pope argues. "Get her out of here."

"Will you shut the fuck up," Nathaniel says glaring at Pope. "Let me handle this."

Pope opens his mouth and I'm sure an argument is about to ensue, but Beast speaks sending the room into silence.

"Everyone out."

Nathaniel looks at me. I can tell his well thought out plans are starting to not look so great to him right now. For some reason, I'm less afraid now.

"I'm okay," I mouth to Nathaniel.

He turns back to the others in the room. "You heard him, get the fuck out."

Slowly the room starts to empty. The last to leave are Pope and Nathaniel. Nathaniel looks at me one last time. I give him a subtle nod to let him know I got this.

"I'll be right out here if you need me," he says before turning and walking out.

Pope tries to stay behind, but Nathaniel grabs his arm and shoves him out the door. The large door closes with a loud clank.

When I turn back around, Gabriel is watching me.

Sucking in a deep breath I try to think of what's the best approach here. I could run through my many characters and see which one sticks, but I think Nathaniel is right. Trying to read Beast won't work. The best approach is to be real. Or as real as I know how to be.

"Do you know why Nathaniel calls me Fem?"

He nods but doesn't speak.

I walk further into the room being sure not to crowd his space. It's then I notice the pools of blood around him. I'm assuming some of those dead bodies Nathaniel mentioned were once in this room.

"I'm really good at reading men and being whatever they want me to be," I go on to explain even though I'm pretty sure he already knows this.

His eyes narrow at my words but still he doesn't speak.

"But I'm not going to do that with you." Holding my hands out at my side briefly, I say. "My name is Albany. Tell me how I can help you?"

Those eyes that many consider vacant stare back at me. One of the things I did pick up from Beast is that he's very smart. A lot of people also think just because he rarely speaks, that Beast is tuned out or not focused. I was seventeen when I met him for the first time, and even then, I knew that was a lie.

Beast is always paying attention. Even when you think he isn't. I also know from my few times of being around him, he's a straightforward kind of guy. If he's freaking out, it tells me something serious is going on.

He's silent for so long I start to second guess my approach to him, but then his shoulders relax and the tension on his face wanes. The man I walked in on is completely gone. It's almost like he switched a channel and turned into someone else. Kind of like what I've been told I do.

A new thought runs through my mind. Nathaniel said that I was a last resort and they'd tried everything to calm him. However, the moment he saw me in the room, his aggression immediately ended.

"You knew he would call me. You did all this to get me here," I say, pointing to the hole in the wall.

A smirk appears on his face letting me know my suspicion is correct.

"Sit down," he demands in that low growl of a voice. "We don't have much time and I need your help."

CHAPTER FIFTEEN

Summer

I wake up and stretch my arms over my head. My body aches all over. My joints are sore, and I feel like shit. However, there is a smile on my face.

Gabriel sexed me so good I don't even remember falling asleep. After he came that first time, he was like the Energizer Bunny. He wouldn't stop. I have no complaints though. However, I will have to do something about the many times he came inside me. Last night, I was on a high with him and threw caution to the wind. Today, I need to be a little smarter.

Rolling over to my side, I scream before sitting up on the couch. Sitting on the coffee table is a beautiful black woman. Her hair is long and parted down the middle. She has smooth brown skin with wide dark brown eyes and a button nose. She's wearing a peach-colored silk blouse and black dress slacks with killer heels. Looking at her reminds me of the disheveled mess that I must look like.

At some point in the early hours of the day, Gabriel must have covered me up. A blanket has fallen down from my bare breasts and pools in my lap. I quickly lift it back up to cover myself.

119

"Who are you, and where is Gabe?" I look around the apartment, but there is no sign of Gabriel.

The woman reaches to the side of her and pulls out a folder. She opens it up and stares at it for a second.

"Two suicide attempts. One from an overdose of Tylenol at fifteen and then it seems you graduated to the harder stuff." I flinch as she reads off my medical records. I won't even question how she got them.

"You've been arrested six times, mostly public intoxication, a couple of disorderly conducts, and I see you have a possession of marijuana as well." She closes the folder and places it down beside her.

Narrowing my eyes at her I say, "You don't know me."

She rolls her eyes. "You will be surprised at all the things I know about you, Summer Jones."

A chill runs up my spine. Without asking, I know this woman is part of Gabriel's organization. For a moment, panic fills my veins. Did I get distracted by the best dick in the world last night only to realize he played me. When he said he wasn't going to kill me, it didn't cross my mind that he could get someone else to do it.

"Are you going to kill me now?"

She smiles, reaches behind her and pulls out a gun. I slink further back into the couch, gripping the blanket to my chest like it's a shield.

"Isn't this what you want?" She asks.

I stare at her like she's crazy. "No."

She uses the gun to point to the folder beside her. "That's not what this file tells me. You see, Beast is part of my family. And right now, he is willing to take the fall for not killing you. That means he's looking at five to ten years in solitary lockdown."

My heart immediately goes out to him. I didn't want him to suffer for not killing me.

"I didn't...."

"You didn't what?" She asks. "Think there was consequences?" I can only look away from her. She's right, I should have known. That organization doesn't strike me as one that will easily let something go.

"The problem is," she continues on. "I don't see why Beast would risk his life for you. It can't be your looks. Your skin is ashy and dry. You also look pale which shouldn't be a thing for a black girl. No matter how light you are. You're entirely too skinny, your boobs are average, your face is bruised, those braids have seen better days, and you have that sunken cheek face all drug addicts have."

It's not like I don't know all these things about myself. Hell, I've said most of them to my reflection in the mirror many times. However, hearing her say them out loud makes me feel like shit. Especially when she looks like a goddess.

"What's your point?" I ask trying to keep my chin from wobbling with my need to cry.

Her face never changes, never showing anything but mild disgust and a little interest.

"My point is, why don't I pull the trigger now and put you out of your misery. That's what you've been trying to do for years, right?".

I shake my head as tears spill down my face. "No."

She once again points to the file beside her. "That's not what this tells me. I mean this is just two documented cases, but we both know there are more. All the drug binges, the dating the drug dealer, even that fire was another weak attempt at ending your life. You're just going about it the long way.

"Eventually the coke and pills won't do it for you anymore and you'll move on to other drugs to get your high like crack, meth, or even heroine. Before long this," she waves her gun up and down my body. "Will be the best you've ever looked. So, I'm here to tell you to either shit or get off the pot. Let me make it quick."

She points the gun at my head. I shut my eyes as the tears pour down my face.

As hard as it is to hear, she's right. Everything I've done has been with the carelessness of someone who doesn't give a shit about their life. That night I burnt the trap house down, I knew I was too high to touch that stove but I did. I even knew the stove was faulty, but I still turned it on.

All the times I snorted coke or took pills I took them with the understanding that at any time it could be my last, yet it didn't stop me. I've been on a slow mission all my life to end myself. To finish what my father didn't.

Why not just allow her to make it quick? A bullet to the head is a lot faster way to go than slowly poisoning my body over time. I didn't see myself moving on to anything stronger, but who says I wouldn't. Who says I won't end up in a ditch somewhere with a needle sticking out of my arm.

"I don't want to die," I mumble as I fight through my clogged throat.

"I don't believe you," she shrugs.

Before tonight, I don't think I would've believed myself. However, after truly staring death in the face so many times tonight, I can honestly say I'm not ready. I don't want to die. Yes, the shit with my father haunts me.

I'll never get over the look in his face when he pulled that trigger, but I've been held hostage to that night for too long. It's time I used the extended life I was given. There is a reason I didn't die that night. I need to figure out why.

"I mean it this time. I'll go to rehab. I'll get clean."

She shakes her head. "You've been seven times already. What's the point? You're just wasting everyone's time. Why should I believe, this time will be different?"

Again, it's hard to argue when she's right, but this time, I really mean it.

I shut my eyes and those green intense one's pop into my head. I'm once again standing in that room with Nic and Gabe. The pills are on the floor and my mouth is watering for an escape. His words play back in my head.

I open my eyes and lift my chin as I stare at the woman in front of me.

"It will be different, because I'm better than this," I angrily wipe at my eyes.

I'm tired of allowing my past to overrule me. Yeah, I got scars, but I'm not the only one that's dealing with shit. I met a man tonight that has more demons than I'd ever imagine, but he saved me in more ways than he knows. I want to be a better person.

She watches me without saying a word. My heart pounds as I wait for her ruling. Finally, a slow smile lifts the corner of her lips slightly. She stands, places her gun at her back and then rakes a hand down the front of her pants.

"Thank you for your assistance. The program you're going to is a one-hundred-and-eighty-day program," she says. "I pulled a lot of strings to get you in this facility. They usually only do ninety days, but I asked them to take extra care of you."

My brows pinch, she already had me enrolled into a program?

"You were never going to kill me?" I ask.

She chuckles. "Oh, I was. It all depended on your response. Just know that if you drop out of the program or come out and fall back into your old ways, my beretta will be waiting for you."

I gulp, knowing she really meant what she was saying.

Running a hand over my fuzzy cornrows, I stand to my feet.

"Can I see him before I leave?"

She cocks her head to the side. "He doesn't want to see you."

Her words feel like cold water being splashed in my face.

Shaking my head, I say. "That's not true. Gabriel wouldn't do that."

She laughs in a mocking tone. "So now you're a Beast expert? You've known him for a total of ten hours. Is it the dick that has you so delusional?"

Her words hurt like hell, but again she's right. I've only known Gabriel for a short time. How could I possibly believe that I meant anything to him? He took care of me, helped me fight my demons, allowed me to take his virginity, and in the end made love to me so tenderly my soul felt it.

He was too good for me, and that should've been my first sign.

"You don't have to be so mean," I whisper the words as I fight the tears threatening to spill down my face again.

She takes a step toward me, lifting my chin with her finger. "You hate me now, but eventually you'll look back on this day and thank me for my harshness."

"I just want to see him."

She smiles but it doesn't reach her eyes. "Never beg a man for something as little as his attention. Walk away with your head up. Trust me on this."

I nod my head, taking her words of wisdom to heart. He didn't want to see me and that's okay. I won't hold it against him.

She lets my face go and turns her back to me. She grabs something off the coffee table, before turning to face me. When she turns around she's holding clothes in her hands.

"Get dressed," she says dropping the clothes on the sofa behind me. "They will be here to take you to treatment in a few minutes."

She heads for the door, but I stop her. "Hey, what's your name?"

She doesn't turn to look at me. "Call me Fem." she says before walking out of the apartment.

I quickly put on the leggings and T shirt she placed on the sofa. I put the expensive shoes back on that Gabriel brought me last night. The last thing I put on is his hoodie. Despite wearing it last night and being knocked around in it, it still smells like him.

Yeah, I should toss his shit in the trash, but she's right. I'm walking away with my head high. I also keep his things as a reminder of last night. It might not have meant shit to him, but it did to me. It told me that I'm stronger than my addiction and I deserve to be happy.

The moment I finish getting dressed, the door to the apartment opens. Fem, and two men walk in.

"Are you ready to go?" She says looking me over.

I take one last look at the apartment. Last night started out as a night from hell. Everything that could have gone wrong did. However, whenever I look back at the night it will only be with fond memories. No matter how disappointing the morning turned out.

Last night will live in my memories for years as the most epic night of my life. It's the night that taught me to live, and the night I spent with a beast.

Act Two
How Its Going

CHAPTER SIXTEEN
Breakout

Beast

Five Years Later....

Stopping in my tracks in the middle of the woods, I tilt my head toward the sky, shut my eyes, and take a deep breath. After five long years, I'm finally free.

The morning after my night with Summer, I watched her sleep for two hours. I thought about taking her and running. I ran the pros and cons through my mind. Gambler did it for years and only got caught when he was ready. I could have done the same. However, not without Hawk, Many, Zel, Lucien and Seth.

I wasn't going to leave the Church and leave my brothers and Priest behind. They are my family. They deserved to be happy. So, I gave up the opportunity to run with Summer in order to free all of us.

It was the hardest decision I've ever made. Even when I turned myself in, I struggled with the choice. That caused me to serve a five-year confinement punishment.

The confinement meant I couldn't leave my prison apartment in Church headquarters. They tried to enforce a no visitor rule, but Priest ended that quickly.

Although I spent five long years staring at the same white walls, it was worth it. I needed that time to prepare. Now I know in order to get everyone the happy ending they deserve I must finish what Gambler started.

Pushing through the rest of the crop of trees, I come out on the other side to find a simple black sedan. Albany is leaning against the car. Her head is down and she's looking at something in her hand. I realize it's a phone when she sticks it back in her pocket. She then looks at her watch.

I purposely kick a nearby rock, causing it to scatter through the foliage on the forest floor causing a ruckus. Albany turns around with her gun aimed at my head.

"Relax, it's me," I say, walking out of the trees.

"Everything went well?"

Dipping my chin to my chest, I head to the trunk of the car ready to get started with my mission. The faster I get it done, the sooner I can get back to her. Mine. My Summer.

Even the memory of her has that fluttering feeling in my stomach going off. I spent a lot of those five years studying every detail of that night, of her. I now know the flutter feeling is my desire for her. I clench my hands into fists at my side.

"How are the guys?"

I ask about my brothers because I have to keep myself distracted. If I don't, I will run to her and him. Now isn't the time. I pull the black shirt over my head and toss it into the trunk of the car. Picking up the new shirt, I put it on.

"Hawk and my sister are safe. Maybe even expecting their first child."

I don't miss the way her tone drops, and her eyes shift down when she mentions her sister. As tough as Albany tries to be, I think the decision she made to leave them all behind eats away at her. But that isn't my battle. I've done all I could to set her on the right track. It will work out. If I know Priest the way I think I do, he will come for her soon.

"Lucien has come to terms with himself, and he and his girls are doing good last time I checked. The kid loves him just like you said she would. Even Many and Zel are in line for their future."

Taking off the heavy combat boots, I place them in her trunk and quickly put on my preferred ones.

"You can relax now. You did everything right. You deserve a break."

Not yet. But she doesn't need to know that. There is still so much that needs to be done.

"And you?" I ask instead.

She laughs. "I already have my future. I don't need anything else."

I don't call her out on her bullshit. She's in love with Priest and won't be happy until she has him back in her life. When she told me she was pregnant and I suggested she fake her death, I already had a plan to get her and Priest back together.

She points to a black duffle inside her trunk. I look inside and find stacks upon stacks of cash. What the hell is this? Most of my money should have gone to Summer and him.

I point to the bag without asking a question.

"It's a going away present."

Shaking my head, I tell her, "No." I go to zip the bag, but her hands cover mine, pausing my actions.

"It's my gift to you."

"Put it with them."

"They are taken care of. I promise they want for nothing."

From the pictures Albany sent me, I can tell that Summer and my son are fine. Before any plans to save my brothers came into fruition, I had to make sure that Summer was okay. I told Albany all she needed to know about Summer in order to get her to go to rehab. It was not an option for her not to go.

When Albany came to me and told me Summer was pregnant, I dealt with mixed feelings. Part of me was happy to know that she would forever have a part of me with her. However, another part of me worried about what my demons would do to my child. I'm flawed.

Even before my mother did her damage to me, I was already different. It wasn't just the autism that made me stand out. Priest and the psychiatrist at the Church are the ones that told me I was on the spectrum.

However, there is something else. Something others don't know about. Something Mother called possession.

I blink, realizing I've been staring at Albany too long without speaking. Zipping the duffle bag, I drop it at my feet. I then turn my attention to the other bag in the trunk. Opening it up, I make sure everything I requested is inside.

"Does it look good?" She asks.

Dipping my chin, I zip the bag and pull it out of the trunk placing it at my feet as well. Reaching in my pocket, I pull out the flash drive.

Albany believes she wants the truth of what happened to her mother. She has no idea the pain that truth will cause her.

She eagerly reaches for the flash drive, but I pull it back.

"You sure this is what you want? Not all answers bring closure."

"I don't want closure. I want the truth and revenge."

No, she wants to belong. She believes that this will help her feel complete. She doesn't realize it yet, but she has everything she needs around her to make her whole. She turns away from me, trying to hide her pain and her truths.

I'm not worried about Albany. I have already put things in order for her happiness too. Everyone wins in this game. Well, everyone but me.

"You're too flawed," my mother's voice taunts in my head.

"She's lying and you know it." Right on time Priest's voice comes in to tell me I'm making the wrong decision. I know he doesn't agree with how I'm handling this thing between Summer and I, but he's wrong on this one.

Holding the drive back out to her, I allow her to take it from me this time.

"How did you even get this?"

She flips the little black rectangular device over in her hand.

"I took a visit to one of the record keeper's apartments. I luckily found two of them together. I cut off the head of one of the record keepers with a box cutter. The other one gave me the information without much argument."

"When they find the bodies, will they know we took it?"

"What bodies?" I ask with a smile. By the time they find those two, they will be nothing but a sludge of liquid.

My time is up. I still have a lot to do. Picking up the two bags at my feet, I turn to walk away.

"Gabriel," I stop when she calls my name. "Are you sure you don't want to see them."

More than anything in this world.

"You got work to do, Boy. Leave that whore and bastard where they are," Mother taunts.

"I have to… feed first. I can't face them without eating." The red haze has been riding me for years. I've been holding onto it, allowing it to build up. I need to exorcise it.

"Be safe," she says softly. "And be careful. Pope isn't going to let you go easily. He's going to make you public enemy number one."

I look back at her over my shoulder. "Pope isn't my concern nor is he my enemy."

I've always known of Fox's plans to use me as his very own puppet. I knew it the moment he first laid eyes on me. But Fox isn't my problem, he's Priest's issue. My job is to finish what Gambler started. It's time I take down the Church.

"If Pope isn't the enemy, then who is?"

"My enemy is higher up." I continue walking.

That is all she needs to know. I'm thankful to Albany for all her help, but she can't help me with this. Her concern now, should be Priest and Charlie.

"Who's higher than the Pope?" She calls out behind me.

I stop, as I remember Gambler's words to me that night five years ago. "When they broke away from the Catholic Church, they didn't go independent, Beast. They aligned with something much worse."

"God," I say. Although, I still had no idea who God was.

Before I turned myself in the morning after I killed Gambler, I went back to his house and collected the information he had. The only thing I was able to take back to the dungeon with me were the three flash drives.

I had Lucien smuggle me in a laptop and cellphone my first week in confinement. All the guards were too scared to come into my space, so no one ever found the contraband. The rest of the info is hidden in boxes at my apartment.

I've studied those flash drives for five years, taking in all the information I could. Now, it's time to clean house.

I leave Albany standing in the road. Her job for me is done.

Making it back to the brick apartment building I took Summer to that night, I use my code to enter the building. I smile at the reminder of her.

Stepping inside, I walk into the foyer. I don't have to worry about neighbors or anyone disturbing me, the entire building is mine.

I take the stairs to my main apartment, not the one I took Summer to. I open the door and walk inside. The place has been cleaned and kept up by the cleaning crew I hired.

As soon as I walk in, I enter the living room. A dark gray sectional faces the wall that separates the living from the one bedroom. There is no other furniture other than a coffee table and a lamp. There are no pictures on the walls or decorations around the room. I only have the basics to survive. To my left is the dining room and kitchen, all open to the living room.

I place my duffle bags down and head into my bedroom. I make quick work of showering and getting dressed.

Not long after entering my main living quarters, I make my way out of the unit and down the hall to my tech-based unit. Other than the main living space, this is my second most used space in the building.

Opening the doors to the remodeled apartment, I'm greeted with a set up similar to my brother Lucien's. In the center of the room is a round table. On top of the table are all the files I took from Gambler. They are still in the boxes he left them in. The rest of the room is one giant computer desk. Nine monitors surround the desk. Four on each side and one large screen in the middle.

Pulling out the chair in front of the desk I take a seat and sign onto my computer. I take the information from the smaller screens and move them to the big monitor.

Gambler spent years tracking down all the menus in Church files that didn't add up. Either the person on the menu didn't fit the crime, or the crime didn't deserve a menu. He had thousands of files like this. However, nothing leads me to a singular person.

It seems that the cases were going through all the right channels to get approved. Bishops are getting the names of the targets; they get them signed off with the Cardinals. Afterwards they place them on a menu and hand them over to a Deacon. All standard practice.

I figured the best way to figure out how these cases are getting into the Church, is to start at the beginning, where the crimes begin.

A picture of a driver's license pops up on my screen. Detective Dennis Chambers. Eight years ago, he found himself on a Church menu. His files said he was a crooked cop that was despised by his fellow policemen. He was charged with everything from abuse of power, to planting evidence, to battery, to wrongful deaths. At first glance it looked as if he deserved everything he got.

However, after reading up on him and the article written after his death, nothing was adding up. Not only did other cops praise him, quite a few civilians spoke on how kind and caring he was.

I decided to look into his last case. It involved the sexual assault of a sixteen-year-old black girl named Tiffany Williams.

A new license pops up on the screen. Jason Averil. The man suspected of raping and nearly killing Tiffany. Not only was Dennis killed before the investigation was complete, Tiffany recanted her story on the stand. While sobbing, she stated that she'd made it all up. She took a lot of heat for that and only six months later, she took her life.

I check the flight itinerary again for Jason. He's flying back home tomorrow. I have plans to meet him there.

I clear the computer screen in front of me. My hand hovers over the mouse. Once again, Summer and Gabe pop up in my thoughts. I promised myself that I would stay clear of them. They didn't need me. I would do nothing but cause them harm.

Even though I know those words to be true, I hit the mouse and open the screen to the camera system. When Albany set up the house for Summer, I had her hire a security crew to come in and set up cameras on the outside of the house. Despite how bad I wanted to put them inside, I refrained. It would have been torture watching her and not being able to touch her.

I access the outdoor cameras.

The first view is from the front porch and driveway. The car I picked for her is in its regular spot. The street out in front of the house is clear. I chose that neighborhood for the low traffic and the safety. I switch to the back door cameras. The yard is clear, other than a few balls lying in the grass and a plastic toy house.

I close out of the cameras, feeling settled even though I didn't see them.

I have work to do. My plans are simple, figure out who is running the Church and eliminate them, make sure my brothers and Priest are safe, set Summer and Gabe up for life, and then disappear forever. I just have to stick to the plan.

CHAPTER SEVENTEEN

Rehabilitated

Summer

"Are you excited to be graduating in a few months?"

Placing my fork back down in my empty plate, I wipe my mouth with my napkin before giving my attention to my lunch companion.

I look over at my sponsor and good friend, Shay. Her long black and honey blonde tipped locs hang down to the middle of her back. Her dark brown skin is flawless and blemish free. Even though she's forty she doesn't look a day over twenty-five.

I lift one shoulder and let it drop lazily. "Yes, I guess. I mean, I've worked for this for four years."

Shay smiles as she leans forward on the table. We are at the restaurant where we always have our monthly meetings.

"It's okay to be nervous, Summer. Remember I told you that just because one goal is obtained, you can always add another goal. Life is all about striving for better."

I don't reply.

I spent six months in the rehab program Fem sent me to. It wasn't easy. Between the therapy sessions and the depression, I spent most of the earlier months crying. I learned that a lot of my issues with relapsing was due to the fact that I was going to rehab to treat my drug problem, but I never fixed the real issue. But I was finally able to heal from my father's suicide.

Before I left the program they connected me with a sponsor in my area. That's how I met Shay Covington. She has truly been the biggest help in my recovery process. Well, her and finding out that I was pregnant. Memories weren't the only thing I took from that night with Gabriel.

"You're still afraid of relapsing," Shay states.

I cut my gaze down to my empty plate on the table before looking back up at her. The thing about addiction is that it forever lingers with you. I've been clean for five years, but every day is a battle to stay sober. It may not require as much fight as it did in the early stages, but it's still a fight.

"You've made so much progress. Don't be so hard on yourself," she chuckles when I grimace at her words. "Why do I have more faith in you than you do?"

"Because clearly you don't know me as well as I do."

She shakes her head as she laughs.

It isn't that I crave the high anymore, I'm past that stage. I fear relapsing because I have someone very important that depends on me now.

"How's the jewelry business?" She asks distracting me from going down my self-pity spiral.

One of the things I was taught during my time at rehab is the importance of hobbies and finding other ways to stimulate the mind. An idle mind is sometimes my greatest enemy.

"The online business is great, and I was able to get my products in two more stores."

"That's wonderful," she says. "Everywhere I go I get asked about my pieces." She touches the jade necklace around her neck.

I made her a matching necklace, bracelet, and earring set one Christmas. Since then, she's been one of my regular customers.

"If you decide not to do anything with your degree in counseling, you can always go into making jewelry your full-time gig."

I smile at the complement and duck my head. It's not that I haven't heard it before. Summer Designs have been incredibly successful. Who knew I had the talent and the eye for jewelry design. However, the shyness comes by way of not being used to being told I'm good at something. That's all new.

Picking up my glass of water, I take a sip.

"Now how is that dating project going?"

I immediately choke on the water in my mouth. I place the cup back down and take a few minutes to pat my chest to keep from dying.

Shay watches me, a smirk on her face.

Of all the suggestions Shay has given me over the years, dating has been the only one I haven't been able to adapt to.

"I…uhhh….it's going."

She lifts a brow and cocks her head. She doesn't believe me. I don't blame her because I'm lying.

I know what this looks like. To someone outside looking in, it seems as if I'm still hung up over Gabriel and that isn't true. Did he show me more kindness in that one night with him than I'd received my entire life. Yes. Was the sex, even as unexperienced as he was, the best fucking sex I'd ever had. Goodness yes. However, I am not caught up on Gabriel.

"Have you been out in these dating streets?" I ask glancing at the beautiful diamond wedding set on her ring finger. "It's like a zombie apocalypse out here. Everyone is walking around aimlessly just trying to rub their body parts against each other."

She laughs but quickly covers it up with her hand.

"It's not that bad."

I roll my eyes. "Holding a conversation with some men is the equivalent of having your brains eaten. And if one more man asks me what I'm bringing to the table or call themselves high valued, I may purposely go back to drugs."

This time she tosses her head back and laughs. Although I was making a joke, it isn't funny. The dating pool definitely had chlamydia infested piss in it. Not that I was that much of a catch. I was indeed an ex-druggy single mother. But damn.

"What about the Mechanic you were dating a couple months ago?"

"Ugh. We went out on two dates, and he kept trying to get me to meet his momma," I say folding my arms over my chest.

"A little early," she shrugs. "But there is nothing wrong with that."

"She's dead."

She once again places her hand over her mouth to cover her smile.

Honestly, most of the men I meet never make it past the first date. The few that have, never make it longer than two months. And trust me, I am definitely the problem.

Every guy I've met these last five years has not held my attention. Even the few that made it to a second date. They all seem to lack something, but I don't know what it is.

If I could maybe figure out what the hell I'm looking for in these men, I might be able to make this dating thing work for me.

"Honestly," I say, shaking my head. "I'd much rather put my time and energy on my business and my baby boy."

The day I realized I was going to be a mother was the day my life changed. I had all the reasons in the world to not keep my son. I mean, I found out I was pregnant by a one-night stand while in rehab. However, as I glanced down at that little pee stick, I remember thinking, for the first time I had something worth fighting for. The day August Gabriel Jones came into this world is the day I found my purpose.

"Part of your recovery is learning how to deal with and maintain healthy relationships. Dating is crucial. Besides, I think it will help you get over that last hurdle."

I've only briefly told Shay about my night with Gabriel. Of course, I left out a lot of key details. It's hard to downplay being held captive, your life being threatened, and the number of murders I witnessed. That would have surely ended with me being in a strait jacket or prison. However, she knows he played a huge role in my recovery process.

"Do you want my opinion?" She asks once my silence has gone on longer than expected.

Not really.

"Sure," I reply instead of the truth.

Shay leans back in her seat, her long locs cascading over her shoulders. "I think you're self- sabotaging with the men you meet, because no matter how much you've changed or how much you've accomplished you still view yourself as that twenty-two-year-old, lost, drug addict that believes she is not worthy of love."

I swallow, wetting my dry throat. My gaze bounces around the restaurant in desperate need to find something to ground me. The words Nic said that night play back in my head.

"She doesn't deserve love. She's incapable of loving."

My watch vibrates against my wrist letting me know that it's time to go. I'm saved by the bell.

"I have to go," I sing, as I grab my purse off the back of the chair. "You know my babysitter is on a tight schedule."

Shay nods knowingly. "But we will pick up this conversation next month."

"Okay," I playfully roll my eyes. Shay laughs as she grabs her things as well. We make our way through the restaurant, waving at our waitress and the staff we know.

"Tell Josiah and the boys I said hi," I say as Shay and I part ways.

She gives me a brief hug before getting into her car. Before she shuts the door she calls my name. I turn to face her.

"You are worthy of love. Don't ever forget that."

I smile and wink at her before walking away. I appreciate all Shay has done for me. However, in this, she and I will always disagree.

I stop in front of my black Volvo.

When Fem picked me up from rehab after my six-month stint, I had plans of going to a halfway house until I could get a job and get my own place. However, I was shocked to my core to find out that not only did I have my own home, I had a bank account to go with it. Two weeks later, after I got my license, there was a brand-new Volvo XC40 parked in my driveway. To say I have been very well taken care of is an understatement.

As soon as I get in and pull off, my phone goes off. I press the handsfree option on the steering wheel. The car immediately fills with the sound of my son crying and screaming.

"Gabe, what's wrong?"

He doesn't reply. He just continues to scream through my car speakers. My heart knocks against my chest and tears fill my eyes. Clearly, he's having an episode.

"I'm coming, baby. I'm coming." I disconnected the call and rush to my mother's house.

The day Gabe was born, I stared down at his little round face and realized I've never loved anyone or anything as much as I did him.

When Gabe turned three, he was diagnosed as being on the autism spectrum. I wasn't too shocked by the diagnosis because after paying attention to my son, I noticed a lot of his father's behavior. I have no doubt Gabriel was also on the spectrum.

His diagnosis made me go harder for him. I wanted my son to know that I didn't give a shit if he saw the world differently, I was going to always have his back and make sure that this world didn't treat him differently.

I make the trip to my mother's house in record time. I pay her $2000 a month to watch Gabe for me if needed. I wanted my son to have a relationship with my mother and sister even if I never did.

Most times, my mother only has to look after him once a month for two hours during my lunches with Shay. However, she still charges me the full price.

I park my car behind my mother's and jump out sprinting to the front door. The sound of my son's cries fuel my haste.

Stepping into the house, my gaze quickly scans the room. Mitchell is lying across the couch glaring at me.

After little MJ was born, my sister and her baby daddy fell on hard times. My mother invited them to move in with her. They've been here ever since.

"You need to take that hollering ass boy home," Mitch shouts.

I ignore him because my concern is and always will be Gabe. I follow the sound of his cries toward the back of the house.

The moment I spot him in my mother's room I run to him. He's sitting on the floor, his back against the wall, his knees up to his chest. He's rocking back and forth, hitting his back against the wall.

I squat down in front of him. "Gabe, I'm here. Mama's right here."

He continues to rock and cry. I place my hand on his shoulder. He immediately goes into defensive mode. He kicks his feet out and swings his hands. I narrowly dodge getting hit in the eye.

"Gabriel. Gabe." I call his name as I try to hold his arms down.

Finally, my words seem to cut through to him. Those gorgeous forest green eyes open and stare back at me.

"Hey, baby." I say softly.

"Mama."

Every time he calls my name it melts my heart. For the longest, Gabe seemed uninterested in talking. He didn't start using real words to express himself until he was nearly three years old. Now, although he speaks, he doesn't do very much of it.

I pull him into me for a hug. He doesn't hug me back, but that's alright.

"I don't know what happened. One minute he was fine and then the next he was having an episode," my mother says from behind me.

I look over my shoulder to glance at her. She has her hands on her hips. My nephew is standing beside her holding Gabe's Iron Man toy.

"You don't know what triggered him?" I glance at MJ's hands and then back to my mother.

She looks to her favorite grandchild before turning to me.

"You have to teach Gabe to share his toys," mom says taking the Iron Man action figure from MJ.

I ignore her parenting advice. She walks over and hands me the figurine. I turn back to my son and give him his toy. He takes Iron Man and smiles up at me. My heart melts even more. I stand and pull Gabe up with me. It's then I pay attention to his arm. Welts go up his arm past his elbow. I move the sleeve of his shirt up and find a large bruise on his upper arm.

"He didn't get those here," my mother immediately starts to defend.

Ignoring her, I squat back down getting eye level with my son. He's busy looking over his toy.

"Gabe, give me your eyes." It takes a second before those beautiful irises look at me. "Who did this to your arm?"

He looks down at Iron Man once again.

"No, Gabe. Give me your eyes." He looks back at me. "Who did this?"

When he glances over my shoulder, I follow his sight. My nephew is sneering at Gabe, but his eyes widen when he notices me looking.

"He's lying. I didn't do it, Grandma," MJ pleads.

Shooting to my feet, I turn and face my mother and nephew. "You little asshole," I shout.

"Now wait a minute," Mama says holding up a hand. "If MJ says he didn't do it. He didn't do it."

"And if Gabe says he did, then he did."

She scoffs and rolls her eyes. "Let's be serious here, Summer. Out of the two, who would you believe?"

I should be hurt by the way my mother is talking about my child, but hell she doesn't even like me. I thought that having her spend time with Gabriel would allow her to bond with him like she never could with me, but I guess once again I'm looking for something from her that I'll never get.

"Out of the two," I say, crossing my arms over my chest. "One has anger issues, he's been kicked out of two daycares, has been suspended from school for fighting, and inappropriately touching other kids. And the other is a four-year-old whose only crime—as you would call it—is that he has autism. You tell me who I should believe?"

Mother's face falls. She knows I'm right. Despite MJ being her favorite, he's a menace to society. I don't think any kid is a lost cause. Hell, I'm a recovering drug addict, I have no room to judge. However, MJ is spoiled and entitled, and no one cares or wants to check him on his shit.

"Fine, I'll tell Raina to talk to MJ about keeping his hands to himself."

Undoing my belt buckle, I rip the belt from around my waist. "No, I'll speak to him in his language." Folding it in half, I yank at the ends causing it to make a snapping sound.

MJ screams and takes off out of the room. I chase after him. Am I overstepping? Maybe. But I will show my son that I am his protector. No one gets to abuse him and not face the consequences.

"Summer, don't you dare," Mother shouts behind me as she follows me out of the room.

"Watch me." I continue to chase my nephew through the house.

I have no intentions of hitting MJ with this belt, but I do want to scare his ass from ever thinking he can put his hands on my son or anyone else's child again.

MJ runs into the living room where his father is still lying on the couch. Mitchell jumps up when MJ runs in.

"What the hell is going on?" He yells.

"I'm going to teach your son some fucking manners."

"She's crazy," Mother cries out behind me. "I think she's on that stuff again."

I ignore her accusations. She claims I'm using again every other day.

I dart around Mitchell to grab MJ, but he sprints away. Just then, my sister walks into the house. MJ runs to her, crying. He wraps his arms around her waist.

"Mommy, Aunt Summer is on drugs again. She's trying to kill me."

"I'm not trying to kill you, you little shit. I'm just going to whip your ass." I grab for him once again. However, Raina blocks me by pushing MJ behind her.

"Don't you even think about putting your hands on my son," Raina shrieks.

"Your demon spawn put his hands on my child."

I hear a scoff from behind me that I know to be Mitch's. "Ain't nobody hit your punk ass boy."

I spin around on my heels and sock Mitch right in the face. I won't acknowledge how bad my hand hurts.

"Fuck, Summer." He grabs his nose.

"Call my baby a name again?" I challenge him.

Although I had no intentions of putting my hands on MJ, I had no qualms about punching his father.

"What the hell is wrong with you?" Raina says, as she goes to her baby daddy's side.

My stomach turns at the way she coddles him. No matter what Mitch does to her she will not let him go. Right before MJ was born, she was cornered and nearly jumped by his other two baby mothers. She lost her apartment because Mitch was causing too many problems. Yet, instead of sending him on his way, they both moved in with mom because he gave her a cheap ring and asked her to marry him. They have yet to make it down an aisle.

"She's jealous," Mitch argues in a nasal voice.

I guess I did more damage to his nose than I thought. He holds his head back pinching his nose.

Snorting, I shake my head. "Jealous, of what?"

"Of me," Raina argues staring me down. "Everyone knows it. Mama even pointed it out."

This is a new one for me. Even in the midst of my addiction, I'd never been jealous of my sister. I may have yearned for the relationship she had with my mother, but I was never jealous.

Looking around the room, I search for what exactly she had that I was supposed to be jealous of.

"Am I missing something?"

She sneers as she takes a step closer to me, making sure to keep her body between me and her son.

"You think you're better than me because you have a fancy house and car? Who cares you went back to school. Everyone knows, once a druggy, always a druggy."

I roll my eyes. "You know the drug jokes don't hit like they used to. Find another insult."

She narrows her eyes at me. I'm pretty sure she thought bringing up my old drug habit would get under my skin. After I got out of recovery, her and mother would always joke about me relapsing.

They would say things like, I'll believe it when you've been clean longer than six months. When six months passed, they changed it to a year. When that came and went and I was still clean, they took away the expiration date, but continued to reference my possible relapse.

Eventually, I started to ignore their insults. My recovery wasn't about proving anything to either of them.

Raina rolls her eyes. "You want to know what you're really jealous of?" She asks, taking another step in my direction. "You're jealous of the fact that my son has a father in his life."

I snort in laughter. "Are you serious? I have dildo's that contribute more to my household than Mitch. How's the job search going, Mitchell? What's it been, four years now?" I ask the last two questions to Mitch.

"No one's hiring," he says in his defense toward my mother.

"I know," she says.

I side eye them both.

"He may not have a job," Raina says getting my attention back. "But at least he loves us enough to be here. Can't say the same thing for Gabe's dad. The man would rather buy you off than to be involved in your shit show of a life."

This time, I have no snarky or quick comeback. Raina had just hit me in the only sore spot I had.

Technically, I know Gabriel can't be with us. From my understanding, he's still in lock down for not killing me. However, it does bother me that my son may never get to know his father.

The quiet voice in the back of my head whispers, *"But if he was here, would he be around?"*

I ignore the hurtful taunt. Turning away from my sister, I spot my son. He's standing in the living room, clutching his Iron Man toy to his chest. He is my only concern and my strength.

"You're right, Gabe's father isn't around," I say, turning to face Raina. "I guess you win. I don't know what the prize is, but you've won it. Does that make you feel better? Is that what you wanted out of this argument?"

She crosses her arms over her chest and turns her head away. I realized a long time ago there was no salvaging our relationship, but I at least thought I didn't have to worry about her being my enemy.

"I'll make it even better for you," I say. "I'm going to take my son home to our fully furnished, forty-three hundred square foot house. With its five beds and 3.5 baths. I'm going to climb into my claw foot standalone tub and take a hot bubble bath and cry over the fact that I don't have a deadbeat man lying beside me in my mother's guest bedroom."

"Go to hell, Summer," Raina whines.

"Gladly. Come on, Gabe." He walks over to me, his head down. "Don't worry. I'll find someone else to watch him next month," I say to my mother.

"Now wait, I told you I'd say something to MJ. No need to find another sitter."

"Let her go, Mama. The money isn't worth it," Raina sneers placing her hands on her hips.

"Be quiet, Rai," Mitch tries to whisper.

It dawns on me, that's the only reason my mother has ever tolerated my son. Not only do I pay her the $2000 a month, but I also give her money for bills anytime she needs it since my son benefits from them. Hell, it's my money that keeps her lights on most months. Gabe means nothing to her but a little extra cash.

The realization hurts, but I'm not totally shocked.

"On second thought, you can all go fuck yourselves. I'll open my own daycare before I pay you to watch him again."

"Summer, don't be that way," my mother calls out to my back.

"Let her go. She'll need us before we need her," Raina shouts.

I walk out my mother's house with my son's hand clutched in mine. There is no love lost here today. I wanted my son to have a relationship with my family because I never did. But he has everything he needs in me and his godmother, Trina. We didn't need anyone else.

I peek my head inside Gabe's room one last time to make sure he's still sleeping. After the shit show at my mama's house earlier, he was anxious. It took a hot bath, four books, and a promised trip to the park to get him to fall asleep.

Closing the door to his superhero themed room, I make my way to my living room. Plopping down on the sofa, I grab my mug of ginger tea off the coffee table, tuck my legs under my butt and turn on the TV.

I'm spending my night like I do most nights, with mindless reality television. After settling on a housewife rerun, I lean my head back on the couch cushions. After all the shit that went on today, Gabriel crosses my mind.

I don't think about him as often as I did when I first got out of rehab. But he was brought up a lot today. I wonder what he's doing right now. I wonder if he ever thinks of me and Gabe. Does he wonder how we're doing?

I'm not stupid enough to believe that he isn't getting updates about us. Until a few months ago, Fem still made appearances. She told me on her last visit that she would be away for a while.

The ringing of my phone has me sitting up, I place my mug on the coffee table as I pick up the device.

"You're late," I say as I answer the Facetime video from my best friend. Like clockwork, Trina calls me every night around eight. Unless she's out of the country or busy with her career as a makeup influencer.

For as little support as I got from my mother and sister during my rehab and after, Trina has made up for it. She has been by my side since I called her from the facility and told her I was going to rehab.

"I was getting some dick from my husband," she says with a smirk.

Three years ago, Trina met a man on one of her many dating sites. He was a widower with no kids. They had a whirlwind romance and got married a year later. He spoils my bestie, and despite her not wanting to admit it, she's madly in love with him.

"You don't have to rub it in," I tease. "Some of us are on a celibacy journey."

Trina scoffs. "Celibacy my ass. You're just still hung up on your baby daddy's dick." She rolls her eyes.

Placing a hand over my heart, I pretend to be offended. "I am not."

"Says the woman still wearing his hoodie."

I glance down at the oversized black hoodie that Gabriel gave me that night. The thing no longer smells like him, but I refuse to toss it out. Strangely enough, it brings me comfort.

Feeling as if I've just been caught with my hand in the cookie jar, I shake my head.

"Whatever. Where's Mr. James?"

Trina sighs and closes her eyes. "Can you please stop calling my husband Mr. It's just James."

"He's old enough to be my daddy. I don't feel right calling him by his first name."

"Girl, he's only forty-five with your awkward ass."

I toss my head back and laugh. There's no better therapy than laughter. All the crap from earlier washes away.

"So," Trina says picking up her glass of wine off the nightstand beside her. "How was your day?"

I quickly filled her in about my lunch with Shay and the incident at my mother's.

"Raina is delusional. I'm starting to think maybe she's the one on drugs."

I snort in laughter. "She's definitely smoking something. But what she said did sting a little."

"Why?" She asks, leaning her back against her headboard.

"I don't know, I just feel like maybe I should have made better decisions than to have a one-night stand with a man that will probably remain absent in his son's life for the rest of his life."

"Do you want some cake?"

"What?" I scrunch my brows trying to figure out where the hell that random question came from. "Why would I want cake?"

"To go along with the pity party you're throwing yourself."

I roll my eyes and sink back into the couch. "I'm serious, Trina."

"So am I. Cut yourself some slack. Women have been having babies by the wrong men for years. The shit happens, it's no one's fault. Plus, as far as absent father's go, yours is doing a damn good job. He paid for you to go to rehab and made sure that when you got out you never had to worry about anything financially. Girl, my daddy lived in the same house as me for ten years and never paid a bill."

Although I laugh, she isn't lying. Gabriel has been good. Not only did he buy me a house and keep my bank account full, I don't even pay the bills. Fem explained that everything would be taken care of, and she meant it.

"You have a point. He's definitely doing his part." I twirl the end of one of my small knotless braids around my finger.

"You know what I think the problem is?"

Leaning forward, I grab my mug off the table in front of me and take a sip. "What?"

"Every time I ask you about that night, you downplay it. You say it was nothing. That he's just some dude you met. Yet, your face lights up every time you talk about him. I think you like this guy and don't want to admit you really want more with him."

I scoff, opening and closing my mouth a few times as I try to come up with a response that will refute her claim.

The night I had with Gabriel was life changing. I won't lie. I felt a connection with him unlike any I've ever felt with anyone else. We were like two broken shards of glass that somehow miraculously fit together.

However, although much about that night is wrapped in a withdrawal induced fog, I am aware that it wasn't the romantic evening my brain wants to make me believe it was. Yes, the way he smelled was real. The rough pads of his fingers brushing against my skin and the growl in his voice when he spoke were definitely real.

The way he truly listened to me and called me on my bullshit wasn't a delusion. The way he spent most of his night protecting me even before he walked into that room with Nic, all of that was real.

But it was also real that Gabriel wasn't stable. The dark look in his eyes before he killed wasn't something I made up. It was the same look he gave me numerous times throughout the night. Reminding me that I was going to be one of his victims.

Gabriel is a dangerous man. A beautiful one, but dangerous no less. No matter how good he's been to me, he and I would've never worked. This is as close of a relationship I can have with him.

"It was a good night," I admit, lifting my shoulder and dropping it lazily. "But no, I don't want anything more with him than what we have. I got the best thing I could out of that night, which is my son. I'm content with that."

I bring my mug up to my lips and take a sip feeling confident in my reply to her.

"Okay, I'll take your word for it. But I know that if Mr. Mysterious showed up at your doorstep tonight, you'd be popping that underused pussy for him by the morning."

I spit out my tea and snort. I swear this girl has no filter.

Rolling my eyes, I lean forward and place my drink back down. "First of all, my stuff is not underused."

"Your toys do not count," She chuckles taking a sip of her wine before continuing. "Speaking of…"

"Ugh," I groan lying my head on the back of the couch before looking back at the screen. "No Trina. No more blind dates. I still haven't recovered from the last one."

"I don't understand why you and Chris didn't work."

"Girl, he showed up to the date in a full face of makeup better than mine."

"First of all, that's not hard to do, your entire makeup collection is just mascara and lip-gloss. Secondly, Chris is metrosexual. He takes pride in the way he looks."

Shaking my head, I go on to explain. "Trina, Chris is gay. And the only person that doesn't seem to know that, is you."

"He is not."

"He told me. And even if he hadn't, I would have known when he gave the valet his phone number. He honestly thought you were playing a prank on him when you set up our date."

She looks completely shocked by this information, despite Chris explaining that he's never kept his sexuality from her. My friend can be a little self-absorbed sometimes.

"Hmm," She hums as if she still doesn't see it. "Well, this guy is definitely not gay, and I think you will like him."

I doubt it.

"He's a friend of James—"

"He's old?" I nearly shout.

She pinches the bridge of her nose. "No, he's not old. He's only thirty-five, he has no kids, a PhD, and specializes in child psychology. He's also 6'2 with gorgeous brown eyes."

"I don't know. I feel like I should give the dating thing a break. With Gabe, school, and the jewelry, I have my hands full."

"No ma'am. We are not making excuses."

Sighing. I shake my head. "Why are you so hellbent on me dating."

Other than Shay, Trina has been on my ass about dating again. She never lets me go longer than two months without setting up a blind date of some kind.

"Because I want you happy."

"I am happy."

"Are you though?" She counters.

I don't reply as I think over her question. I mean what's not to be happy about? I'm clean, I have my son, my bills are paid, I'm about to finish school, and my business is doing great. What could possibly make me happier?

"She doesn't deserve love. She's incapable of loving."

Those fucking words pop up again.

Thankfully, Trina starts back speaking, bringing me out of my head.

"You know I was never the advocate for love and relationships, but I have to be honest with you. Finding James has shown me the importance of being with someone that loves and cherishes you. And I've never been a stingy bitch, so I want that for my bestie."

"Fine," I relent.

Trina claps her hands happily. "Great, I'll set it all up."

Although I knew this date wasn't going to end the way she wanted it to, I have to admit I was a bit intrigued. I wasn't against love, I just couldn't quite see it in my future. But maybe I'm wrong.

"I will also set us up a wax appointment before the date."

"For what?" I asked, my brow pinched. "He won't be seeing that anytime soon."

She narrows her gaze at me. "One can only hope."

I shake my head and laugh. Trina and I talk on the phone for an hour before calling it a night.

CHAPTER EIGHTEEN

Predators

Beast

"You shouldn't be here. Your unclean soul will taint them. Walk away." Placing my hands to my head, I try to push out my mother's voice.

Despite telling myself repeatedly I should leave them alone, I find myself in this park watching them. Summer is sitting on a bench reading a book. She looks so different from the first time I saw her.

Gone are the sunken face and jaundiced eyes. Her cheeks are much fuller, giving her face a more angelic look. Her hair is in long thin braids that fall to her waist. Even her body has filled out, looking much healthier than that night. She is beautiful. More beautiful than I even remembered.

I clinch my hands at my sides with the desire to touch her. The memory of how she felt that night as she rode my cock plays back in my head. The way her skin felt underneath mine. The sound of her whimpers and feel of her nails digging in my skin as she found her release.

I groan as my dick lengthens down my leg.

"The whore has sullied you further. Sex is a sin."

"Not with her," I growl through clenched teeth.

When we were sixteen, Priest sat us all down to give us the sex talk. He explained the basics and had us all practice placing condoms on bananas. He also explained that in two short years he would take us all to the Nunnery to pick out our first Nun. He talked about making a wise decision because we would never get another first-time experience. He said we would always remember our first.

After my experience with Summer, I finally understood what he meant. The memory of her and that night got me through my five years in lock down.

"Hulk," a small voice says grabbing my attention.

I open my eyes, look down, and come face to face with the replica of myself. My son. From the day Albany told me that Summer was pregnant I have both craved and feared this day.

I've wanted to see what she and I created. The two broken souls that were lit aflame one night. What could we possibly create? Would he have her soulful eyes and charming smile. Would my evil rub off on him. Would the darkness that's inside of me reside in him as well. I should've remembered the banana and condom lesson. I'm not worthy of that gift.

Yet, even though I know this, when I look down at his round face, all I see is perfection. He is the best of me.

"Hulk," he says again, holding up a green action figure.

I squat down, getting to his level. My mother is screaming in my head to get away from him, to not ruin him. I take a deep breath fighting her words. I'd rather die than cause him any harm. I've never wanted to touch someone so bad in my life. The desire to wrap my arms around him and hug him to my chest burns my skin.

"You will ruin him. Your darkness will taint his pure soul," Mother growls. I clench my fist.

"Hello, Gabriel."

The young boy smiles at me. My heart knocks against my chest. I wonder how it still beats in my chest even though it's standing before me. He looks so much like me. He has his mother's complexion, only a few shades lighter, but his eyes, smile, nose, even the way he holds his head is all mine.

His caramel golden blonde spiral curls are in a thick afro. Some of the pieces fall into his eyes. I want to push the hair away from his face so that I can see him better, yet my hands remain at my side.

Gabe reaches out a small hand and touches an old scar on the side of my face. I try my best to remain as still as possible so that I don't scare him away.

"Are you hurt?" He asks, looking up at me.

Shaking my head, I reply. "No, not anymore."

He holds out his hand. Slowly, I place my large one in his, swallowing it almost entirely.

"You will hurt him. You are not made to be gentle." Mother warns.

I quickly pull my hand out of his, in fear that I may somehow cause harm to him.

He looks up at me confused with his large hazel green eyes. "Play with me," he demands grabbing my hand back.

I smile at his forwardness. "I wish I could. But not today."

Disappointment fills his face. My stomach turns at the sight. His bottom lip drops and he rakes a hand over his curls pushing the hair out of his eyes. For only a second, he gives me a brief glimpse of his full face.

"Gabe?" His name is shouted across the playground.

From where I'm standing at the back of the park, I was close to the furthest end of the playground near the trash cans. I was able to see Summer, but without knowing where to look she couldn't see me.

Looking down at Gabe, I once again get eye level with him. As much as I want him to stay right here with me, I know he can't. It's for the best. I tell myself.

"Go to your mother. She's worried about you."

He nods his head, before turning and walking away. Before he gets too far, he turns back and waves at me. I stand, and wave back.

I watch as Summer grabs him in her arms and hugs him tight. She squats down in front of him like I did and speaks to him. I'm too far away to hear what she says.

After a brief conversation, she then takes his hand, and they walk out of the park together. I don't leave my spot. I keep my eyes on them, fighting the draw to follow them. Only the reminder of what I need to do keeps me in my place.

Summer places Gabe in the back seat of her car, fastening him into his car seat. She then comes over to the driver's side. She opens the door but stops. Her head comes up and she scans her surroundings. I smile proudly at her instincts as I slip behind the nearest tree. Waiting a few seconds, I look back in her direction. She's in the car now, backing out of the parking lot. I watch her back license plate grow smaller.

Even being this close to Summer has that odd feeling in my chest going haywire. She's like a magnet, and I'm the metal being drawn to her. She's better without me though. I would only mess things up for them.

A gray car pulls out of the parking lot going in the same direction that Summer went. I shake off the suspicious feeling I get watching the car. I have stuff to do. Turning away from the park, I make my way back to my apartment. I've spent enough time being distracted from my mission, it's time I get back to work.

I watch as my victim walks out of the airport. The concierge places his suitcase in the trunk I have opened. I pull my chauffeur hat lower over my head concealing most of my face.

Jason Averil walks up to me, and I open the back door for him. He doesn't glance in my direction as he says, "I don't want to talk. Just get me home."

He climbs in the car, and I shut the door for him.

Keeping my head down, I walk around the front of the vehicle and climb into the driver's seat. As soon as the concierge is done with the bags, I pull away from the airport curb and head to my destination.

Halfway through the ride, I glance in the rearview mirror at my victim as I make my way down the highway.

In my thirty-two years on this earth, I've come to realize the world is made up of predators and prey. When you are at the top of the food chain, you don't have fears. It's why the lion will take naps during the day under the shade and the Zebra will sleep standing. The rich and powerful of the world are like the lion. Their money and status have granted them a security they think is untouchable. It's the reason my passenger hasn't looked up from his phone to realize we are not going in the direction of his home.

"There is no peace, saith my God, to the wicked." My mother says in my head. *"For the love of money is at the root of all kinds of evil. Kill the sinner."*

In this, she and I agreed. He will die a slow and horrible death tonight.

I pull the black Lincoln Town car with tinted windows into the lower garage at the back of my apartment building. It isn't until I turn off the ignition that Jason thinks to look up from his phone.

"Wait," he says finally realizing we aren't at his house. "Where are we."

I don't answer, instead I climb out of the car, walk over to the wall and push the button to lower the garage door. I don't worry about him calling for help, he won't be able to get a signal. I go around to his side of the vehicle and pull his door open. He looks at me for the first time.

"You're not Sam. Who are you?" The right amount of panic has made its way into his voice.

I still don't answer, instead I reach into the back seat and pull him out. He attempts to fight me, but I easily overpower him, hauling him out of the back seat. I shove his body up against the side of the car.

"Listen," he says, holding his hands out in front of him to hold me off. "Is it money you want? I can pay you whatever you want."

I point to the door to my underground work room. It's a metal door with a combination lock on it. It isn't anything fancy, but the way Jason's eyes enlarge when he looks at it you would think it was covered in blood or something.

"Alright, you don't want money," he shakes his head. The rich and powerful believe that money can get them out of anything. I guess in their world it does. Unfortunately for him, I'm not a part of his world.

"Whatever you want I can get it. My uncle is a powerful man. There isn't anything he can't get."

"He tempts you with his wicked wealth. He is an abomination." Mother claims in my head.

"Walk," I demand as I grab him by the neck and lift him off the ground before shoving him in the direction of the door. He falls to the ground, sliding across the concrete floor before quickly getting back to his feet.

"Please, don't do this."

His pleas fall on deaf ears as I escort him to the metal door. After punching the code in, I push him forward. The lights come up as soon as we enter the room.

Jason flinches from the bright lights but once his eyes adjust, he gasps as he looks around the room.

The walls are a dingy beige. No matter how many times I clean them they will not go back to their original white color. Thick metal chains are embedded into the concrete at different levels along the walls from the floor to the ceiling. Large cabinets run along one wall. A fully functioning work bench is in the corner of the room.

Peg boards run along two of the free walls with every tool you can imagine. I have more supplies than your local Home Depot. A dental chair with attached cuffs is in the middle of the floor along with two large drums against the far-right wall. And at the furthest part of the room is my favorite addition, an incinerator that reaches temperatures of nearly 3,000 degrees. It can turn a human body to ash within two hours.

"Sit in the chair," I demand.

Jason looks at me as if I've just asked him to lick the seat of a toilet.

"I will not. Look, I don't know who you are, but you clearly have no idea who I am or the people I'm associated with…"

"You are Jason Averil. Son of Glenda and James Averil. Glenda is the granddaughter of Harold Smith, former CEO of one of the biggest pharmaceutical companies in the world."

Moving away from the door I go to my cabinet and start pulling out the tools I'll be using. Starting with a handheld torch. I place it on the rolling cart beside the work bench.

"You graduated top of your class at Harvard Law School. You are a partner at Smith, Smith, and Stein law firm. One of the youngest partners at the firm. A job you only got because of your family's connections."

I drop a hacksaw on the cart before looking over my shoulder at Jason. He's standing in the same spot I left him, trembling as his gaze stays glued to the objects I've placed on the cart.

"You're married to Vanessa who is currently working with a specialist because she's having issues getting pregnant. Yet, your mistress who is ten years younger than you seems to not have those problems. In fact, you would have at least two kids by now if you'd stop forcing her to get abortions."

Placing the last object on the cart, which happens to be a pair of ratchet cutters, I turn back to face Jason.

"Did I leave anything out?"

He shakes his head, still seeming to be dazed.

I wheel the cart over to the dental chair and start to adjust the straps.

"You see, I know all about you. Even the things you don't want me to know. However, I'm not here to talk about your affair, your gambling debt, or the offshore account you've been laundering money into. I'm here to talk about April 15th your sophomore year in college."

The moment the date is out of my mouth his eyes widen. He turns and runs to the door trying to open it as he screams for help. I don't worry about anyone hearing because not only are we underground, but this room and the entire building is soundproof. Even if anyone else lived in the apartments above they wouldn't hear him.

I finish preparing the chair for him before I walk over and yank him away from the door. He tries to fight my arm off as I haul him back to the center of the room. After slinging his body into the seat, I try to strap him down into the restraints, but he fights and squirms like a fish on a hook.

I give up trying to do this the easy way. Instead, I punch him in the side of the head, the force causing his head to bounce against the headrest. He's immediately put to sleep. Finally, having him still, I go back to placing him in the restraints. His arms are tied to the arm rests and his legs are individually tied to the footrests.

After making sure he's secured, I get the smelling salts out of one of the cabinets and place them under his nose.

He comes awake suddenly gasping. He then flinches and tries to lift his hand to the fast-forming knot on the side of his head. Once he realizes his hands are restrained, panic forms in his eyes again as he tugs against his restraints.

"You're wasting my time," I say.

When his gaze falls back on me his shoulders drop and his head falls forward.

"I didn't hurt that girl. She even admitted to the courts that she lied," he explains.

"Liar. All Liars will have their part in the lake of fire," Mother seethes in my head.

"You raped and brutally beat a sixteen-year-old girl. Then your family and their connections drug her name through the dirt to the point she recanted her story on the stand and later committed suicide."

"No, I…"

I hold up a hand to stop him. I didn't need him to collaborate on the story of Tiffany Williams. I already knew it was true. I wasn't here for that.

"The cop that found her body knew you were behind it and somehow, he ended up dead. I want to know how."

His brows pinch together as he stares back at me. "You're here for the cop?"

I remain silent. He shakes his head.

"I don't know anything about the cop."

I was hoping he would say that. Picking up the ratchet cutters from the cart, I go over to his left hand. Grabbing it with my left hand I hold it still.

"What are you doing?"

Placing his thumb in the circle opening of the cutters I snip the appendage off. It falls to the floor at my feet. Jason screams as he thrashes against the chair. I make quick work of cutting off three more fingers from that hand leaving only his pinky. Once I'm done. I toss the cutters on the cart and grab the blow torch to cauterize the injury stopping the bleeding.

Once that's done, I place the torch down. At some point during that process, Jason passed out. I grab the smelling salts and bring him back. He comes awake abruptly, crying and screaming.

"You fucking psycho," he shouts.

I allow him only a few minutes to get ahold of himself.

"I will ask you only one more time. Who killed the cop?"

"I don't know," Jason shouts as spittle flies out of his mouth. He once again starts sobbing. "My Uncle handled the cop." His head drops between his shoulders as tears and snot run down his face.

"My father tried to pay him off, but the cop didn't want the money, he wanted justice. We tried to find dirt on him, but we couldn't find any. So, my mother called her cousin who's like an uncle to me. He told us not to worry. Next thing I knew the cop was dead. I didn't have anything to do with it."

I don't explain to him that it didn't matter that he didn't directly call for the hit, he was the reason the cop was killed. It's because of his crime against Tiffany, and his attempt to get away with it, that an innocent man died. He will have to face that sin once he meets his maker.

"What's your uncle's name?"

He lifts his head and looks at me before glancing at the wall.

"Timothy Aldean Smith."

I had my next victim. I need to know how Tim was able to get the cop on a Church menu.

I nod my head at Jason. I no longer needed him.

"Will you let me go now, I promise I won't say anything to anyone about this."

"You must punish the wicked for their evil. Your job is not done."

"As you wish, Mother," I agree.

The red haze takes over me and it doesn't let me go until early the next morning.

CHAPTER NINETEEN

Date

Summer

"This is too short." I say tugging at the hem of my black dress that comes to my knees.

"Girl, that dress damn near touches your ankles," Trina says walking up behind me. She glances in the floor length mirror at our reflections.

"But it is missing something." She taps her chin before walking away to look in my closet.

I take the time to study myself in the mirror. My long braids are pulled up into a bun at the top of my head. Trina did my make up. My foundation is light enough that you can still see my freckles. My eyes are lined with black liner giving them even more of a cat shape. The red on my lips make them stand out and look even fuller.

The black body con dress is modest with its crew neck collar and long sleeves. It fits my slim physique like a second skin even making my barely there hips seem prominent. The ankle boots add to the look.

I have to admit, for a first date I looked pretty darn good. Trina walks back over to me.

"Here, this will be perfect."

She wraps a scarf around my neck making it resemble a cowl neck. I freeze at the appearance of the added fabric. It's the scarf Gabriel bought me that night.

I'm tossed back down memory lane. His gorgeous green eyes staring down at me expectantly as he holds out the scarf for me. In my mind I take the time to once again memorize his face. Those old pale scars that cut into his brow and above his lip. His perfect white teeth and those full lips.

I shake the memory out of my head. Nothing good can come from those thoughts.

Turning back to the mirror, I once again admire the work Trina has done.

"What do you think, G?" Trina turns to ask Gabe who is sitting on my bed playing with his action figures.

He looks up at me and I turn to face him. He smiles and gives me two thumbs up.

"Oh, you got two thumbs up?" Trina jokes. "That's hard to come by." Gabe laughs and goes back to his toys.

The alarm on my phone goes off letting me know it's time to head toward the restaurant. I didn't want him to meet me at my house. This was mine and Gabe's sanctuary. I was very picky about who knew where it was.

Plus, I had an issue about having another man in the house that Gabriel bought me. I know it's weird and obviously he doesn't care but it bothers me.

Running my sweaty hands down the side of my dress my nerves start to get the best of me.

"What if I mess this up? You know how I get. What if I say something weird."

Trina raises an eyebrow at me. "You, being awkward as hell, is a given. There is nothing we can do about that."

"Trina," I whine, "I'm being serious."

"Girl, me too."

Admittedly, a lot of my dates never get past the first one because I've never fixed that whole mouth diarrhea thing. And unfortunately, I can't blame my complete awkwardness on the drugs anymore.

I roll my eyes. She laughs.

"Listen. Just be your funny, weird self. He is going to like you."

I'm glad at least one person was confident in this. Walking over to Gabe, I sit on the side of the bed near him.

"Gabe," I call his name and he looks up from his toys. I smile. "I'm going out for a while. Aunt Trina is going to watch you. I want you to be on your best behavior, okay?"

He looks past me to my open bedroom door then back to me.

"Hulk doesn't want you to go on the date."

"Awwww," Trina whimpers behind me.

My son loves his marvel action figures and often uses them to express himself. He's been talking about Hulk since yesterday at the park. He even spent most of the afternoon outside in the backyard playing with his imaginary Hulk.

"Well, can you tell Hulk that even though mommy is going on the date, it doesn't change the way she loves and feels about you. You will always be my number one guy. Okay?"

He looks back at my bedroom door. This time I glance over my shoulder too, only to find no one there.

"Okay. I'll tell him."

I smile, standing from my seat, I push his curls off his forehead and place a quick kiss there. After grabbing my purse off the dresser, I head out of the room with Trina on my heels.

"If he has any issues call me immediately. He's already eaten, but he may want a snack before bedtime. They are in that cabinet. He can watch a movie as long as…" Trina grabs my shoulders and turn me to look at her.

"Stop. I've been watching my godson since he was three weeks old. I can handle G."

I let out a deep breath because she's right. Trina never has issues with him.

"Sorry, I'm just—"

"Freaking out for nothing," she laughs. "You're going to be fine."

She lets me go and taps me on the hip to get me moving again. I head toward the front door. "Remember, be yourself. Try to think before you speak. Oh, and no sex on the first date."

I turn to glare at her. She bursts out laughing.

"What? Don't act like it hasn't happened before. That's how we got G."

Rolling my eyes playfully at my best friend, I head out to my car. I dig through my purse looking for my keys, when suddenly I get the oddest feeling. It's like my entire body goes icy cold. I stop searching for my keys and glance around at my surroundings. However, nothing is out of the norm.

I shake off the odd feeling as I finally find my keys and pull them out of my purse. I push the unlock button and climb into my car.

"Here we go," I say out loud before starting the ignition and heading to the restaurant where I will be meeting Andrew.

I make it to the five-star Italian restaurant in under twenty minutes. Admittedly, not enough time to ease my nerves.

Pulling my car to the front of the building, I open my door as the valet comes around to my side.

"Welcome to Buona Tavola," the young man says before handing me a piece of paper with the number 210 written on it.

"Thank you." I quickly make my way to the front door.

Other than telling me his occupation and that he was tall, Trina didn't really describe this guy to me. Glancing around the foyer, I spot a young couple, a family of four, and a man squeezed into a button up shirt so tight if he sneezed his buttons would turn him into an active shooter. My stomach sinks at the sight of him.

I pull out my phone and text Trina.

Me: Please, tell me Andrew is not this middle-aged balding man with a size youth small shirt on."

Her reply was instant.

Bestie: What? Hell no. But take a picture. LOL!

"Summer?" A deep voice pulls my attention from my phone.

I look up into the darkest brown eyes set into the face of an absolutely stunning man. Tan skin as smooth as a baby, thick dark brows, enticing lips, a well-trimmed goatee and the straightest whitest teeth I've ever seen outside of a toothpaste commercial.

"Holy shit," the words come out of my mouth before I can catch them.

He chuckles, making him even more charming.

"You're definitely Summer,"

"And you are definitely not a balding man with a too tight shirt on."

Andrew's eyes widen. And the man behind me clears his throat. I glance back to find Mr. Tight shirt glaring at me before he storms off.

"Sorry," I mouth even though he can't see me. It's not like he didn't know that damn shirt was too tight.

Andrew starts to laugh. I turn back to him.

"Trina was right, you are funny. She's told me so much about you."

Clearly, she didn't return the favor.

"It's nice to finally meet you," he goes on to say holding his hand out in front of him.

I place my hand inside his for a shake. He brings our joined hands up to his lips and places a kiss on the back of my hand. I giggle like a twelve-year-old in front of her crush.

"You too," I reply breathlessly.

Andrew is absolutely gorgeous. Those square framed glasses perched on the bridge of his nose give him a sophisticated boy next door type of vibe.

"Our table is ready," he says drawing me out of my head.

He holds a hand out suggesting that I walk in front of him. I oblige even though I don't know where I'm going. However, no worries, a gentle hand on my elbow guides me in the right direction.

Finally, we make it to our table, and he pulls out my seat allowing me to sit down. There is already a glass of water sitting in front of me. I take a sip of the cold liquid hoping it will help ease my nerves even more.

"So, what are you thinking about for an appetizer?" Andrew asks as he picks up the menu in front of him. "The food here is really good."

I pick up my fancy leather bound menu.

"How are the mozzarella balls?"

"They're good. I should warn you, they are really big though."

I chuckle. "Not sure I want big balls in my mouth on the first date."

His eyes go round as he stares at me. I realize then how my joke must have sounded.

Holding out a hand as if I'm trying to stop my words from sounding so ridiculous. "Not that I want small balls either."

Andrew chokes on the water he just took a sip of.

"Shit, not saying your balls are small. I mean I bet they are really nice balls."

Never has my brain and my mouth seemed so disconnected. I'm pretty sure when Trina told me to be myself, this isn't what she meant. At this point I wish the ground wouldn't just open and swallow me but politely spit me out onto another continent.

Andrew places his glass down in front of him and pounds on his chest. "Maybe we should move on from the mozzarella. They also have good calamari."

Feeling thankful for his change of subject, I keep my mouth closed. Hopefully nothing else crazy slips out.

"So, Summer," he says placing his hands on top of the table. "Trina tells me you're in school."

I smile, glad to be on a topic other than balls.

"Yes. I'm two and a half months away from graduating with a Bachelor of Arts degree in Psychology."

"That's fantastic. I guess I'll have to take you out somewhere nice to celebrate." He gives me that Colgate smile again and I can't help but blush.

"Hello, Welcome to Buona Tavola," A well-dressed waiter says coming over to our table. He has a bottle of wine in his hands. "Can I start you off with a drink, maybe our delicious house wine?"

Andrew looks at me expectantly. I shake my head.

"Oh, no alcohol for me."

"You don't drink?" Andrew asks innocently.

"No. I ummm, I'm a recovering addict. Alcohol wasn't my vice, but I don't want to put down one addiction for another so, I stay clear."

I don't think I've ever seen the color drain out of someone's face so fast. Andrew goes from tanned to ghost white in 0.2 seconds. I guess Trina didn't tell him everything. Even the waiter looks shocked.

"Don't worry," I say holding up a hand. "I've been clean for five years. No need to hide the silverware." I chuckle but no one joins me.

Clearing my throat, I look up at the waiter. "Sweet tea is fine."

"Uhhhh," Andrew seems to stall for a moment before finally shaking his head and saying. "A whiskey sour for me please. Double it."

The waiter nods before hurriedly walking away. An uncomfortable silence floats between us. Andrew seems to look everywhere but at me.

This is not an uncommon outcome. Many of my dates have hit the awkward silence part after either I tell them about my past or I make a joke that they don't seem to get. I'm used to this.

"You know, we can call it a night. I'm sure you have better things to do than pretend to be interested."

He looks back at me, his eyes widen before he shakes his head. "No, I'm sorry." He holds up a hand then takes a deep breath. "I'm messing this up."

"I doubt you can make it any worse than my confession."

He laughs, as he pushes his glasses up on his nose. "Trina told me you had a past. She didn't tell me exactly what it was. In fact, she told me it wasn't any of my damn business because you aren't that person anymore."

I can't help but laugh because that's exactly what my best friend would say.

"She has such a way with words," I joke.

Andrew chuckles before running a hand through his hair. "Look, you caught me off guard I'll admit, but it doesn't deter me. She's right, it's obvious you are no longer that person. It's in your past."

"Yeah," I say glancing away. "Sure."

For the rest of the date, Andrew and I talk about safer subjects. We discuss our likes and dislikes, movies and tv shows, and he told me about his childhood and his family. Overall, I really enjoyed my time with him.

"I can't believe you actually told your professor that." He laughs.

"Look, math is already my hardest subject. I could not sit in that classroom for an hour with someone who smelled like hot ass on a bed of wild onions."

Andrew tosses his head back and laughs again. He has a nice laugh. It's breathy and deep almost like a chuckle. I wonder what Gabriel's laughter sounds like?

My thoughts come to a screeching halt. What the hell? Why is he popping up in my head? This is not the time or place to get lost in Gabriel.

"Are you okay?" Andrew asks. "You looked a little spooked for a minute."

Planting a smile on my face, I shake all thoughts of Gabriel out of my mind.

"No, I'm good."

"Well, how about I pay for dinner and maybe you and I can go for a walk?"

"That sounds nice."

Andrew reaches across the table and places a hand on top of mine giving it a gentle squeeze.

"Alright, I'll grab the waiter and go to the restroom." He smiles as he stands and walks away. I watch him as he heads toward the bathroom. Turning back around, I grab my phone out of my purse with a huge smile on my face.

Me: Okay, I take back everything I said about your matchmaking skills.

The dots immediately pop up alerting me that Trina is replying.
Bestie: I told you he would be perfect. And he's sexy.
Me: LOL! He is. We're going for a walk after this. I'm sharing my location with you.

I scroll through my apps to find the share location option. I liked Andrew and all, but you can never be too careful. Sooner than expected the chair in front of me scrapes across the floor alerting me that Andrew had returned. I quickly put my phone back in my purse.

"Well, that was qui…." My words die on my tongue as I sit up straight and look across the table. It isn't the well put together Andrew sitting in front of me. It's the one person I was sure I'd never see again.

"Gabriel," his name rolls off my tongue in a breathless whisper.

Although Andrew is attractive with his dark hair and geeky vibe. There is something about the man sitting across from me that puts all other men in the mediocre box.

I take a minute to admire the man that has made cameo appearances in my thoughts since the morning I woke up without him.

In my mind his eyes aren't as electric as they are sitting across from me. The pale scars that mar his face seem less prominent in real life than in my dreams. Those lips that I've dreamt about kissing me are fuller than I remember, so is his size. It feels as if he's gotten taller and even more buff in our time apart.

His long golden blond hair hangs in his face like curtains. For what feels like an eternity he and I stare at each other. It's as if we are both taking in the changes of the other.

It isn't until I start to pay closer attention that I notice the veins in his neck. The way his hands are fisted on top of the table. The way his breathing lifts and drops his shoulders as if he's been running. Even the vacant look in his eyes.

I saw this look many times that night. That is one thing that my memory never gets wrong. Gabriel is battling his mother. It is then I realize that he just popped up on my date. A date with someone that has yet to come out of the bathroom.

I shut my eyes and take a deep breath before reopening and speaking. "Is he alive?"

Silence, and then finally he speaks. "He's breathing."

Feeling relief that Andrew didn't meet an untimely death tonight, I sink back in my chair and shake my head.

I have a lot of questions. They are all swimming around my head at once. I had no idea I'd ever see this man again. For him to pop up now has me a little thrown off.

"So, they let you out?"

"No," he says without any further explanation.

I dip my brows together, confusion etching my face. "You broke out?"

"Yes."

I would say that this shocks me. But I was more shocked when Fem told me that they were holding him. I didn't think there was a prison built that could keep this man down.

Gabriel is like a Tsunami. His presence and energy swallow you up and drags you into him—most likely to your death. Even now, my heart beats so fast in my chest I feel lightheaded just being near him.

One thing becomes blatantly clear, what I felt that night around him was not a one-off thing. And it had shit to do with withdrawals.

My gaze keeps going back to his face. Goodness, this man is gorgeous. And if I was a dumb woman, I'd crawl into his lap and purr like a cat. But, sobriety and time have made me wiser.

"What are you doing here, Gabriel?" There is no way I'm going to believe this is just a friendly visit. He doesn't put me in the mindset of someone that stops by to catch up on old times.

The way his jaw tenses lets me know he either doesn't like my question or doesn't like his answer to it.

"I don't know," he finally says after a while, letting me know the latter was the problem.

Scoffing, I lean back in my seat. I cast my gaze away from him, not wanting him to see the way my eyes are watering.

"Five years." I look back at him and his green eyes are staring directly at me. "It never crossed your mind to call?"

He looks away briefly, but I keep going.

"You could have sent an email, wrote a letter, sent a damn carrier pigeon, or hell even smoke signals asking about your son would have been nice."

He doesn't answer or reply. He just stares back at me with those damn intense eyes. I knew Fem was giving him updates. Gabriel knew about Gabe all this time and not once did he reach out.

I shake my head swiping at the tear that fell. Anytime I allowed myself to think I'd see Gabriel again, I never thought it would be this emotional. I'd long since gotten over him not being around, but I didn't realize how much his lack of communication bothered me until now.

"So, what now? Is this your way of telling me you want back into our lives? Am I supposed to just—"

"No."

His reply catches me off guard. "No?"

"Me showing up here changes nothing. We don't work."

I laugh, even though nothing is remotely funny. His words sting like hell to hear.

"She's incapable of loving."

"Then why come back? What's the point of this?" I ask pointing to him showing up on my date.

He doesn't answer, instead his gaze cuts away from me.

I lean up from my chair. "What about Gabe? Do you even fucking care about your son?"

He slams his fist on the table causing the glasses of water and the silverware to rattle. A few surrounding gazes turn to us, but I don't pay them any attention.

"Of course, I care," he grits out, those seafoam eyes locking in on me. "But I'm not good enough—"

I hold up my hand cutting off his reply.

"Don't. Don't give me your bullshit excuse." He looks away once again, but I chase his gaze with my head. "You want to talk about not being good enough? Imagine fighting your own thoughts to stay alive when you get a positive pregnancy test. Every day I battle depression and my old desires. But I do it for him. I will do anything for my son. I don't get to be a coward and run."

He looks back at me when I call him a coward. His eyes narrow but I don't care. I was once afraid of Gabriel. Don't get me wrong, I still believe him to be as dangerous as he was on our first encounter. However, he no longer scares me.

"Summer." Just from the way he says my name I know that he won't change his mind.

I get it. I see the fear in his eyes. It's the same fear I saw in mine the day that test was positive. I see the same fear every time I look in the mirror and question if I'm strong enough to keep my shit from damaging my son. It crossed my mind to tuck my tail and run. However, I didn't. But I won't fault him for running. My only concern now is the little boy that looks just like the man sitting across from me.

Shaking my head I reply, "Just go, Gabriel. We're good. Gabe and I don't need you."

I wait for him to get up and leave but he doesn't budge. Instead, he remains in his seat, breathing in that labored way from before. Finally, after a few minutes, he stands and starts to walk off.

"Gabriel." He stops at the sound of me calling his name, glancing over his shoulder.

"Let this be the last time you show up at anymore of my dates."

The vein in his neck throbs, his eyes narrow, but he turns and walks away. I let out the breath I was holding.

I feel as if I faced an insurmountable obstacle and came out on top. For the first time since he sat down, my heart has gone back to its regular pace.

The waiter comes over to the table to bring our check.

"Excuse me," I say getting his attention. "My date went to the bathroom, and he's been in there for a while. Do you mind going in and checking on him."

The waiter gives me a sympathetic look. I'm sure he thinks Andrew has run out on me. However, he dips his chin before walking toward the bathroom.

I gather my purse, already aware that the night is pretty much over. That is proven correct when the waiter comes back out with a panicked look on his face demanding another waiter to call 911.

Spending half the night at the hospital was not how I thought the night was going to end. But I'm lucky, because when it comes to Gabriel, it could've been worse.

CHAPTER TWENTY
Too Late

Beast

I should be on a plane right now. Timothy Smith is in France on vacation. I was supposed to be on a flight two hours ago. However, I'm here, in the back yard playing with my son.

"Hulk, throw the ball." Little Gabe says, handing me the football over the fence in his back yard.

Behind Summer's house there is a wrought iron fence that circles her property. The fence comes up to my knees. Giving just enough security so that Gabe can play in the backyard without supervision. In addition to the iron fence, are two rows of evergreen trees that give privacy from the busy road behind her property. It also allows me to hide.

I toss the ball Gabe gave me back into his yard. He runs to go get it. We played the same game yesterday. That's when he told me about Summer's date. I had all intentions of killing the man in that bathroom. However, a small voice of reason told me not to. It took every piece of restraint Priest taught me to leave him alive.

Gabe hands me the ball back and I toss it again. I think I'm playing fetch with my son.

His laughter as he goes to get the ball has me clutching my hand into a tight fist. The sound of it has my heart beating faster. It's the same feeling I got when I first saw Summer.

"Gabe and I don't need you." Her words from last night come back to me. The anger and hurt in her eyes as she looked at me once again caused a tightness in my chest.

I wish I was like my brothers. I wish I could be normal and didn't have this gnawing need to cause destruction. The beast inside of me has to be fed. I can't subject Summer and Gabe to that. We don't work. No matter how much I wish we could.

"Then why are you here?" Mother reprimands in my head. *"You should be out hunting. Not here with the boy. You will tarnish him."*

Placing my hands to my head I try to push her words out. However, those last four words continue to echo in my brain.

"Get out," I growl. Finally, my thoughts were silent. I open my eyes and look down into terrified hazel ones.

"You okay, Hulk?" Gabe's little voice asks.

"Yeah, Hulk is okay."

Gabe dips his chin to his little chest. He tries to hand me the ball back over the fence but before I can take it from him, the back door slides open and Summer walks out. I quickly step further behind the trees obscuring her view of me even more. I once again get lost in the sight of her.

The urge to grab her and take her away last night had me seeing red. I stood outside of the restaurant watching her through the windows. When I saw that guy touch her arm, Mother roared up in my head so quickly I was inside the restaurant before I could stop myself.

I know she doesn't want me around anymore, but I'm not sure I can share her yet. Maybe never.

"Gabe, time to come in, it's getting dark."

"Can Hulk come in too?" He asks.

She laughs, placing her hands on her hips. "Yes, Hulk can come in too. So can the rest of the Avengers."

Gabe turns back to the place I was just standing with a huge smile. I quickly move further away. However, I don't miss the way his smile drops.

"He's gone," he says, turning back to his mother.

"Maybe he had to go home too."

Gabe looks back in the spot I was just standing, his shoulders fall before he turns to his mother and heads back to her. I watch them walk into the house and close the sliding door behind them.

I need to leave this place and never come back. Coming here every day will only make things worse.

Even after that declaration, I stay behind those trees staring at that house until the sun eventually does set, casting the backyard in darkness. Only the muted light from the moon along with the floodlights on the back of the house gives me a view of my surroundings.

I walk from the trees at the back of the house heading toward the front. My walk back to my apartment will take thirty minutes. It crosses my mind to find a place closer by. I quickly shove that thought away.

Stepping onto the curb near the front of Summer's house I spot a gray four door car. It doesn't look out of place. But, I spotted this exact same car the day I saw them at the park.

Walking over to the vehicle, I peer into the back window. It looks to be empty. I walk up to the driver's side glancing through the window. I pause when I spot a gun on the passenger seat. Not just any gun, but a HK .45 with a suppressor.

My gaze goes immediately to Summer's house. I take off for her front door, keeping to the shadows.

I stop at the evergreens by the side of the house keeping me blocked. A man in a pizza delivery uniform and a pizza warming bag in his hands walks up to the door.

He rings the bell and in seconds Summer appears.

"Hey," he says. "Did you order the medium pepperoni pizza?"

"Pizza?" Gabe shouts excitedly as he appears at Summer's side.

"Sorry," Summer says rubbing the top of Gabe's head. "I didn't order pizza."

"Are you sure? What's your name?" he looks at the paper in his hand.

"Summer, and I'm positive."

The man shakes his head. "I'm so sorry about that ma'am. I looked at the address wrong. It's 415 not 514. You two have a good night." The man backs away from the house as Summer shuts the front door.

The scene before me seemed normal. He's a delivery driver, it would explain the need for the gun.

However, there is a niggling in the back of my mind that says something isn't right.

"Hell no, something isn't right. You know that, Kid." Priest's voice says in my head.

Before the pizza driver could make it back down the driveway, I quickly crawl into the back seat of his car and lay down. Within minutes, the front door opens, and he sits down tossing the bag into the back seat hitting me in the chest. Immediately, I notice the bag is too light. I lift the flap and stick my hand in. There is no pizza box inside.

"I think I found your girl," the guy says on the phone. "Her name is Summer, she fits the description, and get this, she has a kid."

My stomach fills with rocks and the hairs on my arms stand at attention. The night I spent with Summer I felt a lot of different emotions. Many being new and foreign to me. While in lock down I studied, not only reading emotions from other people, but also what certain emotions do to me.

However, I didn't need my research for this one. I haven't felt this emotion since I was a child still living with my mother. Fear. For so long in my youth I wore fear like a second skin. Back then, I was helpless against my tormentor. Not anymore.

"The kid's about five or six. Why?" He's silent for a moment, listening to the person on the other end. "I don't know. But he looks mixed. Do you want me to bring them in?" He's silent again. "Alright, I'll keep watching." He hangs up the phone and places it in the drink holder beside him.

Shoving the pizza bag to the floor I sit up in the car causing it to rock slightly. Before the guy can turn around to see what caused the movement, my arm is barred around his neck. I apply just enough pressure to pin his head back against the headrest and keep him in place, but not enough to kill him. He fights against my hold. I grab the wrist of the arm pressed to his neck with my free hand and tug causing a little more pressure to his neck. He stops moving.

"Who are you working for?"

"I'm...not...talking..." the guy grunts out.

They all say that, but in the end, they all talk.

The wicked shall be punished. Rip the truth from his deceitful mouth.

"Yes Mother," I comply.

I apply more pressure to his neck, cutting off his airways. Not enough to kill but just enough to render him unconscious. He fights a little before going stiff.

As soon as he's out cold I climb out of the backseat. Opening the driver's door, I shove the fake pizza guy over to the passenger seat and then climb in. He may not want to talk, but I promise by the end of the night he will.

I smack the fake pizza guy in the face. He comes awake with a start. As soon as his eyes adjust and he notices me, he starts to pull at his restraints.

"Don't," I warn.

"I won't talk," he once again threatens. "You might as well kill me now."

"There is no peace saith the Lord unto the wicked," Mother says in my head. *"Make him suffer."*

"Gladly."

I rip the front of his shirt open, exposing his chest. I then place the sander against his skin and turn it on. His screams roar over the sound of the power tool as his flesh slowly disappears and nothing but blood and muscle remain.

I stop the machine and place it down on the cart.

"Who are you working for?" It takes him a moment to fight through his pain in order to answer me.

"I don't know," he shouts as spittle flies out of his mouth. His head drops and sways as if he might be intoxicated.

Picking up the machine again, I turn it back on. I could do this all night.

"Wait. Wait," he yells halting my movement.

Pressing the off button, I silence the machine.

He heaves a few breaths, his head lolling to the side as if it pains him to keep it up. "I don't know the benefactor. He hired me to find a girl named Summer. That's all I know."

"How did he find out about her?"

"Look, I don't know. All he gave me was a description and a name. An African American woman named Summer, light skinned, around the age of twenty-five to twenty-eight. Anywhere from five three to five four. He said she might have had a drug problem or a record."

The benefactor had entirely too much information about Summer. Even knowing her name was a problem. My question now is why is this benefactor looking for Summer? However, I don't think this man knows anything.

"How did you find her?"

If this guy was able to track her down with so little information, someone else could. I need to know how he did it.

He sighs as if talking is taking a lot of him. "I'm a PI, but I was a detective for fifteen 'years…. I called in a favor from some friends…. they told me they had a few reports on a Summer Jones…. She matched the info the benefactor gave me. Please, I need….to go to the hospital." His head falls forward. I know he's fighting to stay conscious, but I didn't care about his comfort. I still had questions.

"When did the benefactor hire you for this case?"

He doesn't answer right away. Tossing the machine onto the cart, I grab his sweaty hair and lift his head. His eyes are glazed but he's still breathing.

"Answer me," I growl through clenched teeth.

"About……about five months ago."

I release him, before climbing to my feet. I tug at the hair on top of my head. Five months, he's been out there looking for Summer. Getting close to my family. And I've been wasting time.

"Failure. You are a complete and utter failure," Mother taunts.

"Look…." The fake pizza guy says causing me to turn back to him. "I don't mean the girl any harm. The benefactor……. he told me that she was his sister-in-law, and she was in danger. I thought…. I thought I was doing the right thing."

I don't care what he thought he was doing. He got entirely too close to my family.

"Whose fault is that?" Mother chastises in my head. I can hear the disappointment in her tone. *"You left them alone. You don't deserve them."*

I shake my head, forcing her words out of my thoughts. "Where are the records of your search?"

He looks up at me, his eyes rounding at my question. Every PI keeps records or notes of how he tracked down his subject.

"At my home. It's all locked in my safe. Other than calling him tonight to let him know I might have made a positive match, the benefactor has no idea where she is. If you let me go, I vow that he never will. I'll burn everything I have. You can watch me."

I allow silence to fill the space between us. Meanwhile, I study the man before me. He's a trained detective and at one point his job was to serve and protect. Could he be trusted?

"Why do I want her information?"

His brow pinches in confusion. "Wha….what?"

I step closer to him, leaning down so that he can look me in my eyes. "You didn't ask why I want the woman's information? You were hired to find and protect her, yet you would give information to me and not ask why."

He sighs, licking his lips. "Look man, I don't care what you want with her. Just let me go."

I shake my head. "Wrong fucking answer."

Picking up the sander, I turn it on the highest setting before pressing it to his chest. His screams ease the beast inside me. I couldn't set him free. Not only does he know too much about Summer and Gabe, he's proven that he couldn't be trusted with the information.

Once the beast has been sated, I put the PI's body in the incinerator and clean the mess I've made in my special room.

Climbing back in the blue sedan, I head toward the chop shop I use to get rid of cars. Priest taught us to always have outside sources. The Church has their own wreckage company that handles jobs like this. But just as we all have our own cleanup crew, I also have my own source of getting rid of big objects.

After pulling into the shop, the same one I used to get rid of the Lincoln town car, I put the car in park. Immediately, the phone in the cup holder starts to ring.

I answer it hoping it will be the benefactor he was on the phone with earlier. Swiping my hand across the screen, I remain silent. My hope is that he or she starts to speak first.

"Hello?" the voice on the other side of the phone says. I noticed right away it has an accent.

Before I can speak, the person on the other end of the phone chuckles.

"Well, hello, Beastie. I see you found my bait."

Rage boils through me. I fell right into his trap. It never crossed my mind that the PI could've been bait. When it came to keeping Summer and Gabe safe, I allowed my knee jerk reaction to outweigh my thoughts.

"I knew the fastest way to narrow down my search for your girl was to put someone close to her."

It's already obvious that whoever this is, is smart and calculating. He also knew enough about me to know that I would go for the bait.

"Who is this?"

"Who I am doesn't matter. Not yet anyway."

I grit my teeth. "Then what matters?" My questions have to be precise. If I don't ask simple direct questions, I have a feeling he will skate around the answers.

"What matters is you left a lot of breadcrumbs, Beastie. So many people remembered seeing you and her that night. That was very unlike you. I don't think the Church would approve."

"You work for the Church?"

He chuckles. "Don't insult me, Beastie. You and I both know I don't work for the Church."

I grit my teeth at him once again able to read my thoughts. If he'd worked for the Church, he wouldn't use a PI to find my family. I asked the question only to see how he would respond.

"I do have concerns about Summer's safety," the benefactor goes on to say.

"You have concerns about something that belongs to me?" I grit out. My hands tighten around the phone at my ear. The thought of Summer even crossing his mind has me wanting to split his fucking chest open.

"Having something that belongs to you left so vulnerable seems like a bad idea. I knew about the girl, but finding out there is also a child left out there seems sloppy. If the wrong person was to happen upon this information, it could be very bad."

"Stay away from my family."

He gives me another chuckle. "Relax, Beast. I don't want your family. I'm not the bad guy."

"Then who is?"

Twice he's mentioned an unseen villain. I don't believe this man is the type to waste words. There is truth buried in everything he says.

This time when he speaks there is no laughter in his voice. "Someone you are not ready to meet."

The way his voice changes and the quietness after his statement tells me that not only does he fear this person, but he's also angry with them. However, because he didn't give me the name right away warns me there is still some loyalty there.

"If you aren't the bad guy, then who are you?"

I need to know what his plans are with the information he has. Right now, he knows too much about my family.

"I haven't decided yet if I'm a friend or foe," his tone is back to the joking one from earlier.

"And if you decide to be my enemy?"

I had no worries about this man becoming my enemy. I only needed to know what his plans were for Summer and Gabe when I went after him.

"Your family is safe. I don't involve women and children in my affairs."

I don't yet allow his words to bring me comfort. I didn't trust anyone with any information on Summer and Gabe. I also don't like the fact that the benefactor seems to guess my thought process.

"So, what do you want? Why were you looking for me?"

There is no way he would've found Summer if he wasn't first searching for me. Whatever issues he has involves me. I'm assuming it has something to do with Church business because he made a point to mention them.

His laughter floats through the phone. "Now that, is the right question. Let me know when you figure it out."

The line goes dead leaving me in silence.

I slam the cell phone against the steering wheel until pieces of it fly across the car.

"Aye, big man," Pharrell, the guy that owns the chop shop, comes up to my window. "You good?"

Opening the door, I climb out of the front seat. Pharrell takes a step back. Even though I've been working with him for years, he's still terrified of me.

"I need a car," I demand, tossing the broken cellphone back into the car on the passenger seat.

There is no need to take the phone. Most likely it was a burner, and I won't get any information from it. Nor will the benefactor use it again.

"Sure. I can have you a brand-new vehicle with no vin in about three days."

"No, I need one now." I take a step closer to him.

Pharrell takes two steps back before shouting, "Jay, give me your keys."

"What? What do you need my keys for?"

"Man, give me your fucking keys." Pharrell turns and shouts at him.

Jay tosses his keys to him. Pharrell then holds them out to me.

"Thanks. For your help, keep all the proceeds you make from the car."

Pharrell nods. I rush out of the building and onto the gravel parking lot. The light rain that was only barely falling on my way over here is now pouring down in sheets. I don't let it slow me down. Hitting the key fob to unlock the doors. The lights flash on a black SUV. I rush to the vehicle, with only one place in mind.

I may not be good enough for them. And they are better off without me, but right now, they need me.

Summer

I add another bead to the necklace I'm working on. Usually, making my jewelry helps ease my thoughts and settles my mind, but not tonight. A certain someone is stomping through my brain like Godzilla. I drop the necklace to the table and sigh.

"Why can't I get him out of my mind?" I ask myself for the millionth time since meeting Gabriel.

Seeing him last night has not made it easier. Yes, Gabriel is absolutely gorgeous. He doesn't have those supermodel looks like the brother I met that night. He's a bit too rough around the edges for that. However, it isn't his looks that has him traipsing through my mind 24/7.

No, it's something about him. About the way he looks at me as if he's seeing a part of me I don't even see myself. It's the feeling I get when in his presence. As if I'm the safest I'll ever be when he is around me. That is why I can't just forget him like I've been trying to do for five years.

You would think after all this and having him tell me to my face that he's not interested in being in Gabe's life would turn me off from this man.

A loud rumble of thunder claps across the sky and quickly following it is a flash of lightning that lights up the room for a brief second.

"Mommy," Gabe's voice grabs my attention.

He's standing in the doorway, his Black Panther stuffy in one hand while rubbing his eyes with the other.

"Hey, baby. Can't sleep?"

He shakes his head from side to side and stares at the ground.

"I have the perfect remedy for thunderstorms. Do you want to know what it is?"

This time he nods up and down.

"Hot cocoa and a movie."

He lifts his head and looks at me with a big smile. My heart immediately melts.

"Come on," I say, standing from my chair.

I walk over to him, and he grabs my hand, looking up at me with those hazel eyes. We walk hand and hand into the kitchen.

Gabe lets my hand go and takes a seat at the kitchen table. I go over to the stove to prepare our hot cocoa.

"What do you want to watch?" I ask as if I don't know the answer already.

After grabbing the milk out of the fridge, I realized Gabe has yet to answer me. I look over my shoulder to find my son's face pressed to the patio door.

"Hey, what are you looking at?"

"Hulk," he says.

This kid has been mentioning Hulk a lot lately. Usually, it's Iron Man and Black Panther that gets all the attention.

"What is Hulk doing out in this rain? He needs to get back to the other Avengers," I joke.

"He's just watching us."

Something about the calm way he says those words has me pausing with the milk carton in my hand. My stomach tightens.

"Gabe, what does Hulk look like?" I ask, placing the milk down and making my way over to the patio.

"Like me," Gabe says without looking away from the door. "But bigger."

The tightening in my stomach turns to full out pains. I rush to the door and glance out. Just as I do, lightening cracks across the sky illuminating my back yard and the man standing there.

Anger fills me. I slide the door open and stomp out toward him ignoring the cold droplets of rain against my skin. Gabriel's piercing eyes stare at me as I approach. His clothes are soaked and the rain has saturated his hair causing it to lay heavy and flat against his shoulders.

"No," I say marching up to him. "Go away."

"Summer," he tries to speak but I don't want to hear it.

Last time I talked to Gabriel he told me he didn't want to be with us. I refuse to allow him to yoyo Gabe around with his presence.

"You don't get to do this. You can't come and go in and out of his life. Get out of here." I shove him, but I might as well be pushing a brick wall. He doesn't even sway.

"No, Mommy. Hulk stays," Gabe shouts. I had no idea he followed me out into the rain.

His presence and hearing him plead for his father makes me angrier.

"Go," I shout at Gabriel. But he remains in his spot looking down at me.

I shove him once again, putting all of my force into it. Still no movement from him. Balling up my fist, I punch him in the chest. My hand throbs from the impact, but I don't stop swinging.

"No, Mommy. Don't hurt my friend," Gabe shouts behind me.

I ignore him, continuing to pound on Gabriel getting all my frustrations out. I hit him for the fact he thought he could walk in and out of our lives. I hit him because it took him five years to break out and come find us. Also, because in those five years he never thought to reach out to us.

I pound my fists against his chest for all the nights I stayed up running that infamous night through my head. And lastly, I hit him because even though he's unhinged and a reminder of the old me, I missed him.

Gabriel allows me to continue to attack him, never even putting up a hand to protect himself.

"Go away. We don't need you," I sob as my arms lose the strength to strike him again.

I collapse into his chest and cry. The rain has soaked through my braids and my nightgown. I imagine I look like a crazy person.

"I'm sorry, Summer," his gruff voice says, and I can hear the pain in his tone.

I'm not foolish enough to think that my attack caused him any harm. No, something else is bothering him.

Lifting my head from his stomach, I look up into his stoic face. He cuts his eyes away from me briefly before looking back at me.

"They found you."

"What?" I asked, confused about who found me.

"Someone knows about you and Gabe."

My entire world tilts on its axis. I remember the threat Fem told me about the Church and how they would react if they found out about me and Gabe. Fear, like nothing I've ever experienced, takes over me.

I guess all my talk about not needing him just went out the fucking window.

CHAPTER TWENTY-ONE

Books and More

Summer

I came awake abruptly, my jaw stinging. Gabe's hand is across my face. I imagine that is why my cheek hurts so bad. The kid sleeps like he's fighting villains in his dreams.

Gently, I push his hand down to his side. It took a while to get him to calm down and fall asleep.

The events of last night play through my mind. I didn't get much detail out of Gabriel after he dropped that bombshell on me. I think I was too terrified to even ask the right questions. I quickly ushered Gabe back in the house and out of the rain. I eventually fell asleep in his bed trying to get him to sleep.

But this morning I need answers, and the only person that can give them to me is somewhere in my house.

Sitting up in my son's twin size bed, I nearly jump out of my skin when I spot Gabriel in the room. He's sitting on the floor in the corner. His back is against the wall, his head is tilted back, and one knee is bent. From his position he can see the entire room along with a perfect view of me and Gabe.

"Did you sleep there all night?"

"I didn't sleep," he replies without lifting his head from the wall. That doesn't shock me.

I push the covers off and drag my legs to the side of the bed. My feet search the floor for the slippers I took off last night. Finally finding my fuzzy pink shoes, I slip my feet inside.

"You slept restlessly." His voice causes me to look over at him. I ignore the way it has chill bumps covering my arms.

He's watching me now, his gaze on my legs.

"Yeah, well a lot has happened in the last twenty-four hours."

And I meant that literally. Not only did I find out my son's father is back, I also found out that our lives are in danger.

He doesn't reply to my statement. Instead, he climbs to his feet with the easy agility of a large cat.

I get out of bed, stretching my arms over my head.

"We need to talk about last night," I say, walking into Gabe's bathroom to relieve my bladder. I turn to shut the door, but Gabriel is standing in the doorway.

"Umm, can I have some privacy?"

"No," he simply replies crossing his arms over his chest.

Rolling my eyes, I go to the toilet. Apparently, his inability to let me out of his sight wasn't just a thing the night he held me captive. But, if he wants to watch me piss then, whatever.

"So, the Church is after us? Do we need to run?" I ask as I take a seat and use the restroom.

"It's not the Church."

"Then who is it?" I roll some tissue around my hand and clean myself before flushing the toilet and heading to the sink to wash my hands.

"I'm not sure yet." Gabriel comes into the bathroom and stands in front of the toilet.

I turn on the facet and hold my hand under the soap dispenser but get distracted when he unzips his pants. Surely, he isn't about to pull his dick out right here in my face and.... yep, he did. Holy shit.

There is no way that's the same dick I rode to make my son. If there is no other sign that I was out of my mind from withdrawals that night, it's the fact that I was able to take the monster he's working with.

I haven't even seen a penis that beautiful on the porn I watch. Beautiful tan complexion, nice thick girth, throbbing veins, a length that makes your mouth water, and a perfect mushroom head.

"Summer."

"Huh," I ask shaking my head coming out of my trance. My palm is overflowing with the white soapy foam from the hand soap.

"Shit," I mumble as I quickly wash my hands in the sink.

"Did you hear what I said?"

I turn to him just in time to see him placing his pole back in his pants and out of my view.

"No, I was uh....distracted."

He comes to stand beside me at the sink. His large body brushing against mine. It's then I realize how small my son's bathroom is. He reaches past me to get some soap, his arm brushes against my right breast and my body starts to get a fuzzy feeling like a bad cable signal. After reaching over me for some soap, he starts to wash his hands in the sink.

"I said, it seems right now you and Gabe are safe." He turns to face me after turning the water off. I hand him the spider man hand towel I'd just used.

Leaning my hip against the sink, I cross my arms over my chest.

"But?" I ask. I can tell there is a but at the end of that sentence.

"But," he goes on to say after placing the towel on the counter. "I don't like the idea that this person went out of their way to find you. They didn't do it for no reason."

"So what now?" I shrug.

He leans his back against the sink, his palms flat against the edge of the counter.

"I'm going to find out who this person is and make sure no one else from that night talks."

"Basically, you mean a lot of bodies are going to pile up."

He doesn't reply, instead he just stares at me as if that was a dumb question.

"While I'm," he pauses as if he's looking for the right words to say. "Cleaning things up, I need to stay close to you and Gabe."

"And when it's over?" I hold my breath waiting for his reply even though I know where this is going.

"When I know you and Gabe are safe, I disappear. My stance hasn't changed, Summer."

It's not like I didn't expect this response. To be honest, I should be happy. Having Gabriel around is dangerous on many levels. And the most important one has nothing to do with the dead bodies that are going to pop up in the next few days.

It has more to do with the way my heart has not stopped racing since I woke up and saw him in the corner of the room. And how I have the strong urge to touch him as if I need to make sure he's real. Both of those feelings are unwanted and dangerous. Yes, it is best he goes on his way as soon as possible.

"Okay," I say, coming to terms with the fact that I'm stuck with him for now. "But I have a few stipulations if you're going to stay."

His mouth lifts on one side in that minute smirk of his. He turns to face me, leaning up against the side of the sink. He tilts his head as if to say go on.

"I haven't told Gabe who you are yet and I'm not sure I will."

The smirk falls from his face and his jaw tenses.

I hold up my hands in front of me before dropping them back at my side. "It's nothing against you." The way his smile dropped bothered me. I don't want him to think I'm keeping his connection to Gabe a secret because of who he is.

"I may change my mind, but until then I ask that you not tell him either."

As bad as it sounds, I'm thinking about my son right now. Change is already hard for Gabe. If he finds out he has a father just for his father to disappear on him again, it will hurt him. However, I do want Gabe to have the experience of having a father figure in his life for however long he can have him.

"Okay," Gabriel says.

"Good." I nod feeling confident in my choice. "With that being said, for as long as you are here you will spend time with your son. I don't care if it's watching the same Marvel movie 50 times or tossing the ball in the back yard. Whatever he wants to do you will do it."

He rakes a hand down his face. "I don't know if that's—"

I shake my head. "I don't want to hear it. Either you do this, or I'll send you away and call someone else to keep us safe."

I don't tell him that Fem gave me a number. She told me to only use the number in case of dire emergencies. Only if it's a last resort, life or death type of thing. She was so adamant about it, I even taught Gabe how to find the number on my phone. If Gabriel couldn't follow my rules, I had no problem calling that number to keep me and Gabe safe.

The vein in his neck tells me he's angry. I'm not sure if he's angrier at me making this demand or the idea of someone else keeping us safe.

He dips his chin to his chest. I guess that's as much of an agreement I'm going to get.

"My last request," I say, before taking a deep breath. "When we are no longer in danger and your time is up, you have to give us a proper goodbye. Promise me you won't slip out while we are sleep." I hate the sound of desperation in my voice as I give him this last stipulation. But I can't help it. The way he left that last time still lingers with me.

Gabriel's intense eyes stare back at me. They stare so long and so deeply, I feel as if he's trying to tell me something. Like there is a hidden language he's trying to share with me only I don't understand it.

Finally, he dips his chin and turns away from me. "You have my word."

Feeling content with the new arrangements I hold out my hand. He looks back at the outstretched appendage before his half smirk lifts his lips. He places his warm hand in mine, swallowing up my hand. We shake twice before letting go.

"Alright, it's Sunday, which means we are headed to the bookstore."

I turn to leave the bathroom. Gabe appears in the doorway rubbing his sleepy eyes.

"Hulk," Gabe says happily in a groggy voice. The smile on his face lights my heart. He rushes into the bathroom to stand beside his father.

"Gabe brush your teeth so we can head to the bookstore. Hulk," I say getting Gabriel's attention. "There are spare toothbrushes in that top drawer." I point to the set of drawers behind him.

I then leave, allowing the two guys to bond in the bathroom.

Gabe and I make it to Books and More, for their Sunday story time.

"Hey Gabe," Malia says as soon as we walk in.

"Cookie," Gabe sings his nickname for Malia.

He lets go of my hand to runs to Malia. As soon as he gets to her, he grabs her hand. From the first day my son met Malia he has been smitten. The only person he likes more than her, is her daughter. Right on time, Emory walks over to Gabe.

"Em," Gabe beams up at Emory. She waves and signs his name.

He signs her name back to her. She's been teaching him sign language since we started coming here.

"Why don't you two find a spot on the floor. Story time will start soon," Malia says.

Gabe lets go of her hand and takes Emory's. They walk over to the fireplace where story time will take place.

"Is Trina meeting you here?" Malia asks, walking over to the bakery counter.

"Of course. You know she can't miss an opportunity to have one of your strawberry short cake rolls."

Malia chuckles as she goes over to the sink to wash her hands.

"We missed you last week," I say, glancing over my shoulder at Gabe who seems to be caught in a trance as he stares up at Emory.

"Yeah. Life has been a bit complicated lately."

I turn back to Malia. She puts on gloves before going to her pastry display and grabbing a gluten free chocolate cookie for Gabe and two of her strawberry cheesecake crescent rolls for me and Trina.

"Is everything okay?"

Since the first day I met Malia, we've clicked. Not only does my son seem to love her, but she has been so nice and inviting to me and him. Considering I never had many friends growing up—mostly due to me and my issues—it was nice making a new friend.

"As okay as it can be. Em and I had some changes at home with my Grams moving out. And then my boyfriend is having some family issues. His brother is missing."

I've only met Malia's man once in passing. He didn't even notice me as he walked by me and out the door.

"I'm so sorry to hear that. I hope they find him soon."

I follow Malia over to the register where she places two empty cups down beside my food. I've been here so many times and ordered the same thing, she doesn't even have to ask me what I want anymore.

Pulling out my debit card, I hand it to her. She rings up my stuff before handing me the card back.

"If I know Lucien," She continues. "He will find his brother. I just hate seeing him worried."

I could only imagine what her boyfriend must be going through. If Trina ever took missing I'd be crazy. Sadly, I can't exactly say the same thing for my actual sibling.

"Well, if you need anything, I'm here to help. Even if it's passing out flyers or watching Emory for you."

Malia smiles. "Thanks Summer, I appreciate that."

"No problem."

A commotion over by the fireplace has us turning in that direction. One of the kids has fallen and the others are laughing.

"Let me go read this book before these kids get restless."

I grab my bag of pastries and two cups off the counter. Finding a seat by the window, I place my things down before going to fix my and Trina's drink. As I'm walking back to my table my phone pings.

After placing the drinks down, I fish the phone out of my pocket and take my seat before looking at the text message.

Unsaved Number: This is Gabriel.

My heart gallops, knocking against my chest. A smile spreads over my face, but quickly disappears when a thought comes to mind.

Me: When did you get my number?

Unsaved Number: The day I had the phone set up.

I tamp down on the anger that spreads throughout me. He's had my number all this time and never once thought about using it? It never crossed my mind to question who set the phone up. I just assumed it was Fem. As I said, the moment I got out of rehab, I was picked up and immediately taken to a brand new fully furnished house. Along with all my new stuff, was a shiny new cellphone.

I knew Gabriel was paying the bills because I've never seen a letter come to the house or gotten a call from a collector. I just never considered he would have the number and until this day, never used it.

Me: Wow! So you've had my number for five years and it never crossed your mind to call?

I watch as the bubble appears on the screen, I wait for his response, hoping it's a good one.

Unsaved Number: Save this number.

Without him having to say it, I knew this conversation was over. I was never going to get an answer to my question. Rolling my eyes and sucking my teeth I toss my phone on top of the table and sink back into my chair.

"Well hey to you too," Trina says, taking a seat in the chair across from me.

"Hey, girl,"

"What's got your panties all in a bunch?" Trina picks up her cup and takes a sip of the strawberry lemonade that is worth every single one of its calories."

"Gabe's father is back."

Immediately she chokes on the lemonade she'd just sipped. She pats her chest as she coughs up a lung.

"What the fuck, Summer?" she shouts entirely too loud for our current location. Malia stops reading as all eyes turn to us.

"Sorry. She has a condition," I say, apologizing to all the glaring faces.

Malia gets the kids' attention back, and the parents go back to what they were doing.

"Keep your voice down."

She waves me off. "When did he come back? What did he say? Is he trying to get you back? Have ya'll fucked?"

I hold up a hand to stop her. "He came back two nights ago. He hasn't said much, and no we haven't had sex."

Trina leans back in her seat and folds her arms over her chest.

"Then what the hell was the purpose? Did he just pop up after five years to say hey?"

Good question. I still have no idea why Gabriel showed up on that date. I mean I know why he's here now. But why the date?

"He's in town for a while. He has some business to handle and then he's gone again."

"Wait, what about G? He's not sticking around to help raise my nephew?"

I take a sip of my drink. "He's not really the father type." I try to explain as best as I can.

I didn't believe for one second that Gabriel couldn't be a good father to Gabe. Yes, he has issues. I witnessed his demons firsthand. However, I also know that despite what Gabriel thinks, he has better control over them than he gives himself credit for.

"Who the fuck cares. Neither were we, but we figured it out."

I had nothing to dispute that because she was a hundred percent correct. Trina and I made this parenting stuff work. I didn't even know how to change a diaper when Gabe was born but she and I figured it out together. She truly took her role as godmother seriously.

"I agree. But I can't force a man to stay if he doesn't want to."

At the end of the day, I didn't hold any ill will toward Gabriel. He is doing the best he can with us.

"We made a deal, for as long as he's here he will spend time with his son. That's all I ask." That's as good as we were going to get.

Trina sits back in her seat, crossing one arm over her stomach as she props the other up under her chin. "And what about time with you?"

"What do you mean? I don't need his time."

She laughs as if I made the funniest joke in the world. "Let me get this right." She leans forward placing her elbows on the table in front of her. "The man that fucked you so good in one night you haven't been able to ride another dick in five years is back in town and you're not going to even try for a repeat?"

My mouth opens but no words come out. From the outside looking in, it may seem like I haven't had sex in five years because I was still hung up on Gabriel. But in reality, I was busy. He had absolutely nothing to do with my hiatus.

"Okay, Summer." I ignore the sarcastic voice in my head that sounds a lot like Trina.

"First of all, he had nothing to do with my lack of a sex life."

She rolls her eyes and sinks back into her seat.

"And second, I will not go down that road again with him. He and I are better off keeping it truly platonic."

Trina shrugs. "Okay. Whatever you say Summer."

"I mean it," I argue taking a sip of my drink.

She smirks. "I give you three days before he has you bent over your kitchen table taking back shots."

I nearly choke on my lemonade. It takes me a few minutes to stop coughing. It doesn't help that the vision of Gabriel pushing into me from that night makes a reappearance.

"Not going to happen," I state. "I am 100 percent, completely, and fully over that man."

Trina doesn't respond. She stares at me with a smirk on her face. Eventually she shakes her head and reaches into the bag for her pastry.

"Okay. I believe you," she says in the most unbelieving tone ever. "So that means you are ready to move on with Andrew."

I laugh shaking my head. "It would be nice, but I highly doubt it."

Trina puts her croissant down and frowns. "Why doubt it?"

I chuckle. "Maybe because he ended up with a concussion on our first date."

Of course I didn't tell Trina or Andrew that Gabriel was the reason he ended his night in the hospital. Andrew told the cops and hospital staff that he didn't remember anything. One minute he was washing his hands and the next he was waking up with the paramedics standing over him. Thank goodness for that.

"Well, apparently he's not holding it against you because he called James today to get your number."

My eyes nearly pop out of my head I stretch them so wide.

"You're joking right?"

She pulls out her phone and taps on the screen. Turning it to face me, there's a screenshot of a conversation between James and Andrew. True enough, Andrew asked if he could get my number.

I have no idea how to feel about that. I mean, Andrew was definitely attractive. And I had a really good time with him. But I just assumed he had come to his senses after the concussion.

"He was nice," I admit.

"Exactly," she says hitting the table. "Look, if baby daddy is a no go and you are sure you're over him," I didn't like the way she said that last part like she didn't believe me. "Why not give Andrew a chance."

She had a point. I liked Andrew, and I am over Gabriel. It's time to start really putting forth an effort to date.

"You know what, you're right. Give Andrew my number."

Trina shimmies in her seat. "And you know what else. This is a perfect opportunity to make G's dad jealous. Nothing makes a man act right faster than knowing he's lost his position."

At this I shake my head. "Gabe's dad is not the type you want to make jealous."

She scoffs and rolls her eyes. "What is he going to do, kill somebody."

Yes. I think. But I didn't tell her that. Although Gabriel may be upset with my dating again, he's going to have to get over it. I'm a single woman and I deserve to be happy. And if he can't deal with that, then he can kick rocks.

Trina and I spent the rest of our outing talking and laughing.

CHAPTER TWENTY-TWO

Not a hero

Beast

"We need you in room seventeen. Some drunk asshole didn't get the memo we're closed," A deep male voice outside of the room says.

I continue to lie on my back across the bed in the dark room. One hand is across my chest and the other tucked under a pillow.

The benefactor was right. I left entirely too many witnesses that night. Too many people that can be bought or threatened to reveal Summer and Gabe. I failed them.

"*You are a disgrace. You don't deserve them,*" Mother reprimands.

It's time I cleaned up the mess I made. I needed to retrace my steps that night to everyone that saw us together. My first stop, of course, was Ace's night club.

Ace's prides itself on being selective and secure, yet I easily slipped in the back door and found a free room to lay my trap. I once again cut the cameras inside the building.

"Don't worry. You go on home. I'll get this guy out," The man I'm here for says.

The door opens slowly, but I remain in my place. The padded sound of footsteps make their way over to me.

"Hey man, you got to get up," The bouncer from that night five years ago, Curtis, says. He smacks my foot, trying to get me to wake up. I remain in my current state, not moving.

"Fuck, I don't feel like this shit right now," he grumbles before coming to where my head is lying on the other end of the bed. "Big guy, you have to—"

His words are cut off when I spring up from the bed. I grab his neck and bring him down to me. He puts up a small fight, but I use the chloroform I placed on the pillow that covers his face to knock him out.

The moment he stops fighting, I push him to the floor and get up from my spot. Going over to the door, I shut and lock it.

Sunday nights are the only nights Ace's closes at 2am. The cleaning crew isn't due until 9 in the morning.

Glancing down at my watch, I note that I have approximately six hours to get all the information I need from Curtis.

I get moving to prepare the room. Pulling my duffle from under the bed, I grab the plastic tarp from the bag and spread it out on the bed. Once I have the surface covered, I hoist Curtis on my shoulder and drop him on top.

Then, I use the duct tape in my bag to secure his arms and legs to the four posts on each end of the bed.

Making my job even easier, I cut his clothes off leaving him in nothing but his boxers.

"The good book says, we must defend the weak and the fatherless. You must protect them."

"Yes mother," I reply, before waking Curtis with the smelling salts.

He comes awake abruptly. He attempts to move his arms, but immediately realizes something is wrong. He turns his head, looking up from his position to see the tape securing his arms in place.

"What the fuck?" he mutters, tugging against his restraints.

"Five years ago, I came in here with a girl."

"Fuck you, man," he shouts so hard that spittle flies from his mouth.

Letting out a sigh, my shoulders drop. I was hoping this would go by faster. Bending down, I pull the sledgehammer out of my duffle. Raising the tool over my head I bring it down onto Curtis's kneecaps. The sickening crunch of bone precedes his scream. The acidic smell of piss fills the room before his gray boxer briefs take on a darker color in the front.

I allow him a few minutes to gain control of himself. His cries turn from screams to loud whimpers.

"Now, five years ago—"

"Mother fucker," Curtis shouts cutting me off. "I don't remember shit five years ago." He starts to cry again; snot and tears mix on his face.

I start again. "Five years ago," his sobs get louder, nearly drowning out my words. "I came in here with a girl you knew named Summer."

I watch as realization dawns and his eyes widen briefly. The cries immediately die down. His body slumps into the mattress as he shakes his head and wets his lips.

"I didn't tell him anything. I swear, man. I didn't say anything."

"He's lying," Mother snarls. *"He who utters lies is treacherous."*

"He isn't," Priest says in my head. *"Look at the way he's looking directly at you. And how his body sags in relief. He didn't tell."*

Placing my sledgehammer down at my feet and leaning it against the side of the bed, I give Curtis my full attention back.

"Tell me about the encounter."

Curtis takes a deep breath, seeming to calm down even though his body shakes. "A few months ago, I got off work. It was late, around four in the morning. As soon as I got in my car a gun was pressed to the back of my head.

"The guy started asking me about that night. At first, I had no idea what he was talking about, until he mentioned it being the night that City Council guy went missing. He then showed me a picture of you. He asked if I remembered you and if you were here with anyone."

"And what did you say?

"I told him that I didn't remember you. I promise."

I believe he didn't rat me out, but now I want to know why. He had a gun pointed to the back of his head, yet he didn't reveal anything.

"Why did you lie to him?"

His teeth chatter, showing signs his body is going into shock due to the shattered knee.

"Summer," he stutters out.

I dig my short nails into the palm of my hand. I don't like the way he says her name with familiarity.

"You knew she was a whore when you met her. Do not act appalled now."

I ignore mother's taunts in my head.

Before I can ask any other questions, Curtis continues speaking.

"Look, I don't know you and don't give a shit about you. But you were with her, and I've known Summer since we were in high school. She had some issues, but she's good people. I didn't know this guy or what he wanted, but I wasn't about to get Summer involved."

I dip my chin to my chest briefly. His kind words about Summer eases the fire in me a little.

"What did he look like?"

"I don't know. I never got a look at him. But he had an accent, I don't know where it's from."

Before he can finish his statement, I'm shaking my head. "I need more than that."

"I don't have anything else," he whines as new tears fall down the side of his face. I once again give him time to get himself together. Finally, his brows dip as if he's thinking of something.

"The tattoos," he says to himself before turning to me. "When he showed me your picture, I got a view of the tattoos on his forearm. They were tally marks, and from the looks of them there were hundreds of them."

It sounds like the benefactor was the one that asked him questions. Which means, at some point he was actively looking for me. It proves my point that whatever issue he has is with me. But why?

"Did he say anything else to you?"

"No, I swear. After I told him I knew nothing he climbed out of the car."

Standing up straight, I roll my neck back and forth.

"I told you everything," Curtis pleads. "Let me go. Take me to a hospital, I swear I won't say anything to anyone."

I believed him. He didn't rat me out to the benefactor when he had a gun pressed to the back of his head.

"For I have not found thy works perfect before God. You have a job to do," Mother demands inside my head. *"You cannot trust man. Finish the job."*

Although he didn't mention Summer to the benefactor, who is to say what he will admit if he's pressured. I have to protect them.

I pick up the sledgehammer off the floor and raise it over my head.

"Please man." Curtis pleads. "I won't say anything, I swear. Don't do this."

For a second, his plea crossed my mind. They cut through the red haze crowding my thoughts. Could I allow him to survive? Will he keep our secret?

"For nothing is hidden that will not become evident. Kill them all."

"Yes, Mother," I answer out loud.

Without a second thought, I bring the sledgehammer down on Curtis' skull cutting off his cries for help. However, the pull of the red haze has still not let me go. Mother continues to whisper in my head.

"Finish the job."

I drop the sledgehammer to the floor. Reaching in my bag, I pull out a saw. I have more work to do.

Summer

I come awake abruptly. It takes my eyes a moment to adjust to the low light and to remember where I am. I fell asleep on the couch in the living room.

After putting Gabe to sleep, I remember sitting on the couch. My eyes drifted to the clock on the wall numerous times while I watched TV.

I won't say I was waiting up for Gabriel, more like I was just checking to make sure he made it in safely. I texted him before putting Gabe to sleep to see what time he would get back but he never replied.

I kick the covers off my legs and place my feet on the floor. I stand to head into the kitchen.

"Ahh," I scream when my gaze lands on Gabriel standing near the entrance from the kitchen to the living room.

Placing my hand over my heart, I say, "Fuck, Gabriel. You scared the shit out of me."

I head in his direction, stopping in front of him.

"I'm going to have to get you bells for your shoes." I chuckle, but he doesn't respond.

It's then that I start to pay attention to him. He's staring at me with cold eyes. His body seems so tight he would shatter if I thumped him. His hands are down at his side in tight fists. His breathing is labored, his nostrils flaring with each inhale he takes.

"Are you alright?"

"You will be delivered from the forbidden woman, from the adulteress with her smooth words," he says in a slightly higher pitch voice almost as if he's someone else.

Before I could ask him again if he's okay, he speaks letting me know exactly where his head is.

"Yes, mother."

Cold dread runs through my body. Gabriel told me that when he goes to that dark place to kill, he has to let his mother in his head. She's so deep in it, he's speaking in her voice.

"Gabriel—" my words are cut off when his hand wraps around my throat so tightly I feel as if he could crush it.

I fight for my next breath, but his grip is like a snake, every time I try to take a deep breath he squeezes tighter.

"Gabriel.... please..." I choke out.

Yet his eyes remain cold and unfeeling. He's so far in that dark place he isn't even blinking.

Tears spring to my eyes. This is the part about that night I tried to forget. For as special as it was, it was also terrifying. Gabriel is a killer no matter how kind he was to me. This is who he is.

I grab his hand when the spots start to appear in my sight. I scratch at his wrist trying to dig my nails into his flesh hoping to snap him out of it. However, it seems as if I'm barely touching him even though blood is pooling on his skin. He doesn't even flinch at the pain.

It's then I remember that pain isn't going to get that bitch out of his head. He's used to pain. I have to use the only weapon that I have.

"August... Gabriel... Jones." It takes everything I have to get that name out. But the moment it slips out of my mouth, his hand loosen slightly around my throat.

His brows pinch and his jaw tenses. However, that cold look is still in his eyes. I continue giving him all the details he missed.

"Eight....pounds, one.... ounce," his hand loosens even more. "Born July 20th at 4:11pm. He loves superheroes, cookies, and playing outside. And if you hear him laugh it will melt your heart."

Gabriel releases me and takes a step back. I drop to my knees coughing and trying to fight off the urge to pass out. When I finally start to feel somewhat normal, I look up to find those green eyes staring down at me. This time there is so much emotion staring back at me. Gone is the cold vacant look from before.

He now resembles a terrified animal that's caught in a cage. I climb to my feet but stumble a little. My head swims. I'm assuming the lack of oxygen has me thrown off. Steadying myself against the wall, I place a hand against my tender neck and wince. It burns as if it should be bleeding. Yet when I look at my hand there is no blood.

"Gabriel—"

"Don't," he cuts me off. He turns from me, glancing at the wall to his left.

I take a step in his direction.

Gabriel takes a step back, not even looking at me.

"I'm okay," my voice sounds so raspy and speaking feels as if razor blades are wrapped around my words as they come up my throat.

He looks at me with the most pained and defeated look on his face. Common sense would tell me to be scared. The man nearly choked me out, but my heart goes out to him. Maybe those drugs fucked me up. But I just can't blame him for this. So many people failed Gabriel.

"We can—"

"I have to go." He once again cuts me off.

"Gabriel," I call out to him as he storms out of the living room and through the kitchen.

I try to catch up to him, but the lack of oxygen and the fact his legs are much longer than mine has me coming up short. By the time I make it to the back door, he has disappeared into the dark of my backyard.

This is a good thing, I tell myself. He needs time to get himself together. However, I just can't help but think of him being alone out there.

CHAPTER TWENTY-THREE

Errands

Summer

I touch my sore neck gently. The fact that I bruise so easily has never worked in my favor. Especially not today with five very definite fingerprints on my neck. Thank goodness for makeup.

My phone pings on the counter and I rush to grab it hoping it's Gabriel. Unfortunately, I'm disappointed when it isn't his name attached to the text message.

Unknown Number: Good morning, Summer. This is Andrew. James gave me your number. I hope you don't mind.

A smile lifts my cheeks. Not the person I was looking for, but I won't complain.

Me: Not at all. Glad to hear from you.

Unknown Number: I'm not one to beat around the bush, I'd really like to see you again.

My smile turns into a full on blush. I have to admit, there is something different about this guy.

Me: That would be nice.

Unknown Number: How about lunch tomorrow around noon?

Me: Sounds great.

Unknown Number: Good. I'll text you later with the details. Have a great day.

I place my phone back on the counter. A permanent grin on my face. I was so caught up in my conversation with Andrew I didn't hear my son walk into the kitchen.

"When is Hulk coming?" Gabe asks grabbing my attention.

The reminder of last night and the look on Gabriel's face as he walked out of the house wipes the smile and the earlier feelings away.

Gabe has been asking for Hulk since I woke him up this morning. I grab his plate off the counter and walk it over to the table.

"I don't know, Gabe." I say placing his plate of fruit and sausage in front of him.

He pushes the plate away from him. "I want Hulk."

I take a deep breath because I know my son is only acting out because he's confused. This is the reason I don't often make changes to his daily routine.

Sliding the plate back in front of him I take a seat beside him.

"Give me your eyes," I ask.

He turns to look at me. His eyes are so much like his father's. Although they aren't the same seafoam green, they are the same shape.

"Hulk is a very busy man. Some days he will be here when you wake up, but some days he won't be. We have to be patient and understanding to that. Okay?"

He looks down at his hands but nods his head.

"Eat your breakfast so you can finish getting ready for school."

I go back over to the sink, closing my eyes, I take a deep breath. I can only hope that Gabriel will come back. That look in his eyes before he left haunted me all night. I know he's looking for any reason to prove he isn't fit to be around his son. I just can't accept that. Especially when I know he's more than capable.

If I hadn't heard from him by noon today, I was going to call him.

"Hulk," Gabe says happily.

I turn to find Gabriel standing in my kitchen. He's wearing new clothes and looked freshly showered. His hair is pulled back in a low bun. His shorter front pieces fell in his eyes. Never had I seen a more beautiful man. My words made true by the pounding of my heart at just the sight of him. It doesn't matter how flawed he is, there is no one more stunning.

For what seems like an eternity, neither of us speak. We only stare at one another. For a moment I wonder what he's thinking. Can he see the sleepless night in my face? Does the way my heart races for him show up in my eyes? Because I'm looking at him so hard, I notice when his gaze drops down to my neck. I quickly place my hand over it, touching it gently.

I peel my eyes away from Gabriel to look at my son. "Gabe, it's time to go brush your teeth and finish getting ready."

My son quickly gets up and runs out of the kitchen. I grab his plate off the table.

"Where did you go last night?" I take the plate to the sink giving him my back.

"I'm renting a small apartment not far from here."

I take a deep breath before turning around. I'm startled to find him standing right in front of me. I press myself back into the sink. He lifts his hand to touch my neck and I flinch. Not because I'm afraid of him, but because it's very tender today. Of course that's not what he thinks. His hand drops back to his side.

"I'm sorry," his voice is so low I wouldn't have heard him if he wasn't standing in front of me. "If you want me to stay away, I will."

"If I thought you were actually going to hurt me, you wouldn't be in my house right now."

"But you're afraid of me." He looks directly into my eyes when he makes this statement.

Did I think he could hurt me if he wanted to? Yes. Did I think he would? I'm not sure. I don't think he would ever intentionally do anything to harm me or Gabe. But I can't ignore his issues. I'm not an idiot.

"Let's not worry about last night," I say instead. "You can go with me to take Gabe to school."

He's shaking his head before I can finish my statement. "You saw what happened last night."

"Yeah, I did. And we are both here today to talk about it so it's all good."

He runs a hand down his nose toward his chin. "Summer,"

"Just because it's hard doesn't mean you can run, Gabriel."

Because if that was the case, I'd have left all this behind. Trying to fight addiction and suicidal thoughts while dealing with a baby was one of the hardest things I've ever experienced. However, my love for Gabe, pure determination along with therapy got me through it.

He doesn't get to walk away because it's hard. That isn't an excuse.

He nods. "Okay."

The pounding of little footsteps heading in our direction lets me know Gabe is on his way back.

"Guess what," I say when he enters in the room and walks right up to his father's side. "Hulk is coming with us to take you to school."

Gabe smiles so wide, it mirrors on my face. Every decision I make, I do it for him. Even allowing his father in his life temporarily. No matter what it will do to me, it's all for him.

I park my car on the curb near Heartfelt Academy. Climbing out, I go around to the back seat to get Gabe out. Gabriel comes around to join us on the sidewalk.

"Do you have your lunch box?"

He holds up his Iron Man lunch box for me to see.

"Alright, come on." I hold out my hand, but he takes his father's instead. I swallow down the sting, but don't take it personally.

We head toward the large brick building. Parents and children surround the outside of the school saying their goodbyes and getting hugs and kisses.

As soon as we approach the front door, I stop Gabe, kneeling in front of him.

"What are we going to have today?"

"A good day."

"Are we going to use our words?"

"Yes," he nods with a smile.

I place my fist out in front of me. He bumps his fist against mine before turning to look up at his father.

"See you later, Hulk." Gabe holds out a fist for his father.

Gabriel bumps his fist against Gabe's. "See you later," he says.

Gabe walks up the front steps of the school. His teacher and assistant teacher are there to greet him. Immediately, his teacher looks over to me and holds up a hand.

She hurries down the steps toward me. "Ms. Jones. I was wondering if I can speak with you for a moment." She glances at Gabriel.

"Sure," I say giving her permission to speak freely.

She pushes her hair behind her ear. "As you know August has had a real hard time making friends."

"Yeah," I say encouraging her to finish her thoughts.

It isn't that Gabe doesn't make friends, he just prefers to play alone. I try to get him around other kids to help him socialize but it never fails, he will find a quiet spot somewhere by himself. Funny enough, he does better with older kids and adults. He has no problems hanging with Emory.

"Well," She goes on to say. "I notice that August gets more restless during certain times in class. Especially around group learning activities. I took him aside a few days ago to work one on one with him, and I noticed that he's advanced. He's reading well on his own and doing some simple math problems."

The kid catches on to things quickly. It's why after only a few short lessons he's already doing sign language with Emory.

"Okay," I say not sure where she's going with this.

I glance up at Gabriel to see what he thinks about this so far. However, his gaze is busy scanning the street and the surrounding area. To anyone else it may look as if he isn't paying attention, but I know he is.

"I want to place August in the Kindergarten class for about an hour or two for a few days. I think he will do well. But I understand how he does with change and making friends, so if you want to wait on it, I will understand."

"I think if it's only for a few hours and you allow an adjustment period it should be okay. I think he will do well."

She smiles at me. "Awesome. We can see how it goes over the next week and then I'll schedule a conference to talk about it."

"Sounds good."

She waves before walking off leaving us alone. I watch as she disappears back amongst the crowd of students and parents.

"Sorry." The sound of his gruff voice pulls me away from the school and toward him.

"We already talked about last night. You don't have to keep apologizing."

"Not about last night."

Now I'm confused, and my brows pinch to show it.

"I'm sorry," he goes on to say looking at a spot over my head. "For giving him my issues. I wouldn't—"

I hold up a hand to curt off anything else he was going to say. He looks down at me.

"I'm going to stop you right there. The only reason I'm not going to curse your ass out right now, is because I know that bullshit is coming from a place of hurt and pain. But listen to me. There's nothing wrong with my son. He's not a burden, or a problem that you should apologize for.

"He's not some kind of disease that you pass down. He's a kid. A very kind, intelligent, and sweet kid. And yes, sometimes the world gets too loud and too overwhelming for him. And he has a hard time socializing with his peers or keeping eye contact, but that does not make him a burden or something that needs to be apologized for. And I'm sorry no one ever told you the same thing about yourself." He looks away from me again.

I place my hand on his cheek to turn his gaze back to me. "Don't ever apologize for giving me the greatest gift I could ever ask for. Do you understand."

He nods. I let his face go. "Good, I have errands to run.":

"You can drop me off at the house,"

I chuckle and start to walk back to the car. He follows.

"Sorry, I wasn't clear the first time. *We* have errands to run."

"I have stuff to do," he argues as we stop at the car. He's standing by the passenger door and I'm at the driver's side.

"Not today. It's part of the stipulations."

He tilts his head to the side. "That wasn't in the deal."

I shrug. "It is now. If you're going to stay around, you have to help me."

This could backfire. I originally had no plans of spending time alone with Gabriel. This bonding thing had nothing to do with me and all about Gabe. However, as I stand here staring at him, the idea of being around him is starting to appeal to me.

He narrows his eyes, but I can tell he isn't angry. The smirk on his face gives him away.

"What if I say no?"

"You won't." I call his bluff as I climb in the car. He joins me shortly.

"Where to first?" he grumbles.

I fight the smile on my face. Despite what happened last night, I had no fear of being around Gabriel. Don't ask me why.

"You'll see when we get there."

I place the fresh broccoli in the plastic vegetable bag and tie it off before putting it in my cart.

"What's your favorite color?"

So far today after taking Gabe to school, I took some jewelry orders to the post office to be shipped off. I then stopped by the bank to make a deposit. After that, I went to the craft store to restock a few things for my business, and now I'm at the grocery store shopping for the next two weeks.

The entire time Gabriel has been by my side to help. He carried all my mail packages, making it a one-time trip inside the post office rather than the two or three it usually takes me. He stood silently beside me at the bank, helped me pick up material and carry my bags at the craft store, and even now he's pushing the cart as I add things to it.

He's never complained or rushed me, even when I stood in the beads section of the craft store trying to figure out which blue stones to buy. He has been patient and helpful, and it has meant the world to me.

"Black," he grumbles as he follows me with the cart as I pick up a bag of Vidalia onions.

That wasn't hard to guess as I look at his black zip up hoodie and black shiny combat boots. I don't think I've ever seen him in any color other than black and blue jeans.

"Favorite food?" I ask next.

For the last twenty minutes I've been asking him questions to get to know him better. Despite the fact we have a child together and spent one hell of a night with one another, I don't really know this man. This seemed like the best opportunity to do that.

"Pancakes," he says.

Turning to look at him I raise a brow.

"Why pancakes?"

He lifts a shoulder. "It's the first food I had with my brothers."

"Okay, that's going to require further explanation."

He shakes his head but obliges me. "When Priest came and got me from my mother, he took me and my brothers to an all-you-can-eat pancake spot. It was my first time ever eating at a restaurant. However, I was still a bit skeptical of him and didn't want to eat. He bought a huge stack of pancakes for the table. Everyone else kind of dug in but I didn't.

"I think Priest understood I was a bit weary of him. He excused himself to the bathroom. My brother, Lucien, placed a pancake on my plate and told me to eat. When I refused, he said it was fine, but no one else would eat until I ate. They didn't want me to starve by myself. It was the first time anyone ever showed me any type of kindness. So, I ate the pancakes so they could eat.

"Once the stack was gone, Priest came back to the table and finished his food. I realized later that he never really went to the bathroom. Til this day, that is one of my favorite memories and pancakes is my favorite food."

I don't show how that story made me realize how hard Gabriel had it in his childhood. I know enough about him to know that he wouldn't like my sympathy. And he also didn't share such an intimate memory with me so I could feel sorry for him. So, instead of telling him how sorry I was or how much my heart goes out to the lost little boy that needed kindness. I do what I do best.

"Damn, he could have at least taken you to a steak house. I mean pancakes are good and all, but steak is way better."

I felt proud of the small smile he gave me from my joke. It let me know I made the right decision. We moved on from the vegetables and headed down the rice and pasta aisle.

"When's your birthday?" I ask, grabbing a bag of Jasmine rice from the bottom shelf.

"April 22nd."

"You're a Taurus. It means you're loyal and stubborn." I turn to glance at him over my shoulder giving him a pointed look. "Makes sense."

I get another rare smile from him.

"Alright, so I feel like I've asked you enough questions. What do you want to know about me?" I turn to fully face him putting my hands on my hips.

He lifts a brow. "I already know everything about you."

I scoff. "No, I'm being serious." I move to the side so that an elderly couple can get past me in the aisle.

"So am I."

Folding my arms over my chest, I tilt my head to the side. "Okay, when's my birthday?"

"June 27th."

I was shocked, but that was an easy question. You can find that out by searching my Facebook.

"What's my middle name?"

"Elise."

Damn. Now I didn't expect him to know that. I don't have that posted on any social sites. I fire off my next few questions back-to-back.

"Favorite Food?"

"Mexican."

"Color?"

"Green."

"Favorite song?" I finally ask a question I know he won't know. Mostly because it changes on the regular.

"Stevie Wonder, As."

Okay, now this is a bit terrifying. My mouth hangs open trying to figure out how he knows so much about me.

His lips lift up into his usual smirk. "Did I pass?"

"How do you know all that about me?"

"I pay attention."

He must have read the skepticism on my face. He shakes his head leaning his arms against the handle of the grocery cart.

"Getting your middle name and birthday was easy. It's public records. Besides, I needed it to set the house and bank account up." That made sense. I should have guessed that.

"What about my favorite food?" I ask putting my hands on my hips.

He smiles. "I figured it out the night we met. You mentioned not eating much but would never pass up tacos."

"Oh yeah, I forgot about that." I didn't really forget, I just didn't think he paid that much attention.

"Simple observation told me your favorite color," he goes on to say. "Everything you own is some shade of green. Even your bedspread."

"Alright, I'll give you that." I say holding my hands out in front of me. "But there is no way you guessed one of my all-time favorite songs."

"You've been humming it all day. It even came on in the car and you turned it up. Like I said, I pay attention to you. I can also tell you that your favorite flowers are sunflowers. Your eyes went directly to them when we walked in the store."

My mouth hangs open. Here is a man I've known for a total of five days, and he knows more about me than my family. Even Trina doesn't know my favorite song or flower.

I ignore the tingling in my belly and the flutter in my chest. These symptoms are dangerous. And they are unwanted. When all this is over, Gabriel will disappear from our lives. I don't need these feelings. So, I once again do what is common to me.

"You know what I think?" I ask, wiping the shock off my face.

He doesn't respond, instead he cocks his brow for me to finish.

"I think you're spying on me."

He lets out a deep low laugh. I notice it isn't as loud and carefree as Andrew's. Gabriel's mouth doesn't even open, but it's nice. It has the hairs on my arm standing up in attention and a warming feeling in my chest. I ignore the unusual responses.

"Do you have cameras in my house? That is a breach of privacy."

He smirks, running his tongue over his bottom lip. Not seductively, I think he was just wetting his lips, yet it didn't stop me from watching him.

"If I do," he says. "Are you going to move out?"

I squint my eyes at him because he knows damn well, I wasn't leaving that house.

He chuckles, "Didn't think so."

"You think you're so funny." I taunt as I start to move up the aisle toward the pastas. "Let's see how funny you are when I leave you at this grocery store."

"Whatever you say, Elise." I can hear the laughter in his tone as he calls my bluff.

CHAPTER TWENTY-FOUR

I Know You

Beast

I glance down at the picture Summer just sent.

When I gave her my cell number, it was only for emergencies. No one has this number. Other than the phone I used to call in a cleaning crew, I don't use personal cellphones often. I'm not really the calling and texting type. Yet, the odd fluttery and empty feeling in my stomach every time my phone vibrates says otherwise.

I hit the back light on the screen again to re-illuminate the picture she sent. It's a selfie of her and Gabe lying in his bed. I can tell he's getting ready to go to sleep because he's in his pajamas with a silk bonnet on his head. They are both smiling at the phone with their faces close together.

I get that feeling again, the empty stomach one. I had it all day today as I spent time with Summer running errands, even though I had more pressing things to handle.

My phone lights up again, this time with a text message.

Summer: He wanted to say goodnight.

A voice memo pops up and I press play. My son's voice comes through my phone.

"Good night, Hulk. See you in the morning."

I shut my eyes as my pulse races. This feeling is new. One I've never experienced before. I wish I had my brother Lucien here to help me figure it out. It's like my body is out of whack. My brain is fuzzy but still alert. I get the same feeling when I'm near them.

Opening my eyes, I touch the microphone on my text box.

"Goodnight, Gabe." Once I'm done with my voice message, I hit send then place my phone in my pocket.

Going back to my laptop, I once again recheck that I've disabled the camera system on the house in front of me along with the alarm system. Once I've verified my coast is clear, I place the computer back in my bag and slide on my black gloves. Slinging the black duffle over my shoulder I make my way into the large home of Timothy Smith.

The man was still out of the country for the next two weeks, but I wanted to check his home for anything that might give me an idea of how he's connected to the Church.

The house is as grand as one would think a CEO of a Fortune 500 company with old money would have. This is the home he shares with his wife of thirty years. Timothy has two more places in New York, one he shares with his mistress and the other he uses for his temporary flings.

I knew if I wanted to get the most information about him, I would need to check this one first. I entered from the back of the house through the glass French doors into the family room. To my left is an open kitchen.

I make my way through the downstairs area, not really focusing on the decorations. I check the three main bedrooms on the first floor before going into the office. The space is basic. Cherry wood bookshelves and leather furniture.

I rummage through his drawers finding the basics, business and finance logs, a couple of bills, and some receipts. I close the drawers and look on the desk for more information. Hidden under a folder is a black envelope. The front is made out to Timothy but there is no return address.

Opening the envelope, I pull out a black rectangular paper with gold trim. In gold fancy lettering are the words. 'You're Invited." The date at the bottom of the letter was two months ago.

Whatever event he was invited to has passed, yet he held on to the invitation. Even though there is a shredder in the corner that looks full of shredded documents.

His office and desk are clean and well organized. So why would a man keep an invitation like this if the event has passed? It leads me to believe this invitation is important to him.

Flipping the card over for any more information, I come up short. No details of the event or location. Studying the card a little further, something catches my eye in the bottom left corner.

I pull my phone out of my pocket and turn on the flashlight shining it against the black card. Embezzled into the card is a capital R with a thorny crown above it. I have no idea what it means. I've never seen it before, but I documented the image in my memory.

Placing the card back in its envelope, I place it back where I got it. My next stop is to his computer. I start up the laptop and plug in the hard drive I brought with me. The first and easiest trick I learned from Lucien was how to break into basically any personal laptop. Once you start trying to break into large corporate networks it gets harder, but someone's personal computer is lightweight.

The lockscreen appears and I quickly override the password getting into the home page. As I download the contents of the laptop onto my hard drive, I quickly check the basics.

I search his history, his password keys, and his calendar. His home computer links with his work computer.

A date of interest pops up on his personal calendar. It draws my attention because it's classified as a business meeting, but it isn't on his business calendar. It also stands out because the meeting is at ten o'clock at night. And it looks as if it's two weeks from now. At least I know now where to find him. I finish the scan of his laptop and close out of the computer.

I finish my pass of the house. Searching for anything else that may give me clues as to why this man has a connection to the Church. Once I've checked the home from top to bottom, I slip back out of the house as if I was never there.

I make sure to restart the cameras and the alarm before leaving the property. As soon as I climb back into my stolen car, my phone goes off.

That flutter feeling has me reaching for my phone without checking the caller first.

"Hello," I say expecting to hear Summer's voice on the other side of the line.

However, it's not Summer that replies.

"You killed the bouncer?" the benefactor says with a chuckle.

I don't react. Instead, I pull my laptop out of the bag and plug my phone into it. I go to the app Lucien showed me and press record.

I'm not shocked he knows about the bouncer, the body was found this morning.

"You told me to clean up," I say a lot calmer than I was feeling. I have to be mindful of not only what I say, but also how I say it.

"If I didn't know you so well, I wouldn't have guessed who the torso belonged to."

"You know me?"

As always, the benefactor imbeds small nuggets in his conversation.

"Like I know myself, Beastie," I could hear the grin in his tone. "Although, I should tell you. The bouncer didn't rat you out. But I bet you know that already."

"I do."

"Then why kill him?"

"If you know me so well. You tell me?" I ask, attempting to keep him on the phone as long as possible.

He laughs a deep laugh. "See, this is the Beast I wanted to get to know." He pauses for a moment.

It lets me know he isn't worried about me tracing him. Which means he has another burner phone. I expected he'd be too smart to call me on a traceable phone.

"Alright, I'll tell you why," he says. "I didn't put pressure on him. I knew he was lying, but I didn't press for the information. Which you knew. But you thought that if the wrong person really wanted to know about Summer, he wouldn't be as lenient. And pressure burst pipes. So, you killed him because you couldn't trust him to keep that information. It's what I would have done."

I don't agree or disagree. He didn't do anything special, he knew I was going to kill the bouncer before I went to see him. It's why he left him alive. The benefactor wants me to clean up after myself.

However, my interest in the conversation once again piques as he mentions this infamous 'wrong person'. The way he brings it up and speaks about them rings of familiarity.

"Your silence tells me I'm right."

"Who is the wrong person to you?" I ask bypassing the game he's trying to play.

I knew he had some affiliation with the wrong person from our last conversation. The silence after my question proves I'm on the right path.

"Wouldn't you be more interested in how I got your number?"

He's deflecting. Now I know for sure I'm on the right path. Whoever this wrong person is, is connected to the benefactor. Either by blood or some form of loyalty. It puts me in the mind of how we once were with the Church. Yet, he was adamant about not being affiliated with us.

"Considering my number is unlisted," I say to answer his last comment. "And not under my name, I'm going to say you either got it by going through Summer's line, or you were close enough to me at some point to use a device to scan my phone."

He laughs. "I didn't think about going the Summer route. It would have saved me time."

He's been near me. I scan my brain trying to register all the faces I've seen today. I keep track of them all, memorizing small details. I never know who will be a threat or when I'll have to recall a random face in a crowd.

"Trying to see if you've seen me today?"

I don't reply, not giving him the satisfaction that he successfully guessed my actions.

"Let me help you out," he chuckles. "You didn't. Money can buy many things. Including paying an elderly couple one hundred dollars to walk close enough to you in a grocery store."

I immediately remembered the couple from the store. Summer moved out of the way so they could get by us. I grit my teeth at how close he was.

"Friend or Foe?" I ask, tired of the back and forth.

He sighs, letting out a deep breath. "Not sure yet. But I'll let you know when I've made my decision."

The line goes dead. I disconnect the phone from my laptop saving the conversation to study later. I now know that whoever the benefactor is, he's around. Which means I have to be even more vigilant than before.

Starting the car, I break the speed limit back toward Bronxville where Summer and Gabe are.

After stashing the car back where I got it and making sure I wiped down the insides, I headed back to Summer's. I quietly slip into the house. It's not as late as it was last night when I got back but it's still around one in the morning.

The sound of the TV leads me in that direction. It takes her a moment to look up from her phone to notice I'm here. The moment she does, she pauses, staring directly into my eyes. I know what she's looking for. She's trying to see if there will be a repeat of last night.

The memory of my hands around her neck and the obvious signs of the makeup she used to cover it up this morning cross my mind. I look away from her gaze.

"I thought you would have learned your lesson from last night." I say turning back to her.

The smile on her face releases some of the pressure in my chest.

She shrugs. "You and I both know I'm not really known for making smart decisions."

I fight the tug at the corner of my mouth. I don't want her to get too familiar with me. Last night should have proved to her how dangerous I am. She should have gone to sleep and locked her door. However, even as I think those words, all I want to do is sit down beside her.

"I'm good," I say instead of acting out my thoughts. "You can go to bed."

"Well, I kind of thought you'd get back later. I had a shit ton of black tea not too long ago. And now I'm wide awake."

I hate that she felt the need to make herself stay up for me. I don't want to do anything to inconvenience their life.

"Want to watch something? I'll let you pick?"

I should tell her no. Make her get as far away from me as possible. Yet, instead of doing what I know is right, I take a step into the room and drop my duffle down.

"I don't really watch television."

She rolls her eyes. "Why am I not surprised. Come sit." She taps the seat right next to her.

Does she really want me to sit in that seat? I would be so close to her that my body would brush against hers. My dick hardens at the thought of being that close to her. I shut my eyes trying to fight against the wayward thoughts.

The memory of how warm, wet, and snug she felt on my cock floods my mind. The sounds of her soft moans and curses as I drove deeper and deeper into her. I shake my head clearing the thoughts away. I can't think like that. What happened that night with Summer was a one-time thing. There is no way she would want me to touch her now that she's sober.

Opening my eyes, I walk further into the room. Instead of sitting in the seat she indicated, I take the seat on the other end of the couch. Allowing enough space for another person between us.

"We can find a series to watch together," she says sliding closer to me as if it's second nature, taking away the space I purposely put between us.

My entire body stiffens.

"The whore is trying to tempt you like the devil did Jesus in the desert," Mother warns.

"Let her tempt you all she wants," Priest replies.

"Be not moved," Mother Fumes.

"Be. Fucking. Moved," Priest shouts.

I have no idea I'm clutching my head trying to quiet the voices until I feel her small hand on my bicep. Lowering my arms and opening my eyes, I look down at her face. She's not wearing makeup, her freckles splatter across her cheeks and her nose. Those almond shaped brown eyes watch me with concern.

"You're not going to Hulk out on me, are you?"

I shake my head. "No."

"Good." She reaches for the table and grabs a small bag off it.

I'm familiar with the green velvet bags. They're the ones she uses for her jewelry. Earlier today, I picked up three boxes from the post office full of those bags.

She turns to me with a hesitant look in her eyes. She shakes her head as if she's disagreeing with something that crossed her mind.

"Okay look," she starts. "I made you something, but if you don't like it you don't have to wear it. I just thought it would be useful. But if you don't—"

"Give it to me," I say, holding my hand out toward her.

She places the velvet bag in my palm. I quickly pull the drawstring and turn the bag over. The beaded bracelet falls out. It's made up of mostly black round beads with four different color stones in the center.

"The onyx," she says, pointing to the black stones. "Not only represents your favorite color, but also helps soothe anxiety and stress. I thought that could be useful for when you're out doing your thing."

She shrugs as if the gesture is no big deal. However, I can barely take my eyes off the piece. The design is simple, but it's perfect for me. More importantly, she took the time to make it for me.

"What about this one?" I ask pointing to the aqua colored bead.

"That's fluorite. Your son picked it out. It's for protection. He said that all superheroes need protection."

I like the way she smiles any time she talks about Gabe. It's different from all her other smiles. Her eyes light up in a way that is more than just happiness.

"The sodalite," she continues pointing to the dark blue stone, "Is for mental clarity. I picked it out for when that bitch starts talking too much."

She chuckles, causing me to smile too.

"The pink one," She goes on to say. "Is rose quartz. It's for calming and umm….friendship."

When I look down at her, she's looking at me. I don't understand the look in her eyes or why she paused. I feel as if she's waiting for me to say something, but I don't know what. I wreck my brain trying to find the emotion in my memory rolodex. The closest I get is expectation. But before I can respond, the moment has passed. She looks back down at the bracelet.

"The ruby I added to represent Gabe," she says. "It's his birthstone. This way no matter where you are you will have him with you."

My brothers and Priest have given me many gifts. They never miss a birthday or Christmas. But nothing they have ever given me has compared to this.

"Thank you," I say placing the bracelet back in the bag and holding it back out to her.

She looks confused.

"It's not finished yet," I explain. "I need you to add one more bead to it."

"Oh," she blinks. "What do you want?"

"Add a birthstone for June."

Her face flushes and a huge smile brightens her eyes. She takes the bag back and places it on the table.

"I'll have it ready for you by tomorrow."

I nod my head. "Thank you."

"You're very welcome."

She tucks her legs up on the sofa and then pulls the cover down off the back of the couch. She places it over her legs and half on mine. After picking up the remote she starts surfing through the channels. I try my best not to touch her.

She finally settles on a show. It starts with an instrumental beat and what looks like a 3D version of a map.

Summer places the remote down on her lap. She then grabs my arm and puts it behind her head leaning into my side.

"Relax, Gabriel, I don't bite." She smiles up at me, her freckles making her beautiful face stand out. I crave to touch them. To run my finger along the dark spots.

The first night we met she wore make-up. It wasn't until later, as the makeup wore off, that I got to see the smattering of freckles.

"What are we watching?" I ask to distract myself.

"Game of thrones. I heard it's really good. Plus, it has a lot of killing, so I'm sure you'll enjoy it."

She glances up at me and sticks out her tongue before turning back to the screen. Despite having so many more things I could be doing right now, I lean my head back on the couch and watch five episodes of a fantasy show with Summer. For the first time in forever, I felt normal.

CHAPTER TWENTY-FIVE

Hide And Seek

Summer

The last two days have been interesting. Every day, Gabriel goes with me to take Gabe to school. If I have an errand to run, he goes with me. If not, I drop him back off at home while I go to class.

He then spends an hour or two with Gabe after school before leaving for the night to do his thing. Then, at about one or two in the morning he comes home, and we watch an episode or two of Game of Thrones.

If I'm not careful, I'll get used to this. I have to remind myself that this is temporary, no matter how nice it feels to have him here, it won't last forever.

I finish flipping the last pancake in the pan, before turning the stove off. Today is an easy day. Gabe is out of school, and I don't have any classes. My plans are to make a big breakfast and then maybe watch some movies and hang out together.

My phone pings alerting me of a text. I smile as I check it. Andrew and I have been texting and talking to each other for three days now.

We had lunch together yesterday and it was nice. He's sweet and charming, and with him I can ignore that feeling that I'm missing something. Admittedly the feeling is still there, but he makes it easy to ignore.

Andrew: Good morning, beautiful. How's your day so far?

Me: Great. How about yours?

Andrew: Busy. But that's normal.

Me: LOL! That sucks.

Andrew: Well, I'll let you go. I just wanted to hear from you this morning.

Even though I can't see my smile, I can feel the way my cheeks are lifted. I imagine my teeth are all on display.

"Why are you smiling?"

I nearly toss my phone across the room he scares me so bad. I spin around and he's so close to me his body heat makes me feel flushed.

"Jeez, Gabriel. You scared the shit out of me," I place my hand over my rapidly beating heart.

"How did he get your number?"

His question catches me off guard. My initial response to answer him shrivels up on my tongue. I look him over. His eyes are narrowed and the seafoam color is a dark green now.

"I gave it to him," I explain. "That's how dating works."

"Dating?"

"Yes, I'm a single woman and he's a single man and we decided to date."

Gabriel watches me intently; I can't determine what's going through his mind. He stares at me so long I start to worry if his mother is going to make an appearance. However, he blinks and takes a step back.

Once he puts space between us I remember what I was doing before Andrew texted me. I turn around and grab the large serving tray off the counter before turning back to face Gabriel.

"Surprise," I say. He looks down at the tray in my hands and frowns.

"They probably aren't as good as the place you went, but mine have chocolate chips in them and they're gluten free."

I wait for a reaction, but he continues to glare down at the tray.

"Pancakes," Gabe cheers as he walks into the kitchen grabbing our attention. He pulls a chair out at the table and takes a seat. I move around Gabriel and place the pancakes down on the center of the table.

Gabriel's eyes rake over the placement in front of him and then over to the glass sliding door leading out to the backyard. I have no idea what's going through his head. His hands are clenched at his side. He almost looks angry about the gesture. Maybe I read it wrong and this brings back sad memories.

"If you don't want them I can—"

"Thank you," he finally says, cutting me off.

He's silent again. He stares at me for a long moment as if he wants to say something else but doesn't.

"Well, let's eat," I say, cutting through the awkwardness.

Gabriel takes a seat. I grab the bacon out of the oven and plate it before joining the two at the breakfast table. I help Gabe place his food on his plate and cut it up for him.

Gabe's giggles have me looking over to Gabriel. He has the plate slid close to him, one hand covering the plate and with the other he's shoveling food in his mouth.

I forgot about his prison style of eating.

"Hulk, slow down," Gabe says with laughter in his voice.

Gabriel looks up as if for a moment he forgot where he was. He looks over to a smiling Gabe and then to me. His ears turn red as he grimaces.

"Sorry," he says.

"No need to apologize," I hold up my hand. "Eat the way you want. Right, Gabe?" I turn to my son.

"Right," Gabe grabs his fork, places one hand over his plate, haunches his back, and sticks a big bite of pancakes in his mouth.

I cover my laugh as my son imitates his father's eating habits. When Gabe gets a little too excited and starts to choke on a pancake. I pat his back until he stops coughing.

"Are you okay?"

"Yes."

"Drink something," I say with a chuckle as I hand him his cup. "You can't do everything Hulk does. He has a bigger mouth than you," I say jokingly.

Gabe's eyes fall to the table. "But I want to be like Hulk."

"Gabe you can't—"

"Show me how you eat," Gabriel says cutting me off. I look across the table to him and he's watching Gabe.

Gabe picks up a triangle shaped pancake on his fork and places it in his mouth, taking his time to chew it. Gabriel copies him, doing the exact same thing.

"Now, you're eating like Hulk."

Gabe smiles proudly as he continues to eat his pancake with his father copying him. My heart melts, my nipples harden, and my pussy does that little gripping thing like it's trying to hug something that isn't there.

Gabriel is already stunning, but nothing can get my panties wet faster than seeing him bond with his son. Even when I came up with the idea to have him spend time with Gabe, I didn't expect this outcome. But watching him change the way he eats to share a moment with Gabe has me ready to throw all caution and common sense to the wayside and ask him to stay. Thankfully, I know better than that.

We finished our breakfast. Gabe entertained us with all the history of his favorite Marvel Characters.

I grab the plates off the table but get stopped when Gabriel takes them from me. I look up into his eyes.

"I'll do it," he says piling the rest of the dirty dishes in his hand and carrying them over to the sink.

Gabe runs off toward his room, leaving me alone with Gabriel. I walk over to the sink beside him.

"I'll help." I announce before opening the dishwasher.

As Gabriel rinses the dishes I place them in the dishwasher. We work in silence for a moment before I break it.

"If you keep this up, I might not let you leave," I say jokingly.

Gabriel turns to me but continues washing the dishes. You never realize how huge he is until you're standing beside him, and he dwarfs you and takes up most of the space.

He lifts a brow. "Keep what up?"

"Helping me around the house, bonding with Gabe," I explain. "I may hide that little black duffle bag when it's time for you to go."

His lips lift in that minute way of his. He hands me the last plate. I place it in the dishwasher.

"I can always buy another black duffle."

I cut my eyes over to him and roll them. "You know what I mean, smartass."

He turns off the faucet, wipes his hands, and turns to face me. He runs a finger over the bridge of my nose to my cheek. I'm assuming following the grouping of my freckles.

"You don't want me to stay, Summer."

"Oh really. And why is that?" I ask folding my arms across my chest.

"Because if I stayed, Gabe would be the only male other than myself that would be allowed to put a smile on your face without facing the consequences."

My mouth falls open at his threat. Wait a minute, is Gabriel jealous? I mull that over in my head. The man that is adamant about leaving. The guy that never reached out the entire time he was locked up. There is no way he's jealous. Even the thought of it seems silly.

I close my mouth and roll my eyes. "Ha Ha. Whatever, Gabriel," I say taking his comment as the joke I'm sure it is.

Before he can say anything else, my phone goes off.

I turn away from him, drying my hands on the dishtowel, I answer the call.

"Hello?"

"Hello, Ms. Jones. This is Professor Aiken, I was wondering if you still planned to meet with me this morning about your final paper."

I smack my hand to my forehead. No way I forgot about this meeting. I pull the phone from my ear to look at the time before placing it back.

"Oh my goodness, Professor. I am so sorry. I completely forgot."

"It's alright. You're in luck. I don't have anyone coming in for the next hour or so. If you can still make it I'll be here."

"Yes, give me twenty minutes."

"See you then."

I hang up with the professor.

"What's wrong?" Gabriel asks, his brow pinching.

"I completely forgot about my meeting this morning. I can't miss this. It's my final paper before graduation." I rush out of the kitchen into the mudroom to grab my shoes and purse. "I'll be back in an hour."

"What about Gabe?"

"Shit," I groan, running a hand through my braids. "It will take too long to take him to Trina's. And he can't go with me. He will be bored out of his mind. Wait," I say as the idea hits me. "You can watch him."

"No." He turns around and heads back toward the kitchen. I follow behind him.

"Gabriel, please. I need your help. I won't be gone long."

He turns to face me pulling up short. He starts pacing in front of me. I know his thoughts are probably getting the best of him at the moment.

"I can't. What if something happens? What if I hurt him?" He pulls at his hair.

Gently, I place a hand on his arm. He stops pacing and gazes down at me with real fear in his eyes.

"You'll be fine. Your son is not a piece of China. Just ask him what he wants to do and hang out with him. I'll be back as soon as I can." I can still see the hesitation on his face. I play my last card.

"Please, Gabriel. I need you."

He stares down at me for a moment, making me think he may not agree to this. But eventually he nods his head.

"Thank you," I say exhaling in relief. "Gabe," I call for my son and he comes rushing down the stairs.

I kneel down in front of him. "I have to go handle some business. Hulk will stay with you. Be on your best behavior and remember to…"

"Use my words," he finishes my statement.

"Good. I'll be back."

Standing up straight, I give one more glance to Gabriel before grabbing my purse and rushing out. There is no way this can go bad.

It took less than forty-five minutes to sit down with my professor. Other than some minor notes on style and a little more detail, my paper is good to go. I rush back to my car. I wasn't worried that Gabriel would hurt Gabe, but I also respected him enough to know that this is new and out of his norm. I didn't want to push him too far.

As I approach my car, I notice two men standing near it. They aren't threatening or anything. They were only talking. One was sitting in the driver's side in car beside me, and the other guy was leaning against my passenger door. Behind my car was a large pickup truck blocking me in.

I continue to my car, assuming they will see me and move. The one leaning on my car with the baseball cap looks at me before standing up straight.

Climbing in the driver seat, I wait for him to move his truck. When neither of the men move toward the pickup, I realize maybe the vehicle doesn't belong to either of them.

I get back out my car. "Excuse me," I say nicely. They continue their conversation as if I haven't said anything.

"Ummm excuse me," I say once again a little louder.

The guy with the baseball cap that was leaning against my car turns to look at me.

"Hi." I smile politely. "Do either of you know whose truck that is?"

They both look at the truck as if just seeing it.

"It's mine," baseball hat says.

"Great, can you move it?"

"Yeah, in a minute." He turns back to the other guy and picks their conversation back up as if I'm not standing here.

"Well, you see," I say, regaining their attention. "I have somewhere to be. So, I need you to move it now."

Baseball hat chuckles before turning back to his conversation. Oh hell no.

"Maybe you didn't understand me," I try one more time to be nice before I lose my cool.

"Look bitch," baseball hat sneers as he turns back to me. "Sit the fuck down and wait until I finish talking."

"Bitch?" I repeat. "I got your bitch," I say as I pull my braids up into a ponytail. I may not be able to take on both of them, but this mase in my purse was going to help me even the field.

Before I could go for my mase, a man steps in between us. I've never seen him before. He's tall. Not as tall as Gabriel, but taller than average. He's trim but built like an athlete. He is wearing a long sleeve white button up, but the sleeves are rolled up to his elbows.

On one arm from his fingers all the way up to where the shirt started, are tally mark tattoos. There has to be at least two hundred of the groups of five. He has dark brown hair, a jaw line that could cut diamonds, a slight beard, and a roman nose that looks as if it's been broken a few times. I wished I could have seen his eyes, but they were covered in dark shades.

"Are you alright?" he asks, in an accented voice.

"Yeah," I say, caught off guard by his sudden appearance and his voice.

"This has nothing to do with you," baseball hat says.

Tattoo guy turns to the side to look at the two guys.

"I think she asked you to move your car," he says in that deep accent.

The two assholes laugh. "And like I told her, I'll move it when I get good and damn—"

His words are cut off when tattoo guy shoves his elbow into his nose and then rams him, headfirst, into the side of his friend's window. The glass shatters raining down everywhere. When he lets the baseball hat guy go, he slides to the ground in a slump.

"A woman," he says, running his tattooed hand through his hair. "Should never have to ask you to do anything more than once. Now move the fucking truck."

The other guy quickly climbs out of his car, bends down and grabs the keys off his unconscious friend. He then quickly runs to the truck and moves it. I'm still stuck in the same spot.

There is only one other person that I've ever seen move that quickly and that's Gabriel.

"Thank you," I say to the stranger.

He dips his chin at me. "You are very welcome. Now, hurry home."

I don't argue with him. I quickly get in the car and back out of the parking space. Tattoo guy watches me the entire time, never taking his eyes off me. I didn't necessarily get a bad vibe from him or that he was dangerous. I mean, if he was going to hurt me he had ample opportunity. He was actually nice. I was still going to mention the situation to Gabriel just in case.

My car speaker rings when I'm nearly five minutes from home. I answer the call using my steering wheel.

"Hello?"

"What do you think about plays?" Andrew asks as soon as I answer the phone.

"Don't have much to say. I've never seen one. Well, with the exception of those Madea ones I use to watch on bootleg."

Andrew laughs. I notice that as nice as his laugh is, it holds nothing to the way Gabriel's makes me feel.

"What do you think about you and me catching a show this weekend?"

I smile as I turn the corner onto my street. "Yeah. I'd like that."

A male voice is heard in the background of the call. "Hey, Summer," Andrew says. "I have to go. But I'll send you the information for the date later."

"Sounds good. Bye Andrew."

"Goodbye, Summer."

He disconnects the call. I pull into the driveway of my home and let out a deep breath. At least it's still standing. So, it couldn't have gone too bad. Grabbing my purse and laptop bag off the passenger seat, I head into the house.

"Guys I'm home."

I spot Gabriel in the kitchen pacing. His hands are in his hair yanking at the strands so hard I fear he will pull them out. As I walk up on him his yanking turns into him hitting the side of his head.

"Gabriel," I call his name as I approach him. Yet, he seems miles away.

"I'm sorry, Mother. I didn't mean to." He says.

My heart sinks to my feet.

"Gabe," I use the nickname for him that I usually only use for my son. His seafoam green eyes turn to me and there is fear and sadness mixed in. "What's going on?"

"I lost him."

Panic has my heart racing so fast I feel lightheaded. I place my hand on the back of the nearest kitchen chair to keep myself upright.

"Tell me everything that happened."

He starts pacing again, his hands clutched in tight fists at his side. "Everything was going fine. We played outside for a while. Then he asked to play hide and seek and I…"

He stops talking when I start laughing. Relief floods me like fresh rainwater falling after a drought.

"What's funny?"

"He's not lost, Gabriel. He's hiding."

He shakes his head. "No. I've told him to come out. I told him that he won. I lost him."

Turning away from Gabriel, I walk toward the stairs. "Gabe, Hulk said you won. No take backs. You are officially the winner."

His laughter can be heard upstairs somewhere. Gabriel's eyes widen.

"Your son is one hell of a hide and seek player. He used to play with my nephew. Whenever he couldn't be found my nephew would tell him he gave up and as soon as Gabe would come out of hiding, my nephew would tag him and say he found him. It drove Gabe crazy. Now, he will only come out if you swear there are no take backs."

"I thought I lost him," he says in disbelief as if he still doesn't quite believe me.

I pat him on the shoulder. "Welcome to the parenting club. You can't officially call yourself a parent if you haven't had a mini heart attack thinking you lost your child. I had my first one in Walmart when he was two. It took me three minutes to find him. The longest three minutes of my life."

The sound of Gabe's feet running down the stairs has us turning toward him. He stops right in front of Gabriel with a huge grin on his face.

"I won, Hulk."

"You sure did, Kid. You out hid the incredible Hulk," I say, glancing up to Gabriel. He looks ten times better than what he did when I first walked in. Not totally relaxed, but not as stiff.

"Well done, Gabe." Gabriel dips his chin to his chest.

"Again?" Gabe asks hopefully.

"What do you say, Hulk? Want to get your ass handed to you in hide and seek?"

Gabriel stares down at the both of us. I'm pretty sure he's telling himself all the things he has to do today. There's probably some tips he needs to follow and a person he has to kill. But, instead of telling us no and that he had something to do, he turns his back and starts counting.

"One, one thousand…"

"Come on, Gabe." I grab my son's hand and rush out of the kitchen to hide.

For the rest of the day, I spent my time with Gabe and Gabriel. We played games, watched movies, and ate every meal together at my table. Everything else from the day skipped my mind.

I'm on a high. Although, I know it's a false high. I've experienced many of those during my drug use stage. It's that fake euphoric feeling as if you are floating above the clouds. Eventually, I will plummet back to earth. And even though I know this, I still allow myself to float.

CHAPTER TWENTY-SEVEN

The Cheater

Beast

It wasn't supposed to be this way. From his laughter to her smile, I can't get them out of my head.

This ache in my chest whenever I'm not near them was never meant to happen. I wasn't even planning on seeing them. Yet, every time I'm outside of the house I fight myself not to go back.

"You will mess it up," Mother reminds me in my head.

I shut my eyes as the reminder settles in my chest. My hand tightens on the steering wheel causing the leather of my gloves to squeak.

The moan in the back seat brings me out of my head. I glance in the rear-view mirror and adjust it so that I can see my passenger.

The next stop I made the night I met Summer was at the diner. Despite what the benefactor thinks, I did take some precautions that night. The diner didn't have a camera system, but the place across from it did. I deleted the footage of me and Summer walking in and out the restaurant that night. The only other place I had to delete footage from was the shop I bought the shoes and scarf from.

However, even though I deleted the footage of the diner, I didn't need it to track down everyone that was there that night. Apparently after we left, Henry Parks, the owner and cook from that night, called the police. The police took the statements of everyone there along with their name and information.

That's how I found Cody Hampton. The cheater from the diner.

He groans from the back seat of the car. The sedative I gave him is wearing off.

I found him out to eat with another woman that wasn't his wife. After cutting all the cameras in and around the restaurant, I slipped a pill in his whiskey sour before the waiter brought it to the table.

When he stumbled into the bathroom about fifteen minutes later, I snuck him out the back door and into my borrowed car. All without anyone noticing.

I pull the sedan into the garage at my apartment building. After turning off the car and hopping out of the driver's seat, I go around to the back door and lift him out. He puts up a weak fight.

Tossing him over my shoulder in a fireman carry, I walk into my kill room. Leaning him up against the wall, I chain his arms and legs to the cuffs bolted into the cement.

His head rolls around his shoulders, the dosage of meds I gave him were light. I made sure he would be awake for this part. When he looks up at me, he seems to focus a little.

"Who are you?"

I don't answer. Instead, I go over to my shelves and grab my tools for the night. A framing nail gun, a meat cleaver, a blow torch, a box of 16 gauge 1 ½ inch nails, and an ice pick. Once I'm done gathering my supplies. I roll the cart over toward Cody.

"Hey, do you hear me talking to you? Who the fuck are you?"

Once my cart is in place, I grab a metal folding chair on the other side of the room and carry it back to Cody.

"Wait," he says, when I'm in front of him again. "I know you. I've seen you before. The night at the diner. It was you."

"*The adulterer remembers you,*" Mother says. "*The good book says the adulterer should be put to death.*"

Unfolding the chair, I place it down and then take a seat. I still haven't responded to his questions. My answers don't matter. He won't live past tonight.

I grab the nail gun off the cart along with the box of nails and load it up. The gun is rigged so that the safety is off. I don't have to press against anything to fire off a nail.

"What are you going to do with that?" Cody asks.

I glance up at him. His arms stretched out over his head and his legs are spread apart making him form an X shape against the wall.

I place the fully loaded nail gun down on my thigh before leaning back in my seat. I don't have to ask Cody any questions. He will tell me everything I need to know. He has no loyalty to anyone but himself. He will say and do whatever he needs to get out of this predicament. Torturing him would be pointless. I don't need to make him bleed to talk to me.

"Is this about what I told that Russian guy with the tattoos?"

See what I mean?

"Look, I only told him that I saw you in the diner. That's it."

"Did you mention the girl?"

His brow lifts. "You mean the strung-out prostitute?"

I hit the trigger of the gun, and a nail shoots out and hits him right in the thigh. He yells, tossing his head back as spittle flies out of his mouth.

"What the fuck is wrong with you?" He cries. His face is bright red.

"Did you mention the girl?" I ask again.

It takes him a minute to fight through his pain. His teeth are clenched and bared as he breathes through his nose.

"Did you mention—"

"Yes. Fuck. Yes, I mentioned the fucking girl." His anger quickly turns into tears. "I'm sorry." He sobs.

I didn't care for his apologies or his tears.

"What else did you tell him?"

"That's it. I didn't tell him anything else."

"He's lying, kid. I know you can read that bullshit from here," Priest whispers in my thoughts.

I send another nail into his arm. He once again lets out a deafening scream. I send two more out, back-to-back, hitting his shin and his thigh again. He rattles the chains as his body thrashes against the pain.

The second nail in his thigh seems to be bleeding profusely. I lay the nail gun down and stand to my feet before grabbing the blow torch. After turning it on, I put the blue flame to the nail hole.

Cody screams so loud it rings my ears making it uncomfortable. Once I was sure I had stopped the bleeding, I place the torch back down on the cart.

"You lied to me."

Cody's head lulls around his shoulders, his body is limp against the chains holding him up. However, I know he isn't dead.

"What else did you tell him?"

"I told him about the guys that came into the diner and how you protected her." The words fall from his lips slowly. His energy is waning.

"He's weak and an adulterer. He won't last long. Do what you are called to do," Mother says impatiently.

"What did the Russian look like?"

It takes him a moment to get the energy to answer me. "Tall. Tally mark tattoos on his arm. That's all I know."

I don't believe him. "Nothing else stood out? What was he wearing, what color were his hair and eyes?" All details mattered. Anything about the benefactor could lead me to finding him.

"I don't know," Cody shouts as saliva dribbles down his chin.

I allow a minute for his tantrum to pass before speaking again.

"I have over four thousand of these nails and nothing else to do." I prop the nail gun up on my knee aiming it at his crotch. "If I were you, I'd start remembering."

"Okay. Alright," he cries. "His hair was dark, almost black."

"What was he wearing? What color were his eyes?"

"He was wearing a white button up and dress pants. I don't know the color of his eyes because he wore shades. Now please let me go."

Once again, I'm reminded of how close the benefactor got to Summer and Gabe. Even after questioning two people, I still don't have any real way to pick him out in a crowd. But I can't be mad at anyone but myself. I allowed someone to get this close. It's because of me that he was able to get the information that he did. The thought sends fury through me causing that red haze to rise up in my mind like fire.

"Cleanse him of his sins. Send his soul to hell." I allow Mother's words to guide me.

Walking over to Cody, I hold the gun directly in front of his right eye.

"Please," he pleads. "Don't do this. I'm sorry," he begs and cries.

It's no use, Mother has me now. There is no remorse nor sympathy when she takes control.

"Feed," she whispers. I pull the trigger.

Hours passed before mother was sated and the red haze lifted. By the time I'm finished, Cody is unrecognizable. Instead of incinerating his remains, I dump him where he will be found. I need the benefactor to know I'm cleaning up and getting closer to him. My hope is that it lures him out of hiding. I shower in my small apartment near the house before heading back to Summer's.

As I push the back sliding glass door open, my heart races in my chest. Excitement. That's what my studies tell me the feeling is.

I drop my bag near the back door and head into the living room where the television is giving off a dim light. Only, I don't walk in on a smiling

Summer that's making sure I'm not coming back still in the midst of my haze. No, I stumble onto a sleeping Summer, tucked in my black hoodie.

My shoulders slump at the sight of her sleeping. However, my heart still races knowing that she tried to wait up for me.

I pick up the remote and cut the tv off, before turning to the couch. I lift her up in my arms. She turns toward my chest and buries her face in my neck.

Even though she has gained more weight since the last time I saw her, she is still so light and frail in my arms.

"You're going to break her. The whore is too fragile," Mother warns.

I ignore her words as I carry Summer up the stairs to her bedroom. I kick the door open with the toe of my boots and use my elbow to turn on the light. I then carry her over to the bed. After pulling the covers back, I place her down gently.

"You're late," she says in a groggy voice.

"I got a little caught up tonight."

She cracks one eye open and looks me over. "You meant you were having too much fun."

A smile tugs at the corner of my mouth. "Maybe."

She slides back and lifts the covers. "Lay with me."

Immediately the relaxed state I was in disappears and my body stiffens.

"Fornication is a sin," Mother warns. *"You will burn in hell."*

"I don't think that's a good idea," I tell Summer.

"Oh, okay," she says, lowering the blanket. Her face falls a little. "I understand."

"Kid, if you don't get your ass in that bed, I swear I will beat the shit out of you," Priest growls.

Sitting on the side of the bed, I untie my boots and pull them off. I then undo my pants and kick out of them. Next comes my zip up hoodie. I fold my clothes and place them—along with my boots—in the chair beside the bed. I'm left in nothing but my boxers and shirt.

I walk over to the door and turn the light off before making my way back to the bed. Lifting the covers, I slide in beside her. The smile on her face is worth every bit of restraint I will need to endure this without touching her. I lift her up and flip her over me to the other side of the bed.

"What was that for," she asks with a giggle.

"I have to be able to see the door," I explain.

I hope my odd ways don't make her change her mind about lying with me. Trying to sit with my back facing a door is the equivalent to having my skin peeled off.

"Makes sense," she says before moving in closer to me placing her head on the pillow designated for me. Her warm breath brushes against my face. Her cold feet wrap around my legs.

"You're so warm," she coos as she tosses an arm over my side.

"And your feet are like ice blocks."

She laughs. "We make a perfect pair. I'm cold and you're hot."

I don't comment on that. Instead, I relax into the darkness of the room. Finding solace in the gentle sound of her breathing.

"Can I ask you something?" Her voice is light, hesitant almost.

"Yes."

She pauses for a moment before she speaks again. "When you were away for those five years, did you... you know?"

I rack my brain trying to figure out what I'm supposed to know. Is she asking if I killed during our time away? I did. I didn't know I wasn't supposed to. I've always known she didn't like what I did, but I didn't realize she never wanted me to do it.

"Did you not want me too?"

She sighs. "I mean, I guess that would be absurd, right?" she chuckles but it isn't like her usual laughs. "Five years is a long time to wait."

"It's hard to refrain from it, Summer."

She gasps leaning up. I immediately miss her warmth. "Yeah, but I thought I was special."

The sadness in her voice bothers me. It has the same effect that not facing a door does.

"No matter how important you are, I can't hold back. It's part of my job."

She's quiet for a moment. My sight has adjusted to the dark so I can just make out the confused way her brows are dipped.

"What are you talking about?" She asks.

"Killing. What are *you* talking about?"

Because now I have this odd inkling that I did not make the right assumption about what I was supposed to know. Her boisterous laughter makes me believe I am correct in my musings.

"Sex, Gabriel. I'm asking you if you've slept with someone else since we were together?"

This time I frown. Why would she want to know if I've slept with someone else.

"No. I haven't been with anyone."

Her laughter dies down and she goes back to lying peacefully beside me.

"So, you just didn't think about it at all?" She asks once she's regained her position.

"I thought about it."

I don't tell her how much I thought about it. How it kept me sane when those walls started to cave in on me. I don't tell her that I closed my eyes and imagined her scent, her moans, the tightness of her pussy and the warm wet heat it emitted. I don't confess to those things.

"Well, what kept you from doing it? I mean, other than the whole mom in your head thing, you're a great catch for anyone."

I smile at her joke and at the fact that she thinks I'm a catch.

"They don't usually let prisoners make nunnery requests and all my guards were men."

"Oh so you did not succumb to the 'any hole will do' thing?" She laughs, but I have no idea what she's talking about.

"What about you?" I ask and her laughter immediately dies down.

"I thought about it."

"Is that why you have a drawer full of penis shaped silicone toys?"

She lifts up and hits me on the chest. "Gabriel, are you snooping in my room."

"Yes," I confirm, grabbing her and pulling her back down in front of me. She snuggles into me more.

"I'm going to start locking my door."

I don't tell her that it wouldn't make a difference. After studying Priest for so long I can break into any lock she could put on her door.

However, it does lead me to ask another question. "Are the penises in your drawer the only ones you've used?"

She snorts, and her body shakes with her laughter. "Real smooth."

I wait for her to finish laughing to answer my question.

"If I tell you that they aren't, would you be mad?"

I think over her words for a moment. I have no ownership of Summers's body. When I left her that night, I left her with no promises of commitment or agreements of fidelity. She had every right in the five years we were apart to take on another partner.

"No," I say confidently. "But just for my research, I need their names and addresses."

She tosses her head back and laughs as if I was telling a joke. I'm not. I did not require her to be faithful to me in our time apart. However, it does not mean that I will allow another man to live after he has shared the heaven that is between Summer's legs.

Not even Andrew gets a pass. As much as I hate the idea of her dating him, I can't argue. She's right, she is single. But the day he touches her body will be his last. I'm understanding of her feelings and need to date, but not that fucking understanding.

"You know what," she says cuddling back into me. "I'm not even sure if you're joking. But you can relax. There wasn't anyone else."

My body softens. I didn't even realize I had gotten tense.

"Hard to believe. If not for your horribly timed humor, you'd be a catch."

She punches me in the stomach. "You get on my nerves." She laughs before it turns into a big yawn.

I grab her hand and place it back over my side before placing my hand over hers.

"Go to sleep, Summer."

She buries her face in my chest, sliding her body even closer to me.

"Goodnight, Gabriel. And don't be trying to take advantage of me while I'm sleep," she says jokingly.

"If I remember correctly, you took advantage of me that night."

Once again, she tosses her head back and laughs.

For the first night ever, I slept peacefully in a bed.

CHAPTER TWENTY-SEVEN

Too Close

Beast

"Throw it, Hulk. Throw it."

Summer needed to run some packages to the post office and once again left me at home with Gabe. Spending time alone with him is starting to be less terrifying.

I toss the football across the yard. It flies through the air and falls between Gabe's outstretched arms and on the ground at his feet. He bends down and picks it up and runs it into the imaginary endzone.

I'm not a fan of football. I never played it and didn't watch it growing up. Until I met my son, I knew nothing of the sport. But the only thing Gabe seems to like other than Marvel characters, is tossing a football. So, I researched all I could about the sport.

"Good job," I tell him when he rushes back over to me and hands me the football. "Remember, you want to position your body toward the football, and keep your arms together when you go to catch it, okay?"

"Okay," he says nodding.

"Alright, go deep," I tell him.

He runs off, and I once again throw him the ball. This time, it falls right in his arms. The catch seems to shock him. His eyes widen before a huge smile breaks across his face. Gabe is the spitting image of me. Other than his dark skin and curly hair he has my entire face. Only when he smiles, or laughs do you see Summer in him.

He runs back toward me.

"I caught it." He says proudly.

"You did." A warmth spreads throughout my chest. I wonder is this how Priest felt when we accomplished things.

Often times he would stare at us with a grin on his face when we did something correctly or faced something new. Spending so much time with Gabe has me thinking about Priest a lot lately. I miss him and my brothers, but I'm doing all this for them.

"Want to try again?" I ask Gabe, taking my mind off my family.

He nods his head. At that moment, a bee flies between us. Gabe shrinks away from it. When it flies closer to him, he shouts and runs around me.

"Help, Hulk! Help!"

I grab Gabe's shoulder before kneeling in front of him. His eyes are on the circling bee.

"Look at me," I tell him.

He cuts his eyes to me, but constantly glances at the bee.

"Don't be afraid."

"It's going to sting me." He starts to groan louder and louder. Eventually he holds his hand up near his face and flicks his thumb and his pointer finger together.

The action causes a pain in my chest. When I was a kid, I'd pull my hair out when things got overwhelming. Mother would usually mark my skin with her belt whenever I did. Until she started to shave off my hair to keep me from doing it.

"Look at me," I wait until his gaze focuses on me. "The bee might sting you, but not if you calm down. It's more scared of you than you are of it. If you run and panic, it will chase you and may even sting you."

He looks over to the bee and then back to me. His hand lowering back to his side.

"Take a deep breath and still your racing heart." I place my palm to his chest. His little heartbeat is pounding under my hand. "It's okay to be afraid, but there is a strength and a power in facing what makes you scared. When you show fear, you give something else that power."

The bee buzzes around before landing on Gabe's shoulder. His heart rate picks up.

"Keep your eyes on me and breathe through it. Don't show it your fear."

He takes a deep calming breath, keeping his eyes on me. His heart rate slowly lowers. Soon the bee flies away leaving him unscathed.

"See. There was nothing to be afraid of. Sometimes, in order to conquer your fear, you have to face it. My father taught me that."

I repeat the words Priest told me when I was seven years old fighting my unseen demons.

Gabe drops his head and lowers his shoulders. "I don't have a father. That's why I'm such a punk."

I place a finger under his chin and lift his eyes to me. "Don't ever call yourself that."

"That's what Uncle Mitchell and MJ call me because sometimes I cry when I can't figure out my emotions. Uncle Mitchell says if I had a daddy I wouldn't be such a pussy."

I shut my eyes as I tamp down my anger.

"Split their skulls and let their brains spill onto the pavement. You allowed cowards around your son."

"I'm with the crazy bitch on this one," Priest adds.

Shaking off my thoughts and desire to kill, I open my eyes to find Gabe watching me.

"Showing fear or emotion does not make you a punk. Just like bottling up your emotions and denying your fear doesn't make you a man. Everybody fears something."

"Are you afraid of anything?"

I nod my head. "Yes."

"What?" his little brows pinch.

"I fear myself. I fear that one day, I'll get lost to the things inside my head and no matter what anyone does, I'll never come back from it." I imagine that was pretty deep to lay on a child, but I will never lie to my son.

Gabe smiles and places a hand on my shoulder. "Don't worry, Hulk. I'll always bring you back. Me and Mama."

My chest seems to expand with each breath I take, and I'm forced to swallow to relieve the sudden dryness of my mouth.

"If anyone can do it, it's you and your mom." I ruffle the curls on top of his head before standing up straight. "Alright. Want to go long again…." My words trail off when the wind blows the smell of stale cigarette smoke through my nostrils. Just as soon as the scent captures my attention, a twig snaps in the trees behind the house.

My hands fist at my side, yet I don't turn in the direction of the sound. If I acknowledge it, whoever it is will either run or attack. I bend back down to get eye to eye with Gabe again.

"Let's play hide and seek," I tell him. His hazel eyes light up with excitement. "Go inside and hide and remember don't come out until I find you or I declare you the winner."

He nods his head and then takes off running.

"One, one thousand," I start counting until he's fully inside the house.

The moment Gabe is out of view I turn to the trees. It takes only a second for the person hiding there to step out. Shade, a deacon from the church, that specializes in guns and is known for his tracking skills comes into the yard.

"You alone?" I ask, even though I already know the answer. The Church isn't known for group projects. Outside me and my brothers, most Deacon's work alone.

"Yeah, I'm alone." Shade says hopping over the fence, his gun aimed at my head.

I don't make any sudden moves because he's a sure shot. There is only one person that can handle a gun better than Shade, and that is my brother Hawk.

"But at any time, all I have to do is hit this button on my phone," he holds up the phone. "And this house is swarmed with Church members. I don't think we want that do we?"

"No," I say, keeping him in my sights.

He moves in closer feeling more confident. "Let's not make this hard then. All they want is for you to come back. If you come with me peacefully, I won't tell them about your little mini me in there." He tilts his head toward the house. He moves in even closer.

I lift my hands up in a posture of surrender. Shade watches me wearily, he's debating if it's really going to be that easy.

The first thing I learned while in the Church is that competition is encouraged amongst the Deacons. They thrive off being better than the next man. Priest never stood for that. He taught us that a diamond will shine no matter where it is. As long as we did our job and did it well, we didn't have to worry about competing.

Shade will never miss the opportunity of being the one to bring me in. He's feeling so cocky about getting the jump on me, he doesn't realize that with our short conversation he's revealed that not only is he alone, but he also has no back up on the way. He also revealed that he knew my secret.

If he had done just the slightest bit of research on me, then he would know, I could never let him walk out of here alive with that last bit of information.

As I thought he would, he stuffs the phone in his pocket before walking over to me. He moves around me pressing the gun into my back.

"Walk," he demands.

"You shouldn't have put that phone away," I say.

"What?"

I don't answer, instead I lean to the side and reach around with my left hand shoving the gun toward the ground. It fires a round. I spin around to face him, bending his wrist with the gun in it toward his pocket. He fires once again and the bullet hits something hard and metal making a crunch sound. First threat taken care of. In no way could I allow him to alert the Church.

Shade reaches behind him, for what I assume is another gun. It would make sense. Without letting go of his right arm, I spin around him, bringing the arm I'm holding to his back. He's still clutching the gun. Taking my free hand, I shove his elbow up, popping the bone out of place, rendering the appendage useless.

Shade howls in pain and drops the gun in his right hand. He swings around aiming the newest weapon at my head. I move to the side a split second too slow and the bullet grazes my ear.

I grab his arm with the new gun, pushing it out in the opposite direction. I slam my head into his nose. Blood squirts out everywhere. I then chop him in the throat. When he bends down, I use the momentum to flip him over onto the ground landing on top of him. As he's falling, I reach for the bowie in my ankle holster. It was a gift from Seth.

He lifts his arm up to aim his gun at me, I slice the bowie into his arm nearly severing the hand from the wrist. He screams, kicking me off him. I flip over his head, popping up quickly and coming to my feet.

Shade rolls over on to his knees as he cradles his bleeding appendage to his chest.

I toss my knife into my other hand and smile. Shade growls, springs to his feet, and then rushes toward me. I spin out of his way causing him to run past me, I grab him by the back of the neck, yank him back, and then shove the blade of my bowie into his back again and again. Even when his limp body falls to the ground, I don't stop stabbing him.

He thought he would threaten my son and walk free. I raise the blade over my head and bring it down over and over.

"He got too close. What if it would've been a disciple? They would've killed the boy and then taken you. You're a failure." Mother's insults are loud in my ears.

I stab down so hard; my blade goes through his skull and sticks into the ground beneath him.

"*Useless cum stain,*" she continues. "*You are worthless.*"

"They got too close. I failed." Looking down at the body beneath me is a reminder of how much I've messed up. I clutch my bloody hands to my head.

"*Failure.*" Mother taunts over and over.

"They got too close. They got too close," I repeat as I tug at the strands of my hair nearly yanking them out of my scalp.

"What in the hell?"

I shoot to my feet at the sound of Summer's voice. Turning to face her, I find her staring wide-eyed at the body on the ground.

"*Useless failure,*" Mother reiterates.

However, I don't think about how bad I messed up, my first thought is Summer. Blood and dead bodies are triggering for her.

I put a cap on my shit as I take a step in front of her blocking her view of the body.

She looks me over. When I glance down, I realize I'm covered in blood.

"It isn't mine," I quickly explain.

She shuts her eyes, her hand covering her chest.

"Where's Gabe?" She opens her eyes and looks back at me.

"*The whore knows you're a failure. She can't even trust that you kept your son safe.*" Mother snarls in my head.

"Hiding," I say, clenching my hands tightly at my side.

She lets out a breath, dropping her shoulders in relief.

"Okay, well, what happened?" she asks hesitantly.

"They came here."

She looks around me once again, her attention landing on Shade.

"Don't," I warn taking a step to the right to further block her view.

"*She wouldn't have to worry about being triggered if you were doing your job. Instead, you let the flesh lead you. Lying in her bed last night. Allowing your little cock to get hard. You are a failure.*"

I flinch at mother's words.

"Are you okay?"

It doesn't surprise me that Summer caught my reaction.

"I'm fine."

She bobs her head as if she's agreeing with me. "Is he dead?"

"Yes," I tell her.

"Is that it, are we safe now?" I don't miss the tinge of sadness in her tone.

"This guy worked for the Church. He was here to bring me in. He knew nothing of you or Gabe."

I look away from her. The guilt of how close the Church came to finding out about them has me avoiding eye contact. *They got too close.* The thought once again eats away at me.

"Okay, well we need to get you cleaned up. Your ear is bleeding." She reaches for me, but I take a step back avoiding her touch.

"Failure."

Her hand falls back by her side. "What's wrong?"

I ignore her question. "Keep Gabe inside. I'm going to call a clean-up crew to take care of this body."

"Gabriel, talk to me. What's wrong? Why are you…"

"I have to go," I say cutting her off as I turn to leave.

I don't get far before she steps in front of me. She stares into my face, her brows pinched as she studies me. I'm pretty sure she's looking for the red haze. She thinks that's why I need to leave. No, the haze hasn't hit me yet. I feel it around the edges of my mind ready to take over. However, guilt has its grip on me at the moment.

"You're running," she finally says. "You can't leave us."

"A trained member of the Church just showed up at your house. They got too close because I was busy trying to pretend to be a father."

"Pretend?" she repeats, her head moving back as if I struck her. "Your nut fertilized my egg. There is no damn pretending about it."

"You know what I mean."

"No, please enlighten me?" She folds her arms over her chest. I don't need my emotional rolodex to know that she's angry.

"You want me to be something that I'm not. You still think I'm some hero that saved you that night, but I'm not." Her arms fall to her side. She looks away, but I continue.

"Look at me." I hold my arms out at my side. "Look at what I'm capable of. This is who I am."

"It's not," she argues. "It's just who they made you. You're so much more."

I shake my head. "The Church didn't make me a killer, Summer, they trained me to be a better one."

Her brow pinches in confusion. She's still not understanding me.

"I'm not my brothers. I'm not normal and I never will be. There is something inside me that has to be fed. I'm not the hero in your story."

"I didn't ask you to be a hero," her voice catches as her eyes brim with tears.

Part of me is begging to stop. It pleads with me not to hurt her. Yet, I know I have to do this.

"Yes you do. When you ask me to lay with you at night. When you want me to watch TV with you. When you ask me to watch Gabe while you run to the post office. You want me to be something that I'm not. I have a mission, and I can't allow you and him to be a distraction."

I've never said anything that I didn't mean. Every word that ever came out of my mouth has always been true. However, watching the tears gather in her eyes and then track down her face has me resenting my words.

She turns away from me as she bites into her bottom lip. She doesn't even wipe the tears away.

"A distraction," she repeats.

I remain silent, not sure what I can say to fix this. Not even sure if I should say something.

She looks back at me, swiping at her cheeks. Her head lifted a little higher. "I'll keep Gabe occupied." She turns and walks back into the house, closing the door behind her.

"Well, that was fucking stupid, Kid. You handled that about as well as Seth handles people's feelings," Priest says finally coming forward.

"They're better off without you. Do you see the problems you cause. Because God giveth and he taketh away. You are unworthy," Mother quickly reminds me.

Pulling my phone out of my pocket, I dial the private clean-up crew.

"Hospitality," the gruff voice on the other end of the phone says.

"I have a special leak. I'm sending you the address."

"How big is the leak?" The man on the other end of the phone asks.

"One single leak."

"And what makes it special?"

"I need it rerouted."

He's silent for a moment. Usually, a cleanup crew's job is to get rid of the body and make sure no one finds it. "I'm guessing this one is a private matter?"

"Yes. To everyone," I add since all my brothers use the same cleaners.

"Be there in twenty minutes." The line goes dead.

I hide Shade in Gabe's playhouse in the backyard before taking off. I have no doubt that the cleanup crew will handle everything thoroughly. Right now, I need to release this rage. I've contained myself well while I was with Summer, but now the red haze has taken over and I need to exorcise these demons.

"Let's go have some fun," Mother coos in my head.

Using the end of my shirt I wipe the blood from my fist. My breathing is still labored and my throat hurts from yelling. It's been hours since I killed Shade but the haze has yet to leave me. I still feel the fury inside of me. I still have the urge to destroy everything. The walls of my rented apartment took the brunt of my anger.

"You're in here throwing a tantrum like a toddler," Mother fusses. *"You should be out there cleansing the world of its sin. You're a waste."*

The image of Summer's face after I called them a distraction pops up in my head again. The night before, she laid in my arms and laughed, and then today I made her look so broken. I punch my fist into the drywall in front of me, enjoying the bite of pain it caused.

When I was a kid and I would get this dark, Priest would take me to the quiet room. I would destroy everything until I was able to chase the red haze away. However, today it isn't working.

"You need to feed," Mother states the obvious. *"This isn't going to help you. Let me guide you."*

Despite the small voice of reasoning telling me that I shouldn't, I don't refuse.

"Yes, Mother."

Placing my hood over my head, I walk out of the apartment. The moment I step out the door, the older lady in the apartment beside me quickly ducks her head back inside.

"She's called the cops. Did you see the phone in her hand?" Priest asks.

This apartment is now compromised. I won't be able to come back here. The moment she called the cops and gave my description, Lucien will pick up on it and they will be here first thing tomorrow.

I know my brothers and Priest are worried about me. I would be too if one of them took missing. The least I can do is let them know I'm okay. I head back into the destroyed apartment. I have a few seconds to leave them a message.

CHAPTER TWENTY-EIGHT

Baby Daddy

Summer

Three days. I haven't heard from or seen Gabriel in three days. I admit, I was so pissed at him that first day. How dare he call us a distraction. But the longer I thought about it, I realized that to someone like Gabriel we are.

He's the type that sees a problem and solves it. Him going after the people that found us is easy for him. Killing is second nature to Gabriel. Showing emotions and caring for his son is not. He's not used to dealing with us.

So even though what he said hurt me, I'm no longer angry with him. I don't forgive him either though.

"How was it?"

I tune back to my date, looking over at him. When Andrew called and asked to take me to dinner and a show, I was excited. I'd never been to a play before. However, as excited as I was, I've been struggling to keep my thoughts anywhere but on Gabriel.

"It was really good. I loved the music." The music was the only thing I remembered from the show.

We walk side by side as we leave the theater. Once again, the father of my child comes back to my mind. As hurt as I am about our last conversation, I can't help but wonder if he's okay. Is he safe? Where is he sleeping? Is he sleeping?

Andrew's laughter cuts through my thoughts.

"Yeah, you should have seen it when the original cast performed it. It was incredible."

Come on, Summer. You have a good man right here. Get your head in the game. My inner thoughts are right. As much as I care about Gabriel, he chose to run. Right now, Andrew is here, and I should be paying attention to him.

"You go to a lot of shows?" I ask, putting all my focus on him.

He grins and it's adorable. "Yeah, I was a theater kid in high school."

"Cool, I used to buy pot from a theater kid in high school. He had some good stuff."

He laughs. "Man, I love your humor. You're so authentic."

I'm not sure what that means, but I guess it's a compliment.

"Thanks," I say.

We walk a little further chatting about random things. Suddenly I get the oddest feeling. The hairs on the back of my neck stand up. I glance over my shoulder, but no one seems to be paying attention to me. A few of the folks that caught the same show are walking behind us, but no one seems to be out of place.

"Are you okay?" Andrew asks. When I look at him, he's glancing over his shoulder too.

"Yeah, I'm good." I shake off the feeling.

"I'm not ready for the night to end," Andrew admits as we head to the Subway station.

We parked his car in a parking garage and took the train into Manhattan so we wouldn't have to worry about traffic.

"Yeah, me either. I have an idea."

"Oh really. What's that?" He smiles, pushing his glasses up on his nose.

"There's a bookstore not too far from here that has the best pastries in the city."

"Bookstore?" He looks a little surprised.

"Yep, and the owner is really nice."

The smile that slipped a little earlier comes back. "Okay, show me the bookstore."

I take him to Books and More. When we walk in, Malia is there and leaning against the counter is a handsome man with dark brown hair and tattoos. He's in a black T-shirt and dark pants. He turns to look at us when we walk in but quickly turns back to Malia. He looks identical to Malia's boyfriend, but also very different, which is weird.

He says something that makes her blush. He then leans over the counter to give her a kiss that has my toes curling. Well maybe it is her boyfriend and he's just dressed differently. Either that or Malia is fucking twin brothers and if that's the case, she deserves a medal.

The guy wipes her lips after he's done kissing her, he then turns away and walks out of the shop. He walked right by us without glancing in our direction.

"What's the best thing here?" Andrew asks, regaining my attention.

We walk up to the counter together.

"Hey, Summer," Malia says with a smile as she looks over to Andrew. "Who is this?"

"Malia, this is Andrew. He's a…. friend."

"Nice to meet you." Andrew holds out a hand to shake with Malia. She shakes his hand before turning back to me.

"Where's my baby tonight?"

"Gabe is spending the night with Trina. She wanted an excuse to go see the new Disney movie." I say playfully rolling my eyes.

Malia laughs. She's used to Trina's antics. "I have to get him over to the house to hang with Emory soon," she says.

"We can set something up at the next Sunday story time," I add.

"Great. Now what can I get for you two?"

"I was told you had the best pastries around so, I'm excited to try something," Andrew says stepping closer to me.

We ordered two apple turnovers; I got her raspberry lemonade and Andrew got tea. We then found a seat near the window.

"Are you close friends with the shop owner?" He asks as soon as I take my seat across from him.

"Kind of. I come here every Sunday, and our kids adore each other."

He nods before taking a bite out of his apple turnover. His eyes immediately shut, and he moans.

"Good, right?"

He nods his head vigorously while opening his eyes. "Best I've ever had."

"I told you. Malia can't be touched when it comes to baked goods." Every chance I get I tell someone new about her shop.

"Tell me, Summer. What do you do in your spare time?"

We were at this stage of dating where we got to know the deeper details of each other's personal lives. It's my second least favorite part of dating, right after the initial get to know each other conversation.

"I make jewelry."

His brows nearly reach his hairline. I'm guessing that shocked him. "Really? That's cute."

The cute comment makes me grimace a little. "Yeah, I'm pretty good at it. My online shop nearly sales out every few weeks. I have my products in three local boutiques that I have to restock at least once a month."

"Not a bad way to make a little cash," he goes on to say taking another bite of his turnover.

"It pays the bills," which is only partially true. Gabriel pays the bills. But if I had to pay bills, my jewelry income could cover most of my bills.

I don't know why I'm feeling so defensive. He hasn't said anything negative. I just don't like the way he keeps referring to my business as small or cute.

"I thought your child's father left you that house?"

This time it's my brows that reach for my hairline. "Who told you that?"

He shrugs. "Your friend, Trina. She wanted to assure me that you were indeed not a gold digger and that you didn't need my money because your child's father left you a house and a car."

I shake my head. Even though my friend was only trying to look out for me, I'm not sure how I felt about her revealing that information.

"He did," I admit. "But it doesn't mean I don't have bills."

He holds up his hands in a surrender posture with a grin. "You're right, and I didn't mean to offend you. I think it's great the father of your child had the hindsight to take care of you. Many men don't do that. But it makes it easier for the mother to only have to worry about taking care of the child. Because of his forethought, you get to make pretty necklaces."

"Yeah," I say with a forced smile. I turn away from Andrew and glance out the window. This is the reason my dates are usually short lived. Sometimes I think I'm being too picky considering my past.

While I chew on my bottom lip, a tall figure across the street moves. There is a small coffee shop sitting on the corner across the street. Leaning against the light pole is a hooded figure that seems to be staring at me through the window. I lean forward, squinting my eyes.

"Is someone out there?" Andrew asks.

I turn to look at him. "I think there's someone…." My words die on my tongue when I look back out the window and the person is no longer there.

Did my conscious just make up an image of Gabriel out of the blue? I mean, he isn't the only tall wide-shouldered person in the world, but the fluttering feeling I get in my belly is only caused by one person. And the way my stomach immediately started to react after seeing that shadow makes me think maybe my eyes aren't playing games.

But if it was someone, they couldn't disappear that fast. Could they?

I turn back to Andrew, who is glancing out the window moving his head around trying to see what I saw.

"It's nothing," I say.

He turns back to me and smiles. We finish our pastries and head to the house.

The car ride back to my home is silent. Unlike most of the night, I wasn't in the mood to talk. I guess Andrew picked up on it.

"I'm sorry," he says, pulling my attention from the window.

I turn to look at his profile.

"I know what I said at the bookstore came off insensitive. I didn't mean to suggest that your business was something small. The things that you've accomplished are downright incredible, Summer. Especially with being a recovering addict. I'd love to see some of your pieces. I bet they're gorgeous."

For the first time since leaving Malia's, I relax a little. I appreciate his apology and for acknowledging his earlier statements were demeaning. Andrew has proven time and time again that he is worth me giving him the attention he deserves. I've finally found a guy that I actually like.

"Thank you," I say. "And you're in luck. I have some finished pieces in the house."

"I can't wait to see them. Tell me about your jewelry."

For the next ten minutes, I explain my process of making jewelry to Andrew. I discuss how I pick and purchase the stones and what each one represents. I even explain the intricate details of molding and blending polymer clay to make different designs. He listens intently and asks questions. By the time we pull into my neighborhood, I'm excited to show him my work.

"I can't wait to see the obsidian men's bracelet." Andrew says as we turn the corner toward my house.

"You're going to love it. It's masculine without being so over the top..." my words fade as I take in the figure standing on my doorstep. My heart immediately starts racing.

Three days have gone by without seeing this man, and the moment my eyes land on him a feeling of peace washes over me.

"Do you know him?" Andrew asks, but I don't answer because something is off.

I quickly open my door and slide out.

"Summer, wait," Andrew calls out to me.

I, in fact, do not wait. Instead, I rush up the stairs.

"Oh my god, Gabriel," I call out as I get a better view of him.

His black hoodie is covered in something wet. After glancing down at the dark red stains on his jeans, I'm assuming it's blood on the hoodie. He has a new red scar over his eye and his knuckles look like he's been in a battle with a brick wall.

"I'm sorry," he says as he stares down at me. I don't know what he's apologizing for. My concern right now is making sure none of this blood is his.

"Is that blood?" I had no idea Andrew followed me out the car.

I turn around to find him standing behind me.

"No. It's paint." I say quickly even though it doesn't look anything like paint. I turn back to Gabriel trying to see if there are any injuries on his large body.

He cups my face with his bloody hands, those gorgeous eyes seem in so much pain. "I'm sorry." He says again. "You're not a distraction. Neither is Gabe."

I had already come to terms with why Gabriel said what he said. Hearing him apologize does mend my hurt feelings, but seeing the pained and frazzled look in his eyes as he pleads with me to forgive him, has me folding like a cheap lawn chair.

"It's okay. I forgive you."

He shuts his eyes, and his shoulders drop as if a weight has been lifted off them.

"Summer, maybe we should call the cops," Andrew says behind me.

In his defense, if I would have pulled up to his house and a woman was standing on the front porch in blood-soaked clothes looking like she's been to hell and back, I'd have the same response.

"No, everything is fine," I try to make the situation a little less awkward. "He's an artist."

The look Andrew gives me tells me he's not buying the shit I'm trying to sell. He takes a step toward me, grabbing my arm in a gentle way as if he's trying to pull me away.

However, before I can advise him against touching me right now, Gabriel grabs his arm, twists it around his back and has him in a rear naked choke hold. Something I only know about because Mr. James and Trina host MMA fight nights at their house.

Andrew's glasses are skewed on his reddening face. He tries to gasp for help but can't quite get the words out.

"Gabriel, it's okay. Let him go."

Gabriel's green eyes narrow, but his hold on Andrew does not relinquish.

"Please, let him go."

This time, he releases Andrew and steps back. Andrew bends at the waist fighting to breathe. I step forward to help him, but Gabriel's growled "Don't" has me stepping back.

"Take slow deep breaths," I encourage Andrew.

He glares at me. "Who is this guy?" he asks in a raspy voice.

"This is Gabriel, my son's father."

Never has someone's face gone from anger to pure horror and shock in such a short time.

"Summer, I think—"

"Leave," Gabriel warns, stepping forward.

It doesn't take more than that for Andrew to rush down my steps. He goes so fast he completely misses the last one nearly face planting on the ground. He quickly gets his feet back under him and rushes to the car. He pulls out of my driveway so fast the tires make a screeching sound and the smell of burnt rubber assails my nostrils.

"Well, I guess it's safe to say I won't get another date with him," I say before turning back to Gabriel.

However, I don't find that miniscule smile I normally get when I usually make an ill-timed joke. Instead, that sadness is back in his eyes.

"Come on," I say, heading to the front door and opening it for him to enter.

He follows me to my bedroom. I open the door and turn on the light before kicking my heels off.

"Sit," I point to the bench at the foot of my bed.

I continue into the bathroom to grab my first aid kit out of the cabinet along with a soapy warm rag. I carry my things back out to the room. I place the objects on the bench beside him, before kneeling between his legs.

"Is any of this yours?" I ask looking over his hoodie.

He shakes his head.

"Jeez, Gabriel. What did you do?" I unzip his hoodie and push the fabric off his shoulders and down his arms.

"Bar fight," he says.

I shake my head. "You mean to tell me, for the last three days you've just been picking fights?"

When I glance up at him, he's staring at me, but he doesn't answer.

Knowing I won't get any more answers from him about that, I let out a deep breath. Pulling the hoodie further off him, I drop it to the floor. "Take off the shirt," I say next.

He quickly removes the shirt handing it to me. I toss it with his hoodie. When I turn back to him, I notice something new. A tattoo of the number 50 written in thick old English. I was about to ask him about it when something else catches my eye. Actually, it's a lot of something else.

I didn't get a close-up look at his body the night we met. However, I was not ready for the thick and thin lines of scars all over his torso and arms.

My finger runs across a thick scar on his chest right above the tattoo over his heart. It's about two fingers thick and is the length of my hand. The way the skin has healed and stretched leads me to believe it's a very old wound.

Although he has never told me much detail about his childhood, I've been able to put pieces together. The fact that when he goes into this dark place to kill, he allows his mother to take over his thoughts is a huge sign that something was wrong.

Seeing the pale lines makes my heart ache for the small boy with beautiful green eyes that must have endured pure hell to get these. Gabriel's mother didn't only abuse him mentally, she fucked him over physically as well.

Suddenly, Gabriel's large hand covers mine. When I look back up at him, he uses the same hand to wipe the tears off my face.

"They're old," he tells me. "Don't cry over them."

Everything I know about him tells me he's not one for pity. Plus, he doesn't need it. So, I do exactly as he asks. I tuck my chin to my chest, and then wipe my eyes.

"Are you sure you're not injured anywhere," I ask as I go back to looking over his body.

"You don't have to do this."

I roll my eyes, "Shut up, and show me your injuries."

He smirks and shakes his head, before showing me his hands.

"It looks like you punched a wall," I say, grabbing the wet cloth, I run it over his knuckles cleaning the blood off.

"I did."

I glance up at him. His serious face tells me he isn't joking.

"You can't do that, Gabriel. You can't beat yourself up when you're struggling with your feelings."

I knew what this was. I've seen it with Gabe. Although my son usually stims or cries when he's dealing with things. It seems his father's go to is self-harm.

"I need an outlet," he replies. "I have to….. funnel the rage somewhere."

"Pick up a hobby. Try knitting, or hiking. Hell, fuck it out of your system. Just don't do this shit again," I angrily toss the towel to the bench before looking for the ointment I use for Gabe's cuts.

"I'm sorry." He says lowly.

I sigh. "It's okay. Just do better next time."

We're silent again as I rub the cream over his knuckles. Once I'm finished cleaning him up, I place all my first aid stuff back in the box and carry it back to the bathroom.

"Do you like him?"

I startle when his words come from behind me suddenly. I turn to find a still shirtless Gabriel leaning against the open door.

"Who?" I ask, even though I know exactly who he is talking about.

"The psychologist."

Folding my arms over my chest I lean against the sink. "How do you know he's a psychologist?"

The look Gabriel gives me has me chuckling. I don't even know why I asked that question. Dropping my arms down at my side, I shrug.

"He's nice. He's interested in me. And he seems to get my jokes."

"But do you like him?"

I look away from Gabriel, gathering my thoughts. It's not that I don't like Andrew. He's handsome, successful, makes me feel excited, and a great catch. But as always there is something missing between us. Just like it was with all the other guys I went out with. I don't know what it is.

"You know what it is. You just don't want to admit it." My thoughts scream in my head.

"He's okay," I say, finally answering Gabriel. "I can't be too picky. It's not like I have a bunch of options beating at my door." I laugh, before tucking a braid behind my ear.

He's silent for a moment, watching me as if he can read every thought that runs through my mind. I ignore the way my heart races and the fluttery feeling in the pit of my stomach when he looks at me.

"Why don't you?"

I scoff, shaking my head. "Did you forget how we met?" his brows knit together as if he's confused, or he finally remembered. "You couple that with the fact that I'm a single mother, and well, I'm just not at the top of anyone's list."

He's quiet again, watching me. "Fuck their lists."

"Easy for you to say. You have no desire to be in a relationship. I, however, want to be in love. I want to have someone to wake up to every morning and go to sleep with at night. I want to dance in my kitchen, I want to watch sunsets, I want someone to bring me tea without me asking." I turn my back to him, facing the mirror at the sink. I pull my braids out of the half up and half down style I put them in.

"I know it sounds crazy, but I want the type of love that is written about. The kind that inspires others. I want him to not just understand me, but to know my past, know how it shaped me, but don't hold it against me."

I think that is why all my other dates never fully connected. Half of the time I didn't tell them about who I once was, and the few that I did kept saying things like, you're not her anymore and you've moved on. Yes, I'm no longer on drugs but I will always be a recovering addict. My years on drugs may not have been pretty, but they shaped who I was.

"Despite what people may think," I say, finishing my thoughts. "I am capable of love. And one day I'm going to find the right person to show it to."

I turn to face him again. His hands are balled into fists at his side as he silently stares at me.

"When I do, I'll let you walk me down the aisle at my wedding," I joke to ease the tension.

He tilts his head, his brow arches. "Not unless you want to see what the inside of your groom's skull looks like."

I toss my head back and laugh. "You wouldn't dare."

When I glance back at him, he isn't laughing.

"Fine," I tease. "You don't have to walk me down the aisle. You can sit in the back with all the other last-minute guests."

"Won't change the outcome," he states.

"You're so full of shit," I chuckle rolling my eyes.

I don't take these little comments with Gabriel seriously. Do I believe he could kill my groom? Yes. But I won't fool myself into believing he's jealous or that he's saying this because he wants me. He has no idea what he wants, and in the end he will still leave.

"Alright, you're going to shower while I make some popcorn and queue up Game of Thrones. You're not climbing in my bed with all that blood on you."

For a second, he looks as if he's going to argue with me. I know I have no reason allowing him to sleep in the bed with me. But hell, I'm not getting dick. The least I can do is wake up in the strong arms of a man. A girl can dream.

Eventually Gabriel dips his chin at me. I smile as I walk out of the bathroom.

CHAPTER TWENTY-NINE

We Need You

Summer

I push my ass back, trying to move my son's knee out of my back. I don't remember Gabe climbing in my bed last night.

"Gabe," I say groggily. "Move your knee." I scoot my butt back once more, this time coming into contact with a solid surface.

A warm hand lands on my hip.

"I'm not Gabe, and that isn't my knee."

My eyes pop open immediately. Gabriel's voice is already deep and sexy, but when you add that sleepy huskiness to it, it's downright an aphrodisiac. And to a woman that hasn't had real dick in years, it's dangerous.

"You need to tame that damn dragon," I joke. "Some of us don't have as much restraint as you do." I chuckle, but my laughter gets cut off when Gabriel wraps his arm around me and rolls me over on top of him.

I gasp. "Gabriel." I'm lying against his bare chest, my legs straddling his stomach, his dick knocking against my ass. The thin satin shorts and panties I'm wearing allow me to feel everything.

"I think you overestimate my control."

This is the point where I should get up and put some distance between us. Nothing sustainable can come from me continuing this game with him. However, my decision-making skills still require some work.

"Placing me on top of you does not refute my claim." I say, folding my arms on top of his chest and placing my chin on my hands. "You're still in control."

He grips my ass in the palm of his hands and squeezes before he starts to massage it. It feels so good I have to shut my eyes and take a deep breath before opening them. I don't think he realizes what he's doing to me.

"For your safety."

His reply catches me off guard. I squint up at him.

"My safety? Is that your way of telling me you're going to beat up my pussy?" I tease.

Last time Gabriel and I were intimate, he didn't say much. In fact, other than some grunts and randomly asking if he was doing it right, he didn't speak much at all. Having him joke about sex and touch me so freely was a big improvement. One I liked a lot.

"Are you challenging me?" his eyes lower as he stares into my face.

He slips his hands past my shorts and into my panties, gripping my ass in both hands before using one of his long fingers to run down the slippery folds of my lower lips. I should be embarrassed at how wet I am for him already. However, embarrassment is the furthest emotion from my mind.

I bite into my bottom lip and moan when he slowly pushes one finger into my wet walls. It makes a slushing sound, proving just how aroused I am for him.

He hisses at the sound and his eyes become even more hooded.

"Gabriel," I whisper his name when he adds a second finger to the first. They feel divine as they slowly move in and out of me.

"I've thought about you nonstop for five years, Summer."

I rotate my hips gently. He grips my ass tighter. All the earlier jokes have seeped away. I have no teasing rebuttal. I can barely keep my eyes open.

However, there is one thing I have no problem opening and that is my legs a little wider.

"Thinking about the night we made Gabe kept me sane when all I had around me were the walls of my holding unit. I couldn't get the way your warm, wet, slit gripped me so tight out of my head."

He removes his magic fingers out of my passage and down to my hardened nub, smearing my essence as he went.

I want to ask questions. I want to know what he did when I crossed his mind, but every thought is being washed away by the pleasure of his fingers slowly bringing me to my peak.

"Gabriel," I cry out his name again as my body rears up for the first orgasm not caused by me in the last five years.

I bet if my coochie could talk she'd wonder what the hell is going on. This is more action than she's experienced in a long time.

"I know, you're doing good, Summer," He praises as he continues to work his fingers against my clit.

I fist my hands on top of his chest, as my hips continue to grind chasing my orgasm down like a robber that stole my purse.

Gabriel continues to talk calmly as if I'm not about to have a heart attack on top of him. "You haunted me so much when we were apart that I vowed the next time I was inside of you, I wanted to make sure you'd never forget it. I want it to haunt you the way you did me."

"It did, baby. God, it did," I shut my eyes as my body quakes with the ripple of my peaking orgasm. Gabriel's fingers do not relent. They continue their slow motion.

"No," he says. "Not the way I want it to. That's why I studied. I watched every video I could find, I read every article there was on how to please a female. I devoted five years to learning everything I could about fucking you."

The man deserves a PhD for his skills. Hell, a Nobel prize just for his dedication alone. He applies a little more pressure to my nub causing me to whimper. The orgasm that was slowly reaching its climax shoots me to the top of the mountain dangling me over the edge but not yet allowing me to plummet.

"Because," he goes on to say. "If you ever allowed me between your legs again, I would not stop until you could no longer breathe without me. So, I'm restraining myself to protect you."

I open my mouth to beg him to throw all restraint out the window. I didn't need him to hold back. I wanted all of him.

"Come for me, Summer," he growls as he gently squeezes my clit between his fingers.

"Ahhh," I scream as the most powerful orgasm I've ever experienced rakes through me.

It zips through my fingers and down to my toes as if lightning was coursing through my body.

Just when I think I'm coming down from the mountain top, he flips me over on to my back. Gabriel rips my shorts and panties down my legs in one tug. He spreads my legs so wide; you would think I was a gymnast. He then buries his head between my thighs and takes me straight back over the edge.

My back bows off the bed, my thighs lock around his head, and I scream like a banshee as I cream all over his face. If I thought his fingers were magical, his tongue is a damn wizard master.

Gabriel devours me. He eats my coochie like it's a five-star meal at the most expensive restaurant. He laps at my nub, dips his tongue inside my canal, and sucks my pearl. I erupt like a fucking volcano back-to-back. Each time I think I can't come again, my body proves me wrong.

Finally, I whimper, "No more, Gabriel. Please."

I never thought I'd see the day I had to beg for someone to stop making me come.

He places a soft kiss against my lower lips before slowly kissing up my body. It crosses my mind that we are doing all this and neither of us have yet to brush our teeth. But that slips from my mind when he lifts my satin tank top up over my breasts and devours one globe as he tugs at the nipple of the other.

My eyes roll to the back of my head. I run my fingers in his dark blonde hair. At some point the strands fell out of the bun it was in when he went to sleep. The soft strands tickle my skin as they brush against me.

Gabriel sits up on his knees, he stares down at me with hooded eyes. I watch as he tugs his baller shorts down, releasing his massive hardon. With one hand he rubs the head of his cock against my pussy lips, spreading them open with his mushroom tip. The gushing sound is back as he plays in my wetness.

I bite into my bottom lip as I watch his tan erection separate my caramel folds. When he stops moving, I look up into his eyes wondering what happened.

His green eyes stare back at me. This time it doesn't take much to read the question there. He wants permission. He's already told me his plans. If I say yes, he's going to wreck me. I have no doubt that Gabriel is capable of doing exactly what he said he would do. He's going to fuck me until I can't think of anything else but him. He wants me to crave him as if he is the air I need to survive. I know all of this, and it should be enough to make me say no. Yet when I open my mouth, that is not what falls out.

"I'm not on birth control."

He smirks before grabbing my left leg and pushing my knee up to my chest. He lines himself up. I take a deep breath preparing for the stretch my pussy is about to make to accept him back into my walls.

Right as he's about to shove forward, a screeching voice pierces the air.

"Summer, we're back,"

Gabriel glances over his shoulder toward the open door. I have a mini panic attack.

"Shit, it's Sunday." I try to scoot back, but his hand on my thigh keeps me from moving.

When he turns back to me, he stares down at the place where we are almost joined. I can read the hesitation on his face. He's determining if he should continue or not.

I swear, in any other situation I would have told him to keep going. However, I have to keep my child in mind.

"I know what you're thinking, but your son is down there and unless you want to have the "why is daddy on top of mommy naked talk', I advise you to get up."

He narrows his eyes, but thankfully he gets up. I quickly scramble off the bed and find my silk robe before rushing downstairs. My feet hit the bottom step right as Trina was making her way toward the stairs.

"Hey," I say overly loud.

Gabe runs up to me and wraps his arms around my waist. His hugs are rare, and I make sure to enjoy every single one he gives me.

"Auntie Trina and Uncle James took me to see fish," he announces happily.

"We actually took him to a sushi place. However, he was uninterested in everything but the fish tank. I didn't have the heart to tell him the truth," she whispers the last part to me.

"Can I go outside before we go to story time," he asks. I nod my head.

Gabe, who has always loved playing outside, has become more obsessed with our backyard. When Gabriel went missing those three days, Gabe practically lived out there in hopes his father would show up like he did before.

As soon as Gabe is out of sight, I grab Trina's arm and pull her into the kitchen.

"I need a raincheck."

Trina steps back and looks me over. Her eyes are studying my face, my hair, and my robe. She does it so thoroughly, I have to wonder did I miss something. Did I somehow get cum on my face even though he didn't orgasm.

"Biiittccchh," Trina says with a smirk.

"What?" I ask patting at my braids. I cringe at the frizziness of my roots.

"Don't try to act all innocent with me. I know that look." She points a finger at me. "Your face is flushed, your skin is glowing, and you're smiling from ear to ear. You got dick," she shouts happily.

I wave my hands in her face, glancing back over my shoulder toward the stairs.

"Will you keep your voice down."

"He's still here?" she squeals. Suddenly her face falls. "Heifer, you let my godson hug you with sex fluids all over your body."

I pinch the bridge of my nose. "Will you focus."

She smiles again and shakes her head. "My girl finally dusted the cobwebs off that coochie and used it for something other than a toy factory." She pokes out her bottom lip. "You're growing up."

I roll my eyes at her.

"First of all, there were no cobwebs on this cat. And second, I would've gotten dick if my best friend hadn't interrupted."

Her eyes widen. "Oh shit, do you want me to take Gabe on a walk or something? I can keep him outside for a few minutes while you finish getting your back blown out."

I appreciate my friend and all her support but honestly the moment has passed. Also, now that my pussy isn't taking over my body, my brain is starting to make much more sense. What started upstairs did not need to finish. Even though my head says it, my lower lips are still craving what she didn't get.

"No, don't worry about it."

She shrugs. "So, Andrew finally got you to open those legs. Honestly, I didn't think he had it in him."

That would be a reasonable assumption. Considering the last thing she remembers is me having a date with him last night.

"Yeah, about that…" I start, but don't finish because the way Trina's mouth falls open and her eyes widen, I already know who has made an appearance.

I turn to find a shirtless Gabriel in the same basketball shorts he slept in. His hair is back up in its messy bun.

His eyes connect with mine, and the fire in them has me squeezing my thighs together. The ache between my legs intensifies as the memory of him eating my pussy plays back in my head. As if he can sense my thoughts, his gaze drops down to my thighs and takes its precious time making its way back to my face. When it does, he slips his bottom lip in between his teeth.

"Shit, I think I need to change my panties," Trina's whispered words have me turning away from Gabriel.

Clearing my throat, I step to the side so that I can see both Trina and Gabriel, I introduce them.

"Trina, this is Gabriel. Gabe's father. And Gabriel, this is Trina Blackstone. My best friend and Gabe's godmother."

Gabriel dips his head at Trina. She waves demurely at him.

"I'm going to go check on Gabe," he says before heading out the patio door.

Trina and I both stare at his back as he walks out. Although he has been staying with me for a week and a half now, this is the first time I'm actually seeing the tattoo on his back. It's terrifying with its sharp fangs. It almost looks like a depiction of a vampire if not for the large horns. The only color other than black and gray shading are the glowing red eyes of the demon.

For some reason seeing the tattoo doesn't scare me like I think he wants it to. Instead, it comforts me.

Once Gabriel is outside, I'm pulled back to the conversation with Trina.

"I thought we were friends?"

Taken aback by her question, I ask. "What are you talking about? We are friends."

"Why the hell didn't you tell me you were fucking a Norse god. No wonder my baby came out obsessed with the Avengers, his father is got damn Thor."

I toss my head back and laugh. "I can't take you seriously."

"I'm for real. Girl, your pussy has to be world class, ain't no way you took all that."

"Hey," I say jokingly. "Don't be checking out my baby daddy's dick."

"Well tell your baby daddy to cage that thing before he comes downstairs in shorts. For a moment I thought it was going to reach across the room and lasso you to him."

I have to hold my side; I'm laughing so hard. "You need help, Trina. I'm going to take a shower."

"Yeah, you do that. I'm going to see if Gabe needs a new step mama."

"Trina," I playfully shout.

"I'm kidding," She holds up her hands. "But damn it's enough to go around."

I laugh the entire way up to my room and into the shower. My heart is light, and for the first time I feel absolutely happy. I can't explain the feeling. Yes, I've been happy before. The day my son was born I cried tears of joy. However, there is something about this euphoric feeling that feels new. Almost like I'm high.

That sudden thought hits me like a sledgehammer. Because I know all too well, no matter how good the high feels, the crash back down is always hell.

Two hours later, we're sitting at our table at Malia's bookstore. Trina is telling me about her newest collab with a new makeup brand. Usually, I'm excited and totally invested in all her new business ventures, but today my mind keeps going back to Gabriel.

My body still has the tingles from our time this morning. I can still remember how warm he felt pressed to me. The way his tongue felt as he lapped at my essence like it was manna from heaven. Even his scent still lingers in my nostrils. Yet, the reminder that the high will eventually wear off keeps stomping through my head.

"Girl, what is wrong with you?" Trina says, grabbing my attention from the paper napkin I was just tearing up.

"Earlier you were giddy and glowing and now you seem all depressed. And honestly, I've seen that dick imprint, you got nothing to be depressed about."

Scrunching up my nose at her, I say, "No more dick jokes."

"Oh no ma'am. You got about two months of this. Remember how long you teased me about little dick Terry, and I was in love with that boy. Not to mention you still call my husband Mr."

I laugh out loud for the first time since we left the house. She has a point.

"Fair," I finally admit.

Trina sinks back in her seat, eyeing me wearily. "Mmhmm, why are you changing the subject. What's up with you?"

I lean back in my chair mimicking her. After glancing over to Gabe on the story time rug, I give my attention back to my friend.

"This morning with Gabriel was…" I try to come up with a word to describe what I felt but nothing seems sufficient enough. I settle on the closest I can think of. "It was euphoric."

"I bet it was." Trina wiggles her eyebrows at me.

I chuckle but quickly fade back to seriousness. "The way he devoured me and the things he said as he brought me to climax over and over," I shut my eyes as his deep voice plays back in my head. *"I want to haunt you like you haunted me."*

"Okay, so what's the problem?"

I open my eyes and the memory fades. Glancing back over to Gabe, I confess. "He's not staying."

She's silent for a moment causing me to look back at her.

"Are you sure about that? Because the way he looked at you in the kitchen doesn't lead me to believe he's not sticking around. For a moment I thought he was going to toss your ass on the table and fuck you in front of me. And I'm going to be honest, I wasn't leaving."

Rolling my eyes, I snort. "Nasty self."

She shrugs as if she's unoffended by my comment.

"But seriously," I continue. "I know Gabriel. Even if he did want to stay, he won't. He thinks he's not good enough to be with us."

He hasn't admitted it, but I know him enough to know he deals with insecurities. He fears he will hurt one of us. I'm not saying it isn't a valid fear. Gabriel is huge and when he goes to that dark place, he is terrifying. However, I know in my heart he will never allow himself to slip up and hurt us. He just doesn't know it. And because of that, I know he will leave.

"So, just enjoy it while it lasts."

I'm shaking my head before she finishes that sentence. "I can't."

"What? Why?"

Taking a deep breath, I let it out slowly. "You know those apartments Raina use to stay at before she met Mitch?"

She nods.

"One night, I got really high. I was feeling good. I went up on to the roof of the building with this guy. He thought we were going up to fuck, but I wasn't having that. Anyway, we get up there and I'm so out of my mind that I walk up to the edge of the roof. Not only do I have about two lines of raw coke in my system, I'd been doing Tequila shots with it.

"I remember being up on that ledge, looking down at the specks of people walking along the sidewalk feeling like I was untouchable. The guy I was with was pleading with me to get down, but I was laughing as I leaned over the edge."

I shake my head as I come out of the memory. When I look up at Trina her eyes are a bit misty.

"When I'm with Gabriel I feel like that night again. It's as if I'm floating on a high so pure that nothing can hurt me. We are in a bubble when we're together. He makes me want to walk close to the ledge. And for me that's dangerous."

"How?" She asks.

"I've been trying to figure out why I can't connect with anyone else I've dated. It's because I'm chasing the feeling I get with Gabriel.

"He gets me. He doesn't just understand my quirks and lives with them, but he understands me. All of me. The truth is, that man has the ability to break me, Trina." I look over to my son.

Story time is over and they are now doing the craft that goes along with the story. I turn back to Trina. "And I can no longer live that carelessly."

A tear falls down her face. I think she finally understands why this thing with Gabriel is so complicated.

The night we met was insane, but I knew there was something different about him. We had a connection. Having him back in our lives even for such a short period of time has shown me that our connection is dangerous. I won't say I'm in love with Gabriel, but I won't lie as if there aren't feelings there. Feelings that if I don't manage will quickly turn into love. And loving Gabriel is not safe.

Trina pats her face with one of the napkins I didn't rip up before leaning forward in her seat. She reaches across the table for my hand. I place it in her open palm.

"I'm going to say something to you that I never thought I'd ever say in my life. Friend," She pauses as if she has to gather her thoughts. "You can't sleep with that man."

I chuckle but I know she's being serious. She lets go of my hand.

"Seriously, I get what you're saying. And adding sex to your already high emotions won't help. It's going to be hard friend, I know. But trust me, you can't fuck him."

I poke out my bottom lip. "Not even one last time for good measure?"

"No, bitch. You gotta go cold turkey."

We both toss our head back and laugh. Even though we were joking about it, I know that she's right. I have to keep things platonic between Gabriel and me. Which means, no more repeats of this morning no matter how much my body craves it.

We continue our Sunday tradition by ending our day with a trip to the park. That night, after putting Gabe to bed, I sat on the couch waiting for

Gabriel to come home. I had a ton of plans to talk to him about why we couldn't have sex again.

However, when he walked in, I took one look at him and knew that tonight wasn't the night for that conversation.

Instead of talking, I pulled the cover back off my legs and patted the seat next to me. He dropped his duffle and sat down beside me.

"Rough night?" I ask.

"Yeah," he says without further explanation.

"You want to talk about it?"

He turns to look at me. "No, I just want to sit in your presence."

I fight the smile on my face. Without even trying, the man can always make me feel like I'm special, like I'm someone important to him. I bury myself in his side, taking in his warmth and scent. He wraps his arm around me pulling me in closer.

We spend the rest of the night cuddled up on the couch watching Game of Thrones.

CHAPTER THIRTY

The Ring

Beast

I stare down at my sleeping son. His face is pressed into my side, one arm thrown over my chest. Tonight, he wanted me to read him a story before bed and not Summer.

When Summer first made the requirements that I had to spend time with her and Gabe while I was here, I was terrified. I envisioned all the ways I would mess it up. Mother told me that I would hurt them. However, after weeks of being with them, it's become a little easier.

I still have my fears, but each day I allow myself to stay in the moments with them. When I disappear, I will take these memories with me.

Slowly, I lift Gabe's arm up and slide from under it. He rolls over on his stomach. I pause in my movement hoping he doesn't wake up. He quickly settles and falls back to sleep. I stare at his face for a few moments.

"You sure did make one cute ass kid," Priest hums in my head.

"On this I can agree. But even Lucifer was attractive," Mother warns.

I ignore her. My son is perfect.

Finally, I leave Gabe's room, closing the door behind me. I stop by the bedroom I'm sharing with Summer.

There has been no repeat of that morning two and half weeks ago, but every night, I sleep in her bed. She hasn't mentioned that morning again and there has been no sign of her wanting to repeat it. As much as she thought she was ready for that next step, I knew she wasn't. I meant what I said, I was going to make her crave me.

I quickly grab my black duffle out of the closet. Taking it to the bed, I place it down before sitting on the bench seat at the foot of the bed. Grabbing my boots, I start to put them on. The sound of Summer's soft footfalls alert me to her approach. My heart stutters in my chest at the anticipation of seeing her.

I look up at the door as soon as she walks in. She's wearing a long dress with thin shoulder straps. Her braids are hanging down her back. She folds her hands over her chest and glares at me.

"Just because he wanted you to read to him tonight doesn't mean you're the favorite. He asked me to cut the crust off his bread today, so." She sticks out her tongue.

A smile creeps on my face. "We both know you are the leading lady in Gabe's life. I'm just a supporting role."

"Yeah, well you better know it." She laughs, before walking further into the room. "Where to tonight?"

She takes a seat beside me on the bench as I finish putting my boots on.

"Checking out a new source. I may be home late. Don't wait up."

When I look over to her, she has a huge grin on her face. It's out of place in the moment and I have no idea why she's so happy.

"What?" I ask.

She bumps my arm with her shoulder. "You called it home."

I didn't realize I'd made the slip up. I also don't have the heart to tell her that even though this feels more like home to me than any place I've ever stayed, it won't change the outcome. Instead of saying this, I pinch her chin between my pointer and thumb and drop a quick kiss on her lips.

"Don't wait up." I force myself to stand and walk away from her.

That kiss alone has me wanting to sit back down, pull her into my lap as I lift her dress, and push my dick into her.

Grabbing my duffle off the ground, I head for the door.

"Gabriel."

I stop when she calls my name. However, I don't turn to look at her. My restraint won't last but for so long.

"Be safe," she finally says.

My fist unclenches at my side. I hadn't even realized it was clenched.

"Goodnight, Summer," I walk out of the room after that.

I needed to put distance between me and her before I miss my opportunity and decide to spend the rest of my night in her bed.

I've spent the last two weeks going over everything in Timothy Smith's laptop. Other than infidelity, money laundering, paying off politicians and cops to get away with everything from murder, theft, and domestic abuse, there isn't anything that links him to the Church.

I figured in order to get down to the bottom of it, I need to talk to the man himself. Which is why I'm at his office for his late-night meeting.

I got here just as the place was closing down. The meeting tonight is held after hours. I had about three hours to get my stuff in order. I'd already studied the blueprint of the building, making note of all entrances and exits. I had time to scope out all the cameras. This building has over 200 cameras. They were all on different networks, it wasn't as easy to cut all the cameras at once like I'm used to. In the end, I only cut the ones I'd needed. Security also does a sweep of the building every half hour. I had to make sure I timed everything to avoid bumping into them.

I placed a camera and recording device in Smith's office facing the door right over his desk. I don the janitor's uniform I'd pre-ordered and take out the mop bucket.

Nearly twenty minutes before the scheduled meeting the elevator dings. Tim Smith rushes out and hurries past me into his office closing the door.

Not once did he look up at me. If he had, he would've noticed that I look nothing like the usual older black man that cleans his office.

Ten minutes later, the elevator dings again. Two people step off. One is a woman wearing a gray pants suit and blonde hair pulled back into a tight bun. She's tall. With those high heels on, she's about two inches shorter than me. I don't miss the obvious gun she has concealed at her back. She walks with her head high, her eyes straight ahead and her shoulders back. She doesn't glance in my direction as she walks by me. Which tells me she's wealthy, but also deadly.

The male with her is shorter than me, maybe six one. He has a caramel complexion close to my son's color. Not as yellow toned as Summer's light skin. I'm assuming he's biracial. His curly hair is in a similar afro style as Gabe's but with darker browns.

His walk is a little more casual than the female's but no less arrogant. He shows his arrogance by the smirk he shoots in my direction before turning away. He's also wearing a gun underneath his suit coat and a knife at his leg. The leg holster is bulky, but I think he wants people to notice it.

Both the woman and man slip into the office without knocking before closing the door behind them.

I quickly pull up the video on my phone. The over the ear headphones on my head feeds the sound into my ears.

"Victoria?" Tim seems hesitant to see the female. He immediately stood to his feet when she entered.

The guy with her walks around the room as if he's looking it over. His gaze glances at my camera but I'm not worried about him seeing it. Just as I suspect he quickly looks away.

"I thought I would be meeting Maksim."

"That is actually why I am here. Maksim has gone rogue."

Tim gasps and drops back down into his seat. It sems this news about Maksim was unexpected and affects him greatly.

"Corbyn wants all his associates to know that the ties with Sim have been severed. If anyone is seen communicating or doing any business with him, then you are no longer an ally of Corbyn."

Tim shoots to his feet once again. "I assure Mr. Corbyn that I have not seen or heard from Sim."

The mixed guy stops his causal perusing around the room. He turns back to Tim and slowly walks over to his desk.

"What did you call my brother?"

Tim lifts a shaking hand and runs it over his hair.

"Uhh…"

"You called him Sim. Don't ever let me hear you speak my brother's name casually. He may no longer be a part of our team, but you don't get to disrespect the name Corbyn gave him."

Victoria holds up a hand when the mixed guy takes a step toward Tim.

"Easy, Yohan. You have to remember; Timmy is new to this. His bloodline isn't as pure as ours."

"I'm sorry," Tim quickly apologizes.

Victoria smiles, but it doesn't reach her eyes. "Since business with Sim is no longer an option. I will be taking over all his deals."

Tim nods. "Okay. Do you need anything from me?"

"No, not at the moment. I've been looking over your payments with Sim and everything seems good. But I don't have to remind you, I am not my brother."

"I understand. I appreciate all you and Mr. Corbyn have done."

Victoria nods. She turns to walk away but stops and turns back. "I hope that you know that discretion about our brother is of the upmost importance. Corbyn is only telling people that Sim had business dealings with. If the matter was to get out by any chance, well, it would be easier for me to eliminate all that knew than to figure out who told. Do you understand?"

"I do."

"Good. Until next month, Timmy." She turns and walks toward the door.

"Smith," Yohan calls out. "What about your janitor? Can he be trusted?"

"Lawrence?" Tim sounds confused. "He's never bothered anyone. He's been with the company for a while. He's half deaf and a bit touched in the head." I'm pretty sure Tim is describing the older black guy that usually works this floor.

Yohan smirks but doesn't say anything before turning and heading to the door. I quickly stuff my phone away and go back to mopping. I don't turn to look at them when they walk out the office.

"Hey," Yohan calls out to me. However, I pretend to not hear him with my headphones on.

He shouts for me once again. I continue to ignore him.

"Yohan, leave him alone. We don't have time," Victoria calls out to him in a bored tone.

Their footsteps echo off the tile floors until they stop short. I'm assuming in front of the elevator. My suspicions are correct when seconds later, the elevator dings and the swish of the doors opening are heard. I give them time to get on the elevator and to hear the swish once again, before turning back around.

Pushing the mop and broom back into the janitor's closet, I wipe everything down before grabbing the duffle I stashed there. I head down to the empty parking deck making sure to stay clear of the cameras I didn't cut off.

The black Bently Continental is the only car parked on the top floor of the garage. I kneel on the side, away from the door and wait. Fifteen minutes later, Tim's voice appears out of the blue.

"I'll be there in a few. Wait up for me," he says while on the phone. The locks on the car disengage. He pulls the door open and climbs in. I quickly slip in the passenger seat beside him. He turns to look at me confused.

"Who the fuck are you?"

Instead of answering his question, I punch him in the face. His head cracks against the window. He's knocked out.

I slip back out of the car and go around to the driver's side. After opening the door, I pop the trunk and quickly take him out the car. I stuff him in the trunk before getting behind the wheel. I pull out of the building, making sure to check my surroundings just in case I'm being followed.

The trip to my apartment building is quick. I unload Timothy from the trunk of the car, carrying him over my shoulder into my kill room. Once inside, I dump him into the chair. He still hasn't woken up.

I strap his legs down first and then move to his arms. As I'm placing the cuffs on his left hand, I spot a large gold ring. The ring reminds me of those old school class rings. Instead of a school mascot in the center of the red stone, there's a capital R with a thorny crown. The same emblem embossed in the invitation he kept.

I slide the ring off his finger bringing it closer to inspect. Other than the emblem and a few diamonds, nothing else stands out on the outside of the ring. Turning it over there is something scrolled on the band.

I have to squint to make out the writing. 'Smith 1 of 10' the inscription reads. I place the ring down on the table and finish securing Tim. I grab a few tools out of my cabinet and place them on the cart beside my victim. Just as I'm finishing up, Tim slowly wakes up.

His head rolls around on his shoulders as he moans. He'll have a throbbing headache, but he won't have to worry about it long. Finally, he opens his eyes. He looks confused, until he starts to look around the room. I can tell the moment the memory of what happened tonight dawns on him. He starts to tug at the cuffs. His eyes widen as he takes in the scene.

"What the fuck is going on? Who are you?" He asks as his attention lands on me.

I ignore his questions the same as I did in the car. "Eight years ago, a man named Dennis Chambers was killed."

Tim's eyes narrow as he looks me over and then a slow smile spreads over his face. He sinks back in his chair as if he's on a leisurely visit.

"Let me guess, you're an ex-cop or something?" He laughs. "Do you know how much trouble you're going to be in?" He laughs again and shakes his head. "I hate to break it to you, but I didn't kill your cop friend."

I watch him for a moment, studying his posture. Even in this situation he believes his power and privilege still reign. His disposition is completely opposite of what it was back in his office with Victoria and Yohan.

"No," I say. "You hired the Church to do it."

The smile immediately wipes off his face. His brow bunches as he stares back at me. There is no smirk or smug smile this time.

"You're part of the Church?" He asks.

I don't answer.

"Look, I paid for that service. It's a done deal. If you have a problem with it, you can take it up with your Pope." His tone is more serious, like he's handling a business deal. Not so much smugness in it as before. He respects the Church more than he does the police force.

"The Church does not do hire for kill." I knew this to be a lie, but I was baiting him.

This time Tim laughs, albeit not as boisterous as the first time.

"Are you kidding me? That organization has been doing our dirty work for years. My grandfather used them, and his father used them before him. They are always willing to work for the right families." His smirk grows wider.

"How does your family have the Church in their pockets?" I didn't miss out on his use of the word families. But I'll store that information for later.

He gives me another one of those smirks. "Wouldn't you like to know." He leans his head back in the chair. "I'll admit, you got some big balls, kid. Taking me like this takes courage. But when your superior finds out what you did, you won't last a day. Best to let me go. I'll keep your secret." He winks at me.

The smugness is back. He knows the Church, and he knows what we are capable of, but he still feels as if he has more power than they do. Interesting.

"Who is Corbyn?"

All the smugness drains from his face turning it pale. His head lifts and his eyes widen.

"What do you know about that name? Get me out of here." He fights against his restraints.

Funny, he wasn't nearly as terrified of the Church as he was of this Corbyn guy. Yet, he knows the Church's capabilities. This is the first time I've seen true fear in his eyes.

"Tell me about Corbyn," I repeat.

Tim glares at me. "You don't know what you're dealing with. I'm not saying anything."

I believed him. He was too scared of whoever this Corbyn guy was. True fear, the one that has this man nearly wetting his pants at just a name, will make you lock up like a vault. He's willing to die before he betrays this Corbyn person.

I had one more question. I pick up the ring off the table. The moment he sees what I'm holding he panics.

"Give that back," he shouts.

"What's this symbol?" I turn the ring so that the emblem is facing him.

He turns his head refusing to look at the ring. I wait for his answer, but he doesn't speak.

Letting out a deep breath, I drop the ring back on the table with a loud clank and then climb to my feet. I don't believe he will say anything else, but when I'm done he will wish he had.

"Make him bleed," Mother says in my head.

"As you wish, Mother." I reply as I allow her to slip over me and fill my head.

I rip open the front of his shirt, causing buttons to fly everywhere. Grabbing the straight draw knife off the table, I place it at the top of his chest, with light pressure I drag the blade down. His screams rip through the room making my ears ring. I toss the large chunk of skin onto the floor and move on to the next.

By the time I placed Timothy Smith's body into the incinerator, the only skin he had on his body was on his eye lids.

After cleaning the kill room and showering, I drop the car at the chop shop before heading home.

I used the word again. Home. Never in my life did I think that I would feel like any place was my home. Even when I stayed with Priest and my brothers, I never thought of the place as home. However, I'm finding that any place where Summer and Gabe are, is home.

I walk into the house at nearly five am. Summer is fast asleep on the couch. Her tea mug is on the coffee table and a bowl of popcorn is beside it. She tried to wait up for me.

After checking in on Gabe, I head back into the living room. Kicking off my boots, I climb on the couch behind Summer, then lift her up and place her on top of me.

"Gabriel?" she moans my name with her eyes closed.

"It's me. Go back to sleep."

"Okay. Love you," she hums before burying her face in my neck. She quickly falls back to sleep oblivious to the words she's just spoken.

I hold her body close to my chest. If I had it my way, I'd never let Summer go. However, a memory of my childhood pops in my head.

I was five years old. I'd been locked in my crate down in the basement for a month. Those were the worst punishments. When I was locked up upstairs, I could at least talk to Mother and listen to her daily scriptures.

Yet, when I was in the basement, I had no one. Mother only put me in the basement when I'd really done wrong. This time, I smiled at the image of a lady on TV. Mother said I was sinning for lusting after the woman.

I'd been in that crate so long my legs had gone numb. I'd learned early to not complain or cry about my punishments. One night, I heard clawing outside of my cage. Turns out a small mouse had found its way into the house. I named him George after the Curious George cartoon I used to watch.

I remember sharing my food with George and talking to him for hours. I was so desperate for the company. For five days, George was my best friend. He would come out of his hole to greet me. Any time mother would come downstairs I would send George back into hiding.

However, on that fifth day, I did not hear mother open the basement door. I didn't have enough time to send George back to his den, so I grabbed him in my hands to protect him. Mother hated rodents. If she found him, she would've killed him without second thought.

When she pulled me out of the crate for my daily beatings, I clutched George to my chest doing everything I could to keep him safe. However, even at five I was bigger and stronger than most kids. When mother tossed me back in that cage and I opened my hand, I had crushed my friend to death.

Mother found me crying with George's body still in my hands. She reminded me that I am darkness, the son of the devil. She told me that I will always taint and kill the things around me because I was never meant to have love.

As much as I want to keep Summer and Gabe, I know just like George, I will one day hurt them. Even if I'd rather die than cause them any pain. I am evil, and evil does not get the benefits of being loved.

CHAPTER THIRTY-ONE

Henry Parks

Beast

Three days after killing Timothy Smith, I still didn't have the answers I was looking for. There was nothing online that referenced that symbol. In fact, every time I looked it up I got articles about the Illuminati.

The only images I've found are on gravestones. But no reference to what it was. My frustrations were growing.

"It's not the only thing bothering you," Priest says in my head.

I toss the hammer onto the nightstand, walking away from the body lying on the bed.

She loves me. Although Summer has not repeated the words to me since that night, they continue to play back in my head.

"You're going to ruin her. You'll kill her just like you did George," Mother taunts.

"She's lying. You know that, Kid. You're capable of love."

I want to believe Priest, but every time I shut my eyes, I see her bloody body in my arms the same way George's was.

My phone ringing startles me out of my thoughts. I glance down at the screen before answering.

"It's been a minute," I say to the man on the other end of the phone. Walking over to the dresser, I pulled my laptop out of the black duffle. After connecting my phone to the computer, I go to the recording app.

His laughter flows through the speaker. "I was giving you space. You've been busy. After the douchebag, you killed the tramp that was with him that night, and the leggy waitress that served your table. Both quick and simple kills. Is there a reason for that?"

"No," I answer honestly.

The night I killed the call girl and the waitress, Summer asked me to not be out late because she wanted to watch the next episode of Game of Thrones. My quick kills were so I didn't keep her waiting.

"Hmmm," he hums. "You made up for those two kills with the Trucker. He didn't like you much. He thought you were abusing the girl and called you a few filthy names."

I don't tell the benefactor that it was because of those names I gutted him with a jigsaw.

"Did you call me just to discuss my kills?"

He chuckles. "You're talented. I have to admit," he says. "I'm quite jealous of your skill. Your eye for detail and creativity is unmatched. Even the way you channel your rage into your kills. You are a rare breed. Almost as rare as the green eyes you inherited."

"Oddly enough, my son didn't get them," I say casually.

He laughs. "Don't feel bad most don't."

The line goes silent, but I know he hasn't discontented. I wait patiently for him to speak again. I don't have long to wait.

"You know what baffles me the most about you?" he says, sounding as if he's genuinely asking a question. "I can't figure out how you ended up at the Church. How did you slip through the hands?"

"Whose hands did I slip through?"

He chuckles. "Good question, I know you will figure it out eventually."

"Is this still a friendly call, or have you made your decision yet?" I ask once again if he's friend or foe?

He's silent. "I'm still undecided. I'll let you get back to your tasks. But be mindful, the clock is ticking." The line clicks letting me know the benefactor is gone.

I unplug the phone from the computer and stuff it back in my pocket. I run down everything he said once again. At first I thought that maybe he had no idea of all the gems he revealed during our conversations. But now, I think he might be leaving breadcrumbs on purpose.

The mention of the rarity of my green eyes was a big giveaway. The benefactor is connected to me in some way. It further solidified my suspicion when I brought up Gabe not having my eye color and he mentioned not many did. I just have to figure out how he connects to me.

Moaning from behind me draws my attention back to Henry Parks, the diner owner. I turn back to face him. He's nearly unrecognizable on the bed.

"Store what the benefactor said," Mother says. *"Finish your job."*

I do exactly as told, putting the conversation I just had to the back of my mind. Walking back to the bed, I pick up the hammer. With the claw side pointing down, I raise it over my head and bring it down.

I have work to do.

This issue with the ring and the benefactor is messing with my head. I don't have enough answers to my questions and that's slowing down my process. For that reason, I made a much bigger mess with Henry than I had planned. I called in a cleaning crew after I was done to take care of the problem. Afterwards, I quickly went to my apartment to shower first before going back home.

There were too many things still left undone. Although the benefactor isn't an immediate threat, he's still out there and I'm no closer to finding him than I was when he first called. And his warning tonight about a ticking clock had me even more on edge. Whoever it is the benefactor keeps warning me about, is getting closer. I have a feeling if I don't figure this out soon, I am going to have a war on my hands.

"You will lose them in this war," Mother says. *"They aren't built for it. You will fail them again, just like you did once before."*

Her words stop me in my tracks as I stand at the back patio door. I shut my eyes, fighting my thoughts.

"Why do you even try," Mother continues, her voice growing deeper. *"You should just kill them now and put them out of their misery. They will both die in the end."*

It's no longer mother's voice in my head.

This voice is darker, more sinister. It isn't new to me. I first heard it when I was a child. It's the voice that I keep trapped in the darkest recesses of my mind. The voice that only comes out when I am at my weakest and lowest.

"No," I snap at the voice in my head. *"You are not in control."*

"Look where you are, Gabriel," the voice growls.

I open my eyes and realize I am no longer outside on the patio. I am now standing in the kitchen. My duffle bag clutched in one hand and the other hand inside the bag. I yank my hand out of the bag and drop it at my feet.

The clanking noise startles Summer as she walks into the kitchen.

"Jeez," she gasps, placing a hand to her chest. "You scared me." She offers me a beautiful smile, before heading to the stove. "I was just about to make some tea. You want some?"

Just the sight of Summer, has my thoughts clearing. I can feel that sinister voice being shoved back into the furthest parts of my mind. The tension in my shoulders and chest immediately fades away. All the worries and fears I carried to this house are washed away with her presence. She is my sanctuary.

Without saying a word, I walk up behind her. She's wearing the black hoodie I gave her with fuzzy slippers like she does on most nights.

The restraint I've been maintaining the last few weeks flies out of the window. For once, I need her to chase my demons away.

Logic is screaming at me to walk away. This could be dangerous. The way I'm craving Summer could cause me to not be gentle. But logic won't win tonight. The beast needs to feed, but it only wants to sate its appetite with what's between Summer's thighs.

I press against her back, roaming my hand from her hips to the front of her. I slip my hand underneath the hoodie and into her panties. I find her nub and stroke it slowly.

"Gabriel, what are you…" her words die on her tongue as I stroke her faster. She widens her legs, giving me more access to her.

Taking that as a sign, I slip a finger into her tight heat. She's wet, but not nearly as soaking as she was the other morning. The books explain that her lack of wetness means she's not ready for me yet.

Turning her around to face me, I look down into her half-closed eyes.

"Do you want me to stop?" I ask, as I tug the hoodie up her hips to her chest. Although, it might physically kill me, I would stop for her.

She doesn't answer right away. From the moment I first saw Summer I've been able to read her like a book. Her expressions are so open that even I can decipher them. I can see the hesitation in her eyes. Yet the desire has her mouth open and her breathing ragged.

Finally, she lifts her arms over her head allowing me to pull off the hoodie. I toss the fabric behind me. I gave her the only chance of turning back, she will not get another.

She stands before me in her pink silk camisole and matching underwear. She has a lot of these. She wears them to bed every night driving me crazy, taunting me to misbehave. Tonight, she will win.

Dropping to my knees in front of her, I pull her underwear down to her feet but keep my eyes on her.

"Take them off."

She lifts her legs allowing me to remove the silk garment. I finally look away from her eyes, down to her hairless mound. My mouth waters immediately. Getting that taste of her the other morning was not enough. I've dreamed about her flavor every night since.

For the first time, I notice a scar on the bottom of her stomach. It's new, it wasn't there the night I met her. I was so out of my mind that morning I didn't even see it then. I run my finger along the line.

"Gabe," she explains. "He was a bit too big and refused to come out by himself. This was his eviction notice." She giggles at her statement.

I place a kiss on the scar, honoring the hardship she went through to bring my son into this world.

Lifting her left leg, I place it on my shoulder. I turn my head and drop a kiss on the inside of her thigh, before sucking her clit into my mouth.

"Ugghhhhhhh," she gasps and then moans, leaning her head back.

I bury my face in her center working my tongue over her clit. She cries out over my head, as she buries her hands in my hair. My messy bun falls causing my hair to cascade down my back.

Gripping her ass in both my hands, I pull her closer to me. Burying my tongue in her center, I lick up her essence, before going back to the little nub that is now peeking from behind it's hood. Summer's moans and whimpers drive me crazy. Every time she whispers my name it drives me closer and closer to madness.

"Oh, shit. Yes," she screams as she releases in my mouth.

I drink down all of her without wasting a drop. When I'm done, I go right back to her swollen nub, sucking her into my mouth. She screams again, her body convulsing with another orgasm.

The burning need to feel her walls wrap tightly around my length has me springing to my feet. I undo my jeans, pushing them and my boxer briefs down to my knees.

Grabbing her leg, I lift it up to my shoulder. She turns her body slightly giving me better access to her center. Taking ahold of my cock, I bend my knees a little to line myself up to her center. Before I slide in, I look her in the eyes.

The feeling of peace washes over me. There are no voices, no worries, no dark thoughts. It is only she and I. Keeping my gaze on her, I slowly push into her center.

Her mouth falls open as I ease inside. The grip her pussy has on me brings me to the peak of madness. My obsession with this woman grows daily.

Summer shuts her eyes.

"No," I bark. "Keep them open."

Drawing out of her, I roll my hips forward pushing all the way in.

"Fuck, Gabriel," She whimpers as she comes up on her tiptoes her hand pushes against my stomach. "You're too deep. You're too deep."

I slam into her, she cries out and rises up on her tiptoes again. I smack her ass.

"Don't run from me," I growl.

"I'm trying, baby. I'm trying, you're so big," she whimpers.

I stop moving. This is the second time she's called me that nickname. The need to claim her has me pulling out. I can't get as deep as I want at this angle. I turn her around, pressing her front against the kitchen sink.

Holding the back of her neck, I keep her head down before tugging her hips toward me. I once again bend my knees as I push into her until my balls press against her pussy lips.

She lets out a muffled scream. When I look over to her face her hand is covering her mouth. I pull out to the tip and drive back into her rapidly. My hips bounce against her ass making a clapping sound.

Summer reaches behind her and wraps a hand around my wrist, her nails digging into my flesh. The pain spurs me on. With one hand on her ass cheek, I open her up, admiring the way her pink center is swallowing my cock. It puckers with each exit and talks back to me with every entrance.

"Fuuuuccckk," she cries out.

"Will I haunt you, Summer?" I ask. I needed to know if I was in her system the same way she was in mine. I meant what I told her the other day. I wanted to haunt her the way she did me.

I slow up my strokes and feed her less dick allowing her to catch her breath.

"Yes," she moans quickly.

I can feel the start of her orgasm building. Her walls begin to pulse around me as if there is a heartbeat buried inside.

I chuckle. "No, baby," I groan. "Not yet."

Not like I wanted her too. I pull out of her, but quickly lift her up and carry her into the living room placing her down on the couch. I kick off my boots, pants and underwear before joining her.

She spreads her legs, welcoming me between her thighs. I stare down at her. Never have I ever seen such beauty in my life.

Grabbing her legs, I turn her body and slide her to the edge of the couch. I fold her body up, pressing her knees to her face. This angle gives me the perfect view of her.

Getting on my knees, I run a finger in between her folds before strumming over her clit.

"Oooh," she whimpers.

I continue my strokes wanting to see her walls spasm with her orgasm. My fingers move faster. Her hips gyrate and her cries grow louder.

"Gabriel, baby, I can't," she whimpers.

"I want to see this pussy cry for me, Summer. Stop fighting it and let it go."

She squirms beneath me, but I don't stop. She starts to pant my name over and over and then she erupts. Her essence leaks out of her like a leaky faucet. Now it's time, I line the head of my cock to her opening and push in.

She yelps at my intrusion. Her walls squeeze me, welcoming me home. I stare down at her mound, loving the way she's taking me. Her legs are still pushed to her head.

I stroke in her rapidly, my balls smacking against her ass.

"You're doing so good, baby. Taking all this dick like this," her wetness sings out to the room.

"Can I go deeper, Summer? Can I feed all this cock to you?"

"Yes, please," she moans.

I hate not being able to see her face. I part her legs, bending them at the knee, and then tucking them up to her armpits. She's wide open for me.

Slowing my stroke, I watch her face. The way she bites that bottom lip, the way her brows meet, even the noises she makes has my sac tingling.

I stroke all the way in until my pelvis is flushed to hers. She whines, placing a hand on my thigh. If we were in another position she would probably run, but the way I have her she has nowhere to go.

I play with her pearl again, wanting her to shoot off with me.

"No, no," she tosses her head side to side.

"Yes. Yes you will." I continue my rapid flicks over her clit as I speed up my strokes going faster and deeper.

Her movement becomes more erratic, her breathing more labored.

"Give it to me," I demand, wanting us to hit the peak together.

"Gabriel. Gabriel," she cries out and then screams as she comes one last time.

The squeezing of her walls and the way she's become so wet it's soaking the front of my shirt has me shooting off with her. My back locks up and I come so hard my sight goes out and I almost collapse. Instead of pulling out of Summer, I pull her down off the couch on top of me.

Her heart is beating rapidly against my chest. Her body is sweaty. We lie on the floor together, both trying to calm down from that orgasm.

I admire how silent my head is as I stroke my finger up and down her back.

"Do you want to tell me what that was about?"

A smile slips across my face. She lays her hands across my chest and rest her chin on top.

"Why do you ask that?"

She wasn't wrong, but I needed to know how she knew.

She shrugs. "I'm starting to be able to read you a little better. I think your weird magic trick is rubbing off on me."

I chuckle at the old joke from that night five years ago. Wiping a hand across her freckles I sober up.

"Tonight, I had to battle with some old demons." That was as much as the truth I was willing to tell her.

She frowns creating a crease between her brows. "Is everything okay?"

"I'm good."

"Good, now come on." She sits up, straddling my waist. Her center right on my pelvis. I ignore the heat of her pussy so close to my cock. "We need to get up and put clothes on. One of us was rather loud and possibly woke our son up."

"Maybe you should keep it down next time."

She sticks out her tongue at me before standing. I climb to my feet too. I quickly grab my jeans off the floor. The ring I took from Timothy falls out of my pocket onto the floor. Before I can grab it, Summer picks it up and looks at it.

"I need that back," I say reaching for it.

She lifts her head and cocks a brow at me. "I never took you for a royal asshole."

Her words catch me off guard, but I quickly recover. "You know what that symbol is?"

"Well, not really. But I use to work at this upscale club in Manhattan. The owner was part of this very secret society type group. He also had a ring like this."

She holds up the ring to me. "We heard him refer to the group as The Royals one time, so we nicknamed them the royal assholes. Once a month they would come into the club and take up the entire VIP section. We always hated it when they came in because they were rich snobs. And despite what people think, rich people like that are the worse tippers."

"Summer," I place my hands on her shoulders. "Focus. What club was this?"

"It's called O' Cleary's."

Finally, I had a breakthrough with this ring. Even the partial name she gave me was helpful. If that club was still up and running, I had at least one more avenue to search. My doubts from earlier seem like a distant memory.

After grabbing the ring out of her hand and sticking it back in my pocket, I pick her up. She wraps her legs around my waist.

"Where are we going?" She chuckles.

"For round two," I grin.

She shakes her head and bites into her bottom lip but doesn't deny me. I walk her upstairs and into our bedroom where I crawl back between her thighs for three more rounds.

CHAPTER THIRTY-TWO

We Be Clubbin

Summer

"You and Mr. James are spoiling my son," I say to Trina through our facetime call.

It's been five days since the night Gabriel came home fighting his demons. The man sexed me so good that night, I forgot all about my plans to not sleep with him.

When he first pressed up against me, it was on my mind to turn him down. To explain to him how sex would not be a good idea. However, when he turned me to face him, I saw that look in his eyes. I knew he was fighting something. Whatever it was, I knew he needed me to quiet it down at the time. And like a fool I obliged.

Well, I'm paying for it now. Since that next morning, he's been MIA. I have no idea where he is during most of the day. He leaves early in the morning and gets back so late at night I'm not sure the sun isn't touching the sky when he arrives.

I don't know what mission he's on, but it has his head completely occupied.

"What are godparents for if not to spoil our only godchild."

I shake my head at my best friend. I'm in my work room putting the final touches on some custom orders. I glance up into my phone mounted on my desk by the ring light.

"And where do you think he's bringing that giant doll house?"

"First off, it's not a doll house. When James finishes building it, it will be a child size replica of the Avengers headquarters."

I shake my head and roll my eyes at Trina.

"I can't believe you and Gabe suckered that man into building that thing."

Trina scoffs. She pulls the phone down for a second and I can tell she's walking through her house from the flash of the walls around her. She stops, stares down at the phone and then the screen switches. I'm now staring at James and Gabe sitting amongst a giant pile of Legos. They are both fully focused on putting the little pieces together. The camera flips back to Trina.

"Does that look like a man that's being suckered." She's moving back through the house again, I'm assuming heading back to her bedroom.

I toss my head back and laugh. Suddenly my phone vibrates, and the screen switches over to a call. It's Andrew. I hit decline and go back to my FaceTime with Trina.

"Who was that?" She asks, taking a seat back on her bed. Her back pressed against the headboard.

Sighing, I say. "Andrew."

She's quiet for a moment. "When's the last time you talked to him?"

"A couple of days ago. We've been talking on the phone, but he keeps wanting to see me again."

"That's what people who are dating usually do. They see each other."

Placing the necklace I was working on back down on the table, I turn in my seat to give Trina my full attention.

"I know, it's just…Andrew is nice, but—"

"He isn't your baby daddy."

Blinking a few times, I hold up a hand. "Whoa. Where did that come from? You know that me and Gabriel are just—"

"Playing a dangerous game." She takes a sip of her drink. "You can tell me a thousand times he's not staying. Doesn't change the way that man looks at you or the way you glow when you're in his presence."

"Okay, so what. Yes, I like Gabriel."

"Like?" she scoffs. "Baby, you have passed like. You love that man."

Leaning forward I wave my hands in front of the screen. "Pump the breaks." I chuckle. "Don't be ridiculous. He's only been here a month."

"And?" She shrugs. "I knew after the first date that James was special. Two weeks after that, I knew he and I would get married. Hell, the first month I was in love. This is a man that shares a child with you. A man that helped you change your life around after one night with him.

"I don't know what happened the night you made G, and I won't pretend like I don't know it wasn't all rainbows and roses. Something scared the shit out of you. And maybe it has to do with the fact that Nic was brutally murdered that night, but something freaked you out. However, I also know that whatever you shared with that man that night stuck with you. So, no, it's not hard to believe that after nearly of month of him living with you, you have fallen in love."

I slink back in my chair. Leaning my head back, I stare up at the ceiling. She's not lying. Before Gabriel came back, I never knew what kept me from falling for anyone else. He's been back a month and I miss him when he's gone. I can't wait to see him when he comes back. I think of new ways to spend my time with him. And seeing him bond with his son is one of the best feelings in the world. Even when I tell myself that I'm not falling for him and this won't last, I still run headfirst into him.

"We're not good together." Even saying the words out loud doesn't sound believable.

"Keep telling yourself that, maybe you'll start to believe it. But in the meantime, you need to be honest with Andrew. He's a good guy and doesn't deserve to be strung along."

I scoff. "You're right. I have to tell him."

Before Trina and I could say anything else, Gabriel storms into my work room with a black garment bag and a brown shimmery shoe box. He lays the bag and shoes over the hobby table in the middle of the room.

"Get dressed," he says turning to leave. "We're going out." With no further explanation he's out the door.

"What the hell?" I ask turning back to Trina.

"Girl, don't just sit there let me see what he got."

Getting up, I detach my ring light stand from my work desk and carry it over to the table. I place the stand down so that the phone is facing me. I first take the top off the shoe box, inside is a red dust bag. I move the dust bag to the side and pull apart the white paper.

"Holy cow," I sing.

"What? Let me see," Trina demands.

Picking up the black leather strappy heels with the tan insides and the bright red bottoms, I show them to Trina.

Her mouth falls open as she stares wide eyed at the screen. "I have got to see the dress that goes with those shoes."

I gently place the heels back down in the box before unzipping the garment bag. I pause as I gaze down at the emerald green satin dress. I pull it off the hanger and hold it up to my body. It has spaghetti straps and a draped collar. The back is a scoop back and it falls so low I doubt I'll be able to wear underwear with it. Holding it up to my body, the hem of the dress hits mid-thigh.

The dress is sexy but elegant and it will show off my minimal curves perfectly.

"Girl, at this point, you need to just marry that man. He not only picked out a perfect dress for your body type, but in your favorite color. He is a winner."

Never have I agreed with my friend more. It's moments like this that make feel as if I'm falling for Gabriel. My brain is telling me that it's a false high, the feelings aren't real. However, it's hard to remain stoic.

I lay the satin dress back down on the black garment bag.

"This is a bad idea, right? Like, we both agree I shouldn't go."

Trina turns her nose up. "It was a bad idea when you let him move in with you. It's a bad idea that you let him sleep in your bed every night. It was an even worse idea that you fucked him again. Don't act like you're against bad ideas suddenly."

I roll my eyes, placing my hands on my hips. "You're not helping."

She chuckles. "No, I'm being honest. But here are some words of advice. You're going to go shower, put on those expensive shoes and that gorgeous dress. You're going to wear your hair up to show off the back of the dress, and you're going to wear some gold jewelry. And finally, you're going to stop worrying about changing things that you no longer have control of."

Dropping my arms down to my side, I sigh. "You're right."

"I know. Now, go get ready. And take pictures."

The line goes dead, and I stand for a few minutes staring at the dress and shoes. I'm going on a date. I wasn't officially asked, but I was more excited about this date than any other date I've been on.

Grabbing the dress and shoes, I head for my bedroom ready to experience the night.

Coming out of the bathroom, I stop by the full-length mirror. I couldn't help staring at the woman looking back at me. I felt absolutely gorgeous. The green dress looked amazing against my skin and it fit me like a glove allowing my slight curves to show. My braids were pulled up in a high bun.

The girl I was five years ago would be completely shocked to see the woman in the mirror today. She would've never believed that the two were the same. It feels like a lifetime ago that I was that girl.

"You look absolutely beautiful," his deep voice pulls my attention away from my thoughts.

"Thank you. You picked out a...." my words die when I turn to look at him in the doorway. My eyes bulge as I take in Gabriel's appearance. "Whoa."

No one could ever say he isn't an attractive man but seeing him in his black fitted T-shirt that hugs his biceps just right. Not too tight, but enough to show the stretch of the fabric. His dark washed jeans look tailored to his tall frame. His shirt is tucked in and a simple black belt with a silver buckle is an added accent. He's wearing new black biker type boots and on his wrist is the bracelet I made him with the added bead for my birthstone.

If I'm not careful, this man might get me pregnant tonight.

"You look great," I say taking him in one more time.

He looks down at himself as if he's just now seeing his outfit. He looks at me and shrugs.

"Ready to go?"

"Uhh, yeah let me grab my bag." I go to the bed to pick up my small black clutch. "Oh wait, I need to send Trina a picture." I take my phone out of my bag and hand it to Gabriel. "Take a picture please." I quickly strike a pose. He snaps a quick picture and hands me the phone back.

"Come on, let's take one together."

"Why?" he asks confused but follows me to the full-length mirror.

"I want something to commemorate the night. I can look back at it years from now when you're long gone. I'll show my grandkids how good their grandaddy looked."

Although I say it jokingly, it stings a little to know that one day, maybe even soon, he will be long gone.

Gabriel takes the phone from me and holds it up, the flash facing the mirror. I turn my body toward him placing a hand on his chest. He wraps his free arm around my back allowing his hand to rest on my right ass cheek. I don't comment on his hand placement.

He snaps the picture, but instead of giving me the phone back right away, he taps a few times on my phone.

"What are you doing?"

"Sending the pictures to my phone," he simply says.

I blush at the idea of him wanting to have something to remember the night too. He hands me the phone back. I quickly send the pictures to Trina, admiring how good he and I look together.

Stuffing the phone back in my clutch, I follow Gabriel out the bedroom. We make it outside and sitting in my driveway is a smoke grey BMW M4. My mouth falls open as he walks me to the passenger side of the car with a hand placed at my back.

"I didn't know you had a car?" I've never seen Gabriel drive. Even when he goes on errands with me, I'm always driving my car.

"I don't," he says, as he opens the door for me.

"Well, whose is this?" I ask, pointing at the vehicle.

"Just get in the car, Summer," he says.

Without another word, I get my ass in the car sinking back into the leather seat. Gabriel shuts my car door and walks around to the driver's side. I secure myself in my seatbelt and then pop the locks for him. He gets in, his head missing the roof by a few inches.

After cranking the car, he turns to me. "Are you ready?"

I nod my head. He hits a button, and the roof of the car slowly folds back revealing the night sky. Gabriel backs out of the driveway and speeds off. I lean my head back on the headrest, shut my eyes, and enjoy the ride.

Nearly thirty minutes later we pulled into a parking garage. Gabriel helps me out the car and we head out onto the street.

"How far is this place?" I ask.

I'm not complaining, but these heels aren't really made for long walks. He looks down at my feet.

"I should have gotten you flatter shoes."

"Ugh, not with this dress," I laugh. "These shoes are absolutely perfect. Thank you, by the way. I really appreciate the gifts."

"You're welcome."

"By the way, how do you know my size?"

He looks down at me and raises an eyebrow.

"You pay attention," I repeat the words he told me at the grocery store that day.

We walk about a block before things start to look familiar. In my defense this part of the city is a popular spot. Not only are there clubs around here, but there are also bars and a few nice restaurants. So, I had no idea where we would be going.

I stop walking when we turn the curve and come face to face with the familiar brick building. The line for entry is nearly wrapped around the building.

Gabriel stops a little ahead of me, he turns back to face me with a brow raised.

"So, this isn't about a date at all? This is about that ring and the thing you're working on?" I shake my head. We were standing in front of O'Cleary's. "Wow. I should've known."

I turn to walk away but stop when he wraps his hand around my bicep. Damn he's fast.

He stares into my face for a long moment as if there is a hidden message in my features. Finally, he looks away before looking back at me.

"I'm sorry," he finally says. "I should have told you where we were going and not let you get your hopes up."

It isn't just about me getting my hopes up, but I don't explain that to him. Pulling my arm from his grip, I nod my head.

"It's all good. Let's just go."

"We can't. This is the only night the Royals will be here for another thirty days. I need to go in."

Folding my arms over my chest, I say, "Okay. Go in. I'm not stopping you. I'll go into a restaurant and wait for you."

He's shaking his head at me before I finish my sentence. "You have to go with me."

"What?" I shout, dropping my arms at my side. "Why?"

He takes a step toward me, grabbing my hand in his. "I need you in there because places like this are sometimes a lot for me. The flashing lights, the loud noise and the crowd makes it hard for me to focus sometimes. I get overstimulated, but I notice when I'm around you, it quiets the noises. You make everything disappear. I need you in there with me."

Fuck. See. How am I supposed to stay angry when he says things like that to me? He has a way of making me feel so important and so special. I want to be all those things for him that he needs me to be.

"Look, I wish I could. But you don't understand what you're asking of me. O'Cleary's is a breeding ground for my old vices. Since I've been out of rehab, I've stayed clear of places like that. My demons run rampant in that place."

He cups my face in his palms, his green eyes staring down at me. "There isn't a place on this earth you need to fear when you're with me. I got you, Summer. Forever. Do you believe that?"

For some reason, without a doubt, I believed him. I nod my head.

"Good. But you're right. I should have thought about your demons before I brought you here. I'll find another way. Come on." He lets go of my face and grabs my hand, heading back the way we came.

I take a few steps but stop. Closing my eyes, I allow the words of my sponsor to penetrate my thoughts. *"You still fear relapsing."* There is no doubt that even after five years that is a huge fear of mine. I've done well to stay away from places like this.

Even when Trina goes out for her birthday, I usually go to the dinner party but leave before she goes to a club. I'm not saying that I wanted to start hanging at clubs again, but I did want to face this fear. Because if I can fight off those old urges in here, I can do it anywhere. And if I had to face this battle with anyone by my side, it would be Gabriel.

"Alright, let's do it."

He stares at me quietly for a moment. "Are you sure?"

"Yeah, I can do it. But if I need to leave, we will leave right?"

"Immediately," he says.

I dip my chin ready to face the biggest hurdle of my life. Gabriel holds my hand the entire walk up to the club. From outside I can hear the music bumping. I head to the back of the line ready to wait with everyone else. However, Gabriel has other plans. He tugs me to the front of the line. Standing in front of us is a tall woman with a blunt bob. Standing behind her are three bulky bodyguards.

She gives the bouncer at the door her name. He checks the iPad in his hand. Apparently, she was on his list because he handed her one of the VIP bracelets for the Royal's. Once the tall woman and her three companions walk into the club, the bouncer at the front door turns to us.

I was about to tell Gabriel that unless we were part of the royal crew, we wouldn't get in this way.

The bouncer's eyes widen when we step up.

"Sorry Sir, go right in," he opens the door allowing us in without even paying the hundred-dollar door fee. The pounding music engulfs us as we walk inside. I tap his arm and he bends down to hear me.

"How did we get in? They never let anyone cut the line or skip paying."

He smiles before leaning into my ear. "I paid him a home visit. He was very willing to let me in."

I shake my head because I can only imagine what that visit consisted of. Gabriel and I head to one of the only vacant booths. Already the dance floor is packed. Bodies grind against each other; the strobe lights shine across the room casting everyone in colorful hues.

I slide into the booth and Gabriel slips in beside me. His gaze bounces around the room and to the glass divider for the VIP section. Just like I knew it would be, it's filled with the Royals and their bodyguards.

"Are you okay?" I ask Gabriel when I fill his body tense beside me. He looks down at me and smiles.

"Yes. What about you?" I look around the room at the alcohol flowing, and at the tables where the strobe lights don't quite reach. The tables I know to be the supplier of my many intoxicated nights. I look, waiting for an itch or a burning need, yet nothing happens. Turning back to him, I smile.

"I'm good."

He dips his chin at me. Not long after, a waitress comes to the table, one I know too well. If I thought I would get through this night without any hiccups fate has just proven that's a lie.

"Hey Summer," Clarissa sings. "Girl it's been a minute. Where've you been?"

I look over to Gabriel who is watching me cautiously. Sometimes I feel like this man is so in tuned with my emotions he can pick up on them without me uttering one single word.

"Umm, around." I wave my hand in a circle awkwardly.

Clarissa laughs. "I was telling one of the new waitresses about you the other day. Nobody partied harder than you. Remember the time you did those lines off that guys…"

"Coke," I blurt out. "A Coca-Cola would be nice. Gabriel what about you?"

Clarissa turns her attention to Gabriel as if she's just now noticing him. She grimaces before lifting up her tablet.

"Water," he says in that monotone voice.

"That's it, just a water and a pop?" Clarissa looks to me as if she's expecting more.

When Clarissa knew me, I was taking Tequila shots like they were going extinct. I started my day with a bottle and often ended it passed out in the back breakroom. I understand her questioning my order.

"Give us time to look at the menu and we may order some food."

She looks over to Gabriel before nodding her head. "Well just so you know, we have some of our service men in the building. If you want, I can place an order for you." She winks.

Service men is what we called the dealers that were allowed in the club to supply the partiers. I had a pretty good relationship with the service men. I didn't always have the money to pay, but dealers had no qualms about taking a blow job for a small bag of coke.

Swallowing the knot that has just formed in my throat I shut my eyes. The memory of those nights hit me. That feeling of being so high nothing seemed to matter to you. The feeling of floating that a few lines of coke brought you. It's hard to explain.

Then another vision pops in my head. A high so pure there is nothing in the world like it. A vision of Gabe smiling up at me.

I open my eyes and shake my head. "No. I'm good. Just the pop is fine."

"Are you sure—"

"Walk away."

The tone of his voice and the way he's glaring at Clarissa made me feel sorry for the woman. Clarissa, assumingly picking up on his threat, quickly rushes away.

"You didn't have to do that," I chuckle. "I wasn't going to change my mind."

He looks over to me briefly, before looking up at the glass VIP section. "Forever," he says referencing his earlier statement.

Without a doubt, and with not much to base it on, I knew that no matter what, Gabriel indeed had my back.

"Let's dance?" I say, bumping my shoulder into his side.

He looks down at me and then over to the dance floor. "Dance?"

I realized that it might be too much to ask of him. The dance floor is crowded, people are damn near all over each other. The lights are flashing over the gyrating crowd. Just like he didn't want to push me out of my comfort zone, I don't want to force him either.

I lift my shoulder and let it drop. "Don't worry about it."

I was a little disappointed, because I love to dance. And the thought of letting loose and having some fun with Gabriel was exciting.

He places a hand on my thigh. I look over to him and he's staring at me. "Come on."

I smile so big my cheeks hurt. Gabriel stands and then holds out a hand for me. I place my hand in his and slide out the booth. He leads me to the dance floor. Oddly enough, when we get to the crowd, they immediately make a space for us.

The song the DJ is playing is fast paced. I expected Gabriel to stand there and just watch me dance. I would've never thought he could actually dance. He's no Micheal Jackson or Chris Brown, but he stayed on the beat and was light on his feet.

We danced six songs back-to-back, only taking a few breaks to enjoy our drinks. Finally, my feet started complaining. letting me know that unless I wanted blisters in the morning, I had better sit my ass down.

Grabbing Gabriel's hand, I lead him back to the table. As soon as we have a seat, I lean my head on his arm.

"I had no idea you could dance so well."

He looks down at me, briefly before going back to scanning the room. "Priest taught us all how to dance when we were ten. We all thought it was stupid. Only person that enjoyed it was Zel. But, Zel usually liked everything."

I loved when Gabriel talked about his brothers. It always brought a brightness to his eyes and a slight smile to his face.

"Well, that was nice of Priest. Is he like your father?"

He turns to look at me, his gaze narrows as he takes me in. He runs a finger over my dusting of freckles.

"Yeah, he is." He finally says.

We enjoy the music a little longer. Gabriel spends the time texting on his phone and scanning the room. I dance in my seat as I enjoy my second Coca-Cola.

"Okay," I say, putting my drink down. "I think I'm ready to order some food."

He pulls a wad of cash out of his pocket and places it on the table. "Order. I have to take a leak."

I look at his untouched glass of water. "Okay."

He goes to slide out of the bench but stops. He turns back to me. "Do not move from this spot."

Placing a hand to my head in a salute, I say, "Aye aye captain."

He smirks at me before sliding out of the bench. I watch him as he disappears around the corner and into the back hallway where the bathrooms are. For this to be a fake date, it was turning out to be rather enjoyable.

Beast

There are a few people in the restroom when I walk in. They stare at me when I enter. I glare back at them. Two men at the urinals quickly shake themselves off before hastily stuffing their cocks back in their pants and clearing the bathroom. The other guy doesn't even use the urinal before he leaves.

I go to the stall with the white paper that reads 'Out of Order' in black bold letters. I tear the caution tape down and walk into the bathroom.

Taped to the back of the toilet is a clear bag with one gun, a bowie knife and holster, and some construction wire. I place the knife and holster on my leg, the gun at my back and stick the wire in my pocket.

Although the bouncer wouldn't have checked me when I came in, I still had to stash my weapons. Most members of the Church have been trained to spot the bulge of a gun or knife holster. Same way I spotted Victoria's and Yohan's back at Tim's office.

I had no doubt that the Royals' bodyguards could do the same. I couldn't take the risk of carrying my stuff with me.

Just then the door to the bathroom creaks open and two sets of footsteps enter. The click of the lock echoes through the area.

After flushing the toilet, I unzip my pants. I then walk out the bathroom rezipping them.

"Well, well, well, what do we have here, brother? Beast Boy at a Royal Society affair?"

I look up to find two men standing in front of the sink. One almost as tall as me with dark blonde hair shaved low. His eyes are a startling blue.

Not quite as unique as Many's, but still peculiar. The other guy is shorter with dark brown hair. The rest of his features are unsubstantial. Both men have an arm of tally mark tattoos.

"I didn't think I'd ever see the day," Blue eyes reply. "Corbyn's going to be pissed. First Sim goes rogue, and now this."

I've always admired Fem's talents. Out of all the gifts at the Church, I thought hers to be the most special. I wished I had the ability to transform into characters, to be what people wanted me to be. It would have made my life easier.

Thankfully, after working with Fem for so long and seeing her in action, I was able to pick up a few of her techniques.

Taking a step back, I skim through my memory rolodex for a shocked expression. Widening my eyes, I freeze my movements, my hand still stuck at my zipper.

"How did you recognize me?" I ask, causing my voice to pitch up at the end.

Plain face chuckles. "You come in here towering over everyone like a fucking giant and you think we wouldn't notice you?" He looks to blue eyes. Both men laugh.

"That Church made you stupid." Plain face says.

"I heard they are nothing but trained monkeys over there," Blue eyes adds. "Heard they even got a blind guy. That shit sounds pathetic." Both men laugh again.

"What do you want?" I wipe my hands down the front of my pants as if I'm wiping away sweat.

They look at each other and laugh.

"All our lives, we were told you were this giant enigma. A top tier killer," Blue eyes says pushing away from the sink to stand on my side. I angle my body toward him slightly, keeping him from seeing my back.

"You were the big bad bogeyman," Plain face says standing at my other side.

"What do you think, brother? Want to have some fun and take down the incredible Beast Boy?" Blue eyes asks.

"Time to show Corbyn who the real killers are in the f....."

"Aht aht, Boris." Blue eyes says cutting off plain face.

At this point, I can't keep up the façade anymore. I spotted these two as soon as I walked in the club. They've been making their rounds in the VIP section. Every table seemed to know who they were. I even caught the moment they spotted me. It wasn't when I walked in. It was while I was dancing with Summer.

From that point on, they couldn't keep their attention off me. Which is why I lured them into this bathroom. Dropping my shoulders and shaking my head. I let out a deep breath.

"Well, this was easier than I thought."

"What?" Boris questions right before I pull the gun out of my back and shoot him in the thigh. He goes down easily.

Blue eyes rushes me, shoving his shoulder into my chest. He shoves me against one of cubicle doors and we both go tumbling into the stall. I land on the toilet, and he falls over me. Somehow during the tussle, I lost my gun.

I deliver two powerful blows to his side directly over his ribs. He groans and loosens his grip. I shove him off me and he falls out of the stall. He quickly recovers, getting back to his feet.

Standing, I grab my blade out of my ankle, and walk out of the stall.

Boris is up now too, two knives in each hand, his shirt wrapped around his thigh to stop the blood flow. I could have killed him, but then where's the fun in that.

Boris charges me, and I charge straight for him. He swipes his knives at my head. I lean back avoiding nearly getting my head severed. He leans back to lunge at me again. I move to avoid one blade but the other rips into my shoulder drawing blood. I ignore the pain.

I kick Boris in the thigh, reinjuring his leg. He shouts through clenched teeth before falling to his knees. I look up into the mirror just in time to see blue eyes charging toward me with a knife of his own. I move to the side, grabbing his arm out in front of him, I then bend it back toward his face. With my free hand, I shove his head down to meet the end of his blade. It gouges into his eye. He screams so loud it hurt my ears.

Boris attempts to stand up from the ground, but I use my steel-toed boot to kick him in the head. He falls back onto the tile.

Grabbing the back of blue eyes' head tighter, I lean forward to say into his ear.

"Don't ever call my brother pathetic."

I shove his head down toward the sink. The hilt of the knife hits the edge of the counter shoving the blade further up. He falls to the ground motionless.

Grabbing Boris's leg, I pull him from underneath the sink where he landed. He slowly comes awake. Placing my knee on his chest, I pull the wire out of my pocket and wrap it around his neck. He grabs the metal, but I wrap it around my hands and yank in opposite directions.

His face immediately reddens. He claws at my hands, but it's no use. I tug the ends of the wire further apart cutting into his flesh. Boris stops fighting and goes limp.

As quickly as it started it was over. Their arrogance got the best of them. The fight was over the moment they thought they got the jump on me. If they knew anything about the Church, they should have known I'd be prepared.

After cleaning up the scene as best as I could, I take Boris' knife since it had my blood on it. Grabbing my gun near the trashcan I stuff it back in the back of my jeans. I then place both men in the "out of order" stall before heading out of the bathroom.

I quickly make my way back up the hall and toward the dance floor. Passing only one person on my way out. I keep my head down to block my appearance from those around me. I don't have to worry about the cameras, they've been on a loop since I walked in.

When I get back to the table, Summer is smiling at me.

"We need to leave," I say as soon as I reach her.

Her smile falls. "But I just ordered wings."

I grab her arm and gently pull her out of the seat. "Now, Summer."

She stops and looks at my face, taking in everything.

"Okay."

I pull her with me back toward the exit. A loud commotion erupts behind us. We don't stop to see what it is. We walk out of the building and straight toward the parking garage. Once we climb in the car I quickly pull away putting as much distance as possible between us and the club. We ride in silence.

CHAPTER THIRTY-THREE

The Stars

Summer

Staring out the window in the silent car, I watch the lights of the buildings fade by. I was in my feelings about this "date". I felt proud of myself for achieving such a milestone in my recovery.

I'd been clean for years, but there is a different feeling of accomplishment when you can truly be faced with your old demons and still resist. I had no plans to make a habit of facing those demons, but I felt empowered being able to do it at least once.

Focusing on the passing scenery, I notice that we've been driving for a while and nothing looks familiar.

"Where are we going?"

"It's a surprise."

I turn to look at him. For someone that I didn't know up until tonight could drive, Gabriel is a very safe driver. He's not speeding or swerving in and out of lanes. He's actually pretty calm behind the wheel.

"I like surprises," I say, then amend. "Unless we're going to another club. I think one is enough to last me for a while."

He smiles, cutting his eyes to me briefly. "No more clubs."

I felt confident in that. We drive for another twenty minutes before we pull into a nearly empty parking lot. A black SUV is the only car parked in the vacant lot. The windows are down and the speakers are blasting reggae music. The building is small oval shaped with a dome roof.

As soon as we pull in and park, the doors to the SUV open and four black men jump out. Gabriel gets out of the car and before I can open my door, he's there to help me.

He shuts the door and takes my hand walking me over to the sidewalk. One of the four men steps forward. He's tall, handsome, and dark-skinned with a low-fade and goatee. As soon as we approach him, he daps Gabriel up.

"Damn, Big Guy, I didn't know you were into the sistas." He grins showing off his full bottom set of grills. "Wassup, mama," he nods, giving me attention.

"Hi. I'm Summer," I say, holding out a hand.

"Pharrell, but I'm going to hold off on that handshake. He don't seem like the type that wants me touching his girl."

I look over to Gabriel waiting for him to deny what his friend says.

"Thanks for doing this at the last minute," Gabriel says, not disputing Pharrell's claim.

Pharrell and his friends laugh. I drop my hand back at my side and roll my eyes.

"Don't worry about it," Pharrell replies. "As much money as you've made me over the years, this is light work." He holds a set of keys out to Gabriel. "We set everything up inside. The owner told me to tell you, thanks for the donation and enjoy. He'll meet you back in the morning for the keys."

With that, Pharrell and his crew climb back in their truck and back out the parking lot before speeding away.

"I swear everyday you leave me with more mysteries about you," I say jokingly.

"Come on." He tugs me toward the stairs.

Once inside the building I can tell we're at some type of planetarium. The depictions of the solar system and galaxies on the walls give it away. Along with the giant earth inspired globe that hangs from the ceiling and nearly touches the ground. Gabriel leads me to a door to the left of the empty receptionist's desk.

He stops right before going inside.

"You were right earlier. I shouldn't have made you believe we were going on a date only to take you on a job. I didn't think about how that would make you feel." He looks down at his feet. "I have trouble with understanding and sometimes considering other people's feelings. I'm sorry."

Placing a hand on his chest, I grab his attention back. "It's okay. I forgive you."

"Good, because I want to take you on a date."

The smile that stretches my face makes my cheeks hurt. "Well, today is your lucky day. I don't have any plans at the moment."

I love when I can make him smile. He does it so rarely that getting one is like a gift.

"Come on." He pushes the door open allowing me to walk in first.

My mouth falls open and I clutch a hand to my heart. Over my head is a beautiful display of outer space. There are clusters of stars and galaxies above me. In the middle of the floor is a blanket, two pillows, an ice bucket with a bottle of cola inside, two wine glasses, and take out bags.

"Do you like it?" his voice comes from right behind me.

I nod my head, as tears fill my eyes. "When did you have time to set this up?"

"While we were at the club. This is what I was doing on my phone."

I stare up at the screen over our heads in awe.

He points up to the display, while placing a hand at my lower back. I follow where he's pointing.

"That's called the wishing well cluster or Caldwell 91. It is about 1,321 light years away."

I glance over my shoulder at him. "I didn't know you were into astronomy."

He shrugs. "I'm not." Gabriel takes my hand and leads me to the blanket. I kick off my shoes and take a seat. He sits down in front of me.

"My brother, Lucien, loved stuff like this. When we were kids, he was always reading up on stuff and explaining it to us. The others would sometimes get irritated or ignore him, but I always listened."

He takes the coke out of the ice bucket and pours us two champagne flutes with it. I know it's cheesy, but I love the gesture.

"I found this place for Lucien during one of my menus. On his thirteenth birthday, we all snuck out of the house and broke in. We spent most of our night camped out in those chairs." he points to the theater style seats behind him. "Lucien taught us everything he knew about the solar system that night."

"That's sweet. Did you guys ever get caught?" I ask taking a sip of my pop.

A huge grin spreads on his face. "Hawk made a bet with Many that he couldn't reach the top of that giant sphere in the lobby. Many, of course, reached the top but somehow triggered the fire alarm. Priest paid the owner for the damage. The owner turned out to be cool and allowed us back anytime we wanted during daylight hours."

I laugh at his story. I could imagine how bad they were as kids.

"How many brothers do you have?" I remembered Hawk from that night we first met.

Gabriel divvies up the food. "Hawk is the oldest. Then Zel, they are three months apart. Lucien and Seth are next. Just a month after Zel. Then Many. He's five months older than me."

"I'm guessing you guys don't have the same Mother?"

There is no way Gabriel's crazy ass mama was popping out babies that close together.

"I told you, I've been with the Church since I was seven years old. Priest came and got me about three months before my eighth birthday. He raised me alongside my brothers, which were also recruits. The guys and I have no blood ties to each other, but they are my brothers."

I understood that. I can't imagine the stuff they went through with that organization. I imagine it bonded them. Kind of the way life and my habits bonded me and Trina. We were not biological sisters, but you can't tell me that girl isn't my family.

"I want to meet them." Gabriel looks at me with a raised brow. I shrug. "They mean a lot to you. I can tell by the way you talk about them. And technically they are your son's uncles. I know you can't stay, but I would love to have a part of you around him."

A pained expression flicks across his features turning his brow down. I hated bringing up the fact that he's leaving. However, it's a reality that we both need to face. As much fun as I'm having with Gabriel, and despite me not wanting him to leave, I know that he will.

"I'll see," he says.

For the next forty minutes, Gabriel and I eat and talk. We talk more tonight than we have in the past month he's been here. We talk about my family and everything I've done since he was gone. He talks more about his brothers and growing up with Priest. I laugh so much my sides hurt at the trouble they all got into.

We're lying on our backs, side by side staring up as the screen above us shows the rings of Saturn. Turning on my side, I prop myself up on my elbow. I place a hand on his chest. He turns and looks at me.

"I have to admit. This is the best date I've ever been on."

"Even better than a show and apple turnovers?"

I laugh. "Yes, even better than…. wait, how do you know about that?"

He lifts my hand off his chest and places a kiss on my palm. I knew I wasn't crazy that night. I felt like something was off.

"You better be glad I love you because…" The rest of my words trail off.

That was not supposed to come out of my mouth. Gabriel pushes up on his elbows, his intense gaze watching me.

"What did you say?"

I look away from him. "You know, this Mexican food was really good. We have to take Gabe..."

A finger to my chin has me turning back to face him. He's sitting all the way up now. "Do you love me, Summer?"

The reasonable side of me tells me to say no. It tells me there is no way I could possibly be in love with this man. He's dangerous, unstable, and I've only known him a month. It doesn't make sense. However, my heart doesn't care what logic says.

My heart knows that the night I walked into that crime scene five years ago I'd met the man created for me. Even with all his flaws, Gabriel was meant for me. It doesn't matter if no one else understands it.

"Yes. I love you, Gabriel."

His eyes close as if he's in pain. The vein in his head throbs, and the hand that was once under my chin is fisted so tight his knuckles are white.

"I'm sorry," I say, not realizing how this admission may have made him feel. "I shouldn't have..."

My words are cut off when his lips smash into mine. His tongue sweeps across my bottom lip. I open for him, allowing him to deepen the kiss. The hungry way he devours my mouth has my thighs sticky with my arousal. The way my dressed dipped in the back didn't allow for underwear. At least not any I owned.

I moan when he bites into my bottom lip. I tug at the hem of his shirt, pulling it from inside of his jeans. Once I free the fabric, we break apart from our kiss so that I can lift the shirt over his head. I toss it somewhere behind me.

Gabriel doesn't immediately go back to kissing me, instead he stares down into my face. He strokes a finger across my freckles. The same hand moves down to my shoulder and slowly pushes down the strap of my dress.

I pull my arm out, stretching the fabric out a little. He places a kiss on my shoulder and then gently bites the skin there before sucking it into his mouth. My back bows, arching my chest into him. He tugs the other strap down allowing me to free that arm as well. He places a gentle kiss on my lips as he tugs the front of my dress down exposing my round breasts.

He places a hand at my waist and then rolls me onto my back as he leans over me. I stroke his face, loving the prickles of his facial hair against my palm. When he lowers his head to suck one of my puckered peaks into his mouth I whimper. Placing my hand into his hair, I take the top knot out allowing his golden locs to cascade down. The strands brush against my flesh.

Gabriel goes from one breast to the other giving them both equal attention. The way he lavishes one nipple while tugging the other with his fingers has me squirming.

"Yes," I moan.

He leaves a trail of kisses from my chest back up to my lips. Wrapping a hand around my throat, he tilts my head back so that he can deepen the kiss. The fact that five years ago this man knew almost nothing about sex yet now has the power to weaken me with a kiss is crazy.

I move my hands to his waist, unbuckling his belt. Once I've unfastened his jeans, I shove them down, trying to get to the one thing I need. The thing my body is leaking for.

Gabriel grabs my hands stopping me from pulling him out. He moves them over my head, pinning them there with one hand. With the other, he slowly glides my dress further down my body. I lift my hips allowing him to pull the fabric down. Once he gets it over my ass, he slips it down my legs and tosses it behind him.

I lay before him in nothing but the slight sheen of sweat that coats my body.

"You are my weakness," he whispers as if the words were only meant for himself.

He runs a hand down my thigh to my knee slowly pulling my legs apart. My knees fall to the side, the cool air hitting my soaking wet pussy lips. Gabriel licks his lips as he stares at the mound between my legs.

He releases my hands and places his free one flat against my stomach before slowly dragging it down to the apex of my thighs. He cups my center and shuts his eyes. I try to imagine what he's feeling. Can he feel the warmth coming from my lower lips, and the wetness that leaks from me. Does he know how bad I want him?

His eyes shoot open as he runs a finger over my sensitive clit. I hiss at the contact. He strokes my nub, dipping a finger inside of me. My breathing becomes labored, my lower half squirms. He places one heavy hand on my hip, holding me down.

"Please," I beg.

I can feel my orgasm roaring to life. I need to feel him inside of me.

He moves his fingers faster. I should be embarrassed at the music my pussy is making for him. I'm soaking wet.

I claw at the blanket beneath me, my head thrashing from side to side as my orgasm crashes down on me. I scream his name. He holds me down and continues his work giving equal attention to my clit and the penetration of his other fingers.

When I feel as if I can't take anymore, he pulls his fingers away from me and before I know it his head is buried between my legs. He sucks my sensitive nub.

I shoot off to the moon again, this time my mouth opens but no words come out, my head is thrown back and my back is arched so high it's not touching the floor.

I come so hard and long I can feel my release leave my body. Tears fall from my eyes rolling down to my ears.

Gabriel laps up every drop of my essence as if I'm his favorite dessert. Finally, he moves back up my body trailing kisses on his way to my lips. With one arm to prop him up, he looks down at me.

The head of his dick presses against my opening. I close my eyes, preparing for the first push of him inside me.

"No," he growls. "Open your eyes, Summer. See me." I do as he says. Opening my eyes I look up into his green ones.

"Say it again," he demands.

I don't have to second guess what he's asking me. Licking my lips, I cup his face as I say those three words to him.

"I love you."

He pushes into me slowly.

"Uhhhh," I whimper at the intrusion.

He hikes one leg up over his arm as he seats himself in my depths. He starts to stroke, rolling his hips with each entrance.

My moans grow louder but I never break eye contact with him.

"You're mine forever. Forever," he repeats as he moves faster. His balls smacking against my ass.

"Fuck. Shit." I blurt out random curse words. "Don't stop. Please."

He lets my leg go and presses his head to mine placing a kiss on my lips. He rams his hips forward stroking so deep into me, I feel as if he's found a secret tunnel. I toss my head back and scream. He groans before sitting up.

Grabbing both my legs, he holds them out in a wide V, as he fucks me deep. Letting one of my legs go, he uses his free hand to once again manipulate my clit.

I'm so sensitive after my last two orgasms, I try to move his hand. He quickly swats me away.

"This is mine. Do you understand?" He pins my thigh down as he rubs circles on my nub. I buck against him feeling the start of another orgasm.

"Answer me?" He growls.

"Yes," I cry as he continues to rock into me.

"If you ever give my pussy away it won't end well. I need you to hear me. I will kill any man you ever let touch it."

I believed him. I had no doubt that Gabriel would never allow me to be with another man. And if I'm being honest, I didn't want anyone but him.

"It's yours. All yours, baby." The last word is screamed as my eruption explodes causing stars to burst behind my eyelids.

Gabriel pulls out of me, flips me on my stomach, yanks me up on my knees and slams into me.

"Fuuuuccccckkk," I cry out.

He doesn't miss a stroke as he plows through my climax. He slows his movements, spreading my ass apart. Suddenly, something wet hit my puckered hole. I stiffen, there is no way I was about to take Gabriel's length and girth in my asshole. That's an unchartered territory. And you don't just park your yacht in a speed boat parking space without warning.

The press of something blunt presses against my star.

"Gabriel," I warn.

"Shhh," he hushes me. "Don't worry, my cock's not coming out of this pussy. Just relax."

Feeling a bit more confident, I follow his instructions. Once again something blunt pushes against my back door. Once it slips in, I realize it's a finger. Although the feel of it is foreign, it isn't unpleasant.

Gabriel increases his strokes again, slamming against my butt reaching the depths of my cavern. His finger pumps in my ass adding to the sensation of him being inside me.

My toes curl as another peak unfurls in my belly. I try to throw my ass back on him attempting to fuck him back. However, the way his length digs in my guts has me tapping out. I'm not ashamed to admit that I can't handle him.

He smacks my ass. "Fuck me back," he growls.

I whimper, but once again work my hips. I can tell he's nearing his release, his strokes are getting faster and deeper.

I try to move to keep him from going too deep, but he grips my hips so tightly there will be a bruise tomorrow.

With one final roll of his hip, I come undone. I scream as euphoria takes over me. The sound of Gabriel's roar behind me and the hot spirt of his cum inside me signals his release as well.

My body finally gives out and I collapse down to the floor. He lands behind me. His heart is racing against my back. I fight to catch my breath.

"I have to remind you again, I'm not on birth control." The last time we had sex I had to rush out that next morning and get a morning after pill. If we keep this up, I'm going to have to make an appointment with my gynecologist.

I wait patiently for Gabriel to comment on my last statement. I'm pretty sure he didn't want any more kids.

Instead of a reply. He lifts my leg up over his hip, kisses my shoulder, and slides back in me. My eyes roll to the back of my head. This is going to be a long night.

CHAPTER THIRTY-FOUR

Hornet's Nest

Beast

I stare down at Summer, the shower water raining down on her as she's on her knees with my cock in her mouth.

"This is a sin. The whore has corrupted you," Mother growls in my head.

It's been a week since the night of the club when she told me she loved me. Since then, I haven't been able to keep my hands off her. Even though every time I touch her I see George. I'm reminded of his body crushed in my hands. However, I guess mother was right when she said I was evil. Because even though I fear hurting her more than anything, I can't leave her alone. I didn't lie when I told her she is my weakness.

"You will both burn in hell for this," Mother warns.

"Hey, Kid, shut that bitch up and enjoy this got damn blow job," Priest states.

I do exactly as Priest says, silencing my thoughts, I look down into her brown eyes as she sucks me to the back of her throat.

I tug at my hair, not sure what to do with all this pleasure. My many years of studying about sex, I heard and saw how enjoyable this could be. However, having Summer on her knees in front of me doing it feels way more intense than the articles explained.

She hums around me, sending the vibration to my balls. I've had enough. Grabbing onto her long braids, I pull her mouth off me and then drag her to her feet. As soon as she's standing, my mouth descends on hers as my free hand wraps around her neck. Parting her lips, my tongue slips inside to dance with hers.

Bending slightly, I place my hands at the back of her thighs and lift her up. She immediately wraps her legs around my waist and her arms around my neck. I push her back up against the shower wall and without any delay, I press into her. Her gasp has me ready to explode already.

The snug fit and the hot warmth around my length is pure heaven. If this is as close as my tainted soul will come to those pearly gates, I am more than happy.

I lift her up and then slide her back down my cock. She hums her approval. The sounds she makes while I'm inside her drive me insane. It rivals the way the red haze consumes me. Her blunt nails dig into my shoulder as I speed up my pace.

"Yes, baby. Shit." She moans as I lift her up and drop her back down on me rapidly.

Not liking this angle much, I pull out of her and turn her around pressing her front against the shower wall. I grab the back of her thigh opening her up to me wider. Bending my knees, I grab my dick and push into her.

"Oh fuck. You're too deep."

Fisting her braids in my hand I pull her head back to my chest. "You can take it," I growl into her ear.

My pelvis smacks against her butt in a round of applause. Spreading her ass cheeks, I stare down as my length disappears into her pink center. Her creaminess is spread across my dick even coating my course pubic hair. Watching the way she creams for me has my mind going crazy.

Using my arm under her stomach, I lift her easily and carry her to the other side of the shower. I do all this without pulling out of her. Placing her back down, I bend her over the bench seat and then lift my leg onto the seat.

"Ohhhhh, yeah," she moans, going on her tiptoes when I slide my full length all the way into her.

I love watching myself enter her. I love the peek of her pink center I get as I pull out and slide back in.

I smack her ass, watching it redden instantly.

"Fuck me back," I growl.

"I can't," She whimpers as she tries to move up and down on my shaft.

I smack her other cheek. "You came into my shower starting with me. Fuck me like I belong to you."

There really wasn't anything she had to do to state her claim. I was already hers. However, seeing her place her hands against the shower wall and throw her hips back like she's dancing on my cock is well worth it. I look up to the ceiling of the shower, placing my hands behind my head. Her walls squeeze me as she moves up and down my length.

I moan. "Just like that. Keep going for me."

She bounces a little faster, taking my pipe like a good girl. Her moans and whimpers have my orgasm starting at the soles of my feet and slowly riding up.

"Do you like it, daddy," she says over her shoulder.

Every time I'm intimate with Summer I find new things I like, new positions, new sounds, but nothing gets me as hard as when she calls me a new pet name. Hearing her say daddy, has me losing my control.

I grab her hips, keeping her still as I piston into her.

"Fuuuuck, Gabriel," she whines.

"Tell me you love me," I beg, starved to hear those words again.

Reaching underneath her, I lift one of her legs up on the bench so I can get better access to her hardened nub. I rub in a circular motion, knowing it's the fastest way to get her to come.

"Shit," she curses. "I love you. I love you." She repeats as her movements become jerky.

I'm losing my battle with my own orgasm. I'm like a shaken soda bottle ready to explode.

"Come for me. Now, Summer." I squeeze her pearl between my fingers, and she shoots off to the moon with me right behind her.

I let out a roar as my legs go weak. I place my fisted hand against the shower wall to keep me on my feet as I continue to unload inside her. When I've finally given her all that I can, I pull out taking a step back.

She's still bent over the bench. I can see some of my cum oozing out of her, with my fingers I push it back inside, not wanting any of it to escape.

Her laughter draws my attention away from my hand. Summer is looking over her shoulder at me.

"If I didn't know any better, I'd say you were seriously trying to get me pregnant."

I don't comment because she isn't ready for the truth. I turn my back to her and walk under the shower head. I was in the middle of a shower when she walked in the bathroom by accident.

Closing my eyes, I lean my head down, allowing the water to wash over me. Her soft touch on my back has my flaccid cock slowly coming back to life.

"When did you get the tattoos?" She asks as she reaches around me for the soap and body sponge.

"I started the back one not long after I got locked in, and the one over my heart," I pause as I touch the numbers. "I got it right before the back one started."

Summer takes her time washing my back and even running the sponge over my ass and around my stomach.

"What do they mean?"

I look over my shoulder at her. She glances at me briefly with a smile before bending to wash my calves and legs.

"Why do you think they mean something?"

She shrugs. "I know you. You don't seem like the random tattoo person."

I turn back to face the wall, taking my eyes off her. She has no idea what she does to me.

"*She's a poison. A virus. An infestation of the mind. She should be burned at the stake,*" Mother claims.

"*She is mine,*" I reply in my head. "The demon on my back is my promise to you."

Her hands still as she rises back up washing my lower back.

"What promise?"

I turn around to face her. She runs the sponge over my chest while the water cascades over my shoulders.

"I told you to let your demons go that night, that I'd carry them. I'm holding up my end of the deal."

Her mouth falls open. I place my hand over the small of her back right over the dip before her ass curves out. I pull her toward me, not able to get enough of her skin against mine. For years I hated the feeling of being touched or having someone too close to me, but since the night I met Summer, I've always wanted her near me.

"The one on my heart," I lift her hand up and place it on my chest over the number fifty. "It's a reminder that no matter where I am, somewhere out there, your heart is still beating." Her brows lift in confusion. "Fifty is your sleeping heart rate. The night I left you, I watched you sleep for hours. I counted your breaths and your heart rate."

Her eyes fill with moisture, slowly a tear spills down her cheek. I wipe it away even though my hands are wet. I never want her to cry or hurt.

She closes her eyes and takes a deep breath. "You're going to ruin me, Gabriel."

"Good," I lean forward and drop a kiss on her lips. She wraps her arms around my neck. I grip her ass and press her to my erection. I need her one more time.

Five hours after the shower and one more round in the bed, I'm sitting on the ground in a cold mausoleum carving out chess pieces with a smile on my face.

"She has softened you," Mother growls in my head.

I lean my head against the stone wall behind me looking at the work I've done. Last night I found Jayson (Jay) Coats, Antonio (Tony) Parker, Amir (Tiny) Masters, and Demarcus (Dee) Masters. The four men that found Summer in the diner that night.

It took me three days to collect them all. Now, their entrails and body parts help decorate this mausoleum.

I've officially killed everyone that could possibly point out Summer from that night. It took me over a month to do it but she's safe.

Climbing to my feet, I place the Queen and the rook on the shelf at the back of the vault. I know Priest and the guys will find this. The groundskeeper saw me coming in tonight. I'm pretty sure he's going to report this. I need to let Priest know I'm okay.

Despite what this looks like, I haven't gone off the deep end. Although mother is still vocal, my head is clear for the first time ever. And I know why.

Glancing at my watch, my heart picks up an extra beat. It's not too late. Summer will still be up when I get back.

I pick up the bucket I carried the body parts in and my duffle and head out of the crypt. I close the door behind me glancing at the name etched into the marble over the door. Corbyn.

After doing research on the name, I found out that the surname Corbyn is one of the oldest in the world. Also on the list with Corbyn, were the surnames O'Cleary and Smith. Matthew O'Cleary owned the club we went to a week ago. And Timothy Smith was the guy that had the cop killed by the Church.

There is a connection here. The inscription on Timothy's ring comes to mind; 1 of 10. I'm starting to think the Royal Crown has something to do with family ties, especially with these three families.

By decorating this mausoleum, I'm sending a message. One I knew would get to the right person.

Popping the trunk to the stolen Jeep, I place the bucket in the back on top of the plastic tarp. After climbing into the driver's seat, my phone goes off in my pocket. I pull it out glancing at the number.

"It's been a minute," I say to the person on the other end of the line.

"You're off task, Beastie," the benefactor says. "What are you doing? You're supposed to be cleaning up the mess you left behind."

I sit back in my seat. He's angry, the growl in his voice tells me I'm right. It reminds me of how Priest speaks when me or my brothers mess up. He's not happy with me.

"My mess is clean. The last of that night has been dealt with."

There is silence on the other end of the phone, but I know he hasn't hung up. I remain silent as well, waiting for him to speak again.

"Don't start digging under rocks…"

"Or I'll attract the wrong person?" I finish for him. "Right, Maksim?"

He's silent again.

I started to assume that there was a connection to the benefactor and the Royal Crown after talking to Timothy. They both had the same knowledge of the Church and the same attitude toward it.

Finding the guys at the club with the same tattoos that also mentioned a rogue brother, further convinced me. The assumption of the benefactor being the rogue brother Maksim was a leap, but I'm convinced I'm right.

His chuckle comes through the phone. "You're smarter than they said you were."

"I guess we're both full of surprises," I counter.

"A bit of advice, be careful when you kick a hornet's nest, when they swarm, they attack everyone around you."

His threat was clear. He once before made it known that he would not involve women and children in his affairs, however who ever he's running from has no problem bringing Summer and Gabe into this.

I still needed to know one last thing.

"Is that your way of telling me you've made your decision?"

Another moment of silence.

"No, I'm still undecided."

This time when the phone goes silent, I know he's hung up. His words linger with me. I had no doubt that going after whoever this Corbyn person is will cause some backlash. I'm prepared for it.

Now that everyone from that night has been handled and no one else can attach Summer and Gabe to me, I should disappear. That way, when the fall out happens, they will be safe.

However, as I maneuver the jeep back to my apartment to clean it, my only thought is getting back home to Summer.

Two hours later, when I walk into the back door, my thoughts are still on what I should be doing.

I should walk in and tell her I'm leaving. I should hug my son one last time and kiss Summer before disappearing out of their lives.

When I turn the corner into the living room, I spot Summer sitting on the couch. A grocery bag in her lap, a pair of scissors in her hands as she cuts the braids out of her hair.

She looks at me and smiles. "I have a hair appointment in the morning. I have to take these braids out. It's time."

This is it. This is the time to tell her goodbye. It was never meant to last forever. Mother tried to warn me of this numerous times. I'm not made for happily ever afters. I'll never be able to tame the darkness inside me.

"You okay?" Her soft voice asks.

I pause, looking for the right words to say goodbye. To say this is the end.

"Yeah. You need help?" I ask, dropping my black duffle on the floor at my feet.

As much as I know what I'm supposed to do, the words will not come out.

"That demon has you, Boy. Your selfishness will cause her death. You are godless," Mother taunts in my head.

In this, she is right. For once, I'm allowing that darkness in me to win. I can't give them up.

I walk into the living room and sit down on the couch beside her. She gets up and sits on the floor between my legs. She then hands me a comb with a long pointy end.

"Use the point to help you take the braids out," she instructs.

She then turns to our dragon show. For two hours, I help Summer take her braids out. When we are done, I help her wash her hair in the shower, then fuck her up against the wall.

Whatever happens, I'll be here to keep her safe, but I can't let her go.

CHAPTER THIRTY-FIVE
The Run-In

Summer

"I was in the club for over an hour. Not once did I get the itch or the urge. I just vibed and enjoyed the atmosphere. I hadn't been able to do that in years. I even got offered a hit and I turned it down."

Today was my monthly meeting with Shay. Instead of our usual restaurant, she and I were meeting at a park.

I haven't talked to my mother since that blow up a month ago. She's been calling lately but I don't have anything to say to her. Since she was my usual babysitter for these meetings, I had to bring Gabe with me. At the moment, he's going up and down the slide with his Iron Man toy.

"That is incredible, Summer. I'm so proud of you," Shay says. We're sitting at a picnic table not far from the play area.

A warmth spreads throughout my body. Shay has been a big part of my recovery, and I couldn't wait to share this moment with her.

"Thank you. I still have no plans to hang out at a club every night, but it felt good to face that monster."

She chuckles. "It should feel good. You faced a huge trigger and came out unscathed. That should always be celebrated. When I saw my son's father for the first time after rehab, I broke out in a sweat. I ran from that man like he was a rabid dog."

We both laugh at her analogy. Shay's son's father is the person that got her hooked-on drugs.

"Lately, I've just been feeling..." I search for the right words to explain my mood lately.

"Happy?" She questions with the quirk of her brow.

I shrug my shoulders, a smile firmly planted on my face.

"Peaceful," I finally say finding the best description for this feeling.

My son has always brought me joy; a type of sereneness that can't be duplicated. My sobriety brings me happiness and a sense of pride. But Gabriel brings me a peace I didn't know I was missing. His presence around me comforts me and makes me feel protected.

It's been eight days since he came home that night and helped me take out my braids. When he walked into the living room, I could tell something was bothering him. Gabriel doesn't show emotions like most people. There was no look on his face or hidden in his eyes that gave away his thoughts. It was simply the feeling I got when he walked in that let me know. It's the way my heart nearly stopped beating or the hairs on my arms stood up that told me something was wrong.

I feared the worst that night. My soul told me he was leaving. It was something about the way he stood there silently that caused my stomach to drop. However, he didn't leave. He stayed. I still won't get my hopes up though. Even though there is no physical clock ticking down over my head, the one in my heart is telling me my time with him is running out.

"What's going through your head right now?" Shay asks, regaining my attention. "Your entire mood just changed like the flip of a light switch."

Pushing my brand-new goddess knotless braids behind my ear, I say, "Gabe's father is back."

Shay's eyes widen. This is the first time I think I've ever said anything that shocked her. She usually has the I've seen and heard it all attitude.

She sits up straighter in her seat placing her arms on top of the table. "Oh. When did he come back?"

"Six weeks ago."

She nods. "That explains your glow and giddiness."

I roll my eyes and laugh.

"But what does that have to do with your sudden mood change?"

Sighing, I glance over at Gabe. He's moved on to the climbing wall now.

"He isn't staying."

"Why not?" Her brows furrow.

"Because he cares about us." My eyes begin to water. I blink a few times to fight the tears from falling but I lose the battle.

"You're going to have to explain this one to me." She goes into her purse and brings out a small pack of Kleenex. She pulls a few out and hand them to me.

I wipe my eyes, and then ball the tissue in my hands. "Gabriel has issues," I try to explain without going into details.

"Drug issues?" she questions.

I shake my head vehemently. "No. Mental stuff. I guess that's not hard to believe after knowing me." I chuckle but Shay doesn't join me. I take another deep breath before continuing.

"His childhood wasn't good. His mother was a very cruel woman that constantly told her son that he was evil. After hearing something like that for so long you start to believe it."

I sniff and then use the tissue to wipe my nose. "Gabriel truly believes that he's too damaged and he doesn't deserve to be loved. He fears that he will one day do something to hurt us. And because of that, no matter how much he may want to stay, he won't. Because if his mother is right and he does something that causes pain to either me or Gabe, he won't recover."

The hardest part about knowing this, is understanding that it all stems from him caring about us. He would sacrifice himself for us. I have no doubt Gabriel would lay down his life for me and his son. Which is also how I know that he would rip out his own heart to keep us protected. The sad thing is, I can't guarantee his concerns aren't valid.

"So you'll let him walk away?"

I look up at her, before cutting my eyes over to my son.

"What am I supposed to do? Beg him to stay?"

"No, not beg, but you could ask," she says it as if it's simple. "Look, I'm not a therapist, but from one person with childhood trauma to another, you and I both know that sometimes the best way to fight the demons our parents put on us, is to face them." She sits up straighter. "Do you believe that Gabriel would hurt you or your son? I want you to be honest."

I think it over. I even think back to the night he came home and his mother was in his head. As scary as that moment was, I don't think that he would've done it. I know that bitch fucked him up. I won't pretend that he isn't dangerous. I've seen what he can do and how easily he does it.

However, I know that Gabriel has control of his actions. And in the end, he would never allow himself to lose control.

"No," I say truthfully.

"If his mother spent years telling him he's dangerous, then he needs someone he loves and trusts to tell him he's not. And maybe the way you tell him that, is by asking him to stay and showing him that you trust him."

Two hours later, Shay's words were still floating in my head. I understand what she said. Gabriel just needs to know that I trust him, and I have faith in him. But there is a part of me that's afraid to ask. What if I ask him to stay and he still says no. I don't think I can take that kind of rejection.

"Well, hello, stranger." The deep voice has me looking up from my seat at the table.

"Hi, Andrew."

After leaving Shay, I had to drop off some jewelry at one of the boutiques that happens to be two stores down from Books and More. And whenever we are near Books and More, we have to come by, even if Malia is on a leave of absence. I glance over to the fireplace to find Gabe engrossed in the new book I just bought him.

Andrew pulls out the chair across from me and sits down as if I invited him. "My last few phone calls have gone to voicemail. Is everything okay?"

I honestly have been meaning to have a conversation with Andrew. However, it seems every time he's called Gabriel was standing right beside me and it didn't seem like a good time to answer.

"I've been meaning to talk to you about that." I straighten in my seat. "You're a great guy. I mean, I had a lot of fun with you, but right now is not a really good time for me to date. With Gabe and the business…"

Andrew cuts me off with a dry chuckle that doesn't sound friendly at all.

"Let me guess," he says leaning back in his seat. "You're getting back with your deadbeat baby daddy."

To say his words shocked me is an understatement. Never has anyone ever accused Gabriel of being deadbeat. Absentee, sure. But not deadbeat.

"Excuse me?" I ask rolling my neck.

He gives one of those fake ass laughs again. "You know what kills me about girls like you. You swear you want the good guy. The guy with his shit together. But the moment one of us shows you any attention, you run right back to the abusive asshole bad boy."

"Wow," I say astonished by his arrogance. I'm definitely seeing a new side of Andrew today. "You know nothing about me or my child's father. And fun fact, calling yourself a 'good guy' usually means you're not."

"Says the ex-junkie."

His words sting a little, but nothing more than I've heard before. My sister and mother have said much worse.

"This conversation is over." I stand from my seat and grab my purse. Andrew leaps up also blocking my way. I try to go around him, but he grabs my arm.

"Let me go," I grit out as I snatch away from him.

"I had no real intentions of going back out with you after that first date. I don't lower my standards to date single mother drug addicts. But while I was in that bathroom, I thought about it. The least I could get out of this farce is an easy fuck. Because let's be honest, what else are you good for? I know you didn't think I was really interested in you."

Part of me is screaming in my head that he's only saying those words to hurt me. He's lashing out because I didn't choose him. But I can't lie as if they don't hurt like hell.

"Fuck you, Andrew."

I walk past him, heading for my son before he can see the glimmer in my eyes from the tears I'm holding back.

"He's going to leave too, Summer." His words stop me in my tracks even though I don't turn to face him. "As soon as baby daddy gets done using your body, he's going to leave you too. No one keeps trash."

I walk away from Andrew. No matter how much I tell myself to ignore his hurtful words, my heart is not trying to hear it. Old thoughts run through my head. The desire to escape, to run away to that dull place where emotions can't reach me, is so loud I can almost taste the relief on my tongue. After five long years, my demons have made a reappearance.

Beast

Sliding the back patio door open, my heart races with excitement to see her. I now know what the feeling is. As soon as I step into the house, I know something is wrong.

The living room is dark, and the television is off. Glancing at my watch, I notice it's only a little after ten. No way Summer is in bed.

I drop my black duffle by the door and lock up before heading upstairs. I first check on Gabe. He's fast asleep in his bed. I close his door back and head to Summer's work room. The lights are off and she's not there.

A strange feeling takes over me. It causes me to stop in my tracks. I shut my eyes and place a hand over my racing heart. Something is wrong. Opening my eyes, I rush to Summer's room.

Her door is closed, but I quickly push it open. My gaze goes to the bed. It's still made up from this morning. The bathroom light is on, and the door is open. However, the silence coming from the bathroom has my feet feeling like lead.

Summer is not a quiet person. Even when she's working there's always music playing or her humming. This silence feels eerie.

Slowly, I head to the open door. My head throbs in fear. As soon as I walked in, I notice a few things. Her clothes are tossed on the floor. An empty bottle of alcohol is lying near the toilet, and an empty glass is sitting by the tub. Lying in the claw foot tub with her long braids hanging off the back and her arms over the side, is Summer.

I walk over to the bottle first, picking it up.

"It's non-alcoholic," she says just as I read the sparkling grape juice label.

She snorts drawing my attention. "I know, lame right. I needed a hit so bad I had to use the imitation."

She starts to laugh, but it quickly turns into deep sobs. Placing the bottle down, I grab her large white fluffy towel and walk over to her.

"Get out the tub," I demand.

"He's right you know. I'm trash. No matter what I do I will always be the fucked-up drug addict with PTSD. You really should have picked a better woman to have a baby with."

Kneeling beside the tub, I place the towel over my shoulder. Grabbing her face between my hands I use my thumbs to wipe the tears that are rapidly falling down her face.

"What happened?"

She shakes her head, trying to turn away from me. I force her to keep her eyes on me.

"No, I don't want to talk," she shouts, shooting up from the tub. Water runs down her naked body. She grabs the towel off my shoulder. I come to my feet.

She climbs out of the tub in a rush, nearly falling face first. I wrap my arms around her to catch her. After steadying herself she pulls away from me and wraps herself up in the towel.

"Talk to me, Summer," I plead.

She shakes her head. "Why, it won't change anything."

It's clear something triggered her. I try to think back on her schedule for today. She was supposed to go see her sponsor at the park and then drop off some jewelry at the boutiques. What could have happened that upset her.

"Tell me what happened."

She tosses one hand into the air. "I got hit with the truth today. Just a reminder of something I already know."

My brows pinch, I'm still not understanding. What truth? What does she already know.

"What do you know?"

She kisses her teeth. "I ran into Andrew at the bookstore Gabe and I visit. He let me know that no matter what I do I'll never be more than my past. He reminded me of how unworthy I am and I'm never going to be on anyone's list."

"Fuck that list," I growl through clenched teeth.

My anger at her tears and her pain has me seeing red. I shut my eyes to drown out the voices.

"Let me out to play, Gabriel," the deep sinister voice comes out of its cage.

I was expecting mother or Priest. I wasn't prepared for this one. *"Get back. Get back,"* I fight against myself to push the voice away.

"Easy for you to say," she replies cutting into my internal battle.

Her voice is just what I need to refocus. The dark voice is put back in its place. I open my eyes to find Summer pacing in front of me.

"What's that supposed to mean?" I ask.

She scoffs, turning to glare at me. "*You* don't even want to be here."

"Who said I don't want to be here?"

"You," she shouts. "Every day I can see the exit plan on your face. You've had one foot out the door since you got here."

"That's not true."

"Stop it, Gabriel. Stop telling me what you think I want to hear," she shouts. "Be fucking honest and tell me the truth. Nobody wants me."

"I want you," I roar.

Summer goes silent. I never raise my voice. Mother beat that out of me when I was a kid. but watching her tell me that I didn't want her, that my world doesn't revolve around her, has me losing my grip with my control.

My hands clench and unclench at my side.

"Let me loose. Let me take control," Mother whispers in my head. *"I'll teach that whore a lesson."*

I shut my eyes to block her out, glad it was her and not the other voice.

"You talk about being on someone else's list, but you are my list, Summer. There is no one else but you. You are the only thing I thought of for five years. You are the silence in my head, the peace in my damaged mind. I crave your company more than I desire my solitude, and I've thrived my entire life being alone. You say you're unworthy, but to me you are the very thing that keeps me alive."

She stares at me, tears filling her eyes and slowly falling down her face.

"I don't want you to leave," her voice sounds small. It's nothing like her normal tone.

I eat up the space between us, cupping her face in my hands, I stare down into her eyes.

"Then I won't go."

My mind runs rampant with all the ways I could hurt her and Gabe. The vision of George in my hands, the sinister voice in my head, all the things my mother told me would happen. It all plays on a loop in my head warning me this will never work. Yet, I don't take the words back and I have no plans of letting her go.

"Promise me, Gabriel. Promise you won't leave."

I snatch the towel from around her and toss it to the bathroom floor. I lift her up easily. She wraps her legs around my waist before locking her lips to mine in a feverish kiss. I carry her into the bedroom placing her on the bed gently. My heavy body covers hers as I bite into her bottom lip and then suck it into my mouth.

Tears still track down her face. I take my time kissing them away. She takes my hair out of my bun. I've come to realize she likes my hair down when we make love. I ease down her body, giving her breasts attention. I suck the peak of one, then quickly move to the other.

She purrs underneath me like a sated kitten. I nip the flesh of her breast and then suck the sting away.

"Yes, baby," she moans.

I run my tongue from her nipples down to her belly button loving the way her skin tastes against my tongue. When I get to her bare mound, I place soft kisses all over her pelvis.

Gliding my hands up her knees onto her thighs, I push her legs apart. She opens them wide for me. I bury my face into her middle inhaling her intoxicating smell. The vanilla body wash she must have used in the bath compliments her natural scent.

I swipe my tongue up her center, lapping up her essence. She lets out a moan that turns into a cry when I suck her clit into my mouth. I can't get enough of the way she tastes. Pulling her hood back so her nub can stick out further I work my tongue over it. Feasting on her, feeling her body move underneath me, hearing her cries of pleasure and her fingers tug at my hair has my senses overloaded in the best way.

She quickly erupts on my tongue, thrashing against the bed. I continue my attack on her pussy. Dipping my tongue inside her and then back to work her pearl.

"No more, Gabriel. Please," she cries as she tries to scoot my meal away from me.

I yank her hips back down. I remove my mouth but work my way back up her body. I allow my fingers to slowly continue the job my tongue was doing.

She whimpers as I kiss her.

"How could you think, I didn't want you. I told you; you were mine. I meant it. I'm never giving you up Summer."

I continue to slowly make circles around her clit as I use my other hand to free my cock from my pants.

"Don't leave me, Gabriel."

Her words make me pause as I stare down into her brown eyes. I finally realize the damage I did to her by slipping away that night five years ago. I know the reason I did it was valid. Had I woken her up to say bye and she asked me not to go, I would have tossed all my plans out the window to stay with her.

I would have gone on the run, breaking Priest and my brothers' hearts. Plus, it would have left them at the mercy of the Church with no way to break free. Leaving her the way I did was the best option. But it doesn't mean that she didn't hurt.

I place a kiss to her lips before staring into her eyes and making a promise I was willing to die by.

"I will never leave you again." I push into her tight heat.

She gasps as I seat myself inside her.

"I love you," she cries when I grind into her.

"I love you more, Summer," I pant, rocking into her slow and deep. "More than you will ever know."

I don't rush this moment with her. I fuck her slow and deep, feeding her every inch of me before pulling out to the tip. We kiss as we make love, her fingers in my hair. One of my hands is on the bed while the other is wrapped around her neck.

I don't think about my anger while I make love to Summer. I ignore the red haze that is building in my head. I focus all my attention on her.

She slides her hands up my back under my shirt.

"Take this off, I need to feel your skin," she whispers.

Pulling out of her, I climb off the bed and quickly disrobe, leaving my clothing on the floor. When I climb back on the bed, I don't take my spot back. I lie on my back beside her. I lift her up and place her over me.

"Ride me."

She bites her bottom lip but doesn't hesitate to position herself over my shaft. She reaches behind her and lifts my cock up to her opening. Slowly, she lowers herself down.

"Ugh, oohhh," she coos as she settles. She rocks forward slowly with both her hands planted on my chest.

She is so fucking beautiful. I reach up and push her new braids out of her face. She told me they were called goddess braids. She looked every bit like a goddess in them.

She tosses her head back as she rocks forward and back on me. Her wetness smearing all over my pelvis.

"Am I yours, Summer," I ask?

She nods her head, with her eyes closed.

I grip her neck, causing her to open her eyes.

"I asked you a question. Am I yours?"

"Yes."

"Then give me a baby." Her movements halt. Her eyes narrow.

"I know what you've been doing. You're getting those pills from the pharmacy, and you made an appointment with a gynecologist."

She shakes her head. "How do you know that?"

I won't explain how I have access to her phone calendar or how I followed her to the drug store the other day to watch her pick up those plan B pills.

I don't explain any of that to her.

"I didn't get to experience your pregnancy with Gabriel. I know it's my fault. And I know I have a lot of issues that could spread to our child and I'm not talking about autism."

There are a lot of things she still doesn't know about me. Things I should tell her. I never thought I would ever want children, but having Gabe has been the biggest highlight of my life. I want that experience again and I want it with this woman.

"Give me another baby."

She stares down at me, her mouth open and hesitancy dances in her eyes.

She looks to her left. I get the sinking feeling she doesn't want another child with me.

"Okay," she finally says looking back at me. "Let's make another baby."

The euphoric feeling swells my chest, I flip her over to her back, lift her legs over my shoulders and fuck her hard. I want this more than I want my last breath.

"I love you," I whisper down to her as I drive into her. "I fucking love you."

"I love you too," she cries out as she shoots off like a rocket soaking my dick.

I speed up my strokes wanting to reach my end as well. My balls tighten, my eyes roll back and I come undone shooting off inside of her. I don't have the right to pray. Mother says I'm too evil to talk to God, but I close my eyes and ask that this time, gets her pregnant.

I collapse down beside her, immediately pulling her into me. She tosses a leg over mine and places her head on my shoulder.

We lay in silence, trying to catch our breath. My heartrate finally slows.

"You don't happen to have twins in your family, right?" she asks suddenly.

I don't want to admit that I don't know my family. I've never met my mother's family and I don't know who my father is.

"No," I lie for the first time ever to her.

"Good," she says, "because I'm not trying to have two of your giant ass babies at once."

I drag her on top of me as I tickle her sides. Her laughter sounds like heaven to my ears. I pull the covers over us and get us settled in bed.

CHAPTER THIRTY-SIX

Back In Blood

Beast

Summer is passed out on my chest, but my mind can't rest.

"You know what you have to do. Set me free," Mother says in my head.

"Let the bitch out, Kid. It's time," Priest agrees.

Gently, I roll Summer over to her side. She doesn't stir. I make sure the covers are pulled up over her bare shoulders. I place a kiss on her cheek and my pulse races.

I slide out of the bed, my bare feet brushing against the thick carpet. I've held the red haze at bay long enough. Like a light switch, I shut my eyes and allow my mother to come to the forefront.

I quickly dress and make my way down the stairs. Stopping at the back door, I grab my black duffle and head out of the house.

After their first date, I researched everything I could on Andrew Greenly. I know who his parents are, where he went to school, I even know his credit score. Finding his house took less time than his credit score.

I park the stolen minivan around the corner from Andrew's brownstone. Grabbing my duffle off the passenger seat, I step out of the car and shut the door.

The street is quiet for this time of night. Only a few people are walking along the sidewalk. I take the leather gloves out of my pocket and place them on before pulling the hood of my sweatshirt over my head. I then make my way to the back of Andrew's home.

I hop the fence that cuts off his back yard from his neighbors. He has a Ring camera at the front door but nothing back here. There isn't even a motion light in his back yard. He made this easier than it should have been.

Walking up to the sliding glass door, I peer inside. This isn't the first time I've seen the inside of his house. The night he was released from the hospital after their first date, I came to visit him. He was sound asleep as I stood over his bed determined to kill him. It took all of Priest's teachings to get me to walk away and keep him alive that night. All I could see was his hand on top of hers at that table. No one got to touch my Summer.

Now, nothing would stop me from watching the life drain from his eyes. I easily pop the lock to the sliding glass door entering through his kitchen. Closing the door, I listen for any sound in the house. There is music coming from upstairs.

I make my way up the stairs remembering which floorboards to avoid from my last visit here. The closer I get to the sound of the music, I can also hear the light sounds of shower water going.

Pushing the door to the master bedroom open, I walk into the room placing my duffle on the bed. Unzipping it, I stare down into the bag.

"Vengeance is mine saith the Lord," Mother says in my head. *"You are the wrath of God. He made your whore cry. Now you must make him bleed."*

"Yes, mother." I pull out my bowie first.

The weapon was a gift from Priest. Seth got his first Bowie early, but the rest of us got ours the day we graduated into being Deacons. The black leather wrapped handle fit perfectly in my hands. The worn leather was rubbed in certain spots over the years from wear. The blade is made of nine inches of carbon steel. It's my favorite and I only pull it out for special occasions. Tonight was one of those occasions.

The water cuts off abruptly, gaining my attention. I take a seat on the side of the bed facing the bathroom door. He will see me as soon as he walks out.

I don't have long to wait. The door opens wide and billows of steam float out causing the humidity to go up in the room. Andrew steps out with a towel wrapped around his waist. The music is much louder now that the bathroom door is open.

It takes Andrew a second to process what he's seeing.

"What are you doing in my house?" He asks dumbly.

I spin the blade around in my hand, as I stare down at the handle.

"You made her cry," although the words are coming out of my mouth, they sound like my mother's voice. "No one gets to hurt her."

I can feel the dark sinister voice trying to break free. He wants to come out and play. Even though my anger for Andrew is boiling over, I have enough sense to know that allowing that voice to come out will be bad.

"What the fuck is wrong with you?" Andrew shouts.

I cock my head at his tone, but don't reply.

"I'm calling the cops." He turns and heads to the phone sitting on top of his dresser.

I sigh, tossing the blade across the room. It lands in the center of his back lodging almost to the hilt.

Andrew groans and falls to his knees.

"Ahhh, fuck," he cries.

Slowly, I get up and walk over to him.

"Eye for an eye. Tooth for a tooth." I stand over his body and yank the blade out of his back. Andrew howls in pain. "Hand for a hand," I say as I plunge the knife into the back of his hand driving the blade so deep it digs into the wooden floorboards.

Andrew screams as the smell of piss permeates the air. However, I silence the cry by rearing back and kicking him with my steel-toed boot in the mouth. The sound of crunching is preceded by him spitting out blood and teeth. He tries to speak, but the way his jaw is slightly crooked tells me he won't be able to.

Kneeling down beside him, I yank the blade out of his hand. I then flip him onto his back. His bottom jaw hangs causing his mouth to sag open.

I stare into his eyes as tears slide down his face. He tries to speak, but his words are gargled.

"Please."

I make out the single word he pleads. Begging will not get him out of this. Only his death will redeem him.

"She wasn't yours to touch," I explain. "She definitely wasn't yours to hurt. Now the devil has come to collect his due."

"I'm. . ." once again, I have to decipher the jumbled words he's trying to say, "sorry."

"Sshh," I hum placing a finger to my lips. "Your repentance isn't needed. Save it for St. Peter." Placing the tip of the blade right under his left eye, I smile as I push forward.

By the time I'm done with Andrew, he is unrecognizable.

"Well done, Boy," Mother praises proudly as I stare down at his mangled body.

It only took me thirty minutes to appease the darkness within me. I use the towel that was once wrapped around his waist to clean the knife. I place the blade back in my black duffle. Pulling out my phone I make a phone call.

"Hospitality," the person on the other end of the phone says.

"I have a leak."

Forty-five minutes later, after ditching the stolen van and making sure it was clean, I walk up to the sidewalk near my home. All the lights are still out, which lets me know Summer is still asleep.

Knowing my family is tucked safely inside our home has my palms sweating and my body feeling flushed. I memorize the feeling— anticipation. I can't wait to climb back in bed behind Summer. Like always, she will snuggle up to me seeking out my body heat. She doesn't realize she searches for me in her sleep. Her hand undoubtedly goes out all throughout the night reaching for me. She wants me near her. Pride swells my chest.

I make my way around back, ready to call it a night, when something catches my attention. A black Charger is parked across the street. A charger I know too well.

"They've found you," Mother warns. *"They've come to take her away from you. They don't think you deserve her."*

"She's mine," I growl.

"Not after she meets your brothers. They aren't like you," Mother cackles as she fades into the back of my mind.

Dropping my duffle, I walk around to the front of the house, just in time to see Priest step up on the sidewalk. He isn't paying attention to me yet. He's surveying the front of the house.

"No," I say cutting him off in his tracks.

He turns to me, his gaze raking over me. I'd already ditched the hoodie I was wearing inside my duffle. Good thing I did, if he'd seen the blood on it he would've been alarmed.

"Beast, I'm here to help."

"He's not going to help. He's going to take her away. You know this."

"Priest wouldn't do that," I reply.

"You're a fool." Mother sneers. *"He's afraid of you. He doesn't think you can take care of your family. He wants the girl for himself."*

At her words, my hands fist at my side. The urge to kill Priest, rears up in me so strong I can envision my hands wrapped around his throat.

"Wrangle that shit in, Kid." The Priest voice in my head says. *"That bitch is blowing smoke. She's still in your head from that kill. Block her out."*

I noticed I've just been standing here staring silently at Priest. The man that raised me and took care of me. The man that is more of a father to me than the one that dropped his nut off in my mother. I know this man.

His voice in my head is right. Although Priest would want to take control of the situation, he wouldn't take Summer away from me.

"Let me talk to your girl." He takes a step toward the house, and I take one with him remaining in his path.

"Go home, Priest." I say.

I could never hurt Priest, but I can't deal with him right now. His voice is right, mother is still in my head after that kill. She's too loud.

'I'm not loud, I'm right. And you know it."

I ignore her words. I need distance between me and Priest. I turn to leave.

"I'm here to help," he shouts.

I spin around quickly snarling my teeth. The fear in his eyes only calms me a little. I wrangle my anger back. Remembering who he is.

"I don't need your help," I finally say through clenched teeth.

"Then what about the bodies? What about Humpty Dumpty? You were asking for help."

"He thinks you're stupid. He thinks you can't keep them safe." Mother says. *"Kill him. Scatter his brains across this concrete."*

Taking a deep breath I fight against my mother's voice.

"Go back to your family, Priest. I still have much to do to protect mine."

"Let me help you at least," he pleads.

His eyes soften, I can see the love and worry shining back at me. I didn't need my emotional rolodex to know that look. I've seen it many times from him.

"You can't help me," I sigh. "You should be home trying to protect your family."

His brow arches. I knew he was too smart to look over what I'd just said.

"What do you mean?" he asks.

I made a deal with Albany that I wouldn't tell her secret. The fact that Priest was here let me know she didn't hold up her end of the deal. I wasn't angry with her. She loved him. I imagine she didn't like the idea of keeping things from him. However, a deal is a deal.

"Has she told you what she's working on?"

He frowns. "The thing with the DOE?"

A slow smile spreads over my face. He was still so clueless and with so little time left.

"You're running out of time. You better figure it out quick." With that small tip, I turn and walk away. Before getting too far, I stop and turn to face him one last time. "Don't come back here, Priest. When I am ready, you will meet them."

I leave the man that I consider my father standing on the sidewalk. I meant what I said, when I was ready, he would meet Summer and his grandson. I wanted them to know my family, including my brothers. But it was still too soon. I wasn't ready to share them yet.

After making sure Priest left, I make it back inside the house. Summer was still fast asleep in bed. I checked on Gabe before heading into the guest room for a shower.

I had plans to spend the rest of the night between Summer's thighs.

CHAPTER THIRTY-SEVEN

Graduation

Summer

"Summer Elise Jones," Dean Jackson calls my name and I walk across the stage.

"That's my bestie," Trina's voice carries across the crowd. I can't help but laugh at her.

Today is the day. A day I thought would never get here. A day that maybe wouldn't have gotten here if not for the man that dicked me down so good in the shower this morning my legs hurt as I stroll across this stage.

After shaking the university president's hand and grabbing my degree, I smile for a picture. Once done, I scan the crowd while making my way back to my seat. I smile as soon as my eyes land on Gabriel. He's hard to miss.

His golden locks are hanging down today. He towers over most people here, but he stands out even more with Gabe on his shoulders. My son has his noise cancelling headphones over his ears. Places like this with loud noises and a lot of people sometimes overwhelm him. But he's smiling right now as he waves at me over his father's head.

I blow the two of them a kiss. Shay is on one side of Gabriel. She's smiling proudly as if I'm her child. On the other side, Trina wipes her eyes as James tucks her into his side. The most important people in my life only take up five seats. But they are all I need.

When the ceremony is over, I rush out of the stadium to search for my family. I spot Gabriel first. He's standing in the middle of the sidewalk, his arms folded over his chest. People are moving around him as if he's a dark hole.

He watches me closely as I make my way over to him. I have tunnel vision as I hustle through the crowd. The moment I'm close to him he reaches his hand out to me and I take it. He pulls me into him, his body relaxing against mine.

I take in his intoxicating clean scent. His smell and the warmth of his arms bring me so much peace.

"Congratulations," his deep voice says in my ear sending a shiver up my spine.

I gaze up into his beautiful eyes. "I think I prefer your congratulations from earlier this morning."

Gabriel woke me up with his tongue buried so deep in my depths he probably could taste my cervix. As I came down from the high of my orgasm, he slid into me whispering congratulations.

A slow smile slinks across his face. Before he can speak again, I feel a tug on my black robes.

"Mommy, look what Hulk got you."

I look down to find Gabriel holding a large bouquet of sunflowers. The arrangement is stunning and almost as large as my son.

"Oh my goodness," I say placing a hand to my chest. Looking up to Gabriel I fight to hold back tears. "They're beautiful."

"Damn, baby daddy, did you leave any sunflowers at the store," Trina says walking up to us.

She immediately wraps her arms around me giving me a hug. "Bitch, I'm so proud of you." she chokes up.

"I couldn't have done it without you."

She waves me away. "Girl don't get me to crying again. You know I have a flight in three hours."

James has a business trip to Dubai and Trina is going over for an influencer event. I initially thought they wouldn't be able to make it today. However, Trina told me she wouldn't miss this for anything.

"Congratulations, Summer," James says handing me an envelope and teddy bear with a bunch of balloons attached to his arm.

"The envelope is from us, but the teddy bear was left by Shay. She told us to tell you sorry she couldn't wait for you."

I wave him off. Today was Shay's oldest son's baseball tournament. I'm happy she even made the actual graduation. "Thanks, James."

"Okay, so where are you guys going after this? It has to be some place nice." Trina directs her last sentence to Gabe and Gabriel.

"Chick-fil-A" Gabe shouts happily.

"G, we talked about this. Today is supposed to be about your mama."

My son looks to his godmother with the most innocent look on his face. "But mama eats Chick-fil-A too."

I can't help but laugh. Trina rolls her eyes but laughs too.

"Hey Summer."

Trina and I both turn to the new person standing behind us. I almost think I'm hallucinating staring back at my sister. Even before the fallout, I had no plans of ever seeing her at my graduation.

I haven't seen her or anyone from my family since I stormed out of my mom's house two months ago. I've gotten a few phone calls from them, but they've all gone unanswered.

"What the hell is she doing here?" Trina asks, turning up her nose.

I'm not going to lie, I'm kind of taken aback by her being here. We aren't actually on speaking terms. I don't think she would be crazy enough to come to my graduation to start an argument with me. But you never know when it comes to my sister.

Raina ignores Trina. "We've been calling you."

Folding my arms over my chest, I give her my undivided attention. "I know. I thought I made myself very clear the day I left mama's."

Raina's eyes widen as she looks over my shoulder. I don't have to guess who's there. I can feel his body heat pressed up against my back.

"Everything alright?" he asks as he places a hand on my hip.

"We're just trying to figure out why Summer's sister would show up at her special day knowing they don't get along," Trina says before I can answer him.

Raina grimaces, cutting her gaze away briefly. "Well, that's what I've been trying to talk to you about. Can we go somewhere and talk in private?"

"No," Trina and Gabriel say at the same time.

I fight my laughter at their protectiveness.

"What do you want, Raina?"

She exhales, pushing her hair behind her ear. "Okay, umm, I just wanted to apologize about what I said that day."

"What did you say?"

Even though I know exactly what she said, I was going to make sure she repeated it. She didn't get to give me some half ass apology. It doesn't matter that I already know this apology is bullshit. She wants something. It's the only reason she's here.

She shifts her weight and glances over my head before looking back at me. "I shouldn't have said you were jealous. It's obvious you're not."

"Very damn obvious," Trina adds.

Raina bites down on her bottom lip. What is obvious is that Raina is definitely here on some groveling shit. Because there is no way she's not responding back to Trina, those two have never gotten along.

"Anyway," Raina says clearing her throat. "We're having a birthday party for MJ this weekend and we're hoping you and Gabe will come."

I look at Trina, and she's staring at me. Without saying a word, I relay to her how odd this is. And her silent response is that she doesn't trust them.

Turning back to Raina, I plant a smile on my face. "Okay. Text me the details."

She smiles for the first time since popping up. "Great, I'll see you then. Oh and ummm, congratulations." She says the last part as an afterthought before scurrying away.

As soon as Raina is out of sight, Trina turns to me with her arms folded over her chest.

"You know they want something right? That bad ass boy has had five fucking birthdays and they've never invited G."

She's not lying. Usually, mom makes up an excuse about it being too 'loud' for Gabe to come to the party. So why suddenly do they want him there?

"Yeah, I smell BS too. But, I won't lie, I'm kind of interested in what they want."

"Most likely money. Since I won't be in the country, thankfully you'll have baby daddy there with you incase shit pops off." She turns her attention to Gabriel. "You got her back, right?"

I turn in time to see him dip his chin.

"Good," she says. "Because I don't trust them."

Neither did I. However, a curious part of me really wanted to see what they wanted. The other part of me was still hoping that maybe I'm wrong. Maybe, after our time apart they genuinely wanted Gabe around again.

The only way to know for sure is to go to the birthday party.

We parted ways with Trina and James. By now they were probably on their flight to Dubai.

Instead of sitting at some loud busy restaurant, I opted for a more intimate graduation dinner. We were having a picnic at the park. Gabe got his Chick-fil-A and Gabriel and I got barria tacos from a shop not too far from the park.

I was lying on the blanket, belly full, feeling absolutely happy. Gabriel was sitting behind me rubbing his arms up and down my thighs as we watched Gabriel blow bubbles with his bubble wand.

"Are you happy?" His hand stills on my thigh at my question.

I know it came out of the blue, but I was just wondering if he felt the same way I was feeling. This moment, here with him and my baby boy was the purest form of happiness.

"I never thought about happiness before," he says.

Tilting my head, I look up at him. He's squinting as he stares off in the distance.

"Were you never happy with your brothers and Priest?"

"Yes," He answers quickly. "I was happy with them. Although I spent much of my childhood waiting for the happiness to end. I was convinced that it wouldn't last. I knew at some point the happiness was going to be taken away from me. It usually was. Because I was always on guard, I didn't learn to appreciate those times until we were much older."

"And now?" I sit up between his legs turning my body slightly to face him better. "Are you happy?"

He runs a finger across my nose where my freckles are the most abundant.

"I'm at peace. And to me that is more valuable than happiness. Happiness comes and goes, but finding peace is something that stays with you."

I feel like the story of the Grinch where his heart suddenly grows three sizes larger. I lean up on my knees and place a kiss on his lips. He wraps his arms around my waist bringing me in closer. He opens his mouth deepening the kiss.

Suddenly bubbles start floating around our head. We pull apart laughing as Gabe stands over us blowing his bubbles.

I grab for him and he starts to laugh as he plops down on my lap.

"Mama, you kissed Hulk," he chuckles.

I look at Gabriel who has his eyes glued to me.

"Yeah, I kissed Hulk," I say, before looking down at my son. "But do you want to know a secret?"

Gabe nods his head.

"Well, Hulk is your father."

This time when I look at Gabriel there is an intensity to his gaze that I can't read.

But I wanted to let him know that we accepted him. Yes, I know he's got issues, and I don't believe that those issues will ever go away. I heard him that day in my backyard when I found that body. Gabriel is a killer. It's why I didn't question him when Andrew went missing. I knew Andrew wouldn't live to see another day. It's why I initially hesitated to tell Gabriel what happened. I knew what the outcome would be.

However, if I claim to love Gabriel, then I have to love all of him. And I do.

"I already know that secret," Gabe says with a laugh.

Now I'm confused because I never told him. Even Gabriel looks baffled.

"How did you know," Gabriel asks.

"Well, your name is Gabriel, and my name is Gabriel. And you look like me."

Now I know my son is pretty smart for his age, but I had no idea he was doing deductive reasoning like that.

"Plus," he goes on to say. "Aunt Trina told me." He gives a big goofy grin.

Gabriel laughs that low throaty sound that makes my panties wet. I can't help but join him. We spent the rest of our day hanging out at the park and then after we put Gabe to sleep, I rode Gabriel's dick on the couch until he nor I could move.

CHAPTER THIRTY-EIGHT

Birthday Party

Summer

The birthday party is everything I thought it would be. The moment I walked into my mother's house, Raina and all her friends turned up their noses at me. I wasn't surprised nor hurt by their actions.

My mother has been very cheery and accommodating. She even complimented me on my outfit. The most interesting reaction was when I introduced Gabriel to everyone. It seemed to take a lot of people by surprise. I even heard one of my sister's friends say she thought I didn't know who my child's father was.

We've spent most of the party in the small backyard. MJ and his friends were running around and screaming. Gabe was playing by himself at the kinetic sand table I bought him and my nephew to share at my mother's when she used to babysit him.

"He's alright," I say to Gabriel. "He prefers to be by himself."

He hasn't taken his eyes off our son this entire time. There are only a handful of men here. Yet, I can't see Gabriel talking to any of them. They are mostly friends of Mitch.

"I know," he says glancing at me. "I was the same way."

"Until you met your brothers?" I ask.

Lately he and I have been talking more about his childhood. Nothing about his time with his mother though. He only talks about his time at the Church.

"Yes. They found a way to bring me out of my shell."

Looking over to my baby, I get this feeling of hopefulness. My desire is that Gabe will be able to find his people as well. I want him to be able to form a connection like his father did with his brothers. I had no doubt that Gabe would be able to live an independent life without me. However, I've always worried that he wouldn't find his tribe. Being with Gabriel has proven there is hope for that as well.

"Hey, Summer," my mother calls out drawing my attention. "I was hoping you could help me get this cake together in the kitchen."

I frown, slightly. "Where's Raina?"

Not that I didn't want to help, but this isn't my child's birthday party.

Mother waves her hand through the air as she chuckles. "Too busy entertaining her guests."

"Oh, okay. Sure." I turn to Gabriel. "I'll be right back."

He nods his head before turning back to our son. I follow my mother into the house. The kitchen is empty when we walk in. Mother goes to the counter and pulls out a huge sheet cake.

"So, that's your new friend?" She asks.

I go to the sink and wash my hands. "Not really. As I said, it's Gabe's father. We're not really new."

After drying my hands with a paper towel, I join her at the counter.

"Was he on drugs too?" She whispers even though we are in the kitchen alone.

I don't take offense to her question, it's a valid one.

"No. He wasn't."

She nods, before taking the top off the Fortnite inspired cake.

"He seems like a nice guy. Very protective over you two."

I smile. "He is." I answered both her questions. "Gabriel is the best."

"A bit big though," She chuckles. "You sure you can handle all that man?"

I don't know how to feel right now. For so long I have craved this side of my mother. Having playful and joking conversations like this. However, I can't help but think this is all lies. She's only pretending to get what she wants.

I guess my silence may have tipped her off to my mood.

"Sorry," she says. "I overstepped."

Before I could reply, my sister walks in with two of her friends. They get quiet as soon as they enter and see me.

"Dang, Summer. Your baby daddy fine as hell, girl," Lanique says.

Raina and Lanique have been friends just as long as Trina and I.

I laugh. "Thanks. I have to agree."

Raina leans against the counter, propping up on her elbows. "I mean, I guess if that's your thing. I prefer my men black."

I roll my eyes at my sister's attempt to bait me. I won't fall for it.

"Love is love, Raina. It doesn't matter the color of anyone's skin," mother says smiling over at me.

I'm starting to question if she's on something. I mean, she's being a bit too nice.

"Girl, if my baby daddy looked like that and was taking care of me the way he is with Summer, I wouldn't care if he was black, brown, white or green," Tempest, Raina's other childhood friend adds.

Just then a few more of my sister's friends walk into the kitchen.

"What are y'all talking about?" One woman I didn't know asks. She has a pretty pixie hair cut with brown highlights.

"Summer's baby daddy," Tempest provides.

The woman with the wig turns to look at me with her nose turned up. "He's alright."

I chuckle to myself. Even though she says it with a snobby tone, I can tell she's lying. Her eyes were glued to Gabriel when we walked in. I have no problem with a woman checking out my man. They can look as long as they don't touch. I may not be as crazy as Gabriel, but I'll show my ass.

"My question is, how did a crackhead get a man like that? I mean didn't you say she was on dope really bad before she got pregnant?" Another one of Raina's friends says. This one has green contacts and braids similar to mine.

I turn to Raina waiting for her to answer. I'd love to hear her response too. This was all very comical to me.

Raina pushes her hair behind her ears, her face flushing red.

"You know how those Johns be getting turned out by them tricks." Pixie cut says and a few of the woman laugh.

"Ladies," my mother warns.

"Oh no, mom. They're good. This is actually entertaining. It's very rare you get to see a hating ass bitch in her natural habitat."

The silence in the kitchen is priceless. After all the shit Raina talked about me to her friends, she failed to mention that I don't have a problem dragging a bitch across a floor.

"Nobody's hating on you," pixie cut snarls.

I plant a smile on my face and tilt my head. "Of course you're not. You don't even fucking know me. You're just puppets following behind your hating ass friend."

Pixie cut gives me a look as if she just sucked on a lemon. I can't wait to tell Trina all about how my sister and her friends tried to antagonize me. Thankfully, my best friend couldn't make this party. If she were here, the cops would've already been called.

"Who are you calling a puppet?" Green contacts ask rolling her neck.

I could bring up the point that a hit dog will holler, but I don't even care that much.

"You know what," I say, turning to my mother. "I don't have the compacity to pretend like I want to be here much longer. I know you invited me here for a reason, so what is it?" I glance at Raina. "I know your friends are wondering the same thing too. Why invite the sister you talk so much shit about to your son's birthday party?"

"She has a point, Rai?" Lanique says turning to my red-faced sister.

Raina looks at my mother. "You might as well tell her."

"Maybe we should have cake first," Mom says trying to stall.

"What do you want?" I cross my arms over my chest.

Mother sighs before placing the knife down on the counter and turning to face me.

"This isn't the only reason I asked you to this party. I do think we need to form a better relationship with you and Gabe. But, I won't lie as if we don't need your help.

"Raina lost her job a month ago and has been struggling to find a new one. And well, they've cut my hours quite a bit at the post office. Then there is the issue with Mitchell's court fees. We're behind on the mortgage and could use some help getting back on our feet."

"How much do you need?"

My mother's eyes widen. She glances at Raina with a smile on her face. "Nothing too outrageous. Ten grand will definitely set us back on course."

"Ten grand? That's not bad. I have that in one of my savings accounts."

The smile on my mother's face is priceless. The entire room is looking at me now like I'm Beyonce. All the attitudes from earlier are gone along with the tension.

"That's great, Summer." Mom sings.

"I wish I had that type of money in a savings," Lanique adds.

"So, you're going to give us the money?" Raina asks the most important question.

I chuckle, "Hell no. Are you crazy?"

Immediately the smile on my mother's face fades.

"I can't even get you people to show up for my graduation, and you want me to give you ten thousand dollars? I don't care if I have it just to wipe my ass with, I won't give it to you. I told you the day your son put his hands on mine, I was done. And I meant it. Now you want me to pay for a house I'm not even welcomed in, you guys are insane."

"I can't believe she would be that selfish," Pixie cut says.

I shrug. "You better start believing."

"I told you not to invite her mama. Nobody is going to kiss her ass for…"

Her words are cut off when MJ storms into the kitchen with tears in his eyes. "Mommy! Mommy! Come quick, Aunt Summer's crazy boyfriend is beating up daddy!"

My heart sinks to my feet. Gabriel doesn't beat up anyone. If he's fighting Mitchell, he's trying to kill him. Everyone in the kitchen including myself makes a mad dash to the backyard. I hope I can get there before it's too late.

Beast

The moment Summer walked away, I went over to the sand table with Gabe. Squatting down near my son, I scanned the yard.

"Are you okay?"

He looks up at me. "Yes."

"What are you doing?"

"Building Stark Tower."

I'm pretty sure that's something from that superhero movie he's made me watch a hundred times. The structure he's built is about a foot long. It's rectangular in shape with some type of rounded structure sticking out from the side. Gabe has been working on it since we got here.

"It looks good," I say.

I've noticed that it's no longer hard for me to conversate with my son. I'm not searching my head for the right things to say or being mindful of if I'm standing too close or could possibly hurt him. All those concerns are still there, but much quieter now, more natural. It seems I am capable of being a good father.

"Hell yeah you are. You learned from the best, Kid," Priest says in my head.

"I'm almost finished with it," Gabe says proudly grabbing my attention.

Suddenly, the little boy Summer pointed out as her nephew comes over to the table with two of his friends.

"Aye MJ, what's wrong with your cousin?" One of the boys asks.

I notice Gabe tenses a little but doesn't look up from his project.

"I told you he's slow," the cousin says and the boys with him laugh.

"Kill the little shits." Mother growls in my head. *"You must protect the boy."*

I close my eyes and take a deep breath trying to keep my mother at bay. I don't kill kids.

"So he's retarded?" One of the friends ask.

"That's not a nice word," Gabe says speaking for the first time to the boys.

The young boys laugh again. I have to shut my eyes again and breathe. Mother is pressing hard to come out and teach the boys a lesson.

"He's a retard," the nephew sings.

"Leave me alone," my son pleads breaking the small restraint I had against my mother.

"You know what to do, Boy," Mother grits out.

I open my eyes, my hands at my side in tight fists. I stand to my feet towering over all the kids.

"Get the fuck away from this table before I forget that you're only children."

Despite mother telling me to crack their heads together like eggs, I refrain. The little boys' eyes widen before all three of them scurry away to the men on the other side of the yard.

I squat back down to my son. "Look at me kid." He turns and gives me his eyes.

The sadness in them has my mother roaring back up in my head. The same way I would leave a trail of bodies for Summer, I would do for Gabe.

"Are you having fun at this party?"

Gabe shakes his head no.

"Good," I say glancing up at the men that are heading our way. "Because we're about to get kicked out."

Gabe's smile lifts his cheeks. "Hulk Smash?"

"Yeah kid. Hulk's about to fucking smash. Stay back, okay?" he nods, taking my hand.

I stand just as the five men approach me.

"Aye, muthafucker, did you curse my son out?" one of MJ's father's friends asks.

"Yes, I did."

The men look to each other confused.

"And why the fuck did you think it would be okay to curse out little kids?" MJ's father asks. I think Summer said his name was Mitch. The three little boys were all standing behind the men with smirks on their faces.

"Why don't you ask your son."

"I'm asking you?" Mitch snarls.

The way the other men are surrounding Mitch and allowing him to do all the talking leads me to believe he's the ringleader. Which means, he will throw the first punch just to maintain his dominant role amongst his friends. The one to his right wearing the red shirt will be the next to jump in. He was also the first one to say something to me.

Striped shirt to Mitch's left probably thinks he's the biggest threat. He's not as tall as me, but he's muscular. He believes he's my match. It's why he's trying to come off calm and relaxed with his hands across his chest.

The guy in the back with the shades seems to be the smartest. He's keeping his distance. He doesn't know for sure what I'm capable of, but he's smart enough to know something isn't right in this situation. The guy standing directly behind Mitch in the white tank is on the fence. He will probably jump in if they are winning but if not, he will run.

"Your kid called my son an ugly name."

"All I said was that he's a retard."

The men laugh as if the kid told a joke.

Mitch grins at me. "You can't blame the kid for telling the truth. I mean, what did you expect having a baby by a crackhead." Once again, the men's laughter ring out in the back yard.

"Actually," I say. "I don't fault your kid at all. He did exactly what I wanted him to do."

Mitch's brow's pinch in confusion. "And what is that?"

"Well, I can't beat your kid's ass. So, I wanted him to bring me his bitch ass father."

My last statement changed the dynamics. All the laughter is swiped off their faces. Red shirt widens his stance. For a minute I think I might've been wrong, and he might throw the first punch. However, that's short lived when Mitch cocks his hand all the way back and swings it at me.

I saw the hit coming from yesterday, yet I allowed him to throw the first punch. It lands on my chin and had I not been looking at it, I wouldn't have known he'd hit me.

A slow grin lifts my lips into a smile.

"Whip his ass, Kid."

For this lesson, I allow Priest in my head instead of mother. When my fist connects with Mitch's face, he crumbles to the ground. Just as I thought, red shirt swings second. However, I easily dodged that blow. I only needed one person to start the fight to prove self-defense. Stepping back, I grab the arm he swung at me, lifting it up over his head, I send a powerful blow to his ribcage. The cracking sound echoes over the backyard. The following ooh's from his friends adds to the atmosphere.

Striped shirt steps up next. I don't even let him swing before chopping him in the throat. He bends forward. I grab the back of his head and shove his face into my knee. He screams out. When I lift his head back up blood is pouring out of his misshaped nose. White tank takes off running leaving shades guy alone.

Shades guy tosses up his hands in surrender. "I don't want any problems, big guy."

I dip my chin at him. Gabe runs in front of me and wraps his arms around my knees. "That was awesome, Hulk."

Pride feels me, but it is soon replaced by rage when I see Mitch toss a chair across the yard at me. I have only seconds to grab it out of the air before it hits my son.

Immediately, Priest disappears in my head and mother appears. *"Time to play. And make it hurt."*

Tossing the chair to the side, I step out of Gabe's embrace as I charge at Mitch. He tries to run, but I'm on him before he can get away.

I slam into him, knocking him to the ground. I stand over him, grab the front of his shirt, rear my arm back and then punch him in the face, repeatedly. Even when he goes limp in my hands, I continue to pound my fist into his mangled face. All I see is that chair flying through the air and if I had been a second too late it would have hit Gabe. Anger and rage cloud my thoughts as my fist flies through the air.

"Don't stop. You are the Lord's wrath. He is the serpent," Mother whispers in my head.

"Yes, Mother."

I was in the thick of the haze. This was dangerous around so many people. Even though I knew this, I couldn't drag myself out of it. The voice of Priest in my head was so faint I could barely hear him.

A soft touch on my arm, had me pausing my fist in mid strike.

"What are you doing? Finish him," Mother demands.

Before I could attempt to swing again, an angel speaks.

"Gabriel, baby, that's enough. It's done."

I turn my head to the sound of the angel, but I've yet to see her face.

"Ignore the call of the wicked. Do your job," Mother shouts.

I turn back to the bloody and bruised body beneath me.

"No, Gabriel. I'm here. Come back to me," the angel speaks again.

I shake my head, wanting to clear my thoughts so that I could be with the angel. Mother screams in my mind as I force her away.

Finally, the fog clears. I'm in Summer's mother's back yard. Terrified faces surround me. But I search for the only two that matter. I find the first staring back at me. Big hazel eyes with no fear in them. He smiles at me when he notices me looking at him. I dip my chin before turning to find my peace.

Her smile is contagious.

"Hey," I say, dropping Mitch to the ground and standing up straight to face Summer.

"Are you okay?" She scans my body up and down as if she's checking for injuries.

"He hit me first," I don't tell her that I purposely allowed him to and that I was banking on it.

"Bet he won't make that mistake again," her grin is everything.

We are pulled out the moment by the sound of a female wailing. Lying over Mitch's prone body is Summer's sister.

"What the hell happened," Her mother asks.

"Apparently, Mitch doesn't know how to keep his hands to himself," Summer replies. "Which doesn't shock me."

"That doesn't make sense, Mitch would never," Summer's mother argues.

Shades guy steps forward. I glare at him, watching him visibly swallow.

"She's right, Ms. Jones. Mitch started it. But it didn't escalate to this level until he threw the chair." Shades grimaces as he glances down at his unconscious friend.

I was right, Shades is the smartest out of the group. Had he lied in any way, I would have found him later and gutted him in his sleep.

"I don't care, I'm pressing charges," Raina cries still clutching Mitch to her chest.

"Try it," Summer says.

"Enough," her mother shouts. "You know you can't call the cops, Raina. Mitch is not supposed to be around kids."

Her mother turns back to Summer. "Look, just go. I'm sorry about this entire thing. We shouldn't have invited you here just to beg anyway."

Summer nods her head before turning and holding out her hand toward Gabe. He rushes over to her and grabs her outstretched hand.

"I can't believe you're letting her off that easy," Raina shouts.

"Come on," Summer whispers to me.

I follow behind my family making sure no one tries anything. The other two men are still rolling around on the ground groaning in pain.

"That's right leave, take your psycho boyfriend with you," Raina shouts.

Summer spins around on her heels. "Who the fuck are you calling psycho," She takes a step toward her sister, but I place a hand in front of her, blocking her path.

There will never be a time I'll let Summer fight, even for me. Although seeing her stand up for me did fill me with pride.

Raina stands, her fist at her side. "I don't care what you change about yourself. You will always be the fuck up. The family disgrace. No wonder he's the only man you can get, he's fucked up just like you."

This time, I turn back to face the sister. I have no problem with her calling me names, but I'll never let anyone get a pass at calling out Summer.

"You know what's so funny," Summer says without laughing. "You've lied to yourself so long that you really believe you're the perfect daughter."

"Fuck you, I am perfect. I wasn't the dead-beat drug addict that stole out of my mother's purse just to get her next high."

Summer tilts her head to the side. "You're right Raina. I used to be on drugs. Coke, pills, and weed. I used them as an escape because when I was a little girl my mother left me with my bipolar father in the midst of one of his episodes. And I was not only shot by my father, but I watched him blow his brains out in front of me."

A few of the women around Raina and her mother gasp. Her mother looks away. It takes me a moment to run through my rolodex of emotions to pinpoint what I see on her face. Guilt.

"I have no issue claiming my past." Summer goes on to say. "It made me who I am. But what I'm no longer going to do is sit back and let you pretend you're some perfect angel. Because although I have no problem admitting I used drugs, maybe you should tell mama who I was buying them from? That little CNA job came in handy when you were friends with the med tech."

Raina's mouth falls open.

"Raina," her mother shouts. "Tell me she's lying?"

Raina stands in her spot. Her eyes glued to Summer with so much hatred in them I'm shocked they aren't shooting lasers.

"No, mother dearest, I'm not lying. You had one daughter using drugs and one daughter dealing. And you might want to run some blood work on her now, I know the signs. Looks like the dealer is now the user." With those final words, Summer turns her back on her family and starts to walk away.

"I hate you," Raina screams so loud Gabe startles.

Summer tosses the middle finger over her head. "The feeling's fucking mutual, bitch."

Once again, I follow my family out. We climb into the car, me on the driver's side, and head back home where we spend the rest of the day watching movies and hanging out.

CHAPTER THIRTY-NINE

All Falls Down

Beast

Summer moans underneath me. Her beautiful light brown skin is covered in sweat.

The curly pieces of her braids stick to her glistening body. Her mouth is open and her brows are pinched. My hand is wrapped around her neck as I thrust into her. Each movement causes her round breasts to jiggle. She looks absolutely gorgeous.

"This is a sin. You will burn in hell for this," Mother growls.

"Gladly," I murmur.

Four days after the events at her mother's house we spent our morning like most mornings. Instead of me waking her up with my tongue buried in her sweet pussy, I awoke to her warm mouth wrapped around my cock. I quickly flipped her over and buried myself inside her.

Staring down at the woman I love more than life itself as she takes my dick fills me with a sense of calmness. I lift her hips higher off the bed, folding her even more in half. Her knees are pressed against her chest and her feet are near my left ear.

"You're too loud, Summer. I don't want my son to come in here," I tease as I drill into her rapidly. My balls clap against her ass.

She continues to moan and whimper.

"Take some out, baby. Take some out," she cries.

I slow down my strokes, only feeding her half of my cock.

"Are you telling me what I can and can't do with my pussy now?" I growl.

She tries to shake her head, but my hand around her neck tightens. I smack her ass and then rub the sting away.

"Is it mine, Summer?"

"Yes, Gabriel. Yes," she whimpers as I continue to slowly move in and out of her.

I grin as I run my hand through my hair, pushing the wet strands out of my face.

"Then don't tell me how to fuck it," I push all the way in until my pelvis is pressed against her.

I go back to my fast pace, drilling into the ecstasy that is between her legs. Sticking my finger in my mouth, I get it good and wet before bringing it down to her puckered hole. Slowly, I press it at her star before pushing it in.

She coos and bucks as I work her bottom with my digit. She's nearing her third release.

"Come on my cock," I demand.

"I can't. I can't do it again."

"Don't tell me you can't. Yes, you can." I stroke into her faster. "Wet my dick up, baby."

I look down at where our bodies connect, getting a glance at that pink center. My dick is soaked in her moisture, but I want more.

Summer starts to shake letting me know she's right where I want her to be.

"Gabriel," she squeals my name.

"That's right. Be a good girl. Come all over me."

She screams as she soaks me up. Her walls convulse around my length squeezing it tighter than a lover's embrace. I lose my control. I let her neck go as I pin her legs to the side, allowing me a different angle. Summer claws at the sheets as I piston into her depths.

"Yes. Yes, don't stop," she cries as I drive into her faster and faster.

I can feel my release coming. The soles of my feet tingle. The feeling works its way up causing my stomach muscles to tighten.

"Tell me you love me," I plead as I chase my own ending.

"I love you….Uh….yes….. I love you," she cries out.

My toes curl, my back bows, and with a roar, my cum shoots out of me and bathes her walls. I unload everything I have inside her.

I collapse down to the bed beside her, immediately pulling her into me. While placing kisses on her lips, I run my hand down her sweaty back.

"Good morning," she says with a huge smile. I grin too.

"I can get use to a good morning like this."

She leans in to kiss me again just as a soft knock interrupts us.

"Mama, Hulk, are you two finished playing?" My son's soft voice comes through the door.

Summer looks at me and then buries her face in my chest. Her body vibrates with her laugher.

"We're done now, kid." I call out to him.

"Well, can I have some cereal now."

Summer lifts her head. "I'm coming, baby. Go on downstairs."

Gabe's footsteps retreat from the door. Summer goes to get up, but I pull her back, not ready for her to move.

"Gabriel, I have to go," she chuckles. "Your child needs to eat."

I place another kiss on her lips, this time running my tongue over hers. She moans, making my dick hard again.

"Oh no," she says pushing up off me. "Ms. Kitty is tapping out. She needs a break." I let her get up. She grabs my shirt off the floor and puts it on.

"I'm going to feed him. You can shower and meet us downstairs." I watch as she walks out of the bedroom, the bottom of my shirt touching her knees.

I quickly climb out of bed and stretch. My phone goes off on the nightstand, but I ignore it. I head to the shower to wash this morning's festivities off.

Twenty minutes later, I walk out the bathroom fully dressed. Once again, my phone rings on the nightstand. I don't have to guess who it is. There are only two people that know that number and one of them is in the house with me.

Picking up the phone I answer as I make my way downstairs.

"It's been a while, Maksim."

I immediately notice his heavy breathing through the phone. It sounds like he's running.

"Beastie, you didn't listen," he huffs.

"And what was I supposed to listen to?" I ask as I step off the bottom step and into the kitchen.

"I told you what would happen if you kicked a hornet's nest."

I freeze in my tracks. My body goes on high alert.

"Everything okay?" Summer asks. She's standing by the stove flipping pancakes.

I nod my head, trying not to alert her, as I walk past Gabe at the kitchen table to the patio windows. I scan the backyard.

"Is this the phone call when you finally tell me your decision?" I keep my eyes on the yard scanning between the tree line behind the house.

"Yes," he says, with a grunt as if he hit something or fell.

"Well, what is it? Friend or Foe, Maksim?"

A beat of silence floats between us as I continue to take in the surroundings of the backyard. Then I spot it, a light flash from the roof top a few houses down.

"Friend," Maksim says. "Now get your family down."

I drop the phone and immediately turn in the direction of the two most important people in my life. It's then I spot the red dot on Summer. I take off running toward her just as the patio doors shatter. Leaping across the table in one bound, I tackle Summer to the floor.

"Get down, Gabe," I shout to my son.

Another bullet flies through the air hitting the wall over my head. I pull Summer around the corner before going to grab my son. He's on the floor with his hands over his ears rocking. I scoop him up in my arms and dive back around the corner rolling Gabe on top of me.

He climbs to his feet, and I kneel in front of him.

"When I tell you to, I want you to run up the stairs to your mom's room and hide in the closet until I come for you. Do you understand." He looks down at my shirt.

"You're bleeding, Hulk." I look down at the bloodstains on my shirt. My head drops and fear like none other hits me.

"It's not mine."

He tries to look past me at his mother. I block his view. I don't want him to see her like that. I'm not even ready to face her.

I swallow around the lump forming in my throat. "Are you ready to run?"

He nods his head with tears in his eyes. I have to fight back my own emotions.

"Run," I tell him as I step around the corner to block the stairs. If anyone else shoots, it will be me that gets hit. I wait for the pain of the bullet. Yet, nothing happens. Gabe rushes up the stairs and to the bedroom. As soon as I hear the bedroom door shut, I turn back to Summer.

Her body is so still. I drop to my knees at her side, a puddle of blood is surrounding her. There's a bullet wound in her upper chest. I place my hand over it applying pressure.

"No. Please no," I beg.

My brain flashes to images of George's crushed body in my hand.

"I told you, you're not meant for happiness. That demon in you can never touch the light." Mother cackles. *"Let me in, Boy. Let me stay."* Her voice turns into that deep sinister voice.

The same voice that told me at three years old to stab the neighbor's mean dog forty-two times.

When mother found me covered in blood with a bloody ice pic in my hands, she immediately locked me up. That's when the abuse really picked up. That's when she knew I was evil.

As I watch the rise and fall of Summer's chest slow down more and more until it stops. I can feel every part of me that was sane slowly seep away. Finally, only the true beast remains.

ACKNOWLEDGMENT

I want to give a big thank you to my readers. I know you guys waited a long time for this book. I appreciate your patience and understanding.

Beast and I went through a lot. I started this book in 2022. In that time, we loss my Nanny, got devastating health news, sent two kids to college, and recently preparing to say goodbye to my dear Bumblebee.

I can only hope this book is worth it in the end.

To the crew, I couldn't have done it without you. Thank you for the sprints, plot breakdowns, the listening ear, and the encouraging words.

To Nanny, my guardian angel, I'm still writing.

To my husband, who is my Beast—minus the mental problems—I love you. And last but never least, to my three babies. All I do, I do for you.

ABOUT THE AUTHOR

Tiya Rayne is an avid reader and writer. She has an unhealthy relationship with coffee and is known to enjoy a glass (or two) of wine on a regular basis. When she is not reading or writing—which is rare—she's trying to master this thing called parenting. She's married to her high school sweetheart, and they live in North Carolina with their three—subjectively wonderful—children.

Thank You

Wait, there is more to come! You can stay up to date with my latest releases, and learn more about me, the author, by subscribing to my newsletter at www.TiyaRayne.com
If you enjoyed Beast: Part One, I'd love to hear your thoughts and please feel free to leave a review. And when you do, please let me know by emailing me at TiyaRayne@gmail.com or leave a comment on Facebook https://www.facebook.com/AuthorTiyaRayne/ or Instagram @AuthorTiyaRayne

Until the next time.
Bye!

Made in the USA
Middletown, DE
03 July 2025